THE DRAGON LORD

"I want a dragon," said the king. "I want a thing that will fall out of the night onto a Saxon village, rip the houses apart . . . leave everything that was alive torn for the neighbors to find in a day or a week."

The king's voice began to rise. "I want a thing that can breathe on a field at harvest time, can turn its grain and beasts and the men among them to ash! Can you do that for me, wizard?"

The other could have been merely a frail old man, except for eyes that bit what they stared at. "You have your army," he replied.

"Oh, I can *beat* the Saxons," said the king offhandedly. "I can beat them a dozen times . . . but I'd have to, wizard because they won't surrender to me and there's too many of them to kill them all. If the Saxons stood in rows for a week, my Companions' arms would be numb with throat-cutting. And there still would be Saxons in Britain.

"I'll give them a symbol, since they won't surrender to a handful of horsemen. But I want it to be a symbol that kills and burns for a thousand years unless I tell it to stop—or nothing remains. I want a dragon."

"There have never been many who could raise dragons, Leader. The knowledge it takes, and even with the knowledge, the very considerable danger, yes . . ."

"Can you do it or can you not, wizard?" the king demanded. "Can you raise me a dragon?"

The older man had heard that tone too often in the past to dally with his answer. "Yes, my lord Arthur."

Baen Books by David Drake

Hammer's Slammers
The Tank Lords
Caught in the Crossfire
The Butcher's Bill (forthcoming)
The Sharp End

Independent Novels and Collections
The Dragon Lord
Redliners
Starliner
Ranks of Bronze
Lacey and His Friends
Old Nathan
Mark II: The Military Dimension
All the Way to the Gallows

The Belisarian series (with Eric Flint)
An Oblique Approach
In the Heart of Darkness

The General series (with S.M. Stirling)
The Forge
The Hammer
The Anvil
The Steel
The Sword
The Chosen

The Undesired Princess and the Enchanted Bunny
(with L. Sprague de Camp)
Lest Darkness Fall and To Bring the Light
(with L. Sprague de Camp)
An Honorable Defense
(with Thomas T. Thomas)
Enemy of My Enemy
(with Ben Ohlander)

THE DRAGON LORD

DAVID DRAKE

THE DRAGON LORD

This is a work of fiction. All the characters and events portrayed in this book are fictional, and any resemblance to real people or incidents is purely coincidental.

A Baen Book

Baen Publishing Enterprises
P.O. Box 1403
Riverdale, NY 10471

ISBN: 0-671-87890-5

Cover art by Charles Keegan

First Baen printing, September 1998

Distributed by Simon & Schuster
1230 Avenue of the Americas
New York, NY 10020

Printed in the United States of America

A preview of

In The Heart
of Darkness

by
Eric Flint
&
David Drake

Human evil directed from beyond time.
The sequel to *An Oblique Approach*.

Available in Bookstores Now

Prologue

When the lavish dinner was finished, and the servants sent away, the spymaster broke the bad news.

"Belisarius is alive," he said curtly.

There were seven other men in the room. One, like the spymaster, was foreign. From the blankness of his face, it was obvious he had already heard the news. Of the Romans in the room, five rose up on their couches, their faces expressing various degrees of consternation.

The seventh man, the last of the Romans, simply curled his lip, and satisfied himself with shifting his weight to the other elbow.

He had been disgusted the entire evening.

The two churchmen in the room disgusted him with their sanctimonious prattle. Glycerius of Chalcedon and George Barsymes were deacons, acting on behalf of Rufinus Namatianus, Bishop of Ravenna. They were rabidly orthodox. But, at bottom, their orthodoxy was nothing but a veil for ambition. The Bishop of Ravenna sought the papacy, and his underlings sought the patriarchates of Constantinople and Alexandria.

Ambition was the seventh man's motive also, but he did not disguise it with false piety. (A ridiculous piety, to boot—allying with Hindu heathens against Christian heretics.) The seventh man counted many sins against his soul, mortal and venial alike. But hypocrisy was not among them.

1

The two noblemen in the room disgusted him with their swaggering braggadocio. Their names were Hypatius and Pompeius. They were brothers, the nephews of the former emperor Anastasius. By any formal dynastic criterion, they were the rightful heirs to the imperial throne. But Romans had never worshipped at the altar of heredity. Competence was the ultimate standard for wearing the purple. And if there were two more feckless creatures in the entire Roman empire, they were hiding themselves well.

The other high Roman official in the room disgusted him. John of Cappadocia, his name was, and he was Emperor Justinian's Praetorian Prefect. A ruthless and capable man, to be sure. But one whose rapaciousness and depravity were almost beyond belief. Murderer, thief, extortionist, torturer, rapist—all these things John of Cappadocia had been named. The names were all true.

The two Malwa spies in the room disgusted him—Balban the oily spymaster even more than Ajatasutra the assassin—partly for their false bonhomie and pretense of comradeship, but mostly for their claim of disinterested concern for the best interests of Rome, which no one but an idiot would believe for an instant. The seventh man was very far from being an idiot, and he took the Malwa air of innocence as an insult to his intelligence.

The seventh man was disgusted with himself. He was the Grand Chamberlain of the Roman Empire. He was one of the most valued and trusted advisers of Emperor Justinian, whom he planned to betray. He was the close personal friend of the Empress Theodora, whom he planned to murder. He would add the count of treason to his sins, and increase the counts of murder, and all for the sake of rising one small rung in power. He was a eunuch, and so could never aspire to the throne himself. But he could at least become the Grand Chamberlain of a feckless emperor, instead of a dynamic one, and thus be the real power in Rome.

The seventh man knew, with all the intelligence of a keen mind, that his ambition was stupidity incarnate. He was an old man. Even if he realized his ambition, he would probably not enjoy its exercise for more than a few years.

For that stupid, petty ambition, the seventh man risked the possibility of execution and the certainty of eternal damnation. He despised himself for that pettiness, and was disgusted by his own stupidity. But he could not do otherwise. For all that he prided himself on his iron self-control, the seventh man had never been able to control his ambition. Ambition rode the eunuch like lust rides a satyr. It had ridden him as far back as he could remember, since the days when other boys had taunted and beaten him for his castrated deformity.

But, above all, the seventh man was disgusted because the Malwa and the Roman reactionaries in the room had insisted on dining in the archaic tradition, instead of sitting on chairs at a table, as all sensible people did in the modern day. The seventh man's aged body had long since lost the suppleness to eat a meal half-reclined on a couch.

His name was Narses, and his back hurt.

The Indian spymaster's eyes had been fixed on Narses from the moment he made the announcement. Months ago, Balban had realized that the eunuch was by far the most formidable of his Roman allies—and the only one who was not, in any sense, a dupe. The churchmen were provincial bigots, the royal nephews were witless fops, and John of Cappadocia—for all his undoubted ability—was too besotted with his own vices to distinguish fact from fancy. But Narses understood the Malwa plot perfectly. He had agreed to join it simply because he was convinced he could foil the Malwa after he had taken the power in Rome.

Balban was not at all sure the eunuch was wrong in that estimate. Narses, in power, would make a vastly more dangerous enemy for the Malwa than Justinian. So Balban had long since begun planning for Narses' own assassination. But he was a methodical man, who knew the value of patience, and was willing to take one step ahead of the other. For the moment, the alliance with the eunuch was necessary.

And so—

"What is your reaction, Narses?" he asked. The Indian's Greek was fluent, if heavily accented.

The eunuch grimaced as he painfully levered himself to an upright posture on his couch.

"I told you it was a stupid idea," he growled. As always, Balban was struck by the sound of such a deep, rich, powerful voice coming from such a small and elderly man. A eunuch, to boot.

"*It was not*," whined Hypatius. His brother's vigorous nod of agreement was intended to be firm and dignified. With his cosmetic-adorned and well-coiffed head bobbing back and forth on a scrawny neck, the nobleman resembled nothing so much as a doll shaken by a toddler.

The eunuch fixed muddy green eyes on the nephews. Against his bony face, surrounded by myriad wrinkles, the effect was utterly reptilian. Deadly, but cold-blooded. The brothers shrank from his gaze like mice.

Narses satisfied himself with that silent intimidation. Much as he was often tempted, Narses never insulted the brothers. One of them would be needed, in the future, for his puppet emperor. Either one, it did not matter. Whichever summoned up the courage to plot with Narses to murder the other first. So, as always, the eunuch maintained formal respect, and allowed his eyes alone to establish dominance.

"I told you all from the beginning that the plan was pathetic," he said. "If you want to assassinate a man like Belisarius, you had better use something other than common criminals."

Ajatasutra spoke, for the first time that evening. He was the Indian mission's chief agent. A specialist in direct action, a man of the streets and alleys, where Balban manipulated from the shadows. His Greek was also fluent, but, unlike Balban's, bore hardly a trace of an accent. Ajatasutra could—and often did—pass himself off as a Roman citizen from one of the more exotic, outlying provinces of the empire. A dark-complected Syrian, perhaps, or a half-breed Isaurian.

"It was a well-laid plan, according to the report," he murmured. His tone exuded calm, dispassionate assessment. "Belisarius was ambushed shortly after landing in Bharakuccha. At night, in darkness. While he was alone, without his cataphract bodyguards. By no less than eight dacoits. Seasoned killers, all of them."

"Really?" sneered Narses. He was quite happy to insult the Malwa, within reason. So he allowed his lip to curl ferociously, but refrained from spitting on the polished, parquet floor. "Tell me, Ajatasutra—I'm curious. How many of these—what did you call them?—oh, yes! 'Seasoned killers,' no less. How many of them survived the encounter?"

"Three," came the instant reply. "They fled after Belisarius slaughtered the first five. Within seconds, according to the report."

Narses' sneer faded. Ajatasutra was immune to the Roman's contempt. The agent's dark brown eyes were filled with nothing beyond professional interest. And the eunuch well remembered that Ajatasutra had expressed his own reservations at the meeting, many months earlier, when the decision was taken to recommend Belisarius' assassination as soon as he reached India. (Recommend, not order. Lord Venandakatra was the one who would make the final decision. Balban ranked high in the Malwa Empire's hierarchy, but he was not a member of the imperial dynastic clan. He did not give orders to such as Venandakatra. Not if he wanted to live.)

Narses sighed, as much from the pain in his back as exasperation.

"I told you then," he continued, "that you were grossly underestimating Belisarius."

A rare moment of genuine anger heated his voice. *"Who did you think you were playing with, for the sake of God?"* he demanded. "The man is one of the greatest generals Rome has ever produced. *And* he's still young. *And* vigorous. *And* famous for his bladesmanship. *And* has more combat experience than most soldiers twice his age."

A glare at Balban. *"Real* combat experience, against *real* enemies. Not"—the sneer was back in full force—"the 'seasoned killer' experience of a thug backstabbing a merchant." He stopped, hissing. Partly from aggravation; mostly from the sharp pain which streaked up his spine. He sagged back on his couch, closing his eyes.

Balban cleared his throat. "As it happens, it may have turned out for the best in any event. The report which we just received—from the hand of Lord Venandakatra himself—also says that Lord Venankatra believes Belisarius may be open to treas—to our mutual cause. He has developed a friendship with Belisarius, he says, and has had many conversations with him in the course of their long voyage to India. The general is filled with bitter resentment at his treatment by Justinian, and has let slip indications of a willingness to seek another patron."

His eyes still closed, fighting the pain, Narses listened to the conversation which suddenly filled the dining chamber. An agitated conversation, on the part of the Romans. A mixture of cold calculation, babbling nonsense, scheming analysis, wild speculation, and—most of all— poorly hidden fear.

All of the Romans in the room, except Narses, were torn and uncertain. To win Belisarius to their plot would greatly increase its chance for success. So they all said, aloud. But to do so would also make their own personal prospects that much the dimmer. So they all thought, silently.

Narses said nothing. Nor, after a minute or so, did he pay any attention to the words. Let them babble, and play their witless games.

Pointless games. The Grand Chamberlain, old as he was, eunuch that he was, knew beyond the shadow of a doubt that there was no more chance of Belisarius betraying his oath to Justinian—less chance; much, much less chance—than that a handful of street thugs could cut him down from ambush.

The image of Belisarius came to his mind, as sharp as if the Thracian were standing before him. Tall, handsome, well-built. The archetype of the simple soldier, except for that crooked smile and that strange, knowing, subtle gaze.

Narses stared up at the ceiling, oblivious to the chatter around him, grimly fighting down the pain.

Balban's voice penetrated.

"So, that's it. I think we're all agreed. We'll hope for the success of Lord Venandakatra's effort to win over Belisarius. In the meantime, here in Constantinople, we'll step up our efforts to turn his wife Antonina. As you all know, she arrived a month ago from their estate in Syria. Ajatasutra has already initiated contact with her."

Narses' eyes remained fixed on the ceiling. He listened to Ajatasutra:

"It went well, I think, for a first approach. She was obviously shaken by my hint that Emperor Justinian is plotting with the Malwa to assassinate Belisarius while he is in India, far from his friends and his army. I am to meet her again, soon, while she is still in the capital."

John of Cappadocia's voice, coarse, hot:

"If that doesn't work, just seduce the slut. It seems the supposedly reformed whore hasn't changed her ways a bit. Not according to Belisarius' own secretary Procopius, at any rate. I had a little chat with him just the other day. She's been spreading her legs for everybody since the day her doting husband left for India."

Lewd laughter rippled around the room. Narses rolled his head on the couch, slightly. Just enough to bring John of Cappadocia under his reptilian gaze.

Not for you, she hasn't. And never will. Or for anyone, I suspect. Only a cretin would believe that malicious gossip Procopius.

Narses levered himself upright, and onto his feet.

"I'm leaving, then," he announced. He nodded politely to all the men in the room, except John of Cappadocia. Courtesy was unneeded there, and would have been wasted in any event. The Praetorian Prefect was oblivious to Narses. His eyes were blank, his mind focussed inward, on the image of the beautiful Antonina.

So Narses simply stared at the Cappadocian for a moment, treasuring the sight of that twisted obsession. When the time came, the eunuch knew, after the triumph of their treason, John planned to finally sate his lust for Antonina.

Narses turned away. The Cappadocian's guard would be down then. It would be the perfect time to have him murdered.

Fierce satisfaction flooded him. In his own bitter heart, hidden away like a coal in his icy mind, Narses had compiled a list of all those he hated in the world. It was a very, very, very long list.

John of Cappadocia's name ranked high on that list. Narses would enjoy killing him. Enjoy it immensely.

The pleasure would alleviate, perhaps, the pain from his other crimes. The pain from killing Belisarius, whom he admired deeply. The agony from Theodora's murder, which would leave him, in the end, shrieking on his deathbed.

The servant helped him don his cloak, before opening the door.

Narses stood in the doorway, waiting for the servant to fetch his palanquin from the stables in the back of the villa. He glanced up. The night sky was clear, cloudless. Open. Unstained.

Murder them he would, nonetheless, or see to the doing of the deed.

Behind him, dimly, he heard John of Cappadocia speaking. He could not make out the words, but there was no mistaking that coarse, foul voice.

Foul noise and unstained sky swirled in the soul of Narses. Images of a murdered Cappadocian and a murdered Thracian vanished. The cold, still face of the eunuch finally twisted, unbridled. There was nothing reptilian in that face now. It was the face of a warm-blooded beast. Almost a child's face, for all its creases and wrinkles, if a child's face had ever borne such a burden of helpless rage.

Cursed, hated ambition. He would destroy himself for that cannibal.

The palanquin was here. The four slaves who carried it waited in silent obedience while the servant assisted Narses into the cushioned seat. The palanquin began to move.

Narses leaned back into the cushions, eyes closed.

His back hurt.

Chapter 1

RANAPUR

Spring 530 AD

Belisarius watched the stone ball arching through the sky. The trajectory was no flatter than that of a ball cast by catapult, but it slammed into the brick wall surrounding Ranapur with much greater force. Even over the roar of the cannon blast, the sound of the ball's impact was remarkable.

"A least a foot in diameter," stated Anastasius.

Belisarius thought the cataphract's estimate of the cannonball's size was accurate, and nodded his agreement. The other of his veteran bodyguards, Valentinian, grimaced sourly.

"So what?" he grumbled. "I've seen a catapult toss bigger."

"Not as far," countered Anastasius, "and not with anything like that kind of power." The huge Thracian shrugged his shoulders. "There's no point fooling ourselves. These infernal Malwa devices make our Roman artillery engines look like toys."

Menander, the last of the three cataphracts who had accompanied Belisarius to India, spoke up.

"What do you think, general?"

Belisarius turned in his saddle to reply. But his quick answer was interrupted by a muttered curse.

Anastasius chuckled. "It's amazing how quickly we forget old skills, isn't it?"

Belisarius smiled ruefully, for the truth of the remark could not be denied. Belisarius had introduced stirrups into the equipment of his cavalry only a few months before his journey to India. Already he had half-forgotten the little tricks of staying in a saddle without them. The ambassadorial mission which Belisarius led had not brought the new devices to India, however. Stirrups were one of the very few items of Roman military equipment which were superior to those of the Malwa Empire, and Belisarius had no intention of alerting his future enemy to them.

But he did miss the things, deeply, and was reminded of their absence every time some little motion caused him to lose his balance atop his horse—even something as simple as turning in his saddle to answer the young Thracian behind him.

"I agree with Anastasius, Menander," he said. "Actually, I think he's understating the problem. It's not just that the Malwa cannons are superior to our catapults *at the moment*. What's worse is that our artillery engines and techniques are already at their peak of development, while the Malwa devices are still crude and primitive."

Menander's eyes widened. "Really? They seem—"

The young soldier's gaze scanned the battleground. Belisarius and his entourage had arrived at Ranapur only the week before. But the northern Indian province of which Ranapur was the capital had rebelled against their Malwa overlords two years earlier. For more than a year now, Ranapur itself had been under siege. The once fertile fields surrounding the large city had long since been trampled flat and then re-elevated into a maze of trenchworks and earthen fortifications.

The scene reminded Menander of nothing so much

as a gigantic ant nest. Everywhere his eyes looked he
saw soldiers and laborers hauling supplies and ammu-
nition, sometimes with carts and wagons, but more
often through simple brute labor. Less than thirty yards
away, he watched a pair of laborers toting a clay-sealed,
tightly woven basket filled with gunpowder. The basket
was suspended on a bamboo pole, each end of which
rested on the men's shoulders. Despite being clothed
only in loincloths, the laborers were sweating heavily.
Much of that sweat, of course, was the product of the
blistering heat which saturated the great Gangetic plain
of north India in springtime, during that dry season
which the Indians called *garam*. But most of it was
due to the work itself. Menander estimated the basket's
weight at sixty pounds, and knew that it was only one
of many which those two men would have been
hauling for hours.

That scene was duplicated dozens of times over,
everywhere he could see. The entire city of Ranapur was
surrounded by wooden palisades, earthen walls, trenches,
and every other form of siegework. These had been erected
by the besieging Malwa as protection from the rebels'
catapult fire and occasional sallies.

Menander thought the Malwa were being excessively
cautious. He himself was too inexperienced to be a good
judge of these things, but Belisarius and the veteran
cataphracts had estimated the size of the Malwa army
surrounding Ranapur at 200,000 soldiers.

The figure was mind-boggling. No western empire could
possibly muster such a force on a field of battle. And the
soldiers, Menander knew, were just the fighting edge of
an even greater mass of humanity. Menander could see
only some of them from his current vantage point, but
he knew that all the roads in the vicinity of the city were
choked with transport bringing supplies to the army.

Glancing to the south, he could see barges making their

slow way up the Jamuna river to the temporary docks which the Malwa had erected to offload their provisions. Each of those barges weighed three to six hundred tons— the size of the average *sea-going* craft of the Mediterranean world. They were hauling food and provisions from the whole of northern India, produced by the toil of the uncountable multitude of Malwa subject peoples.

In addition to the freight barges there were a number of equal-sized, but vastly more luxurious, barges moored to the south bank of the Jamuna. These were the accommodations for the Malwa nobility and high officials. And, here and there, Menander could see slim oared craft, as well, moving much more rapidly. The galleys were powered by fifty or so rowers, with additional troops aboard. The Malwa maintained a careful patrol of the river, closing Ranapur's access to water traffic.

Most of all, Menander's gaze was drawn by the huge bronze cannons which were bombarding Ranapur. He could see eight of them from the slight rise in the landscape where he and the other Romans were watching the siege. Each of the cannons was positioned on a stone surface, surrounded by a low berm, and tended by a small horde of soldiers and laborers.

"Magical, almost," he concluded softly.

Belisarius shook his head. "There's nothing magical about them, lad. It's just metalworking and chemistry, that's all. And, as I said, crude and primitive metalworking and chemistry."

The general cast his eyes about. Their large Rajput escort was not far away, but still out of hearing range.

Belisarius leaned forward in his saddle. When he spoke, his voice was low and intent. He spoke loud enough for all three of his cataphracts to hear him, but his principal audience was Menander. Out of all the hundreds of cataphracts who constituted Belisarius' bucellarii, his personal retinue of elite soldiers, there were none so deadly as Valentinian and Anastasius. That was why he had selected them to accompany him on his dangerous mission to India. But, for all their battle skills, neither of the veterans was really suited for the task of assessing a radically new situation. Young Menander, even with more experience, would never be Anastasius or Valentinian's equal as a warrior. But he was proving to be much quicker to absorb the new realities which the Malwa were introducing into warfare.

"Listen to me, all of you. I may not survive this journey. Whatever happens, it is essential that at least one of us return to Rome with what we've learned, and get the information to Antonina and John of Rhodes."

Valentinian began to make some little protest, but Belisarius waved him down.

"That's stupid, Valentinian, and you know it better than anyone. A thousand things can kill you on the field of battle—or off it—and I'm no more immune to them than anyone. What is important is the *information*."

He glanced again in the direction of the Rajputs, but the cavalrymen were still maintaining a polite distance.

"I've already explained to you how the *cannons* work," he said. He cocked an eye at Menander. The young Thracian immediately recited the formula for gunpowder and the complex series of steps by which it was properly prepared. His words had the singsong character of one repeating oft-memorized data.

Belisarius nodded. "It's the wetting and the grinding that's key. Remember that." He made a small nodding gesture toward the distant cannons. "The Malwa gunpowder is really pretty poor stuff, compared to what's possible. And so is their metalworking."

Examining one of the cannons, he sat slightly straighter in his saddle.

"Watch," he commanded. "They're about to fire. Watch the trajectory of the cannonball."

Menander and the other two cataphracts followed his gaze. A moment later, they saw one of the Malwa soldiers take a long iron bar out of a small forge. The bar was bent ninety degrees at the tip, and the protruding two inches glowed red from heat. Gingerly, he inserted the firing bar into a small hole in the breach of the cannon. The mouth of the cannon belched a huge cloud of smoke, followed almost instantly by the roaring sound of the blast.

The recoil jerked the cannon back into its cradle. Menander saw the gunner lose his grip on the firing bar. The bar was spun against another of the Malwa soldiers, who backed up hastily, frantic to avoid the still-glowing tip. Menander did not envy the Malwa gunners. Theirs was a risky task. Two days earlier, he had seen a recoiling cannon shatter its cradle and crush one of its gunners.

Menander and the other Romans followed the cannon-ball's trajectory all the way to its impact against the great wall of Ranapur. Even from the distance, they could see the wall shiver, and pieces of brickwork splinter and fall to the ground.

Belisarius glanced at his companions. All of them were frowning—the veterans with simple puzzlement, but Menander with concentration.

"It didn't fly straight," announced the young cataphract. "It shot off at an angle. It should have hit the wall fifteen or twenty feet to the east."

"Exactly," said Belisarius with satisfaction. "If you watch carefully, and keep track, you'll eventually notice that the cannonfire is very erratic. Occasionally they shoot straight. But more often the ball will sail off at an angle—and the elevation's just as haphazard."

"Why?" asked Menander.

"It's the clearance," replied the general. "What's called *windage*. In order for a cannon to shoot straight, the ball has to fit snugly in the bore. That requires two things—

an even, precise bore all the way through the cannon barrel, and cannonballs that are sized to match."

Anastasius puffed out his cheeks. "That's a tall order, general. Even for Greek artisans."

Belisarius nodded. "Yes, it is. But the better the fit, the better the fire. The Malwa don't even make the attempt. Those cannonballs aren't much more than crude stones—they'd do better to use iron—and the cannon barrels are simply castings. They're not machined at all. Even the casting process, I suspect, is pretty crude."

Valentinian scowled. "How would you machine something that big in the first place?" he demanded. "Especially metal."

Belisarius smiled. "I wouldn't even try, Valentinian. For cannons the size of these, sloppy accuracy isn't really that much of a problem. But let's examine the question from a different angle. How hard would it be to machine a very *small* cannon?"

"Very hard," said Anastasius instantly. His father was a blacksmith, and had put his boy to work at an early age. "Any kind of machining is difficult, even with wood. Almost nobody tries to do it with metal. But—yes, if it was small enough—"

"Hand cannons," said Menander excitedly. "That's what you'd have. Something small enough for a single man to fire—or maybe two."

"One man," pronounced Belisarius.

"I haven't seen any such weapons among the Malwa," said Valentinian uncertainly. "Maybe—" He fell silent, coughing. There was a soft wind blowing, and the cloud of gunsmoke emitted by the recent cannonblast had finally wafted over the Romans.

"God, that shit stinks," he muttered.

"Better get used to it," said Anastasius, rather unkindly. For a moment, the giant Thracian seemed on the verge of uttering one of his frequent philosophical homilies, but Valentinian's ferocious glare made him think better of it.

"You haven't seen any handcannons, Valentinian, because the Malwa don't have any." Belisarius' voice was soft, but filled with confidence. "They're not hiding them from us. I'm sure of that. They've kept us far from the battlefield, but not that far. If they had any handcannons, we'd have spotted them by now."

He waited for the roar of another cannonblast to subside before continuing.

"And that's the wave of the future. *Handcannons*. If we can get back to Rome—if *some of us* can make it back to Rome, and get this information to John of Rhodes, then we've got a chance. We'll have better powder than the Malwa, and our artisans are more skilled than theirs, on balance. We can build an entirely new kind of army. An army that can defeat this colossus."

For a moment, he considered adding some of the ideas he had been coming to, of late, concerning the structure and tactics of such a future army. But he decided against it. His ideas were still only half-formed and tentative. They would confuse the cataphracts more than anything else. Belisarius needed more time. More time to think. And, most of all, more time to learn from the strange mentality that rested, somehow, in the bizarre "jewel" that he carried in the pouch suspended from his neck. The mentality which called itself *Aide* and said that it came from the far distant future.

His musings were interrupted by Valentinian.

"Careful," muttered the cataphract. "The Rajputs are coming."

Belisarius glanced over, and saw that a small group of Rajputs had detached themselves from the main body of the elite horsemen and were trotting toward them. At

their head rode the leader of the escort, one of the many
petty kinglets who constituted the upper crust of the
Malwa's Rajput vassals. This one belonged to the Chauhar
clan, one of the most prominent of the Rajput dynasties.
His name was Rana Sanga.

Watching Sanga approach, Belisarius was torn between
two sentiments.

On the one hand, he was irritated by the interruption.
The Rajputs—following orders, Belisarius had no doubt—
never allowed the Romans to get very close to the action,
and never for very long. Despite the limitation, Belisarius
had been able to glean much from observing the siege
of the rebel city of Ranapur. But he would have been
able to learn much more had he been allowed closer, and
if his observations were not always limited to a span of
a few minutes.

On the other hand—

The fact was, he had developed a genuine respect for
Rana Sanga. And even, in some strange way, the beginning
of friendship, for all that the Rajput lord was his future
enemy.

And a fearsome enemy at that, he thought.

Rana Sanga was, in every respect except one, the
archetypical model of a Rajput. The man was very tall—
taller, even, than Belisarius—and well built. The easy
grace with which Sanga rode his mount bespoke not only
his superb physical condition but also his expert horse-
manship—a quality he shared with every Rajput Belisarius
had so far met.

His dress and accouterments were those of a typical
Rajput as well, if a little finer. Rajputs favored lighter
gear and armor than either cataphracts or Persian lancers—
mail tunics reaching to mid-thigh, but leaving the arms
uncovered; open-faced helmets; tight trousers tucked into
knee-high boots. For weapons, they carried lances, bows,
and scimitars. Belisarius had never actually seen Sanga

wield those weapons, but he had not the slightest doubt the man was expert in their use.

Yes, the ideal image of a Rajput in every sense, except—

Sanga was now within a few feet. Belisarius smiled at him, and found it impossible to keep the smile to a polite minimum.

Except for that marvelous, dry sense of humor.

"I am afraid I must ask you and your men to leave now, general Belisarius," said the Rajput, as he drew his horse alongside. "The battle will be heating up soon, I believe. As always, we must put the safety of our honored guests above all other concerns."

At that very moment, as if cued by the Rajput's words, an object appeared above Ranapur. Belisarius watched the bomb—launched by a catapult hidden behind the walls of the city—as it arched its way toward the Malwa besiegers. Even from the great distance, he could spot the tiny sparks which marked the bomb's fuse.

"You see the peril," announced Sanga.

The fuse, Belisarius saw, had been cut too short. The bomb exploded in the air, well before it struck its intended target, the front line of trenches encircling the city. Which were at least a mile away from the little knoll where they stood.

"The deadly peril," elaborated Sanga.

"Indeed," mused Belisarius. "This is perhaps the most dangerous moment in my entire life. Or, perhaps not. Perhaps it takes second place to that terrifying episode, when I was eight years old, when my sister threatened me with a ladle."

"Brutal creatures, sisters," agreed Sanga instantly. "I have three myself. Deadly with a ladle, each and every one, and cruel beyond belief. So I have no doubt that moment was slightly more dangerous than the present one. But I must still insist that you leave. The safety of our honored guests from Rome is the uppermost concern in our Emperor's mind. To allow Emperor Justinian's official envoys to suffer so much as a scratch would be an irreparable stain upon his honor."

The Rajput's expression was solemn, but Belisarius suddenly broke into a grin. There was no point in arguing with Sanga. For all the Rajput's invariable courtesy, Belisarius had quickly learned that the man had a will of iron.

Belisarius reined his horse around and began moving away from the siege. His cataphracts followed immediately. The entire Rajput escort—all five hundred of them— quickly took their places. Most of the Rajputs rode a polite distance behind the Romans, but a considerable number took up positions as flankers, and a small group of twenty or so trotted ahead to serve as the advance guard for the little army moving through the milling swarm of Malwa soldiers and laborers.

Rana Sanga rode alongside Belisarius. After a moment's silence, the Rajput remarked casually:

"Your Hindi is improving rapidly, general. With amazing rapidity, actually. And your accent is becoming almost unnoticeable."

Belisarius repressed a grimace, and silently cursed himself for a fool. In point of fact, Belisarius could speak Hindi fluently, when he chose, without the slightest trace of an accent. An almost magical capacity for language was one of the many talents which Aide provided him, and one which Belisarius had used to advantage on several occasions.

And one which, he reminded himself again, was useful in direct proportion to being held a close secret.

He sighed, very slightly. He was learning that, of all the difficult tasks which men face in the world, there is perhaps none quite so difficult as pretending to be semicompetent in a language which one speaks perfectly.

Belisarius cleared his throat.

"I am pleased to hear that. I hadn't noticed, myself."

"I thought not," replied Sanga. The Rajput glanced over his shoulder. "Given that your Hindi is becoming so fluent, I suggest that we might speak in Greek from now on. My own Greek, as you know, is only passable. I would much appreciate the opportunity to improve it."

"Certainly," said Belisarius—speaking, now in Greek. "I would be delighted."

The Roman general pointed back toward Ranapur with his thumb.

"I am curious about one thing, Rana Sanga. I notice that the rebels seem to lack any of your *cannons*, yet they obviously possess a large supply of gunpowder. It seems odd they would have the one and not the other."

The Rajput did not reply, for a moment. It was obvious to Belisarius that Rana Sanga was gauging the limits of what he could tell the Roman.

But the moment was very brief. Sanga was not given to hesitation. It was one of the many little things about the man, Belisarius thought, which indicated his capabilities as a military commander.

"Not so odd, General Belisarius. The cannons are under the exclusive control of the Malwa kshatriya, and are never stationed in provincial cities. Neither are supplies of gunpowder, for that matter. But cannons are very difficult to manufacture, and require special establishments for the purpose. By law, such manufactories may not be created outside our capital city of Kausambi. Gunpowder, on the other hand, is much simpler to make. Or so, at least, I am given to understand. I myself, of course, do not know the secret of its manufacture. None do, except the Mahaveda priests. But it does not require the same elaborate equipment. So long as one possesses the necessary ingredients—"

The Rajput broke off, shrugged slightly.

"—which I, needless to say, do not—"

Fibber, thought Belisarius. *I doubt he knows the exact process, but I'm sure a soldier as observant as Sanga knows the three ingredients and their approximate proportions.*

"—and the necessary knowledge, gunpowder can be made. Even in a city under siege."

"I am surprised that Mahaveda priests would join a rebellion against Emperor Skandagupta," remarked Belisarius. "I had the impression that Malwa brahmins were utterly devoted to your empire."

Sanga snorted.

"Oh, I have no doubt their co-operation is involuntary. Most of the priests were undoubtedly killed when the province revolted, but I'm quite sure the lord of Ranapur kept a few alive. It is true, the Mahaveda are sworn to commit suicide before divulging the secret of the Veda weapons. But—"

The Rajput tightened his lips.

"But the priests are perhaps not completely free of the weaknesses which afflict we lesser mortals. Especially when they are themselves the *objects* of coercion, rather than—"

He fell silent entirely. Belisarius completed the thought in his own mind.

Rather than the overseers of the work of their mahamimamsa torturers.

Their conversation was the closest Belisarius had ever managed to get to the subject of the Malwa secret weapons. He decided to see how far he could probe.

"I notice that you refer to these—incredible—new weapons as the *Veda* weapons. My own men tend to believe they are the products of sorcery."

As he had hoped, his last words stung the Rajput.

"They are not sorcery! Magical, perhaps. But it is the reborn power of our Vedic ancestors, not the witchcraft of some modern heathen."

That was the official public position of the Malwa Empire: *Ancient weapons from the time of the Vedas, rediscovered by diligent priests belonging to the new Mahaveda cult.* Belisarius was fascinated to see how completely it was accepted by even Rajput royalty.

But perhaps, he thought, that was not so surprising after all. No people of India, Belisarius knew, took greater pride in their Vedic ancestry than Rajputs. The pride was all the greater—a better word might be ferocious—for the fact that many non-Rajput Indians questioned the Rajput claim to that ancestry. The Rajputs—so went the counter-claim—were actually recent migrants into India. Central Asian nomads, not so many generations ago, who had conquered part of northwestern India and promptly began giving themselves airs. Great airs! The term "Rajput" itself meant "sons of kings," which each and every Rajput claimed himself to be.

So it was said, by many non-Rajput Indians. But, Belisarius had noted, it was said quietly. And *never* in the presence of Rajputs themselves.

Belisarius pressed on.

"You think so? I have never had the opportunity to study the Vedas myself—"

(A bald lie, that. Belisarius had spent hours poring over the Sanskrit manuscripts, assisted in deciphering the old language by his slave Dadaji Holkar.)

"—but I did not have the impression that the Vedic heroes fought with any weapons beyond those with which modern men have long been familiar."

"The heroes themselves, perhaps not. Or not often, at least. But gods and demi-gods participated directly in those ancient battles, Belisarius. And *they* were under no such limitation."

Belisarius glanced quickly at Sanga. The Rajput was scowling, now.

A bit more, I think.

"You must be pleased to see such divine powers returning to the world," the general remarked idly.

Rana Sanga did not respond. Belisarius glanced at him again. The scowl had disappeared, replaced by a frown.

A moment later, the frown also disappeared, replaced by a little sigh.

"It goes without saying, Belisarius," said Sanga softly. The Roman did not fail to notice that this was the first time the Rajput had ever called him by his simple name, without the formal addition of the title of "general."

"It goes without saying. Yet—in some ways, I might prefer it if the Vedic glories remained a thing of the past." Another brief silence. Then: "*Glory*," he mused. "You are a soldier yourself, Belisarius, and thus have a better appreciation than most of *everything* the word 'glory' involves. The ancient battle of Kurukshetra, for instance, can be described as 'glorious.' Oh yes, glorious indeed."

They were now within a hundred yards of the Roman encampment. Belisarius could see the Kushan soldiers already drawing up in formation before the pavilions where the Romans and their Ethiopian allies made their headquarters. The Kushans were vassal soldiers whom the Malwa had assigned to serve as the permanent escort for the foreign envoys.

As always, the Kushans went about their task swiftly and expertly. Their commander's name was Kungas, and, for all that the thirty or so Kushans were members of his own clan and thus directly related to him by blood, maintained an iron discipline over his detachment. The Kushans, by any standard, were elite soldiers. Even Valentinian and Anastasius had admitted—grudgingly, to be sure—that they were perhaps as good as Thracian cataphracts.

As they drew up before the tent which Belisarius shared with Dadaji Holkar, the Maratha slave emerged and trotted over to hold the reins of the general's horse. Belisarius dismounted, as did his cataphracts.

From the ground, Belisarius stared up at Rana Sanga.

"You did not, I believe, complete your thought," he said quietly.

Rana Sanga looked away for a moment. When he turned back, he said:

"The Battle of Kurukshetra was the crowning moment of Vedic glory, Belisarius. The entire *Bhagavadgita* from the *Mahabharata* is devoted to it. Kurukshetra was the greatest battle ever fought in the history of the world, and uncounted words have been recorded discussing its divine meaning, its philosophical profundity, and its religious importance."

Rana Sanga's dark, heavily bearded, handsome face seemed now like nothing so much as a woodcarving.

"Eighteen million ordinary men, it is also written, died in that battle."

The Rajput drew back on the reins, turning his horse.

"The name of not one of those men was ever recorded."

To Karl Edward Wagner—

Excellent friend, excellent writer, and an excellent inspiration for a would-be novelist.

"Yet, be warned; call not to you that which you may neither hold nor forbid."

Acknowledgments

This book owes a great deal to a great number of people. Among them are:

Joanne Drake, my wife, and Glenn Knight, who read portions of the work in progress and pointed out several forests which I couldn't see for the trees;

Sharon Pigott, who proofed the typescript and found four pages of errors I had missed;

Dave McFerran, an Irishman and a godsend to my research;

Karl Wagner, MD, a source—among other things—of crucial medical data;

Andrew J. Offutt, whose request for a plot outline was the proximate cause of my sitting down to write a novel;

Dave Hartwell, who pointed out a problem and then stepped back to let me fix it my way;

and Prof. Jonathan A. Goldstein, who taught and I trust still teaches his classes to enter the minds of ancient peoples through their own writings.

Prologue

"I want a dragon," said the king. His voice was normal, almost too soft to be heard by the man across the table. "I want a thing that will fall out of the night onto a Saxon village, rip the houses apart . . . leave everything that was alive torn for the neighbors to find in a day or a week." The king's voice began to rise. Centuries under Roman rule had smoothed the accents of most British tribes, but the burr was still to be heard among the Votadini. "I want a thing that can breathe on a field at harvest time, can turn its grain and beasts and the men among them to ash!

"Can you do that for me, wizard?"

The other man waited with a half smile for the echoes to die. He was small and should have shaved off his beard. It was dirty, sparse, and ridiculous. He could have been merely a frail old man, except for eyes that bit what they stared at. "You have your army," he replied, using the willow switch he carried to dabble in the ale spilled on the intarsia tabletop. "Your Companions kill and burn well enough."

"Oh, I can *beat* the Saxons," said the king off-handedly, "but that won't make my name live a thousand years." He was lying Roman fashion on the bench, his long cloak pinned at the shoulder and draped so that it completely covered his feet. He always hid his feet if possible, though all men knew that the right one was twisted inward from birth. The Saxons had named him Unfoot in derision when they first saw him leading a troop of cavalry against them. The name had stuck, but by now it had the ring of Hel or Loki in Saxon ears. "I can beat them a dozen times . . . but I'd have to, wizard, because they won't surrender to me and there's too many of them to kill them all. I can bring fifteen hundred men to the field at a time. If the Saxons stood in rows for a week, my Companions' arms would be numb with throat-cutting. And there still would be Saxons in Britain."

The wizard looked down at the parquet table and muttered something under his breath. The spilled beer shimmered. For an instant the liquid showed two armies facing each other. The ripples were sword edges and silvered helms, teeth in shouting faces and the jewel-bright highlights of spurting blood.

The king pretended to see nothing. "I'll give them a symbol, since they won't surrender to a handful of horsemen. But I want it to be a symbol that kills and burns for a thousand years, kills unless I tell it to stop—or nothing remains. I want a dragon."

The willow whip nodded, throwing nervous shadows against walls where years had cracked away most of the frescoes. The paint had been replaced by patterned fabrics, tapestries, and brocades. The wizard said, "There have never been many who could raise dragons, Leader. The knowledge it takes, and even with the knowledge, the very considerable danger, yes . . ."

The king's beard and hair were cut short—hacked short, rather, for he could not bear a blade in another's hand to lie so close to his throat. Perhaps he would have let the hair grow and run across his torso in rich, syrupy waves had he not once seen a man try to dodge back from a dagger point—and find that his enemy gripped a handful of his beard. The king's moustache alone was full. "Can you do it or can you not, wizard?" he demanded. "Can you raise me a dragon?"

The older man had heard that tone too often in the past to dally with his answer. "Yes," he said, "I can raise a dragon—and control it—if you can get me the ingredients I need and cannot supply myself." The wizard toyed with the beer and murmured again. A thing trembled on the inlay. Its neck was as long as its body, and its tail was as long as both together to balance it on its two legs. There were no forelegs. From the shoulders sprouted a pair of scaly black wings. The beast could have seemed childish, but it did not, even before one realized that the irregularities beneath the feet of the illusion were Saxon longhouses.

Nodding, reaching through the simulacrum for the ale pitcher to refill his jeweled bronze cup, the king said, "Of course, of course. What will you need?" His forehead glistened with sweat, but he still said nothing about the illusion.

"The major thing . . ." began the wizard. He paused to rephrase his thought and continued, "My magic works from lesser to greater; for a matter of this magnitude, however, 'lesser' by no means implies 'little.' There are monsters in the Pictish lochs. I need the skull of one of them."

The bronze cup gouged the tabletop as it slammed and splashed. His cloak swirling as he leaped erect, his eyes bright with sudden fury, the king shouted, "Am I God Almighty that you ask this thing of me? Or—" and his hand dropped to the hilt of the long dagger thrust through his brocaded belt—"do you think this is an easier thing than saying no to me? Wizard, if I believed that . . ."

Except for tiny lines around his eyes, the wizard's face was unwrinkled. He kept it bland as a waxen death mask as he said, "Leader, I will not lie to you." He paused, holding the willow branch so still that not even the leaf eyes at the tip, bared when the wizard had stripped away the bark in long threads, trembled. "I need a skull."

The king let out his breath and with it much of his anger. "I can't fight the Picts," he admitted. He stepped over to a side table set with napkins and a wide clay bowl for washing. The king's limp and the thick-soled buskin that gave his right leg back its height were evident when he moved. "The Saxons fight like a big slow bear. My troopers can prick an army of Saxons and run off, prick it again and again until all the blood runs out and the army dies without striking a blow. But the Picts, now . . . the Picts swarm like bees. My horsemen don't have enough hands to swat them."

He tossed a linen napkin to the dining table. The wizard mopped at the ale shining in pools on the parquetry, never taking his eyes off his king. The club-footed man continued, saying, "They dismounted me. A naked Pict rolled out of a clump of heather that couldn't have hidden a toad, and he put a spear up into the belly of my horse. Then I was on the ground and I tried to stand . . . and they swarmed at me. . . ." The king slipped his foot out of its buskin and rubbed its calloused knob on his left calf as he remembered. "Cei got to me before they did, swung me over his saddle. That time. Oh, the Picts can be beaten—" his voice changed as he spoke and he was again the strategist and not the frightened cripple—"and one day I'll do it, send an army of Saxons against them to trample their heather flat and spear them in their burrows. But not yet, wizard. I still have the Saxons to conquer. And there isn't any way I can bring you a monster skull from the middle of the Picts."

The wizard pursed his lips. A thin line of bark still traced down the side of his switch. He began to worry it loose as he thought. "Can you get a man into Ireland?" he asked.

"Perhaps."

"They say the creatures once swam in Irish lakes. I don't think they still do now, but all *I* need is the skull of one."

The king sat back down on the bench. His dark face lost a little of its hardness. "Yes," he said. "I couldn't send one of my captains . . . any of my Britons, I think. Matters between us and Ireland are well enough—given what they were ten years ago, or a hundred. But there are men on that island still with long memories and long swords. Men who haven't forgotten that raids on Britain stopped when I drowned them in Irish blood. Still, I've got a few Irishmen in my squadrons. If they sold themselves to me to fight Saxons, they ought to be glad of a job this easy. One of them will be able to bring you what you need." The king got up, calmly this time. He walked to the door of the entrance hall and threw it

open. His six guards looked at him, scarred men
whose eyes were as hard as the iron links of their
mail. In its case in an alcove behind them, meant
by its builder for his household gods, waited the war
standard of the army. It was a tube of red silk, ten
feet long from mouth to tapered end. When the wind
filled it, the scales of gold writhed and whispered
on the fabric. Uther, the king's father, had borne it.
It was the Pendragon, the King of War Standards,
for which both Uther and his son were named. But
its history was longer than that, longer than any man
now living could recite. Four centuries before, the
standard had come to Britain with a squadron of
Roman cavalry. It had remained on the island,
victorious and venerated, ever since.

From behind the king, the wizard asked curiously,
"A mercenary? Do you think you'll be able to trust
a hireling with something as important to you as this
is?"

The king's eyes were fixed on the dragon banner.
He was not seeing it as it was, but rather waving over
greater triumphs than any it had yet known. The
guards looked away uneasily, aware that their Leader's
expression was skewed a little to the side of madness.
"Well, wizard," he said, "we'll have to make him
trustworthy, won't we? Find one with a wife, say, or
a son . . . or perhaps a comrade he loves more than
life itself. I'll have my dragon, Merlin. Depend on
it."

Behind him the wizard nodded slowly. "Yes, my
lord Arthur," he said. There was no doubt at all in
his voice.

Chapter One

The amphitheatre had been built as a rich man's toy in the palmy days after Constantius Chlorus had replaced a British usurper with a Roman emperor, when for the first time in decades the armies of civilization were able to fight pirates instead of each other. The structure had never been richly adorned; it was only an oval arena fifty feet by a hundred, surrounded by a five-foot curtain wall of native sandstone. On either side sloped turf mounds which once had been laid with wooden bleachers. In the early days all the countryside, slave and free, had turned out to watch the shows. Sometimes there would be imported gladiators, the acts alternating with local boys battling with quarterstaffs. There were beast hunts, too, though they only used bulls. The bulls were dangerous enough, to be sure, and available—but even more important, they could not

7

leap the low wall the way a hungry wolf had done on one long-remembered afternoon. Gymnasts had performed in the arena, horse-trainers and fire-eaters as well. Once a magnate of intellectual pretensions had even imported a troupe of Greek mimes to put on a comedy of Terence. The actors' Latin had been so pure that the West British crowd had howled them offstage as foreigners mouthing gibberish, as indeed they had been to the listeners.

Those were the good days. Time passed. Bit by bit, the Empire had passed as well. Trade slowed as markets burned. The amphitheatre became used mostly as a sheepfold, and the bleachers rotted away. The villa of which it was part was too far west for the Saxons to raid it, too far south for the Picts to be a problem. Its owners and their friends met in the evenings and murmured about the state of the Empire, vowing to plant more wheat the next year since the wool market was so uncertain. Then, in the night, Niall and his reavers had landed.

The metal and fabrics, the tools and the weapons, the women they wanted—all those things the Irishmen sent back to their curraghs. The humans they did not take were marched to the amphitheatre where their throats were slit, thirty-seven of them. The Irish joked that a man as fat as the owner of the villa should have had so little blood in him.

Arthur was the first man in a hundred years to find a use for the enclosure after Niall had left it.

There had once been a gate at the western end of the curtain wall, but it had long since rotted away. The men who now entered the dark arena did so through the gap. There were thirty of them of two distinct groups. Six of the men were of Arthur's Companions, afoot now but obviously horsemen from their rolling stride. Despite their evident discipline, they marched no better than did the shambling recruits they accompanied. Their dress was uniform: leather breeches and jerkins, polished black by the links of iron mail that covered the leather in battle or on campaign. The rounded leather caps were padding for helmets. Though the Companions did not wear their full armor, a sword hung from the belt of each.

Except for their captain, the Companions themselves were as uniform as their garb. They were all stocky men of middle height with faces darker than exposure alone could account for. Arthur had men of all races among his Companions, but for a variety of reasons most of his training cadre was British. They carried flaring torches, the only light in the amphitheatre since the moon was new. The breeze was channeled by the viewing mounds. It whipped the yellow flames. Occasionally it lifted a droplet of pitch to bring a curse from the man it touched.

The chief of the Companions was set apart by more than his arrogance. He stood six feet six, almost a foot taller than the tallest of his subordinates. He was slim at the hips, thick in the wrists and the shoulders. While the other Companions cut their hair short to fit safely under their helmets, the chief's curled out in long auburn ringlets which had as much of art as of nature about them. The tall man had no torch, nor was there a real sword on his belt. In his left hand he carried a buckler with an iron boss, and in his right was a pair of training swords. Each of the swords was a yard long, fashioned of thick wood and strengthened by a rod down the center. The captain swung them one-handed with a nonchalance that belied their weight. In the middle of the arena he paused, looking over the recruits. He let his lip curl under his moustache, forming the quick sneer that came so naturally to it.

The recruits were varied but by no means despicable. Man by man, they looked to be as formidable a pack of killers as could be hired. Most of them were Germanic—half a dozen Franks besides Goths, Vandals, and Herulians—but there were other folk represented as well. A Moor in a robe of stinking black goat's wool, his fingers nervous because they no longer held his pair of knobbed javelins; a Greek with a black beard to hide a neck scar, still wearing the accoutrements of the Eastern Empire; and the Irishman who called himself Mael mac Ronan and whose six-foot frame was utterly dwarfed by the huge Dane who stood beside him.

Starkad Thurid's son was as tall as the captain of the Companions in the center of the arena; he looked twice as broad. For a game, the Dane sometimes straightened horseshoes with his hands and flipped the resulting bars to gaping onlookers. The torsion-heated metal would sear the men who caught it as surely as if Starkad had plucked the horseshoes from a fire. A buckler swung from Starkad's neck on a leather strap, ready to be raised if he wished it. Generally he waded into battle swinging his axe with both hands. Even now the Dane stood with the weapon's head on the ground before him, its oaken helve upright beneath his cupped palms. All the other recruits had obeyed the command to turn out with shield and padding only, leaving their mail and weapons at their tents. Starkad's hands and the carnage his axe left behind had earned him the nickname Cruncher; alone of the men in the amphitheatre, he would have said his Irish friend was the more deadly of the two of them.

For ten years Mael—who admitted to being of the Ui Niall and would change the subject if pressed further—had closed the Dane's back in battle, drunk him cup for cup in peace, followed Starkad's whimsies or led the Dane where a black Irish fancy called. The two of them had spent the decade as soldiers and merchants, pirates, and even for one season farmers. That had ended in strayed cows and seven men dead in the garth to which the cows had strayed. Mael and Starkad were outlawed in Tollund for that, but they had made it to the coast before the posse was raised. It was neither's first outlawry.

The chief of the Companions cleared his throat, a signal to his men. They stilled their banter at once. The murmuring among the recruits, low-voiced and uncertain at all times, died away as they too realized something was going to happen. "Get in a line," the tall captain ordered in Latin. He sneered again, watching the recruits form awkwardly against the crumbling wall. Some had not understood the order; if they did not guess its meaning from the others' motion, Companions thrust them into place. The Irishman whispered in Starkad's ear and the two took places at the end of the line. There they waited, giving the nearest of the Companions stare for stare.

"I am Lancelot," rasped the chief of the Companions. For five years he had greeted in this same way each gathering of the mercenaries who sold their swords to Arthur. He explained to his peers that his "demonstrations" served a double purpose: the recruits learned to respect the unfamiliar techniques in which they were to be trained; and they learned to respect Lancelot himself—Arthur's chief adviser and Master of Soldiers. There was a third reason that Lancelot admitted only to himself. He took great pleasure in humiliating barbarian warriors. All the recruits were symbols of the tribes which had brought down the Empire in two continents and eviscerated it even in the East. To Lancelot, Arthur's dream was not an adequate substitute for the past, but it was a suitable tool for revenge.

"I am the chief of Arthur's Companions. It's therefore my duty to start you on your way toward becoming . . . not Companions, I suspect—there's few men anywhere up to that standard and probably none among you—" his lip writhed again—"but fair soldiers, perhaps."

Mael had heard the speech eighteen years before. Then it had been spoken in Irish on the training grounds of the Ard Ri's Guard. He knew what Lancelot was leading toward and he listened with only half an ear. With his right sandal, the Irishman scraped at the soil to test the footing it would give. It was an amalgam of sand and sheep dung rammed into the clay substrate, a pocked, irregular surface but hard as concrete and unlikely to slip out from under a lunging man.

Starkad leaned toward Mael. In Danish and in a voice not really meant to be private, he rumbled, "What does he say, brother?"

"You!" Lancelot called, pointing at Starkad with his right index finger instead of the practice swords he held in that hand. "Do you speak Latin?"

Mael cleared his throat. In Latin as good as the Companion's, he said, "Starkad speaks your British tongue well enough."

For a moment Lancelot did not reply. When he spoke there was an edge in his voice. "He'll speak Latin soon." The captain's eyes swept the line like a challenge. "You all will—because Latin is the tongue Arthur's Companions speak. There's no time in battle for a translation, no place for a missed command. And you'll learn to shoot a bow, ride on horseback, thrust with a sword—all these things, because that's what Companions do. And you think you can be Companions." Again he glared at the recruits, one by one. This time he spat on the ground. "You should live so long," he said.

"He's both self-important and a fool," observed Starkad almost soundlessly. His lips were pressed close to the Irishman's ear. The two men had spent years together in situations where concerted action meant survival. That long experience made the burr of sound intelligible to Mael where another man would not even have known the Dane was speaking. "Let's you and I walk away from here."

Mael leaned his shoulders back against the stone. He knew—as perhaps Starkad did also—that Lancelot, for all his posturing, was no fool. "I think," Mael replied in the same battle whisper, "that the lancers on guard out there would ride us down in a hundred yards. They make a god of order, here."

Staring at Lancelot as if he were really listening to the harangue about the necessity of training, Mael waited for the Dane's reply. At first it was only a sigh. Then, "You were right when you warned me, my black-headed friend. But I was so sure the war pickings would make up for the trouble . . ."

"Right now I'm going to teach you how to use a sword," Lancelot was saying. The interest of the recruits revived. They had been restive though silent during talk of discipline; swords were another matter. "Most of you carry one, don't you? And I'll wager there's not a man of you who knows how to use it— by thrusting, not slashing. 'The edge wounds, the point kills.' *Always* remember that."

"I've killed my share with the edge," retorted a Herulian in the middle of the line. His hair was black but there were gray speckles in his ruff of beard. Though he was of no more than middle height, he was broad and had the arms and shoulders of a blacksmith.

The Herulian's jaw was cocked up, expecting a snarled insult and ready to reply in kind. Lancelot instead smiled and said, "Fine. I thought somebody would be stupid enough to say that. Come on out and show me how you use a sword." The Companion tossed one of the training blades so that its polished sides made a yellow ripple in the torchlight.

The Herulian caught the hilt in surprise. His own face lit in a slow grin. Just below the edge of his deerskin cap, a long scar crossed the recruit's forehead. It flamed like a white bar as he flushed with anticipation. His eyes took in the ground, its irregularities and the heavy blocks of sandstone that had fallen from the wall. "Not much of a surface," he grumbled.

Lancelot's smile was as cold as a king's thanks. "Before we next fight the Saxons," he said, "shall we have them rake and roll the field?"

The Herulian slipped his left arm through the loops of his iron-bound target. He began to advance on Lancelot without replying. The torch-bearing Companions were spread in a forty-foot arc around their captain. Lancelot raised his light buckler in his left hand, gripping it by the double handles on the back of the metal boss. Other than their shields, the antagonists were similarly equipped. Lancelot wore only his gambeson and a cap. The Herulian's cuirass was similarly of leather, boiled and sewn with half a dozen iron rings the size of large bracelets. The two men eased together with the mutual confidence of persons who had killed frequently and were both sure they knew the techniques of the business.

Ten feet from Lancelot, the German shrieked and charged. The Companion moved with the lethal grace of a stooping hawk. His right leg slid forward while his left straightened to give him thrust. Lancelot's left arm and buckler swung back slightly, just enough to balance his right arm and the thick practice sword which stabbed out unstoppably. Its tip caught the Herulian in the middle of the right thigh, just below the edge of the shield. The rounded end of the sword did not penetrate, but its impact—doubled by the victim's own momentum—was as bruising as the kick of a horse. It spun the Herulian to the ground. His own overhand swing had slashed the air harmlessly.

Lancelot backed a step as if to let his opponent rise. The Herulian rolled to one knee and winced as he put weight on the right leg. He touched his shield rim to the ground to steady himself. Lancelot lunged again, smashing his point into the center of the German's chest. Even through the reinforced leather, a rib cracked. The Herulian was flung backward. He groaned but tried to stand again. Though the fight was already over, the battering had just begun.

"Shift your footing with your weight," Lancelot said, demonstrating by skidding his right foot forward as he drove at the Herulian's pelvis. Wood and bone clacked together. The Herulian's skin, torn between the hardnesses, began to leak blood onto his linen tunic. "Never, never let yourself lose your balance," the Companion continued. The Herulian had kept his feet after the last blow, but a feint at his thigh brought his guard low. The real thrust broke the left side of the German's collarbone.

Screaming more with frustration than pain, the Herulian dropped his lath sword. He let the target slip from his useless left arm, then seized the heavy round of wood and metal by its rim and hurled it backhand at the face of his tormentor.

Even that was expected. The Herulian's fury and thick shoulders spun the shield with enough force to kill, but it sailed harmlessly over Lancelot's head as he ducked away. When the shield struck the ground thirty feet distant, it clanged.

"You can drive down a battlefield, killing a man at every step," Lancelot said to the other recruits in a conversational tone, "if they're all as inept as this fool." He lunged a last time, his body a perfect line from his left heel through his extended right arm. The sword point buried itself in the pit of the Herulian's stomach. The German doubled over, somehow keeping his feet though his knees wobbled. He was retching uncontrollably.

"There's one other thing that we'll take up later," Lancelot said as he rose gracefully. "Since you've already seen it done wrong tonight, though . . . shield fighting. Your shield is a useful weapon, but don't *ever* let it out of your hands." The captain stepped to the bent-over Herulian and clubbed him behind the ear with the metal edge of his buckler. All the Herulian's muscles went slack as he dropped. "You see?"

None of the recruits made a sound, not even the two remaining Herulians.

Lancelot's chest was heaving but his voice was under perfect control. Its timbre was normal as he demanded, "Well, do any of you women think you could do better than this one did?"

Starkad turned his head and spat deliberately into

the darkness beyond the wall. He faced back around without speaking.

Lancelot pointed the wooden sword at him. "You, Dane!" he said in German. "Can you take me?"

"I can kill you, Roman," Starkad said without raising his voice or lowering his eyes. He matched the Companion's angry stare.

With his foot, Lancelot indicated the lath sword the Herulian had dropped. "Pick it up, Dane," he said.

Starkad's knuckles tightened, but he did not shift his grip on the axe helve. "I won't fight you with toys, Roman," he said. "Get yourself a real sword and we'll holmgang."

No one in the arena doubted that the Dane seriously meant his offer to go to an island for a death duel with the Master of Soldiers. The recruits drew up, weighing the alternatives of mutiny or brutal exercises like the incident they had just watched. The six Companions tensed as they awaited decisions over which they had no control.

Mael stepped forward. "I'll fight you," he said to Lancelot in Latin. He scooped up the wooden sword. Lancelot smiled at him; but then, the captain had never let his smile slip, even when baiting Starkad.

Mael could have been a model for Lancelot in nine-tenths scale. He was six feet tall, large-boned and covered with muscles that looked flat until they tensed and stood out in knotted ridges. In battle the Irishman wore a mail vest to mid-thigh and a rimless steel cap. Tonight he had turned out as ordered, bareheaded and with only a gambeson of laminated linen covering his torso. Without headgear his one affectation became obvious; he still shaved the back of his head to above the ear peaks, in the fashion of the High

King's Guard. Whenever someone asked Mael about it, he told them loudly that he was a coward who feared to be seized from behind when he fled, and Mael's eyes dared any listener to believe him. The shield the Irishman carried was a heavy target like the Herulian's, a round of plywood three feet in diameter with an iron boss and a seamless rim of the same metal. The rim had been shrunk on like a tire to a fellie. The shield was plain and serviceable— and of course new. A good sword was an heirloom that father might pass down to son through several generations. A good shield served once in a hot fight, and its owner thanked his gods then if it got him through that one encounter without disintegrating.

Mael and Lancelot edged toward one another, rotating counterclockwise to keep their shield arms advanced. The Irishman refused the first blow. Lancelot thrust from six feet away, his long sword and longer arm flowing in one supple motion that brought the sword tip to within an inch of Mael's chest. The Companion recovered as smoothly as he had struck, but there was a glint of surprise in his gaze. Mael had jerked back at the waist, just enough for the thrust to clear him—and no more. There had been no counterattack though, neither the roundhouse swing to be expected from a barbarian nor the lightning thrust of which Mael's cool precision suggested he might be capable.

Lancelot feinted at Mael's face and lunged low at the left shin which only the high-laced sandal protected. The point should not have rung off the Irishman's shield boss, jarring every bone in the Companion's lower back, but somehow the shield was there. Still Mael did not strike back. Lancelot's smile was as stiff now as the leather of his jerkin, but he kept his curses within him as he and the Irishman circled tensely.

Lancelot's third thrust was smooth and precise and guided cleanly past Mael's face by the edge of the Irishman's sword which redirected it harmlessly. The missed stroke almost threw the Companion off balance, but practiced reflexes allowed him to recover. The Irishman's reaction seemed to give Lancelot his first real opportunity, however—Mael screamed something Gaelic and bloodthirsty, raised his sword high over his head, and let his target swing to the side where it did not cover his body.

This was the fatal error Lancelot had expected from the barbarian, the triumph of bloodlust over discipline. He reacted instantly, lunging again in a spray of sand even though his weight was not perfectly centered nor was his left leg set with the care he would have demanded of a trainee. The captain had been rattled by the Irishman's skill, after all, and he needed a quick victory to retain the prestige that was his life.

Mael's timing was dangerous but perfect. His left foot lifted as if drawn to the Companion's blade by magnets. Even if Lancelot had seen the parry coming, he was already hopelessly committed to his lunge. Mael's hobnailed sandal caught the sword. The weapon and the man holding it spun to their left. The point glided past Mael again. This time Lancelot's shield was no longer between him and his opponent but rather on the other side of his body. Lancelot could have left the buckler in his room for all the good it did in stopping Mael's sword.

The Irishman's practice blade scissored down in the same motion that had brought up his left foot to block Lancelot's thrust. The sound Mael's sword made on the Companion's cap was like the first slap of lightning before the full weight of thunder rolls across the sky. The oaken blade shattered, leaving the hilt and reinforcing rod in Mael's hand. Lancelot skidded on his face, driven by his own lunge and the force of the blow. His head stopped inches short of a block of stone. There was a collective intake of breath from the other men in the amphitheatre, recruits and Companions alike. For the first moments after the blow, there was no sound at all from Lancelot.

Mael backed toward his place in line beside Starkad. There was a wild light in his eyes. He looked at the vibrating remains of his practice sword and giggled. "'The edge wounds . . .'" he quoted. He giggled again. Then he flipped the rod over his back into the darkness.

Lancelot raised himself to one elbow and stared at Mael. The Companion's nose was broken. Blood from that and from his sand-abraded face smeared the ground. It shone black in the torchlight. If the Irishman's eyes were wild, then Lancelot's were hell-lit. Without taking his eyes off Mael, the captain felt for the block of stone and grasped it with both hands.

The block was coarse sandstone, a rectangular piece of the wall larger than a man's torso. Lancelot faced it and locked his right knee under him. He was a big man and hugely strong even for his size, but there should have been no way a single human could have lifted that mass of rock. Grunting, Lancelot gripped it by the ends and cleaned it, bringing the block to chest level and rotating his palms under the edges. The right side and shoulder seams of his gambeson ripped. The leather flopped loose over muscles as stiff as the stone they lifted.

One of the Companions dropped his torch and ran

to Lancelot, his hands washing each other in the same
terrified indecision that knotted his tongue. Lancelot
ignored him, did not even see the man although his
eyes were open and staring. Before Lancelot was only
the red blur of sandstone and the brighter red of
the blood bulging the veins behind his retinas. The
captain straightened his legs and arms together,
jerking the monstrous weight overhead.

There was silence in the arena save for the peeping
of frogs in the low spots beyond the wall. Lancelot
stood, a caryatid whose face was no redder where
blood smeared it than where the blood suffused the
flesh within. Then the towering figure took a step
forward, toward the Irishman who no longer laughed.
The Goth to Mael's left blundered away from him,
stumbling because his eyes were fixed on Lancelot.
It was a scene whose like had not been played out
in the fifteen centuries since Ajax lifted a boulder
and advanced on Hector beneath the walls of Troy.

Lancelot took a second step. Dust puffed from his
boot toe and the hard ground shook. He was eight
feet from Mael and only a chest's width more from
the wall against which the stone would pin his victim.
Mael crouched, his shield raised but useless.

Starkad stepped forward, his buckler swinging like
a bangle on its neck strap. The Dane had gripped
the four-foot shaft of his axe with both hands. Using
the doubled strength of his arms, he brought the ten-
pound head up in an arc that shimmered because
speed blurred its glittering highlights. The peen led,
square and blunt and tempered to take shocks that
would shatter the glass-hard cutting edge on the other
side.

The axe struck the center of the sandstone block.
It rebounded, ringing with a shrill sound that was

nearer a scream of anguish than a chime. The metal could shriek and leap back; the rock had no such resilience. It would hold or would crack, and the weight of Starkad's blow left no choice but the latter.

Lancelot's breath *whuffed* again with tension released as the stone split in the middle. It fell backwards out of his hands. The twinned blocks thudded to the sand together and rolled once, dice that gods might have thrown. Lancelot, his balance gone and with it the hysterical strength that had worn his flesh like a cloak, toppled and fell back between the stones. He lay there, his eyes beginning to focus for the first time in minutes.

Starkad's right hand had been leading on the axe helve. That whole arm was numb to the shoulder. With his left hand alone, the Dane raised the axe over his head. Its bearded edge still quivered like a live thing with the shock. "They call me the Cruncher, Roman," Starkad boomed in British. "Shall I show you why?"

The tension broke in the shadow of that axe. Like a force of nature, a storm or an avalanche sweeping all before it, the weapon was for the instant a thing that no man present could imagine withstanding. Surrender brings an absence of conflict; recruits and Companions relaxed accordingly. When the six mounted cataphracts rode through the entrance to the arena, the men gathered within were too drained of emotion to do more than glance at the newcomers. Minutes earlier, their arrival would have jangled nerves and led to bloody mutiny because the recruits would have thought they were about to be attacked.

The six riders were Companions in full armor. Their gear jingled as they cantered into the amphitheatre. They were of normal height for West Britons, averaging around five and a half feet tall, but in armor and mounted they bulked larger than life. Two of them wore scale mail, tiny leaves of iron sewn individually to a leather backing where they lay in overlapping rows. The result was not as effective as a fabric of rings, each interlocked with four others, but it was within the capacity of any smith and seamstress to manufacture. Scale armor was both cheaper than ring mail and far more readily available.

The four other horsemen wore rings, however; their chief's had been washed with silver so that his torso danced in the torchlight. Among Arthur's Companions, as in most professional armies, it was customary to flaunt wealth in fine equipment. The only proviso was that one's arms must not appear more valuable than one's ability. Besides their mail shirts, the cataphracts wore leggings faced with scales or rings on the outer sides. The insides of their thighs were covered only with leather, not simply because armor was unnecessary there but because iron would have robbed the riders of the firm grip they needed to stay on their horses. Their saddles had four low horns, two front and two behind—and no stirrups at all. Keeping mounted in a fight was a major part of the training each Companion received.

"Lancelot, what in the name of the crucified God are you doing?" demanded the silver-armored horseman.

Lancelot used the broken stone beside him as an anchor and pulled himself into a sitting position. He tried to speak but blood or a dry throat choked him. He spat out a tooth on the ground. One of his own men knelt beside the Master of Soldiers and ripped a strip of linen from the hem of his tunic. Another Companion splashed the rag with beer from the goatskin bottle hanging at his waist. Together, as carefully as artificers preparing a pharaoh for eternal burial, the two soldiers sponged away at the damage to Lancelot's face.

"Lord Gawain," one of the training cadre blurted, his eyes flicking back and forth from Starkad to the mounted man, "it was—"

"I'll wait for your captain to tell me, thanks," interrupted Gawain with a mildness that bit. The trooper bobbed apologetically. No one else spoke aloud while the two Companions worked on Lancelot.

Nearer the wall, two Herulians and a Frank were tending to Lancelot's object lesson. The remaining recruits had drifted toward them. The nursing gave the men something to focus on instead of the cataphracts and their battered officer. Hot looks came out of the motley throng, directed against the isolated Mael and Starkad. The torches had burned down to embers and a trickle of fire, but they had dimmed gradually enough that those present could still see each other.

"1 think they've just written us out of the human race," Mael said to the Dane. He tossed his head toward the recruits in lieu of a more respectful gesture. "They think they'll all be punished for what I did to that prancing dandy . . . and they've seen enough of Arthur's discipline to worry about it."

"What we did to that one," Starkad corrected softly, staring at his right hand as he clenched and unclenched it. Feeling seemed to be returning. "Men and dogs, Irishman, men and dogs . . . Give me a wolf pack any day. Wolves tear out no throats but their enemy's— or their dinner's, of course. But wound a dog and the ones he's been running with will be the first on him. Since they're the nearest." The Dane flexed his hand again, turned it over to show curls of hair as heavy and dark as copper wire crawling down the back of it. Even Starkad's fingers were hairy, except for the skin over his knuckles. Those patches gleamed pale in the torchlight for not being shadowed by hairs. "We could run," he said in the same tones of bored unconcern.

Mael had been watching the riders with a frank, friendly smile on his face. The Irishman looked as if he could not imagine what their dismounted fellows of the training cadre were telling them in low murmurs. "No, I don't think so," Mael said. "I don't feel quite like I'm about to die yet, and I surely would die if we ran." He grinned sidelong at Starkad. "Of course, *you* may be about to die, my friend. That stone was probably a valuable Roman relic—and you've heard how this Arthur is about Roman things."

The Dane chuckled, reaching across to knead Mael's skull brutally. They were in this as in most things— together. Call it friendship or a wish to die. "Next time I'll have sense enough to use the edge on his skull," Starkad said. "At least I'll be able to use both hands if I have to, later."

Mael continued to study the Companions. Men in armor were no rarity now in any army apart from the Irish. Long past were the days in which Rome's legions faced hordes of shrieking Germans protected by no more than a loin clout and a wicker shield. Rome had educated her barbarian neighbors. Part of the process had been by example, survivors around camp fires telling how their points skidded from bronze corselets. Even more destructive of Rome's superiority had been her practice of hiring enemies as auxiliaries, training them in armored tactics for twenty-five years—and all too frequently having the men return to their tribes across the Rhine or the Danube to pass their training along. When the naked mobs became effective heavy infantry, Rome's own period of lordship was soon to end.

But while the Companions' armor was common enough for warriors who could afford it, their array of weapons was not. From the right side of each saddle, just ahead of the rider's knee, hung a quiver of arrows. A bow was cased to the left, balancing the quiver. Horse archers had been a staple of Oriental warfare for centuries, but they had never been popular among the armies of Western Europe. Even in nations to whom mounted bowmen were standard, the nobles who could afford full armor carried swords and sneered at the drudgery of daily archery practice. These Companions were equipped with both armor and bows. Either Arthur had issued expensive mail to all his forces, or his discipline was so rigid that even the wellborn were forced into finger-burning, muscle-knotting archery exercises. Perhaps both were true. Brief experience suggested to Mael that they both were. The Irishman wondered where Arthur got the money and the authority to put such a program into effect.

Like the dismounted cadre, the riders all carried swords sheathed along their left thighs. The varied richness of the weapons suggested the rank and wealth of the bearers. The hilts ranged from plain wood, in the case of the two troopers wearing scale armor, to Gawain's, which was of iron forged in a single unit with the blade and quillons. The metal was carven and heavily inlaid with gold and ivory. Its owner's calloused hand had smoothed the hilt to a perfect fit for him, proving the weapon was no useless toy for ceremony.

One further weapon completed each cataphract's arsenal, a weapon which Mael knew for the most deadly and difficult to master of all. In tubular sockets hanging from the right rear of the saddles stood twelve-foot lances. The heads were four-sided pyramids, narrow and a foot long. A tang joined each point to an ash shaft two inches in diameter and as smooth and straight as an artisan could fashion.

Lances have only rarely in history been popular. A lancer gets the first stroke at an enemy, but if he misses, the speed of his charge thrusts him into the hands of his foe with no way to strike again. A light javelin can be flung from a distance or its shaft raised to block a hostile blow. A lance is like a glacier, massive and unidirectional. It is too heavy to throw, too clumsy for protection. Worse, when saddles lacked stirrups as these did, a clumsy lance thrust was as likely to dismount the lancer as to slay his opponent.

And yet trained lancers were the terror of every field on which they fought. Lances killed with the unanswerable certainty of catapults, but even greater than their material effect was the moral. A line of glittering lance-heads plunging nearer, backed by dust and thunder and tons of armored horsemen, was soul-shattering.

Mael frowned inwardly, though his face remained bland. He could appreciate the Companions, for he had been raised a fighting man and spent his life in the service of war. But these men were simply too good, too perfect. To conceive of and train them had been works of genius—but a damned bloody genius it must be. It was natural for men to kill and, aye, to make a business of killing. But to turn slaughter into an intellectual exercise was as warped as for a woman to lust after a bull, and the progeny was apt to be as evil. Lancelot sucked beer into his mouth, wincing at its astringence. He spat after swizzling it around. The second mouthful he swallowed. Only then did he look up at Gawain who was waiting with a hunter's patience while his men fidgeted. "Well?" Lancelot said, shaping the word very carefully.

"The Leader needs to talk to two of the new recruits," Gawain said. Both men spoke Latin but with markedly different accents. The variation was less regional than a matter of education. Although Britain had scholars and orators the equal of any on the Continent, Gawain had never been trained by such. The Votadini, his tribe and his Leader's, valued other skills than those of civilization. "He sent us to bring them now—the Irishman, Mael mac Ronan, and the Dane who joined with him."

Mael looked at his friend. He popped the big man's shoulder with the heel of his hand and said "See? That's why I hate to do anything final. You just can't tell what's going to turn up."

Starkad snorted, oblivious to the staring faces around them. "They could still be taking us out to chop us."

"They didn't have any reason to chop us until now," Mael responded cheerfully, "and nobody got a message out of the arena to those guys." Tugging Starkad by the left shoulder, the Irishman stepped toward Gawain and his half squad. "Here we are, friend. Much as we hate to leave this happy gathering."

Gawain's chuckle was full and appreciative without being in the least friendly. "I'd intended to put you both on pillions to get you to headquarters," the slim captain said, "but now that I've seen your friend I'll be damned if I have a horse try to carry him and one of my boys besides. You can walk, and we'll all be happiest if you don't waste time at it." Gawain glanced back at Lancelot. "Good night, Master," he said with an ironic salute. Then, to his men and their charges, "Let's go."

...one of my boys had just...

Chapter Two

The horsemen wheeled and rode out of the arena. Gawain set a pace that brought Mael and Starkad immediately to a jog. Beyond the gateway the Companions formed two lines abreast. With the recruits sandwiched between them—as much escorted as under guard, but under guard beyond doubt—they rode back through the darkened countryside toward the villa that was Arthur's main base and headquarters. The nearest town, Moridunum, the market place for the region, was five miles southward. There were no civilians closer than that except for dependents.

The route to the villa took the company past the recruit lines near the arena. They were of wattle and daub with thatched roofs, recently built and broken up internally into tiny one- and two-man cubicles. There were a hundred units in blocks of

31

ten with common walls. Each had a door in front facing the latrine, a window in the back, and barely enough floor space for beds and the personal effects of the occupants. Only transients and trainees were quartered there; veterans had billets attached to the main building. The semi-private rooms were not intended as benefits to the recruits. There was no enclosure in the area in which more than a dozen men could gather and conspire because of the separation. When the trainees assembled, it was either under the eyes of the cadre or during meals in the huge mess hall in the main building. Then the new men were mixed with no less than equal numbers of hard-bitten veterans.

Arthur was under no illusions as to how his discipline would be received by mercenary recruits, and had the recruits not been bloody-handed killers already, they would have been of no use to the king. His control measures were as carefully considered as every other part of the training.

Mael jogged along with the horses easily, holding his shield close to keep it from battering him at the end of its neck strap. His legs were long, his chest large, and if the Irishman had not deliberately trained for running in the decade since he left the Ard Ri's Guard, then still he was not a man to be concerned about a half-mile jog. He looked over at Starkad. The Dane had dropped back two steps and caught the nearest horseman's quiver in his left hand. Using the horse to smooth his own pace, a psychic rather than physical crutch but no less real for that, Starkad was pounding along without evident concern. He and the horseman had exchanged brief glances when he attached himself. Sensibly, the Companion had made no protest. The Dane was ignoring the light shield, letting it flop against his breast. In his right hand he carried his axe at its balance near the head. Its shaft worked up and down behind him like a pump handle as he ran. Mael grinned and stopped worrying about his friend.

The villa they approached was a two-story building of stone and stucco. A taller block of apartments had been recently constructed of lath and plaster along the back. The kernel of the villa had been raised in the time of Trajan and expanded piece by piece over the centuries following. At the villa's zenith and that of Roman Britain in the early fourth century, the building had been filled by slaves who lived in its rambling halls and turned raw wool into fine woven cloth under awnings in the central courtyard. With the change from sheep to wheat, the surrounding country had been broken into tenant holdings and the slave gangs had disappeared. Rooms were closed. In earlier ages the owners had been occasional visitors from London or the Continent; now they became permanent residents.

Then the Irish came. Though they did not burn the building, for the next century it was occupied only by travelers and the bandits and deserters who were an increasing feature of the times. When Arthur grasped power, he found in the villa his safe base in the center of what remained British in the face of the Saxon onrush.

Gawain drew up at the front entrance. Once a portico had led to it, but the columns had been wood and long since burned in cooking fires. The high oak doors had been replaced. They stood open, displaying the lamplit hall and the remainder of the squad on guard duty that night.

"Pass on through," Gawain said to Mael with a

sardonic smile. Turning a little further he added to
Starkad, "You'll have to leave your axe."

"I'd as soon die holding it," the Dane replied. His
chest was heaving and his face was flushed from the
run.

"Well, that's the choice," Gawain agreed without
emotion.

"Give me the axe, lunk," Mael said. He reached
out, touching the shaft with his fingertips but not
trying to grasp the weapon. "Indeed, they may kill
us. Assuredly they will if you insist on posturing."

Mael spoke in Danish, softly enough and more
quickly then he thought the Companions could follow.
"This one doesn't posture, my friend. He'd as soon
kill us as not. And that'd be a damned foolish way to
die." The Irishman closed his hand over the axe. "If
they attack us, I'll let you use my rocky head for a
club." He lifted the weapon from Starkad and handed
it to Gawain.

The British captain weighed the axe and tried its
balance. "Sometimes I wish I had the size for one
of these," he said to Mael with a grin as lethal as a
wolf's. Mael grinned back, knowing that if he had
toyed with this man as he had with Lancelot, one or
both of them would already be dead. Gawain would
simply not have accepted any conclusion short of
death in such a challenge.

Mael and Starkad passed through the doorway and
its gauntlet of lounging guards. The roof of the hall
was opened by an impluvium which funneled
rainwater down into the decorative cistern in the
center of the hall. The architectural design was
normal in Italy, miserably uncomfortable during
British winters. The concession that Mediterranean
style had made to northern weather was to close

the three doorways off the hall with solid panels instead of leaving them open.

One of the Companions tapped deferentially on the left-hand door, then opened it to an order grunted from within. Mael started through. Starkad touched his shoulder and said, only half in jest, "No, I lead and you cover my back. Just like any battle." He entered the room ahead of the Irishman.

There was no obvious danger inside, only two men reclining at the head and side of an intarsia table. Neither man was prepossessing, Mael thought. There was certainly nothing in the younger of them to make fighting men refer to him so naturally as Leader. And then the two looked up, and Mael felt their eyes on him. The Irishman grinned, because he had to do something with his face before these men, each in his own way as deadly as Gawain.

"Starkad Thurid's son," Arthur said, not a question but a vocalization of notes jotted somewhere inside his skull. "Starkad Grettir."

The Dane nodded, stiff-backed and hostile. He had already measured the distance to the king. He knew he could leap it in time for a single skull-cracking blow, even if a spear from behind had gone through him.

"And Mael mac Ronan." Arthur was not the hulking bear of a man rumor on the Continent had him. The Saxons who returned from Britain needed an excuse for their fears, a snarling monster to lead their enemies, a beast with swords the length of flails and muscles that could lift an ox. This man, forty and slim except in the shoulders; more gray-haired than gray-bearded, but with much of gray in his beard as well; three or four inches less than Mael's height, though the unclasped cloak over his lower legs hid the exact length they stretched—this was no creature for whom a Saxon warrior could articulate a terror that his fellows could understand.

Mael didn't care who understood. He had seen the Companions and had now seen Arthur himself. Both the man and what he stood for were frightening.

"I need an Irishman to take a trip home for me," the king said. "Merlin here—" he nodded toward the older man on the side bench. The wizard's lips had been working silently ever since Mael and Starkad had entered the room—"needs the skull of a water monster as lived once in your lakes. Have you heard of such?"

Very formally and carefully, Mael said, "I left Ireland for reasons that seemed good to me—and better yet to some who stayed home. I have no wish to die and less to return to Ireland—which may well be different ways to say the same thing"

The king took a swallow of ale and brushed foam from his moustache with the back of his hand. Merlin beside him continued to mutter, using the butt of his willow whip to divide a puddle of ale. The two dollops of thin fluid stayed separate after the wand passed instead of flowing back together. Arthur was saying, "You're Irish, after all. You can blend in, not attract attention as Lancelot would or Gawain. Call yourself something—oh!" And the king broke off with a gleeful chuckle at his insight. "Of course, of course—you already do. It's a matter of only a few days and back, you see, nothing to tax a disguise."

Merlin said *something* aloud and the puddles of ale rejoined with a pop of blue fire.

"Well?" Arthur demanded.

"Perfect," said the wizard. "Exactly what you wanted." The old man looked up at his king "None of my spells kept the two pools apart after I'd given the names of these two. Not women nor wealth— nor fear. They won't abandon each other."

"And duty?" the king asked as if the two mercenaries were not in the room.

"Duty means standing by your friends," Starkad rumbled in German before Merlin answered.

Arthur laughed. "And trust means being sure of what a man will do," he said, "not thinking that he's a friend and so he'll back you. Sit down, Irishman— and you, too, Cruncher, though there's no work for you in this except for waiting here until your friend returns. I'll explain what it is we have in mind. . . ."

◈   ◈   ◈

The fishing village—six houses, each owner kin to the other five—had been built at the higher end of the rocky beach. Above, the long, rank grass stretched eastward over the Cambrian hills, furring the spine of the promontory so that there was no one place on which a man could stand and see why it had been named Octapitarum—Eight-headed.

To the inhabitants, the baylet was a separate thing and not merely one facet of the seven of the headland. Indeed, the village was part of the greater world only as it chose—in normal times. About once a month the villagers emptied their drying sheds of the fish stacked there, layered with salt baked from tidal pools by the sun. They loaded the fish on oxcarts which then creaked along rocky paths in an all-day journey to the nearest of the great farms. There the fisherfolk would barter their catch for cloth and metal-work and sometimes ale better than their own sour, salty brew.

Had the villagers wished, the magnates inland would as willingly have come for the fish themselves. The price would have been effectively greater, since then the fishermen need not have kept oxen. But little as they cared to leave their notch in the island's wall, their home, the fishermen cared less to show visitors to it. Thus the arrival of King Muirchertach's embassy had been almost as unpleasant a shock to the villagers as if the fifty strangers were hostile, as they thought at first.

Mael listened to Arthur's account of the landing, grinning broadly. "What did they do?" he asked the king. Like Arthur, the Irishman had remained on his horse when the column halted. Starkad had dismounted as soon as the glittering sea announced they had reached their destination.

"Oh, they sent a boy running to the nearest villa," the king said also smiling. "They don't run very well either, you know. The owner of the villa whipped off a messenger to me and ran along behind with all his household as quick as he could. *He* thought it was a raid, too, and he knew these hovels—" Arthur nodded to the drystone huts—"weren't going to occupy the murdering Irish long. So . . . I took the half squadron I had on hand, rode thirty of the horses to death or to bonebreak, got lost twice pushing on at night. We got here at dawn, just in time to see these damned fishermen lugging their nets to their boats, pretending there wasn't a curragh pulled up on the shore and fifty men trying to sleep around greenwood fires while the locals ignored them. If we'd been half an hour later I wouldn't have seen the fishing boats. I'd probably have killed everybody on the shore." Arthur looked sidelong at Mael. "And then how would we have gotten you to Ireland, my dragon-snatcher?"

"Oh, you'd have found something," Mael said, his

humor chilled at the thought of his mission. They were a huge company for this quiet opening to the sea. The Irish embassy had been loaned mounts for its return to the shore. Arthur accompanied Muirchertach's men with two hundred of his cataphracts, fully equipped as he himself was. The king's mail was silvered and the general sheen picked out by links washed in gold instead. A helmet with a long nose-guard covered his head. The helm had a faceted appearance because it was made of welded steel plates, carefully resilvered after each time dents had to be beaten out of it. To either side flared a gilded wing. Behind Arthur, a bearer raised the ancient war standard to snap and snarl in the wind.

"If this is such a peaceful embassy," Mael remarked, "why does it look like they're being escorted back to the coast by a warband?"

Arthur chuckled. "Oh, just honor due a fellow monarch, perhaps. Muirchertach's more than friendly, yes—to me. It seems there's trouble in Ireland—" and again Arthur's eyes darted unexpectedly at Mael—"and though he's not king of the Laigin yet, Muirchertach has notions for the future. He needs help. For the time, I've sent him one sword as a gift by way of his war chief Dubtach there." Arthur nodded at the burly leader of the embassy. The chieftain's red hair was bound back with a linen fillet and his chest was deliberately bare to display the battle scars on it. "Muirchertach hopes that one day I'll send more swords—and men of my own to carry them."

"You want Ireland, too?" Mael asked bluntly.

"It's part of the world, isn't it?" the king replied, and his words were too offhand to be a joke. Arthur looked out over his accompanying troops. They had formed in a double row as soon as the terrain had opened enough to position a hundred men abreast. To the right, the ground hung in terraced pastures sufficient for the goats and oxen; goats ran loose beyond as well, supplementing the grass with mast from stunted hardwoods. The Irish, with Gawain alone of Arthur's men riding along with them, were filing down the gentler slope toward the houses and the shoreline beyond on foot.

"In the meantime, I thought this would be a good time for a little . . . friendly demonstration," Arthur continued, obviously pleased at a chance to flaunt his abilities in front of a new listener. By now the king had to have heard about Mael's destruction of Lancelot the night before, but he had made no reference to it on the ride to the coast—unless requesting that Mael and Starkad be placed beside him was in itself a comment. "Thanks to you Irish becoming Christians—"

"Some Irish becoming Christians," Mael cut in sharply.

"Most of you Irish becoming Christians," the king went on smoothly, "and Vitalis' daughter marrying your High King . . . and most of all, I suppose, the Plague and the squabbles on your island that seem to have left fewer cutthroats to amuse and more at home to amuse them—" Arthur paused but Mael said nothing, only grinned across at the slender king. Arthur was baiting death as he dreamed of empire— "perhaps there wouldn't have been many raids here even without my Companions to deal with them. But it can't hurt to get word back that the Companions *are* here—and can deal with raiders—can it?"

Arthur nodded to his cornicine. That tallish Briton raised a coiled bronze horn to his lips and blew a single note. Downslope, close to the nearest out-building of the village, Gawain bent to speak briefly to Dubtach. Then the Companion cantered over to a smokehouse built of heavy timber. The building stood a score of yards to the right of the main path. Using the neck strap, Gawain hung from the ridgepole the plain shield he was carrying in place of his usual ornately studded one. He waved up the hill to Arthur, then rejoined the Irish. Dubtach challenged him, though the words of their argument were not intelligible at the distance. The Irish waited, bunched together, while Gawain and their leader spoke. Some of them watched the shield, their hands a little tighter than usual on their own weapons. The low, slate-roofed houses of the village had their shutters latched as if the visitors were a storm, but the boards trembled sideways and eyes within caught the light in stray reflections as the women looked on.

Arthur himself was in conversation with Cei, the two men leaning together so that their shoulders and helmets touched Their hands twitched in gestures that meant nothing except to each other. Starkad tapped Mael lightly on the right knee and used a tiny gesture of his head to indicate on the other side of Arthur the six riders who had moved up when the horn blew. Now they waited, talking among themselves in mild, high-pitched voices. They sounded from a short distance like the sing-song giggling of a girls' school. Their horses had no reins or saddles. The riders held bows with nocked arrows in their hands.

"Oh, yes. . . ." Mael said quietly. He had not noticed these men on the march. Perhaps they had been used as outriders, scouting the line. It was the sort of work they gloried in.

"You know them?" Starkad asked.

"I know of them. Huns." Mael stared openly. They were little men with black, coiled hair and flat faces. One was bare-chested. His skin was hairless and almost of a color with his breeches of supple leather tanned from rabbits or other small mammals. Only in size and the ease in which they sat on their mounts, knees high and calves flexed sharply backward, were the Huns uniform. Two more wore leather corselets, black from being hardened in boiling vinegar. The ancient bronze medallions of a dead legionary, traded eastward over the centuries and so polished with age that the reliefs had been worn almost away, glittered against one corselet.

Two of the other Huns wore mail, but while one set was of the highest quality—each ring a double coil that left almost no interstices for a point to enter—the other shirt was of scales of a type almost unknown in the West. They were large, up to three inches across the base, and made of aurochs' horn instead of metal. The scales were translucent gray and they shimmered as if still alive.

The sixth Hun wore no more armor than the first, only a linen tunic over his breeches, but despite the warm sun, he had a cape of marmot furs pinned at his shoulder. Its cowl was thrown back and the lustrous brown fur rippled down behind him.

"I fought them once with Hjalti's army," Starkad said. He ran an index finger along the peen of his axe as he counted silently. "Fourteen, fifteen years ago, that would be. Maybe if I live another hundred years or so, I'll want to fight Huns again."

Gawain shouted to the king from the midst of the Irishmen. The Companion waved his helmet as an all-clear signal.

"Now," said Arthur. His cornicine sucked a chestful of air, then blew a long note. The six Huns fanned forward at a gallop without noticeably directing their horses. The riders were shrieking like files on stone, each a different note and as bloodcurdling as the cries of the wounded when crows alight on their faces. The Huns shot as they rode, reloading in a single, natural motion with the draw and release. Their bows were short but heavy, recurved and stiffened with plates of horn and bone The staves averaged between a hundred and a hundred and twenty pounds of pull, so that only the flicker of points and white fletching was visible as the arrows slapped out at the target.

At the first shout and volley, half a dozen of the Irish dropped flat. But the Huns' target was the shield and the men standing twenty yards from it were as safe as if they were in Ireland. Despite the range and the gallop, none of the Hunnish arrows was more than a hand's breadth off the mark.

The shield wobbled. Arrows hitting it squarely made a double *thunk* as the shafts penetrated and struck the shed behind. Arrows that missed the shield sank to half their length in the heavy timbers. The target area was suddenly a deadly garden, the feathered ends of the arrows trembling like horizontal flowers in the sunlight.

As the riders yipped and thundered downslope, they opened gaps of about six feet between each man and his neighbor. For those on the ends of the line, the final volley was almost an edge-on shot at the shield as the charge swept around the smoke-house, three men to a side. The last arrows smacked into the target as surely as the first had.

In the gravel yard between two buildings, the Huns drew up and reformed. They cantered back around

the shed, laughing and gibing among themselves. They
utterly ignored the Irishmen who now clustered
around the shield. There were over twenty arrows
in or near the target. Dubtach tried to pull one out
of the timber and found that the shaft splintered
before the barbed head would release. There was
awe in the faces of those who looked at the swarthy
little men. Two of the Christian Irish surreptitiously
crossed themselves.

"What do you think of my demonstration?" Arthur
asked.

Mael jumped to realize that the king was again
speaking to him. The Irishman smiled. His right hand
rested on Starkad's shoulder in an unconscious
gesture of affection, and from his saddle he looked
across the big Dane's head toward Arthur. "Very
nice," he said. "There's not a man down there—"
his thumb generally indicated the Irish—"but
believes every one of your Companions can ride and
shoot like that. At home they'll spread the story and
piece fable onto it—though by the Dagda's club, the
truth is enough! You'll have an island defended by
devils, here, and no place at all for a pirate to think
of landing."

"But you aren't fooled," said the king, his lips still
curved in what was either good humor or the start
of a snarl.

"I've heard of Huns—and I've seen your . . .desire
for discipline," Mael replied. "If you could find
anybody else to do the job they do, you'd never in
hell let these Huns parade like a troupe of buffoons,
would you?"

It was a smile. "Yes," Arthur said, "and when they're
drunk—which is generally—it is a devil's job to keep
them from cutting every throat in reach before raping

the warm bodies. But they have their uses, as you say."

The king looked back at the beach where the Irish were gathering about the curragh, preparing to launch it. "Time for you to join your kinsmen," Arthur said. He drummed his fingers, thin and paler than the backs of his hands, on pommels. "Bring me back what I need, Irishman. Bring me back the skull. . . ."

Mael swung off his borrowed horse. "I'll walk, I think," he said.

Starkad echoed, "We'll walk. To the boat."

Arthur made no response. His eyes were as unfocused as a drugged man's, though his seat on his horse was firm.

Flints in the soil clacked beneath the hobnails in Mael's sandals as the friends trudged toward the sea. Starkad's huge feet were encased in boots sewn from single pieces of cowhide, supple and silent as he walked. They were laced around the outside. In colder weather the boots could be stuffed with rags for insulation and tied with one or two fewer wraps of the thongs.

Gawain rode past on his way back to Arthur, giving Mael a nod and a grin that could have meant anything. When they were beyond him but still long out of earshot of the Irish, Starkad said, "If we both got in the boat, friend, we could be well out to sea before any horsemen reached us. I've always wanted to see Ireland again."

"Umm," Mael said. "You watched that little archery practice just now?"

"They'd kill half the embassy if they started shooting at us in the middle of the boat," Starkad protested, starting to raise his voice.

"That's going to bother Huns?" Mael asked. "Or Arthur?"

The Dane chuckled. He said, "Umm. Yeah, he is mad, isn't he?" Then, "I wish I were leaving with you, friend. I really do wish that."

They were among the houses now, square, one-story buildings. Their east walls, away from the sea and the salt droplets the wind lashed from it during storms, were high and moss-furry. The doors and windows were there, now shuttered but able to be opened to the sun when it rose over the harsh ridge line. The roofs of the houses were slate, black stone frosted with the gray-green lichen despite the salt scouring. They sloped seaward more steeply than the hillside, so that the exposed western walls were only two or three feet high.

Mael glanced back at the seaward lines as they passed. The walls were blank, courses of limestone laid without mortar or even mud to fill the chinks. They were not relieved by windows or openings of any kind. Did the women of these fisher-folk not look up from their evening cooking, the eternal fish stew and bread baked in the coals from bartered flour, to see if their men were returning? To watch for the bobbing coracle that held father or brother or husband—or all three, perhaps, in the same man?

But the walls were as blind as the cliffs from which they were quarried, as expressionless as the sea they faced. And perhaps that was the explanation: the sea would have her way. To search her face for disaster was to multiply that certain disaster by as many days as she, laughing, withheld it. A stoic who ignored fate could be hurt only once—at a time.

"I wonder," Starkad said, wagging the axe on his shoulder just enough to call his friend's attention to it, "why Arthur let me and this so close to him today? Last night it was our lives or our weapons before he'd let us come near. Does he think I love him now for making me a hostage?"

"I doubt he thinks anyone loves him," Mael said after brief reflection. "Mad, yes, but not stupid. . . . But you've noticed his foot?"

"He was whelped when the clay of his flesh was too wet," the Dane said. "Back home, a brat like that— well, the nights get cold on the kitchen middens, even in the summer. And there's always something hungry prowling there for what might be thrown out of the back doors."

Mael touched his lips in what could have been distaste, but man differed from man, and customs differed among peoples. One individual and another could cross lines of race and tribe to find friendship— but that did not make the differences less real. "On his horse," Mael explained, "Arthur's as steady as any other man with four legs under him. On his own feet, he—fears."

"He was born with more than his foot twisted," muttered Starkad.

The Irish had carried their curragh ashore rather than simply drawing it up on the beach at high tide. The crew had leaped into the surf when the boat grounded and put their shoulders to the hull while their hands found such purchase as they could on the slimy oxhides. When the men heaved upward the whole vessel came, dripping and lurching as the bearers lost their footing on the stones or a wave swept the legs from under several like a soft flail. Shouting and laughing, their steps quicker and more certain as they advanced beyond the slick buffeting of the sea, the Irish had carried their boat up to where the house walls announced safety from the waves of even the fiercest storm. As Mael and Starkad approached, the crew was launching the curragh again as easily by reversing the process.

The curragh was lightly built but not light. Its transport was a function of the fifty strong men beneath it, rather than an absolute lack of burden. There was no true keel or skeleton of ribs, only a wicker lattice anchored in the center to a thirty-foot sapling. The flexible ends of the tree had been bent up to mold the identical stern and prow. Over the framework were stretched oxhides, sewn to the lattice and to each other with linen cord. The seams and thread holes had been carefully tarred, leaving a shiny black pattern superimposed on the brown and black and white blotches of the hides. The seams still leaked, of course, but most of the water that would slap in the vessel's interior would come over the low sides.

If the outside of the hull was simple, its interior was almost nonexistent. There were no oar benches or true thwarts, only withies crossing from gunwale to gunwale every yard or so. With luck, that flimsy bracing would keep the wicker frame from opening out at sea like a bud in springtime. There were no oarlocks or even oars; the curragh was paddled like a huge canoe, twisting and snaking across the waves. It was as limber as a sea serpent and as large. In its crew, the vessel carried a venom more lethal than anything with scales could match.

"Well, do as you please," Starkad said as he eyed the Irish who were beginning to load the curragh. It quivered in the surf. "You will, anyway. But I'd rather that if you have to throw yourself in with those fine ambassadors that you'd at least go armed."

"Oh, I'm armed," Mael laughed, tapping the dagger

in his belt sheath. It was a serviceable weapon with a twelve-inch blade, unmarked but of good steel. Its thick tang ran the length of the sharkskin grip to the butt cap. The knife was not a toy, but neither was Starkad's concern misplaced. Besides the dagger and the leather scrip balancing it on the other side of his belt, Mael wore only a tunic and breeches of dark wool, his sandals, and a cloak he carried rolled and slung under his arm. His sword and coat of ring mail, his shield and steel cap, all were back in the room he shared with Starkad in the recruits' barracks. "After all," Mael said, "If I'm to be safe where I'm going, I've got to look harmless and Irish. In all my gear, I wouldn't look either."

Dubtach, soaked to the waist, stepped out of the sea and noticed them. "You're going with us?" he demanded. "They told us one. Gets damned crowded on one a' these bitches, though I don't suppose a land-lobster like your king up there'd know."

"I'd know, wouldn't I?" said Mael speaking the liquid Irish of his youth. It was a tongue that already had more of a lilt and a bubble to it than the remainder of the Celtic language stream. "Haven't I raided the coast south of here in a boat no bigger than this and with twice the crew?" And Mael had, of course, twelve years before, in a force led by Cearbhall, the High King's brother. Cearbhall, a few years older than this Dubtach but with the same bright hair, the same muscular chest and arms . . . "The Dane is here only to see me off; I'll be going back with you alone, and you'll have no need to worry for my stomach."

"Irish, are you? I'd taken you for a Briton," said Dubtach. In his eyes was a glint that further increased his resemblance to the Ard Ri's dead brother. Nor had the reference escaped the war chief—there had been few raids in recent years. "And you say you sailed with Cearbhall? He was the last real man Ireland raised so near the throne, Manannan knows. The day of his murder was an ill one for the country."

"He's dead, then?" Mael asked in lying ignorance. The speech and the warriors around him were pulling his mind back to another beach, another curragh, and it was all the same except that now there was no blood. . . .

"Dead?" repeated Dubtach. "Of course he's dead, throat cut in his own tent ten years—say, if you sailed with him, how is it you wouldn't know that?"

Starkad stood a step to Mael's right and a little to the rear, as inconspicuous as a 250-pound axeman could be. The Dane's eyes were measuring the distance to Dubtach. Mael spread his hand, palm backward, as if just stretching the fingers, and told the war chief the first outright lie, the planned lie: "Oh, I didn't come back from the raid, I took a block of stone on the head the night the Britons ambushed us. . . . You've heard about that?"

Dubtach's nod was agreement, and the smile spreading across his horsy teeth was proof that he had heard the rest, too; the payment Cearbhall had drawn from the villagers who had dared defend their goods.

"For seven years I was a slave," Mael continued, "and for five more a freedman. Now the king is letting me go home." And the strangest thing about the lie, Mael realized, was that in a psychic way it was no lie at all. He had not been wounded on the raid, but something of him *had* stayed behind in the West Country. It had been nailed to the hut-walls like the villagers themselves—men, women, and children. The lucky ones had been dead. Of the rest; some were screaming and some were silent, but all of them screamed when Cearbhall gave the order and his men began thrusting torches into the roofs of the plundered huts. That screaming was a thing to which Mael could have grown hardened in time; he could have come to accept it as a necessity of life, like the shriek of a pig on the butchering ground or the grunt of a warrior who has just taken your point through his rib cage. Even twelve years ago, Mael had known he was no better a man than most of those around him. The shock, the realization of what he had been helping to accomplish, was just too sudden, that was all.

And as the flames rose, Cearbhall had turned so that Mael could see his eyes. There was nothing behind them but arrogance that would not brook the slightest hint of opposition. Mael had collapsed. His fellows thought it was a delayed reaction to a blow, but in reality Mael had been bludgeoned by an insight more damaging than a stone could have been.

Later he had dreamed about the empty eyes, nightmares that at first had ended in sweaty terror. Then, as months and a year went by, Mael woke in red killing rages instead. About two years later, the dreams and Cearbhall had ended together.

Red-haired, scar-chested Dubtach clapped Mael on the shoulder. "Ireland needs more of the old breed," he said. "Come and see me after you've looked about your homeplace long enough to satisfy kinship. Muirchertach's an open-handed man, and he'll have a need for men to follow him soon. Real men."

"Gear's stowed," shouted one of the crewmen standing in the curragh while a dozen others held the hull parallel to the shore and steady. The boat bobbed in the shallows, waiting for the burden of men to fill its mottled sleekness.

"Then start boarding," Dubtach called back. "You too," he said to Mael. He turned to supervise the boarding.

Mael looked at Starkad, then up the slope toward the cataphracts. The sheen of their points and armor would, by Arthur's design, be the last image the Irish carried away from Britain. Mael rapped Starkad in the middle of the chest and said, "See you soon."

The Dane caught the outstretched wrist and squeezed it. "Make sure you come back," he said quietly.

"I wouldn't leave you," replied Mael, hurt that Starkad thought he might abandon his friend to Arthur's whimsy.

Starkad snorted, nodding his head contemptuously toward Arthur and his troops. "Think I care what *they'll* do to me if you don't show up? Don't worry about that. But I've gotten used to having you around." The big man squeezed Mael's wrist again, then used its leverage to turn the Irishman toward the sea and the waiting curragh.

The vessel was riding thirty yards from the line of wet gravel. Waves staggered Mael twice as he strode outward. The second time the water rose mid-thigh and almost threw Mael down with its purchase on his tunic. Out of practice, he thought, not that he cared. Reaving in skin boats was, like plucking hens, a skill with which Mael had some acquaintance but no desire for proficiency. Besides, half the men trying to restrain the curragh had gone down in the last wave, too.

Most of the crew was aboard by the time Mael gripped the flexible gunwales and let the men to either side of his handhold pull him in. It was not a hard pull since the loaded vessel showed only a foot of freeboard. Last within were the two wolf-hounds who until then had paddled around the curragh in happy circles. The dogs launched themselves out of the water like hairy porpoises, buffeting men aside as they landed. Somehow they managed to avoid impaling themselves on spear points. One hound shook itself and turned around three times before flopping down with its head across Mael's feet. Its tongue lolled. The grizzled paddler beside Mael glanced over and said apologetically, "Blood and old Terror, here, they can't bear for a boat to put out without they're aboard. Even though we aren't raiding."

Mael nodded and grinned back at the rangy dog. He knew why the beasts accompanied raiders. The long, toothy jaws were not to kill but to hold ransomable fugitives. The dogs' masters would do the killing if whim and economics required.

"Stroke, damn you, *stroke!*" Dubtach was shouting from the stern. There was no rudder or steering oar on the curragh, but stern or bow were the natural places for the captain to seat himself anyway. Loaded with fifty men and their gear, the vessel drew considerably more water than it had empty. Furious paddling thrust the curragh forward, but the next wave cost all of the gains. The bottom scraped. Every man aboard knew what the shore would do to the oxhide hull if it caught them fully.

Up the slope, Arthur's warhorn sang. Mael looked back, saw the six dark-skinned riders detach themselves from the group around the standard and ride for the beach. Mael saw Starkad, too, his axe-helve slung through the double loops on his back and the ocean hammering his chest with foam from about the

curragh's stern. The curved stern-post slipped backward despite all that fifty straining paddlers could
do. Then the Dane's great hands blocked it. The supple
wood gave a little but Starkad did not, despite the
weight surging against him. The sea turned and the
curragh shot outward beyond the shelf of the shore.
The next swell only lifted it. Starkad turned and the
Huns drew up, even before the horn ordered them
to recase their bows.

Mael let his breath out very slowly. Dubtach kinked
forward again, still shaking his head in amazement.
"A strong man, your friend." he said.

"He's that, all right," Mael agreed. "One day he's
going to decide he's strong enough to live with a dozen
arrows through his chest, though. I'll be sorry for
that day." And for the men who kill that foolish blond
bear, Mael added bleakly, but that was to himself
and unspoken.

Chapter Three

It was a normal voyage by curragh: wet, cramped, and queasy. Without a sail—the vessel was too flimsy for a mast to be stepped, much less to take the strain of a filled sail—the crew had to paddle constantly in shifts to make way. In theory, the men not paddling could have slept. In practice, the chill sea sloshed across the open belly of the craft and made sleep both unlikely and dangerous. Part of the crew bailed at all times. If the water within rose too high, the curragh would sink like a stone. It was lightly built but not of positive buoyancy.

"I had a piece there in Arthur's camp, one of his captains' wives," Dubtach began when they were out of the surf. "So blond she looked white as an old lady. But when she threw her cloak back she hadn't a stitch on under it and there wasn't a wrinkle in her skin. I swear by the MacLir . . ." The rest of the story was a paradigm of the conversation for the whole of the voyage. It was, indeed, the conversation of every group of soldiers since war began. Only the languages change.

Muirchertach's men were a relic of older times, still normal in Ireland. Their shields were light, generally of oxhide strapped with bronze or iron. Almost none of them wore body armor. In the ancient past, battle nudity had been of magical significance, an ultimate sign of faith that the gods would save the man who trusted in them. Now even in Ireland it was more conservatism and braggadocio, acceptable enough on an island whose only contact with other peoples was at the islanders' choice. Niall's reavers, for all their savagery and their king's reputation, would have fared no better arrayed against a legion than had Boudicca's naked warriors three centuries before. But the reavers had proven quite adequate for murdering civilians while Rome's sparse troops marched from the site of one raid to another.

When Mael fled Ireland, he had considered armor and made his own decision about it. If he were to earn his living by war, he would arm himself so that he could fight at the front of any battle on earth. That meant weapons which would cut without breaking or bending, a shield that could last an afternoon of strong men and hard blows—and a good coat of mail, for in the midst of war no man could avoid all blows from his blind side. But now, looking at the naked warriors around him, a fierce surge of freedom shook the exile. He grinned in its throes, and the grin was unpleasant.

The voyage took half a day, lasting from daylight to dusk and then three miserable hours of pitch darkness besides. Dubtach tried to make sense out of the stars. Finally the shore loomed up, richly odorous and—for all its dangers—still home to Mael.

Dubtach and his chiefs held a lengthy, querulous conversation as they tried to decide where the curragh was about to fetch up. Most of the other crewmen joined in. Even the hounds, smelling land and a chance to run, began to whine loudly until a frustrated warrior booted them to whimpers.

"We'll land," Dubtach said finally. "If it's not Muirtaig's reach, it's Eoghan's, and we've no foes so great in the Laigin we need fear to camp on their beach for a night."

They drew in, the men in the stern paddling while those in the bow poised to leap into the grumbling surf at the least tremor from the bottom. To the right was a headland jutting high enough that a clump of three stunted junipers could grow in despite of the salt spray. One of the crewmen called out, pointing to the landmark. Dubtach cawed in triumph, "Who says I can't navigate, hey? Not fifty feet from where we put her in the sea, are we?"

No one contradicted the war chief, least of all Mael. Having listened to Dubtach wrangling about their bearings with men equally ignorant, Mael knew the curragh might as easily have made landfall in the Hebrides.

Mael joined in the quick dash for the beach with the hull of the curragh flexing over his shoulder like a silent drum. Laughing in relief at their safe return, the crew carried the vessel high up on the beach to where the grass displaced the pebbles. The night was warm and friendly, lighted by the silver moon just edging up over the sea. A trio of wattle huts in a palisade were within a hundred yards of the beached curragh. No one came to a door despite the halloos of some of the men. Well, thought Mael, he wouldn't have come out himself to meet such a mob. At least not until dawn or an attack required it. The exile smiled, thinking of the householders tremblingly alert, each with a fish spear or a gutting knife clenched in his hand. This time the residents would be lucky.

"These are Muirchertach's lands?" Mael asked, stretching his arms high to ease the cramped muscles of his back.

"King Muirtaig's," Dubtach corrected him. "He sends his tribute to the Laigin as we do not. But we have no coast, so we borrowed this curragh from Muirtaig against a dozen horses pledged for its return."

"Can you show me the road for Lough Conn?" Mael asked, naming a lake in the shadow of the Ox Mountains, far beyond where he intended to go. He wanted to be clear of Dubtach and his troupe as quickly as possible. With them Mael was an outsider— always dangerous when among armed men. Besides, he was sure to attract comment as "the man from Britain" so long as he accompanied those who had brought him over.

"We'll be heading west tomorrow," Dubtach said. "Travel with us."

"Umm, I'll be back when I've done the business I need to do," Mael replied mildly. "For now—well, I've been gone twelve years, and I'd not add another hour to them for choice."

The war chief shrugged. "I'll point you to the road, then," he said. "It's past the orchard, is all."

They walked together between the rows of apple trees on the high ground west of the shore. The trees were well kept but as gnarled and ingrown as only old fruit trees become. In the flat moonlight they looked more mineral than alive. The air among them was a little warmer, a little sweeter, than that of the shore. The trilling of katydids in the branches washed away the raucous jollity of the warriors below.

"Right there's the track," said Dubtach, pointing to a dirt path bounded on the far side by hedgerows. "Go left here and just follow whichever branch seems western at a fork if you can't get better directions. Now, I think there's a spring here if—umm, hel-*lo!*"

Figures moved, two horses and a woman standing in the shadow of the hedge to the right. Dubtach shrugged as if to loosen clothing from about his bare torso. Mael touched his tongue to his lips, darting his eyes about the darkness and silently cursing the katydids. Their sound, so welcome a moment before, would cloak the rustle of bandits creeping to attack. The woman's presence made sense only if she were a decoy.

The woman walked closer while the horses stood where they were on their dropped reins. She was not tall, perhaps a little over five feet, nor was she heavy. Her slim fingers were loosely intertwined in front of her. She wore a gray cloak pinned at the right shoulder. The shift beneath it was of linen, but it was bleached and silver-gilt by the moon so that it showed as a gleaming wedge. Then the woman shrugged her cowl back and Mael could see the shift was no brighter than her hair. Her face was perfect and unlined. Glancing at the contrast, Mael was reminded of Dubtach's tale of his ash-blonde conquest in Britain. Mael was surprised at the sudden hatred for the war chief that boiled through him at the thought.

Dubtach stood, arms akimbo, and said to the woman, "And what would you be doing here, *lady*?"

Mael was behind him, but even there he could feel the tooth-baring smile in Dubtach's voice.

"Waiting for a man," she said, looking at Dubtach and looking away to Mael. Her voice was full without being either deep or loud. "I've found him now."

"That you have!" brayed Dubtach. He reached out his long, thick-muscled arm and drew the woman closer by the shoulder. "Two of us, indeed."

"No." The woman nodded at Mael. "I'm waiting for him." she squirmed, which should have made no difference to Dubtach's heavy grip, but the cloak rippled under his fingers, leaving the woman free and a yard away, staring coolly at the war chief's fury.

Dubtach's left hand toyed with his sword hilt, raising it an inch or two to free the blade in the scabbard before dropping it back. The gesture was unconscious and a suggestive one. Dubtach reached out again with his right hand. Mael touched his elbow. "Wait a minute," the exile said quietly.

The red-haired warrior snapped around like a released spring. "You're going to tell me she's kin to you?" he shouted at Mael. "That she knew you were coming here when I didn't myself?"

"I'll tell you damn-all but the truth," Mael said, his own voice controlled and as tight as the muscles of his rectum. They were drawing up and chilling his whole body with the fear of death. "She's no kin, she's no acquaintance—by the Dagda's dick, she's not even Irish, you can hear that in her voice." Which was true; the syllables were perfect but too flat for a native speaker's. "But this I will say, I'll not be a part to a rape in a stranger king's territory, not with me not an hour landed in Ireland again."

"You just hold her bloody arms and leave me to

worry about Muirtaig," Dubtach snarled. He turned back to the woman.

Mael caught him again by the arm. Dubtach cursed as he jerked his hand down to his sword hilt. Mael kicked him in the groin, his hand locking Dubtach's down so that the war chief could not draw. Dubtach's gasp as he doubled over choked the call for assistance that was already halfway up his throat. Mael hit him on the back of the head and cursed as Dubtach ignored the blow and tried to rise. Mael kneed him in the face, then drew his own dagger and chopped the red-haired man with the butt of it twice behind the ear. This time Dubtach sagged all the way to the ground.

Mael spun, crouching, his dagger out to take the charge and the life of anyone who might have followed him and Dubtach through the orchard. Breeze and the terrain blocked all sound of the men at the beach. Mael prayed that all sound of Dubtach's struggles had been masked as well.

He turned again, both fearful and threatening. The woman with white hair had not moved, nor had the hedges spilled her suspected companions. Mael was breathing heavily. "I need one of your horses," he said, pointing his dagger downward. He did not sheath it, not yet. "I'll pay you for it, a fair price."

"I brought it for you," said the woman. "I've been watching for you to come."

"That was a fine story the first time, " Mael snapped sarcastically. "It nearly got me killed and you raped by a boatload instead of the chief only. But it's no good with me, you see. You don't know me and you can't have been expecting me."

"I've been waiting for Loeghaire o'—"

"*Don't say that name!*" Mael shouted. For the instant

he forgot the men on the shore and the others a cry might bring to find him over the bludgeoned Dubtach. He forgot everything but the far past and the icy fear of discovery. Mael had convinced himself that it would not happen on a brief return. After all, there had been a decade for men and memories to age.

"Come," said the woman, "we have to ride."

That was good advice. Besides, Mael was beyond planning for himself, not then. He sheathed his dagger as he followed her, two quick steps and a vault that took him astride the larger of the two horses. The woman mounted the bay mare as easily. Mael's stallion walked, then trotted to quick heel pressure. They were following the path westward as Dubtach had directed.

"Where are we going?" the woman asked, keeping station to Mael's right and half a pace behind.

"Don't you know that, too?" Mael retorted. The measured gait of the horse was a comfort to the exile's mind, especially after the greasy smoothness of the curragh in the waves.

"I was told to meet a man," the woman said, her tone quiet and certain. She sounded like a mother drawing an answer out of an unruly boy. "And if you don't want me to call you by the name you were born with, you have to tell me what you go by now. I'm Veleda."

"Mael mac Ronan," Mael said unwillingly. Veleda was not an Irish name, but that was no surprise. German, perhaps? But not really that, either. There was no accent at all in her speech; rather, she had a suspicious lack of accent. And—but Mael broke into his own thoughts to add, "I'm riding to Lough Conn," repeating his lie to Dubtach.

They went on in silence for almost a mile, through

a landscape of small fields and occasional small turf houses. Most of the dwellings were surrounded by fences that served both as corrals and for protection from attack. Once a horse whinnied as Mael and Veleda passed, but their own mounts made no reply.

They reached the first fork in the road. Veleda pointed to the right without hesitation. They continued on. "What are you?" Mael demanded abruptly without looking at his companion.

"A woman," she replied.

He turned in his saddle and her eyes were on him already, her face shadowed by the silver frame of her hair. "There's ten thousand women in Ireland," Mael said, "and not one of them but you knew where I'd be landing—any more than I myself did. What are you?"

"We're all of us together in the world," Veleda said, "all of us a part of it and of each other. Some are born a little more aware of that togetherness than others. I hear things, I'm told things. I was told that I should meet you, and where I should and when . . . and I did. I don't know who or what it was that told me, or why—not really. If all that makes me wise, then I'm a wise woman, as some have called me. But they've called me a demon, too, and a goddess—and I'm none of those things. I'm a woman."

She smiled and tossed her head. The road jogged south at the same moment, and the thin moon lit Veleda's face like a still pool in the sunlight. Mael grinned back, then laughed aloud as he found himself believing her. A pressure lifted from him. "I won't complain that you hear voices," he said, "if they've saved me a hike I was dreading."

For a while Mael's face sobered, but it did not fall into the grim lines it had worn at the beginning of

the ride. He held his horse for the half step that
brought Veleda abreast of him, then asked, "What
are you going to do, then?"

"There's something very important and very near,"
Veleda said. "Very . . ."

"A king rising?" interjected Mael into the pause
with his mind on mad, brilliant Arthur and his
boasting. "An empire?"

"No," said Veleda with the curtness of one who
understands something completely for one who never
would. "Not men, not anything of men. That's like
saying the sun sends down its light to warm us. We're
not that important. But whatever is about to happen,
you're a part of it. I want to stay with you, at least
until I understand more than I do now." she smiled
again. "That's a fault of mine. I like to know things."

"Umm," murmured Mael as he considered. Indeed
she was a woman. An attractive one who had done
him a favor. Clearly it was not safe for her to wander
alone in a country as unsettled as Ireland now. Even
the leaders, unless Dubtach was the exception,
seemed to think it no disgrace to rape in peacetime
as if they were at war. . . . "We'll see, then," Mael
said. "Do you have any relatives around here?"

"None at all."

"Well, we'll see then," Mael repeated. "For now, I
think we're far enough from Dubtach and his friends
for safety, and I, at least, could use a soft place to
sleep in. Though I doubt we'll do better than a
haystack. It's damned late, and nobody with good
sense is going to open his house to strangers."

"I've slept in haystacks before," said Veleda. "There's
one a quarter mile ahead on the right—near the path
and far enough from the house that we won't trouble
the owners. Or they us."

"Oh, you've been this way—" Mael began. He stopped himself when he realized that if the answer were "No" he would not want to have heard it.

The haystack was where Veleda said it would be. It was a six-foot dome notched by use to half that height on one side. The two of them unsaddled their horses. Mael stripped the reins off his mount and started to use them as a makeshift hobble, but the woman said, "No need—they won't stray." She had already unpinned her cloak and was wrapping it around her in place of a blanket.

Mael shook out his own cloak, a thick, gray-white rectangle of wool. It had not been either bleached or dyed. The lanolin still in the wool made the garment almost waterproof. He eyed Veleda as he worked, fascinated by her grace and the economy of her movements. Odd—generally he liked his women tall, with a little more bone showing than was most men's ideal. Mael's mind flashed him a memory of a tanned, rangy woman, her eyes and hair black and welcoming. He shivered with the force of the thought, shaking his head as if to free cobwebs from his hair.

This woman, Veleda. Was it her hair that drew him? It fell in silky perfection to the small of her back when she shook it from beneath her cloak. Or again, the attraction might be her face; serene and smooth, its youthfulness was a stunning contrast to the white tresses around it. Veleda's lips were thin—thinner than those other lips—though not cruel. But a knife blade is not cruel either, only lethal, and there was a quality of lethal determination in the blonde woman's lips and face. Veleda's hands were small and gentle, as delicate as filigree brooches. They clasped the cloak about her in the moonlight.

Mael grunted and rolled himself down in the

yielding hay. He found the woman interesting as a person, and the fact concerned him. Interest in women as people was a practice Mael thought he had given up ten years before, in a bloodstained bedchamber. That was not a scene he ever wanted to repeat.

Sleep was a longer time coming than it should have been.

Chapter Four

In the morning Mael told Veleda their real destination, the wide slough of the Shannon that was Lough Ree. The roads were crooked and narrow, frequently muddy ruts where their course followed a creek. Mael and Veleda moved as fast as the well-being of the horses allowed, but Mael knew it would be at least an honest three days' travel to the wayside shrine that was his goal.

Though travelers were rare, the two of them attracted little attention. Veleda generally rode with her cowl up to hide her striking hair. They were both too simply dressed to arouse greed. Mael, though not heavily armed, had a killer's look about him that twice turned casual bullies to look for other prey. All around were signs of an unsettled land. Men tilled their fields with spears lashed to their plows where they could be seized at need. Women called their

67

children sharply out of the road when the strangers appeared. But two riders who gave no trouble and looked able to defend themselves were safe enough anywhere.

Veleda traded brass armlets for boiled mutton and porridge along the way, bargaining with the householders while Mael stood back with just enough of a frown to encourage a quick resolution. They dipped water from springs when there was no house nearby to barter them beer.

And each night the two of them slept on the ground, close enough together that Mael could feel the heat from the woman's body—or thought he could. Mael's knee had swollen where Dubtach's tooth had cut it, but the pain and swelling had disappeared when Veleda applied a poultice of leaves and spider silk. Mael's only pain was that of his groin which was as tight as an inflated bladder. It ached, especially when his mind wandered back to times past. Mael talked incessantly as they rode.

Late in the afternoon of the third day, Mael and Veleda topped the wooded ridge that overlooked the black waters of Lough Ree a quarter mile away. There had to be some current, but the surface seemed still for as far as the watchers could see. Reeds grew so thickly in the shallows that the shoreline was hard to determine. The western slope of the ridge on which Mael stood was covered with rhododendrons that linked themselves impassably to either side of the path. From the water's edge at the end of the path, a rickety pier thrust out beyond the reeds.

Halfway down the hill, between the crest and the pier, stood a tiny stone chapel whose peaked roof made it look taller than it was long. "The shrine of the Unknown Hero," said Mael in satisfaction. "They say a traveler jumped into the lough with nothing but a sword and beheaded the monster there. Quite a hero tale about it—as there are about lots of things, of course. More to the point, there was a shrine built at the spot—here—and the monster's skull inside it. I saw it once."

"And you're going to kill a monster yourself?" Veleda asked mildly.

Mael snorted. "I won't go swimming with fish that size," he said, "not when somebody did the work for me already. Besides, there aren't any of the beasts around, not any more."

He felt Veleda's cool eyes on him. He turned to her, frowning. "Look," Mael said, "it happened a long time ago. There's stories that the hero was Niall, but that's not true—the skull was old even when he was the High King. Maybe it really was Lugh or some other god that killed the thing—that's what the oldest songs say. I don't know. But I don't have years to spend out there in a rowboat, proving that the skull in the shrine was the last one there was to be had, either. I don't care to rob a shrine, and if your voices tell you to go—go. I didn't plan to drag anybody here anyway.

"But the gods can take care of their own. I've got a friend depending on me."

"A man does what he must," Veleda said.

"A man does what he can, you mean," Mael said, and he faced back to the shrine. But of course it was not what Veleda meant, and it galled Mael more than any open condemnation could have.

The chapel was of ashlar-cut limestone. The roof was formed by heavy timbers because its slope was too sharp for slates. There was a suggestion of a wooden lean-to built against the far side, but the angle

made it hard to see for sure. On the uphill side toward
Mael was a wooden door and a slit window. The latter
was unshuttered but too narrow to pass a man or
even a boy. A yard of sorts had been cleared of
rhododendrons. A solid oak bench sat in the clearing
against the wall of the building. It was a moment
before Mael noticed the stone cross that now stood
at the northern peak of the roof.

"Christian?" he blurted incredulously.

"Many of the old places are now," Veleda replied.
"It's coming, you know, all over Ireland."

Mael shook his head. "I've been away too long,"
he said. He grinned and added, "Or maybe not long
enough. Well, this may change things, but we won't
know till we check." He clucked to his horse, leading
the way down the narrow path through the twisted
shrubs.

Chance or the thud of hooves on the peaty soil
brought motion at the window. Then the door flew
back and a short man stepped out of the building to
await them. He was a priest—or a monk, perhaps;
there was a difference but Mael did not know quite
what it was. The man was old and wore a cassock of
black wool in startling contrast to his white beard
and hair. His face was more shrunken together than
lined, its expression bitter and proud and inflexible.
He could have been fifty years old or eighty, but he
still moved like a bird.

Mael smiled and waved his right hand, empty, in
greeting. The priest nodded stiffly in reply. He
stepped to the side of the door. A balding giant seven
feet tall walked out of the shrine behind the priest,
ducking to clear the lintel.

Mael was not small himself, and he had been around
even bigger men for most of his life. This fellow would

be, he thought, the biggest man he had ever seen. The giant was barefoot and clad in a plain linen tunic with a wide sash. He seemed to taper toward both ends like a skein of wool. Mael's first thought was that the giant was fat, since his smooth limbs seemed stuffed like sausages and his torso a tun of lard. Then the fellow moved in front of the black-garbed priest. His flesh rippled and bulged instead of dimpling as fat does. The giant was muscular, and there was an awesome bulk of those muscles.

"Fergus!" snapped the priest. "Did you finish your prayers?"

The giant stopped. He opened his mouth and drooled slightly on his tunic. Mael could see that the cloth was already damp. "I forgot," Fergus rumbled, looking at the ground instead of the small man questioning him.

"And do you want the Lord Almighty to forget you in the day of your need? Is that what you want, Fergus?" the priest demanded.

The giant began to twist his right index finger into his left palm. He concentrated wholly on the process and did not speak.

The priest sighed. He wiped spittle from the giant's chin with the end of the sash, then said, "Oh, go sit down. But you *must* be more careful." Obediently Fergus walked to the bench and sat. The oak creaked loudly. The giant's round face was as expressionless as his bare pate.

The giant's appearance had startled Mael out of his original plan of tying the priest, stealing the skull, and fleeing before a chance wayfarer stopped by the shrine. Instead, the exile reined up at the edge of the clearing and said, "Ah, sir . . ." but he could not think of a way to continue.

The little priest nodded. "Yes, yes, I'm Father Diarmid. And you're pilgrims to the shrine, I see— since this path doesn't lead anywhere else."

Mael dismounted, still trying to frame a useful opening. His body no longer blocked Diarmid's view of Veleda. The priest's breath hissed in. His wizened face took on the look of a man who has caught his wife making love to the potboy. "Witch!" he cried with loathing.

Mael blinked in surprise and looked back at Veleda. She was calm, not even frowning. There was nothing unusual about her except her hair—and that, if unusual, was no certain witch-mark.

But the priest was right.

Diarmid pointed at the woman and his voice, never pleasant, rasped like a corn mill as he shouted, "You! God seared Ireland over the coals of his wrath for your sort, witches and druids! He brought the Plague on us as upon the heathen Egyptians, that all this land should know His name and follow Him. Your gods are false, dead and stinking with the corruption of their falsehood. How dare you try to enter this holy place wrapped in sin and error?"

"Men will do as they wish, think as they wish, pray as they wish," said Veleda. She leaned a little toward the old man and added, with a distinctness as forceful as his own shouted polemic, "and god is still the same in all his aspects. For myself, I don't worship a god who died on a tree, and my god doesn't drown the earth with the blood of innocents to fill his churches— and his coffers!"

"Get away from here," Diarmid said, almost calmly. The leash on his tongue snapped and he screamed, "Get away from here, whore of Satan! Cease defiling ground blessed by the feet of the Holy Padraic!"

"Now wait a minute . . ." Mael began. He stepped forward with his left hand raised as much for attention as a sign of peaceful intent.

Fergus moved also. He reached under the bench on which he sat and twitched out what Mael had thought was a loose building block. It was a forty-pound wedge of soapstone, a small boat anchor. A three-inch hole had been bored in the center to reeve through a line. Fergus had fitted the stone with an oak shaft as long as Mael's arm. The streaked, gray mace head was utterly steady though Fergus held it one-handed.

The giant stood. Mael smiled and brought his left hand around in a slow arc to the side, nothing threatening, just an easy motion to draw eyes away from his right hand and the dagger in his belt. He could slip the knife out and throw it point first, knowing that at seven feet he could bury it to the hilt in Fergus' chest. Mael knew also that while the dagger would kill the giant, it would assuredly not stop him. The sweeping counter-blow of the mace would literally tear Mael's head off if it connected. His fingers poised—

"Wait! " Veleda cried. Mael froze, turned his head toward her. She was white with the same fury that was shaking Diarmid, but the command in her voice was certain. "This isn't a fight between men," she said, "and I'll not stay to make it one. But I've one last thing to say before I leave, priest: men get the sort of gods they deserve." She wheeled her horse. "Mael," she added, "I'll wait for you at the top of the hill."

Mael and Diarmid both watched her ride off. Fergus simply grunted and flicked his mace back under the bench as easily as he had taken it out.

"Wipe your mouth, Fergus," the priest said. Fergus stared at him blankly. Diarmid muttered, then daubed spittle from the slack chin. Then the giant sat down again.

"You aren't Christian, either," Diarmid said, "but you're not a witch. What brought you here?"

"I came to see the skull of the monster," Mael said. "The one the Unknown Hero slew."

"The monster which God Almighty slew at the behest of the Holy Padraic," the priest corrected him, sharply though without rancor.

Mael blinked. "Padraic killed one of the water monsters, too?" he asked in perplexity.

"There was only one of the creatures," snapped Diarmid, "a child of Satan—as *all* things heathen are. It pursued one of the followers of the Holy Padraic as he swam toward a coracle." The priest gestured vaguely toward the peat-black waters in which his own skiff bobbed at the end of the pier. "The Apostle prayed to God to save his disciple, and the hand of God struck down the monster in answer to the saint's prayer."

"I hadn't heard the story," Mael said mildly. Nor had his father, who had seen the relic before Padraic had returned to Ireland to preach in the year Mael was born. The year Loeghaire was born, that was, but he must not think of that . . . "Father," Mael said aloud to the stern-faced priest, "I've traveled a long way to see this skull."

"You'll find your journey to Hell much shorter unless you repent," the older man gibed, but he motioned his visitor to follow as he stepped into the shrine. Fergus stood also.

Diarmid crossed himself at the threshold. He looked at the giant. "Fergus," he said.

"I forgot, Father," Fergus said. He crossed himself carefully.

With Fergus' huge body blocking the doorway behind him, Mael's eyes took a moment to adjust. There was little enough to see. A wooden crucifix had been added above the altar. It was of rustic workmanship but was carven with surprising vigor. The Christ's eyes bulged as he writhed against the nails. Mael could almost hear the scream from his open mouth. The altar itself was of plain stone, the same slab that had been there when Mael had seen it as a boy. The casket on the altar was the same also. It was a foot and a half long and about a foot in width and depth, constructed of bronze-bound wood. It was so obviously ancient that Mael shot a quick glance to Diarmid to surprise signs of embarrassment at his lie about it being a relic of Padraic. There were no such signs. The priest was obviously sincere, even though his claim for Padraic being the monster-slayer was untrue on its face. Religion, Mael thought sourly. He grinned.

The design on the casket was a rendering of the monster. Its head formed the latch which opened from pressure on the plate set cunningly between its open jaws. The head of the beast was oval, with a blackish-green patina that even looked wet. Around it was a circular fringe like a stylized lion's mane or a gorgon's frill of snakes. The neck writhed around the edge of the casket to the left, while the pointed tail rejoined the head from the right side. Presumably, the creature's torso and limbs, if any, were inlaid on the back where they were out of sight for the moment.

Diarmid murmured a prayer, then reverently touched the latch. He lifted the lid of the chest.

The interior was padded with heavy scarlet wool—

a trophy itself, cut from the cloak of a high Roman officer in the days when the conquest of Britain was still in doubt. The skull within was flat, about a foot long and nine inches broad. The brain case was small, no more than the size of a clenched fist. Mael realized that what he had originally taken for large eye sockets were only sinuses in the bone to lighten it. The real eyes had been set far back and to either side of the head. The sockets were smaller than a man's.

Most of the skull, in fact, was jaw, or attachment for the jaw muscles. The maxillaries were set with a pincushion of teeth, conical and rear-slanting. The longest—and they varied little from the mean—were only about half an inch long. Fish-eater, Mael thought. He suddenly remembered the big salamander he had once plucked from beneath a rock in a stream so cold it numbed his fingers. That one had been black, slimy, and almost blind, a squirming monster in its way, though only eight inches long. A beast of that sort and this size—well, it would be nothing to meet in the water, whatever its choice of diet.

"Behold the power of the hand of God," the priest was saying.

Mael nodded. There were three vertebrae in the casket along with the skull. Two of them were notched and the third was half-missing where a blade had severed it. That bone had other blade nicks in it. The hand of God should have sharpened its sword, Mael thought to himself, but that was unfair. The drag of the water would prevent a proper stroke, and the thick sheath of muscles and cartilage would dull any edge before it reached the bone.

"Thank you," Mael said aloud. Diarmid's deep eyes burned him as if the priest knew what his visitor was planning . . . but no, that was only Diarmid's normal expression. Men get the gods they deserve. . . . "A man beholds the relics of ancient heroes that he may follow in their footsteps," Mael added sententiously.

"Follow in the path of God," Diarmid corrected, but with a hint of approval in his voice. The priest gestured. The room brightened as Fergus moved away from the door. Mael stepped back into the sunlight, hearing the latch click as the priest closed the casket behind him. Blinking with the light, the exile mounted his horse which was nibbling such grass as it could find at the edge of the rhododendrons.

"Thank you," Mael repeated. As he rode back up the slope, he could hear Diarmid scolding Fergus again for missing a prayer. For some reason, the scene chilled him.

◆   ◆   ◆

Veleda had built a small fire on the far side of the ridge, out of sight of the shrine. Mael unsaddled his horse without saying a great deal. He began to knead ash cakes from the barley flour they had bartered that morning. Veleda used her small knife to prepare a chicken for roasting. She skinned the bird instead of trying to pluck it without a pot in which to scald it first.

"He's crazy, isn't he?" Mael said at last. "Not the big one, he's just lack-witted . . . but that priest, that Diarmid, he—what he's saying is like he said the sun shines here at midnight. But he really believes it."

"Why does that bother you?" the woman asked, her hands still for the moment as she looked over at Mael.

He opened his palms. "I've never been much for gods," he said. "They may be, they may rule me and everything else—I don't know and I don't much care. I don't care much about Christians, either, in a way . . .

but even when I, ah, left Ireland, they were turning everybody to them. Now this. They don't just convert the men, they convert the holy places that have been there as long as there've been men at all on the island. And they tell lies, and they *believe* their own lies!" Mael clenched his fists in frustration. "Why is everybody going crazy?" he demanded. "Or am I?"

Veleda smiled. She spitted the chicken on a twig. "Men don't want to die," she said quietly. "People don't want to die."

"Nobody wants to die!" Mael blazed. "And everybody dies anyway. What does that have to do with it? Padraic didn't bring all this about by threatening to slit all the throats of those who wouldn't pray to his god."

"No, though that may come later," Veleda agreed. She laid her hands over Mael's, her fingertips touching his wrists. "Do you remember the Plague?"

"Yes," Mael said. The Plague had wracked Ireland only a few years after Mael was born. Limbs blackened and began to decay even before death; abscessed lungs filled with fluid and drowned sufferers; high fevers cooked brains and left behind inhuman things that died later as the rest of their systems disintegrated. Isolation had preserved Ireland for centuries from the diseases which ripped the Mediterranean Basin, but past safety was cold comfort when death began to ricochet back and forth between the narrow shores. "Yea." Mael repeated, "I don't think I'll forget that soon."

"Nobody will," Veleda said. "Most people come to religion for comfort, not truth. There are truths, but they're not for most people to know. Whole villages died then, from the Plague. Half the people on the island died, and the bodies rotted in the fields because there were too few hands left to bury them. The idea that cycles are infinite and that souls are reborn in other bodies—doesn't have any appeal after so much pain. Even though it's true. Especially because it's true."

Veleda began turning the chicken over the coals while her left hand still touched Mael, sending prickles up and down his arm. "The old faith could handle death in people's minds, but not death on that scale. You know that the emperors of Rome were worshiped as gods?" Veleda continued.

Mael nodded.

"That didn't start in Rome for a political reason," she said; "it started in Gaul, men bowing to the power that had slaughtered their kinsmen by tens of millions. And that would have happened here, people praying to death and disease because there was no other power in the land. Except that the Christians had come at the same time."

"Padraic didn't make the Plague stop," Mael argued. "Hell, he died himself just last year. A sailor in Massilia told me that when I asked for news from home."

"But death doesn't matter to Christians," Veleda explained. "They learn that this world is only a doorway to the real existence in their heaven. I don't know where that heaven is or what it is—but people don't need truth. They need a way out of a charnel house, and that Padraic and his teachings promised them."

Mael swore in frustration. He prodded at the coals to scatter fat that had dripped and flared up. The sky above them was growing dim as the sun set making the orange flames brighter. "You mean their god Christ is false," Mael said flatly.

"No." Frowning again, Mael looked up at Veleda. "No," she repeated, "I don't mean that at all. Padraic's truth wasn't my truth, but he had a power. His vision was beyond that of all but a few of the men who have ever lived. Even the little man here, Diarmid . . . Mad? Of course. But he has a window to truth of a sort. He knew me for what I am, though his twisted mind put twisted labels on what he saw.

"So I won't say their Christ is false. But sometimes I wonder at minds that can take comfort in a truth of death and torture and misery in this world."

Mael chuckled grimly. He shifted his seat a little so that he could lean back against the pine tree beside which they sheltered. "I always wanted to come home," he said. "Oh, I knew I didn't dare, but . . . I was looking for an excuse like this one that Arthur offered me. But now that I've seen Ireland again, I—well, I'll be glad enough to leave it to its Christians."

Chapter Five

Two hours after sunset, Mael slipped down the pathway afoot and alone. He would have liked to wait longer, but the moon would be rising soon. No light spilled from the priest's quarters. Probably Diarmid and the giant went to bed at sunset, vaunting a poverty that did not allow even an oil lamp. If they were awake praying instead, Mael knew he would have to take his chances. He touched his dagger hilt; they would all have to take their chances.

Mael had left his cloak behind with Veleda and the horses. His tunic and trousers were a dark blue, invisible in starlight. He had considered blackening his face and hands with mud but had decided against it. That was too clear a badge of crime to any chance-met traveler later, and Mael did not want to waste time washing if his theft was successful. Theft. Well, he'd done worse things in his life than steal from a holy place.

Before he entered the clearing, Mael crouched beside the rhododendrons that formed a solid palisade along the trail. A fitful breeze was blowing from behind him toward the water. He strained against it to hear any sounds that might be coming from the shrine. There was nothing, though a fish slapped the surface of the lough. Mael took a deep breath and stepped swiftly to the door of the building.

He had drawn his knife to force the latch, but that was unnecessary. A simple slide bolt on the outside held the door against the wind; there was no lock. Mael pushed the door open gently. At first he thought he heard a tiny tinkle of sound. He froze, but the sound was not repeated. He opened the door the rest of the way.

The casket was still on the altar under the tortured Christ. The room was otherwise empty. Mael's tautness eased. He had been more afraid than he would admit to himself that Diarmid would have removed the relic into his sleeping quarters overnight. Even worse, the priest or Fergus might have been waiting in the shrine. Mael stepped forward to take the casket and run. The room darkened.

Fergus stood blocking the doorway. The mace was in his right hand.

Mael cried out, slashing at the giant's eyes. Fergus bellowed and seized Mael with his left hand. The doughy fingers wrapped themselves in the front of Mael's tunic. He jerked upward as if Mael were weightless. Mael's bare head rang on a roof beam. The giant swung his mace to finish the smaller man, but the weapon caught in the narrow doorway. Flakes of rock spalled off the outside of the shrine.

Mael held his dagger in a death grip that had nothing conscious about it. Fergus flailed him against the walls of the stone room, roaring in his own mindless pain. Blood from his slashed face spattered over Mael and the shrine. The casket had been knocked from the altar. It lay on its side, still fastened.

"Out!" Diarmid cried. "Bring him out!"

Either the words penetrated or Fergus acted without hearing them. He stepped back, wrenching Mael through the doorway in the same motion. Mael's tunic ripped and the battered man flew free. Mael bounced numbingly on the ground. The dagger sprang from his hand. It fell, gleaming softly, a dozen feet downslope where the path continued toward the pier.

Diarmid darted into the fane to examine the precious relic. He came out with the casket a moment later. Snuffling in wild frustration, Fergus turned toward the priest for the first time since Mael had cut him. No major blood vessel had been severed, but a sheet of gore, black in the dimness, had spilled down the giant's face. It was collecting to drip from the rounded chin. Both eyeballs had been destroyed. Clear humor from the eyes emphasized the upper cheeks by washing the blood away from them. "Oh Christ, *Christ*!" Diarmid cried. "My son, *my son*!"

Mael tried to get up. He could not. His whole left side was numb, as much beyond his control as if it belonged to another man. The first shock had been to his skull. That and the repeated pounding of his body against the wall of the shrine had stunned both his muscles and nerves. He could see the sheen of his knife through a haze. He rolled toward it.

"Fergus!" the priest ordered. There was grief and rage in Diarmid's voice, but he was controlling them. The reliquary was under his right arm. His left hand guided his son's arms and weapon upward, then turned him to face Mael. The priest took a step forward, maneuvering the giant from the side. "Now!" the old man said, and he twitched at the mace arm. Fergus struck down with his full strength.

The soil was peat, compacted by the feet of pilgrims for ages. The wedge-shaped stone buried itself to its haft, brushing Mael's chest as it passed. Mael's good hand snatched up his dagger. Fergus effortlessly tore his mace free and started to take another step forward. "Back!" Diarmid cried, and Mael's blade snicked air an inch from the giant's right ankle as that foot halted.

Mael crawled backward, down the trail, putting another few feet between himself and the deadly mace. He used the heel of his right hand to propel him while the locked fingers still pointed the dagger at his enemies.

"A little forward, Fergus," the priest crooned. "No, no, boy. Don't lift your feet, slide them. That's right, now—"

Mael pivoted his body. His feet caught in the impenetrable wall of rhododendrons. The exile shouted, arching backward like a wingless insect. The mace thudded into the ground again. Fergus cleared it with a sideways flick that netted the head among the dense branches. He bawled angrily and tore the weapon free—into the tangled rhododendrons on the other side. Despite Diarmid's cries, Fergus began to slash his weapon from side to side, scattering stems and branches with every sweep. He paused only when an arc in front of him had been cleared and further strokes met no resistance.

The giant was breathing heavily. Still, he held the mace out at arm's length with no perceptible strain or weariness. Mael had scuttled a dozen feet further down the trail, temporarily out of danger. He was unable to take his eyes off the awesome destruction. Diarmid's hand touched Fergus inside the elbow. "A little forward," he said.

Mael's left side was still almost dead to him. A few prickles of sensation were returning, but he had no real feeling. In a way that was just as well. He had long since scraped away a patch of his trousers on the ground, and the skin of his thigh was rapidly going as well. Bluffing, Mael thrust himself up on his right knee and stabbed. "Back!" the priest ordered. Then, seeing the exile was still only half a man, Diarmid shouted, "Strike!" Fergus' blow was harmlessly short. Mael had bought a few more moments toward the time he would have full use of his limbs again. He backed further, to where the trail ended at the pier.

The breeze wrapped Mael in the effluvium of Fergus' body: hot, dry—the odor of an ox which has been plowing in the sun, not so much offensive as overpowering. Mael knew that he himself must stink of blood and fear like a pig in the slaughter pen. The moon had risen. It silhouetted his assailants, the giant and the black-robed priest. They hunched forward together.

Mael made a choice that was no choice. The pier was narrow and uneven, giving him even less room for maneuver than the path had done. But to either side quaked the mire of the slough margin where reeds replaced rhododendrons. To dodge to the side meant to be held in gluey muck while Fergus pounded his body into something of similar consistency. Cursing, Mael backed onto the flimsy boards.

Splinters tore at him. In another minute or two he might be able to stand or even strike back—if he could avoid the sweep of the mace until then. Mael did not even consider throwing his knife. It was the only thing that kept Fergus at a distance. The giant did not need a weapon to kill a man Mael's size. Once the threat of the dagger was gone—even if it were buried in Fergus' heart and inexorably bleeding his life away—Mael was dead. The giant would seize him barehanded and pluck his limbs off one by one, like a boy with a cricket.

The pier swayed as Fergus stepped onto it. He halted. In chillingly normal tones he said, "Father, you never wanted me to walk here."

"This once we'll go together," Diarmid said softly. "Be very careful now, Fergus. I'm right behind you." The older man paused, then added, "When I tell you, I want you to swing your club sideways."

The giant slid his right foot forward, the bare toes gliding over the irregularities of plank edged against plank. There was nothing clumsy about his advance. The pier showed no signs of imminent collapse but it creaked and sagged with the strain. Fergus was too big—and too much of his bulk was muscle—for Mael even to guess at his weight.

The pier had been constructed by driving double lines of posts into the mud of the slough, then pegging stringers to the inner face of each line. The plank flooring was attached to the stringers by leather thongs tied through holes in the wood. Where the leather had rotted away, the planks were loose and ready to spill a man who stepped on the edge. Diarmid's gentle touch kept his son centered safely and lethally.

Mael slashed quickly across the thongs holding three planks to the right-hand stringer. He twisted stiffly, ignoring the fanged splinters as he reached for the ties on the other side. If he could rip a big enough gap in the boards, he would be safe. Blind Fergus could never jump an opening. If the giant tried, his weight would carry him through into the water. He would hit the boards on the far side like a battering ram hitting the wall of a woodshed.

"Step, " Diarmid ordered, then, "Now! " and the mace whistled out toward Mael's flattening body. The edge, blunt as it was, stripped away Mael's breeches with both the skin and the underskin fat of his left buttock. At the other side of its arc the mace clipped a post. The post was four-inch oak, a recent replacement for one that had rotted away. Where the anchor stone struck it, the wood sheared off as cleanly as if sawn. Transmitted impact was still great enough to skew the remainder of the piling in the bottom muck and pull it loose from the stringer. The flooring sagged slightly to the side.

Mael was dazed and weeping with pain. He crawled backward more from instinct than from conscious volition.

The priest said, "Hold your mace in your left hand, Fergus. . . . That's right. Now, put your right hand on this post. Keep very close to the side . . . now, step, step . . . let go the post and slide your right hand—*right hand*—that's right, hold the post and wait for me, yes. . . . Now you don't have to hold the post any longer. We're past the bad section. Step, step. . . ."

The weakened portion of the pier had cried under the giant's weight, but it had held. Now Mael had nothing around him on three sides but water. On the fourth, the soapstone mace was rising for a final blow.

Mael was unable to swim in his present condition. He would sink like a stone in the water. If he clung

to a piling, if he even tried to flutter toward the coracle
floating ten feet away at the end of its tether, Diarmid
himself would throw the mace down on top of him.

"Step," said the priest. *Now—sideways, Fergus!*"

Mael threw himself outward, catching the end piling
in the crook of his good arm. The mace arced straight
down to where Mael had lain an instant before. The
pine planks exploded upward without slowing the
weapon in the least. The mace plunged on into the
slough like the anchor it was meant for. Fergus
followed it, his bald skull caroming off the post to
which Mael clung. The giant's hands still gripped the
shaft of the mace as the water sprayed up at his
impact. Not even a bubble returned to the surface.

Diarmid stared at the shattered pier and the roiling
water. The disturbance was the only marker his son
would ever have. Mael was wrapped around the lone
piling like a monkey on a stick. His left hand still
lacked strength, but he had managed to bend its flesh
onto the wood in a semblance of gripping. The priest
moaned deep in his throat. He turned.

Veleda leaped down from her horse at the other
end of the pier. "Mael!" she cried. She had a knife
in her hand.

Without hesitation, Diarmid flung himself and the
reliquary into the lough. When he surfaced, he began
kicking toward the boat. The casket floated. Diarmid
pushed it in front of him, making headway despite
the drag of his billowing robe.

Mael cursed. He squirmed to bring his right foot
onto the stringer so that he could stand instead of
hanging by one arm. Veleda was pattering down the
pier toward him, but she would be too late to stop
Diarmid from reaching the coracle and casting off.
The monster's skull would be gone and the priest would

be free to raise a posse to avenge the desecration. Under the circumstances, Mael would be lucky if they burned him alive.

The coracle bumped before Diarmid reached it. The priest's vision was blocked by the reliquary so he did not notice the boat move. Then the black water humped as something opaque and equally black rose through it, spilling the coracle to the side. Diarmid screamed. A head lifted in front of him on a five-foot neck, a column as thick as a man's torso. Only in comparison to the swollen bulk of the body did the monster's neck appear slender. A stiff fringe like a ruff of coral fronds sprouted from behind the creature's skull. They were the gills of a huge, neotenous salamander which never needed to surface in order to breathe. It was not at the flaring gills that Diarmid screamed. It was at the mouthful of needle teeth lowering on him. The priest continued to scream until the jaws closed on his head and pulled him under. This time there were bubbles. They would have been red in better light.

The coracle had overturned and sunk. The reliquary casket rotated alone in little eddies as the water slowly calmed.

Mael looked across the four-foot gap between his piling and the rest of the pier. The stringer, still festooned with the stubs of shattered planks, connected them. "Veleda, I'll fall if I try to get across," Mael said.

"Of course you won't," the woman replied sharply. Her knife disappeared into her scrip. She held out both hands to Mael. "Your left leg will hold you. It's just one step. Now, walk."

Like Diarmid and Fergus, Mael thought, and look what it got them. But the black joke settled the terror that had paralyzed him for a moment after the real danger was past. He stepped onto the stringer, then to the planking. Veleda was right. His leg did hold.

Mael clutched her to him like the only buoy in an angry sea. "There, there," she murmured as her fingers brushed over his wounds. She winced more than Mael did at his left hip where the skin still curled in tendrils that had dried to his trousers. "We'll have to do something about that," Veleda said. Her touch brought a quick flash like that of cautery. Mael was not sure whether it seemed hot or cold. Then, though feeling returned, the pains were less than those of the hard ride from the seacoast.

At last Mael broke away. The reliquary floated a body's length from the pier. To Mael's surprise, he was still holding his dagger. He sheathed it, then unlaced his sandals and kicked them off with his trousers. His tunic, ripped all the way down the front, slipped off without needing to be lifted over his head. "Next time, I strip naked first and grease myself," he said ruefully. "At least that'll leave me decent clothes to be buried in." He set his dagger between his teeth, careful not to gash his lips with the edges, and crouched to lower himself into the water.

"No," said Veleda. "Leave the knife."

"Umm?" Mael took the blade out of his mouth and stared at his companion in surprise. "Didn't you see that thing that—got—Diarmid?" he asked.

"I've seen them. That one I called to us. There are very few left."

"Oh." Mael lowered his eyes to consider. "Well, if you called it—" and he did not like that idea in the least, but that could not show in his voice—"then it won't hurt me, I suppose. . . ."

"I can't promise that," Veleda said flatly. "I don't rule those old ones—or any other living creature. I can only talk to them, sometimes. But there aren't so many of us who follow the old truths, Mael, that we should plan to slaughter each other when we meet."

"I don't follow any gods, old or new," Mael said. Veleda met his gaze but made no reply. He grunted, then laid his dagger on a dry plank He slid into the lough. Nothing touched him but the cold water, and that was further balm to his wounds.

Mael handed the chest up to Veleda and followed it awkwardly. "I should poultice your cuts," she said to the battered man as he began drawing on his clothing.

Mael shook his head. "I want to be at least ten miles away before we stop," he said. "I don't look forward to the ride, but they'll flay the rest of me if anybody catches us here."

Still he took the pad she handed him, linen folded over layers of herbs, and rode with it between his torn hip and the saddle. The casket was tied to Mael's pillion after they had checked it to make sure the skull within was undamaged. Mael found he liked the look of the rows of teeth even less after he had seen similar ones in use.

"We'll ride south to mBeal Liathain," he said. "There's enough trade through the port that I'll be able to buy passage back to Britain. Besides, I don't want to go back the way we came."

Veleda mounted without replying. Mael looked at her in brief doubt, then mounted as well with only a spurt of agony. Except for brief comments where the trail forked, they rode for two hours in silence. At last Mael said, "If this isn't far enough, nothing is. We've put half a dozen farms between us and the shrine."

"There's a grove of pines at the top of the next hill," said Veleda. "The ground there is smooth. The horses can be out of sight, and there's a spring there, too."

The grove was just as she said it would be. There was no altar within it, but in the recent past the ground beneath the big trees had been swept clean of twigs and needles by someone for some reason. Veleda soaked another cloth in the spring. Using it and her little knife, she cleaned Mael's buttock while he bent against a tree, digging his fingers into the coarse scales of the bark.

"I, ah . . ." he began. Carefully formal, he tried again. "When I held you there on the pier, it was because I was, ah, frightened. I didn't mean anything by it. Didn't mean to offend you, that is."

"You didn't." Veleda looked as helpless as a rabbit in a ferret's den, soft and warm and gentle. She laid the cloth down and bound another poultice over the wound. Her touch made Mael's whole body shiver. "There," she said. "It'll be weeks before it really clears up, but you'll be able to ride. Ride further."

They spread their cloaks on the ground. Mael set his saddle at the head of his cloak for a pillow. He lay down on his back, staring at the starburst pattern of pine branches against the moonlit sky.

"When I use my saddle like that," Veleda said from very close beside him, "I wake up in the morning with an aching neck. It's a little too high."

Mael turned his head. Veleda was facing him leaning back on her left elbow. Her hair shimmered about her arm and pooled on the cloak beneath her. He stretched his arm out, under her head. After a moment's hesitation, he curved his hand around her neck and pulled her to him.

"I told you I was a woman," she said before she answered his kiss.

And she was, but like no woman he had ever known before. The last thing Mael remembered as he finally fell asleep was the thrill of her slim, white fingers as they urged him to heights he had not dreamed a man could reach.

⟐   ⟐   ⟐

In the morning, Mael rode bare-chested until they reached a farmhouse. There he traded a copper bracelet for baggy trousers and a tunic of gray homespun. Britons had minted coins before the Romans came, but it would be another four centuries until an Irish king did the same. The remnants of Mael's old tunic were wrapped around the reliquary to hide its unique decoration. Mael whistled a good deal as he and Veleda cantered southward. Occasionally he broke into song.

"Ruadh, but it's been a long time!" he said suddenly, turning toward Veleda with a dazzling smile.

Veleda smiled back. She had thrown off her hood so that the fresh sunlight exploded in her hair. "Since you last had a woman?" she asked, as naturally as another man might have done. The question was incongruous from someone so feminine, but Mael found that it did not bother him.

"I would have said, 'Since I've been in love,'" he explained. "But there's a little of the other, too, since I . . . since a woman last mattered to me more than a few minutes." He was remembering things now which pain had kept him from willingly recalling before. "Ten years," he said. "Ten years."

"She left you?" asked Veleda, not really a question,

only an offer to let someone who mattered drain off a part of what had been eating away his soul for a decade.

"She died," said Mael. His voice was normal, but his eyes were now fixed on the road instead of meeting Veleda's. "Or rather, she got killed, but the end was before that, that just resulted . . ." He took a deep breath and, still without turning his head, said, "Her name was Kesair. She had black hair and she was just the same height as me for all our lives. We— grew up together, you see.

"At fourteen I was sent off to train with the Ard Ri's Guard. When I came home on leave—and after the first six months that was frequent enough—it was just the same as it had always been between us. There was never another woman for me until now, until you." Mael looked at Veleda. She reached out and touched the back of his hand with her cool, perfect fingers.

"You didn't marry," she said.

"No, we didn't do that," Mael agreed grimly. "But neither of us married, not for a long time. Then, ah, her father—her father was an important man"—and Mael's whole body was cold, trembling with the recollection of what he had almost said, but not quite, not quite—"a king in fact, though a client himself of the Ulaid. Every third man's a king in Ireland, doesn't it seem? Her father was a king, as I say. When the High King needed a wife for his brother Cearbhall, to make an alliance an edge more secure, where should he look but to Kesair, my lovely, black-haired Kesair?"

Veleda's fingers squeezed Mael's. He bent in his saddle to kiss her hand before continuing. "There were two years of that. I talked with Cearbhall, ate with Cearbhall—even fought at his side, if you can believe that. And I never once touched Kesair, never." Mael looked straight at Veleda. "And when we saw that it wasn't going to work, we . . . met again. And it was just as good as it ever had been. Only Cearbhall walked in when he was supposed to be a hundred miles away.

"He had his shield and a drawn sword. I suppose some of the servants had guessed and told him. But he didn't bring anybody else with him, either. He didn't want that talk in the barracks, and I guess he figured he could handle the matter himself. Which maybe he would have, except that Kesair threw herself onto his sword point before he could get it into me. And then I beat him to death with a bronze candlestick." Mael grinned like a skull. "No, I didn't put it through his helmet; but it was hard to live in a steel drum, and anyway, the helmet slipped off after a time . . . ."

Mael wrapped his fingers around Veleda's, letting them writhe in active contact for the first time since he had begun speaking. "See," he said with a false smile, "that's the kind of person you're running with."

Veleda leaned over and kissed him, startling a shepherd watching the travelers from the shade of a wayside oak. "It won't happen that way again," she said. "I promise. And I'm a witch, you know."

Chapter Six

mBeal Liathain was considerably farther from Lough Ree than Mael's landfall in Leinster had been. Despite that and the battering Mael had taken, he and Veleda rode the distance in the same three days. Both fear of pursuit and a desire to finish a task thus far successful drove them. mBeal Liathain was a fortified village nestled on an inlet, a port and as near to a city as Ireland had at the time save for Cashel and the High King's seat at Tara. There was even a true wharf, though many of the round-bottomed vessels were simply beached to avoid the toll. Men from Gaul and Spain traded on the waterfront. In the market square you might find a blond-bearded Geat bartering with a Phoenician through an interpreter. The pelt of a great white ice bear for silk brocades woven in war-torn China . . . This was the funnel through which Ireland moved her exports: horses and fine woolens, linen and metalwork the like of nothing cast elsewhere west of the Scythian steppes. But mBeal Liathain was more than that as well. The little village in Munster provided a stable freeport for much of the North Sea and the Atlantic, where migration and the dissolution of the Empire had left very little stability.

Mael and Veleda found a suitable ship at once. The vessel was a beamy, shallow horse transport about fifty feet long. She had been beached parallel to the shore, not only to save the wharfage fee but also because that was the only practical way to load her cargo. Sandbags cocked the shoreward gunwale down. Planks made a ramp up the side along half the boat's length. The six horses of her cargo would be walked aboard without difficulty. There they could be harnessed between the thwarts before they realized they were no longer on dry land. The crew had already started loading when Mael, after a whispered discussion with his companion, dismounted and walked over to them.

"Who's your captain?" the exile called.

The burliest of the six sailors, a black-bearded man whose forearms and legs looked as curlingly hairy as his face, turned from the horse he was prodding forward with the butt end of his quirt. "Who the hell wants to know?" he demanded.

"Two people who need to buy passage to Britain," Mael said, as calmly as if he had not been challenged.

"Well, go find another bloody ship," the sailor snarled. "This one's headed for bloody Gaul on the next tide."

"I said 'buy,' " Mael remarked, knuckling his purse so that the heavy coins within gnashed together.

The sailor looked around with a somewhat different

expression. He tossed his quirt to a companion. "I'm Vatidius," he said. "I'm the captain. Let's go get a drink and we'll see." Back over his shoulder he roared to his men, "Get 'em loaded right or I'll have your bloody hides when I get back!"

While Veleda sold the horses to a drover with a string of twenty, Mael and Vatidius bargained over bad beer and worse wine respectively. Vatidius was not the owner of the transport, merely a captain hired by a Breton consortium. He had no authority to do anything but sail straight for home with his cargo. Mael found the shipmaster brutal and stupid, but also venal. They struck a bargain after two cups of the wine. The bribe was sizable, but Vatidius swore he would have to pay his five seamen out of it for their silence as well. It was Arthur's money, anyway, and with as little direct trade as there was between the islands, Mael was willing to call the price fair.

Veleda and the cloth-covered reliquary, their only baggage, were waiting with the loaded freighter when Mael and Vatidius returned. Mael wondered briefly at Veleda's income—not until she sold the horses had it occurred to him that she must somehow have bought them as well. But that was no great matter; perhaps she told fortunes for the rich. Mael took her hand and nodded. Vatidius was already shouting, "Get your bloody asses on, then, and don't get in the way!"

The ramp had been dismantled so the three of them splashed aboard through the foul harbor water. Mael and Veleda watched in silence as the vessel was poled off shore. When the water was deep enough, four men began to work the sweeps. The remaining seaman watched the harbor over the tall cutwater, while Vatidius himself knelt astern at the steering oar.

The ship—if she had a name, Mael never heard it

spoken—was a dozen feet wide amidships. Passage forward or aft was too tight for safety from the teeth or hooves of a nervous horse. All the beasts stood crosswise, their heads to port, lashed to reinforced thwarts intended to hold even horses frightened by tacking or bad weather. The sail was a single square of linen, hoisted to catch the fitful west wind as soon as the vessel cleared the harbor. The two men on the forward sweeps went astern as soon as they had shipped their long oars. The lookout followed. Mael and Veleda were left with only three of the snorting horses to keep them company forward of the mast.

"I don't like either the ship or the crew," Veleda said, her back cushioned from the gunwale by Mael's right arm. There was no chop, so even in the extreme bow they were dry.

"Who could?" Mael agreed with a shrug. "But we'll be shut of them soon enough if the wind holds. Are you tired?"

"Go ahead and nap," she answered. "You're still healing."

Mael smiled and squeezed her. He managed to nod off almost at once. Veleda did not let a frown of concern show on her face until after she was sure the Irishman was asleep. From time to time her eyes locked with those of one or more of the polyglot seamen as they worked the ship. None of the sailors came any nearer than was necessary to feed and water the horses. Horse dung lay where it fell. The breeze blew the green odor toward the bow.

Clouds rolled up from the west to catch the sun before it reached the horizon.

⊕   ⊕   ⊕

The sky was pitch-dark when Mael awakened to the crash of the falling spar. He snatched at his dagger left-handed. Embarrassed, he immediately resheathed the weapon when he realized the crew was simply taking in the sail by the light of a horn lantern. Vatidius gave his passengers a wave and a gap-toothed grin. After a moment he came forward, still holding the lantern. His men appeared to be furling the sail. It was difficult to see the crewmen because of the darkness and the intervening horses.

"Don't want to go driving up on the bloody shore, do we?" the shipmaster said cheerfully. "That's not the kind of arrival you paid for, is it?"

Mael gave a noncommittal grunt. Veleda said nothing, but her body tensed. Vatidius squatted down in front of his passengers anyway, talking enthusiastically. "Going to be glad to get back to Britain, I suppose."

Mael nodded. He had told the shipmaster only that he was returning to Arthur. It didn't matter that the Gaul mistook him for a Briton. He said, "Glad to be back on dry land, anyway."

Vatidius' hand on the lantern kept the light from his own eyes, shrouding his whole face. Not far away the water slapped, making one of the horses whicker in response. "Yes," the captain went on, "I know you landsmen. I never had any luck on shore, myself, and little enough at sea. . . ." His voice trailed off. Then he added, "Tell you one thing that does surprise me, though—that box you carry." Veleda was murmuring under her breath, the words only a bone-felt vibration to Mael. He stiffened. The reliquary lay between his legs and Veleda's. As unobtrusively as possible, he cleared his right arm.

"I mean," Vatidius was saying, "most people'd have baggage for as long a trip as you're making. Folk of quality like you, you know. But the box, it's not real baggage, now, is it? Just wondering, of course."

"It's just got some bones in it," Mael said. "Just some saint's relics, that's all." Did one of the sailors around the mast hold a javelin?

"Now isn't that something?" said Vatidius. "Now me—you know how sailors are. If you hadn't told me, I'd have imagined there were, oh—jewels, say, in the box from the way you carry—"

"Mael!" Veleda shouted. There was a huge splash behind them. Mael's feet lashed out, skidding the casket hard against Vatidius' knees and spilling the lantern. Even as Mael kicked, he was turning. A Syrian seaman was lunging over the rail with a knife in his right hand. The sailor must have slipped into the calm water and pulled himself along the boat's side while Vatidius occupied the passengers. Mael's right elbow caught the sailor in the throat with all his strength behind the blow. Gurgling, the Syrian pitched back into the sea.

Vatidius struck in the darkness. He rang an oak belaying pin off the side of the Irishman's skull. Mael bounced against the gunwale and fell back. He was conscious, but none of his limbs seemed to work. The captain's black bulk raised against the sky, readying a finishing blow.

At first Mael thought that Veleda had cried out and thrown something. She stretched her right hand toward Vatidius. A worm of purple fire uncurled from one slim finger and struck the Gaul. The flame-thing did not seem to move swiftly, but even before Vatidius could scream, its flattened ribbon had wrapped about his throat. One end of it buried itself deep in the captain's chest. Then the scream came and purple fire burst with it out of the burly man's mouth and nostrils. The flash lit the whole forepart of the ship.

The purple glare caught the remaining seamen

running toward the prow. Each had an upraised weapon. The sailors froze as their captain, his torso shrinking in on itself and the fire licking all about him, threw himself overboard. Steam hissed when he struck the water. Veleda spoke again. Two more serpents of fire rippled from her hand. One of the sailors hurled his javelin. The metal popped and sizzled as the purple flame coursed through it The air stank with the harshness of a lightning strike.

All six horses went mad together. The harness and attachments that might have been adequate in a storm disintegrated as supernatural terror drove the animals. Showering wood fragments, the beasts plunged into the sea in near unison. They carried two of the sailors with them in their rush. A third seaman overbalanced when the three-ton cargo leaped to port and sent the vessel pitching. That man flipped over the starboard rail. The last crewman deliberately jumped, an inch ahead of the flame that had darted for his eyes. The purple light winked out as the intended victim cleared the rail.

The moon came out from behind the clouds. There was no longer any sign of the living flames. One of the seamen was still afloat, swimming blindly away from the vessel. He was dwarfed by the frothing horses. They neighed in panic as they kicked white pools of foam in the calm water around them. The beasts could swim well—for a time—but the immensity of the sea terrified them. They tried to lunge higher in the water to sight the shore. Two of them reached the sailor at almost the same moment. They battled viciously with their teeth and front hooves, each seeing the man as a place to rest. Long before the horses had parted, their feet had pulped the sailor and driven his remains deep into the sea.

The boat rocked and pitched at the fury of the big animals around it. One of them approached the vessel. The horse's fear of the witch flames had been dwarfed, as everything else was, by the huge expanse of salt water.

Mael pulled himself upright. A javelin stuck up from the planks halfway between him and the mast. He stepped to it and tugged it out. The blade was warped and dulled by the fire that had touched it, but its point was sharp enough to serve. The nearing horse, a chestnut stallion, kicked upward. Its hoof rang on the hollow side of the ship. Its head sank, then rose again from the water in a froth of effort. This time the horse swung its left foreleg over the rail. The vessel lurched toward its weight.

Mael lunged, driving the javelin into the horse's chest at the junction of neck and shoulder. The beast's jaws started and it screamed like a human. Both forelegs kicked straight up, the left fetlock shattering the railing as they glanced together. Mael jerked his weapon free. The chestnut dived backwards into the water. It did not come up again. Two more of the horses paddling frantically around the vessel came nearer.

A bow and a spilled quiver of arrows lay amidships. Mael saw them and judged the distance of the approaching horses. He tossed the javelin sideways to Veleda, shouting, "Hold them off a minute!"

"But they're *horses*! They'll *drown*!"

"Hell drink your soul, woman!" the Irishman cried. "They'll drown *us* by trying to get aboard!"

Mael snatched up the bow. Veleda, weeping, slapped the nearest horse across the muzzle with the spear shaft. The horse shied back and sank to nostril height. Its companion, a black mare, kicked and knocked the spear away. Mael shot the horse behind the ear. The animal went limp and sank without a sound.

The arrows were crooked and the boat provided a shaky platform to shoot from. Mael locked his hip against the rail and leaned outward so that the point of his arrow was almost touching the other horse before he released. The arrow penetrated half its length but missed the brain. The beast turned away, whinnying and leaving a swirling trail of blood.

There were twelve more arrows in the quiver. Mael fired them all. When he was finished, the sea was clear of all life but himself and his companion. Mael set the bow against his knee and snapped the staff into halves. Then he leaned the halves against the gunwale and broke them again with his foot. When he was finished, he hurled the fragments as far as he could into the sea. They floated over the bodies of their victims.

Mael leaned against the rail. Veleda's cool hands touched his neck and right biceps. Memories of her fingers skittered through Mael's mind; comforting him with their pressure—stroking his groin to unbearable lust—*burning Vatidius' lungs away with a ribbon of fire*—

Mael screamed and jerked away from the woman.

Veleda stared at him as if he had slapped her. "I had to!" she cried.

"I'm sorry," Mael said, pressing his hands together to have something to do with them. He would not meet her eyes. So delicate, so . . . "I know you had to, I really do, it was your life and mine and maybe Starkad's, too. . . . And I'm really glad you could, could do something about those sailors, because I sure as hell couldn't. But just for now I, well, my mind is . . ."

He looked up at Veleda and bit his lower lip. Then he burst out, "Manannan MacLir, woman, I just don't want to b-be touched right now! That's all."

Veleda stepped back from Mael's pitiful anger. "No," she said, "that's not all. But it's not your fault either." She looked back at the western sky. "I think we're going to get some wind soon," she said. "If we can get the sail up, we can get out of this . . . stretch of ocean. I think we'd both be happier for that."

The breeze was sudden and strong. The vessel was squirrelly with neither cargo nor ballast, but the wind was dead astern. There was no real danger even in their undercrewed state. Mael wondered briefly whether that was a result of Veleda's art, too, but he put the thought aside hurriedly.

Veleda had saved both their lives.

Mael steered by the stars and an inner compass that failed him about as often as it brought him where he wanted to go. At the moment he felt he would be just as happy if the boat gutted itself on a rock in mid-ocean, so of course his luck carried him straight to his destination with an accuracy no practiced navigator could have guaranteed. Seas rustling on the shoreline to the north brought Mael to steer that way. Half an hour later, Veleda pointed to the river mouth that gaped blackly between the fringes of surf to either side. "That's the Tuvius," she said. "We're within ten miles of Moridunum and the villa."

Mael did not bother to ask her how she knew.

A mud bank brought the ship to a halt that seemed fairly gentle, until the mast snapped and went crashing over the side. Mael was jarred off his feet. He stood, picked up the reliquary, and walked to the bow. It rested a dozen feet from shore. Veleda followed, her face calm. Mael looked over the rail, then back at

Veleda. "I'm sorry," he said. "I really can't tell you how sorry I am about—the way I acted." Very deliberately, he extended his right hand to her. "I'll lower you down, then I'll jump."

Veleda smiled with tears bright in the corners of her eyes. Grasping Mael's big hand with both of hers, she lowered herself into the shallow water and waited for him. Mael tried not to shudder at the touch of her fingers. The two of them waded to shore together, into a small crowd that the noise had brought out of bed with torches and half their clothing.

One bulky spectator was mounted on a good horse. He trotted forward and demanded, "What happened? You aren't just going to leave your ship like that, are you?"

Mael eyed him flatly. "No," he said, "I'm going to trade it to you for two horses."

The rider blinked and pulled his maroon cloak closer about him. He was fully dressed but his tunic was inside out. "Trade?" he repeated. "Why, that's—I mean, how do I even know you own the thing?"

"Look," Mael snapped, "either I own it and you're getting one hell of a bargain, or I cut the throats of the people who did own it and you aren't wearing a sword. Now, do you have another horse handy or—"

In ten minutes Mael and Veleda—on a pony that was adequate for her weight and the short distance— were riding north along the east bank of the River Towy. The casket was again lashed to the back of Mael's saddle.

Chapter Seven

The night was warm. The six guards on duty at the villa's front entrance were outside, under a torch. At that distance the sounds of their dice game would not disturb the chieftains quartered within the building. When the guards heard the approaching horses, they swept up the dice and checked their weapons. A messenger was more likely than a sudden attack, but—it was cheap enough to be ready, that was all.

Mael reined up in the circle of torchlight and dismounted, He began to unstrap the reliquary. "We've got to see Arthur," he said. "At once."

Two of the guards laughed. None of them answered.

Mael pulled the last tie loose and turned in fury with the casket in his hands. "Look, ye cunt-brains," he snarled, a little of his Erse lilt quivering through the anger in his voice, "it's five hundred miles your

Arthur has sent me to fetch this back—with my friend's life the forfeit if I failed. I'll have Arthur awake now to see it, do you hear?"

Hands hovered near weapon hilts. The guard officer said, "No, I recognize him. He's the one we escorted off to Ireland. Godas, knock on the Leader's door and see if he wants to talk to this one now."

Doubtful but obedient, the named guardsman slipped into the villa. A moment later the door reopened. First through it was the guard. To Mael's amazement, the second man was Arthur himself. The king must have been asleep, but even so he had slid into his boots and pulled his coat of mail on over his bare shoulders before coming to the door. The links would be uncomfortable without padding beneath them, but they were less uncomfortable than a spear thrust through naked skin. Kings had died before through neglecting to arm themselves as they rushed out into the night. Behind Arthur was his seneschal Cei, a short, stocky man who was also in armor. He carried a drawn sword in one hand, in the other a lantern. Cei blinked in its radiance, looking as logy as a denned bear and as ill-tempered.

There was soft motion from the darkness to Mael's right as well. Mael turned and squinted. Unsummoned but not unexpected, Merlin stepped into the converging spheres of torch and lantern light. The wizard was barefoot and wearing the same simple tunic as before. His fingers toyed with another willow switch. Merlin's eyes searched Mael and the casket eagerly. Then his peripheral glance at Veleda penetrated and he froze. He glared at the woman. She stared back at him, overtly as calm as a stone.

"What's *she* doing with you?" Merlin demanded of Mael.

The Irishman's eyebrows rose with his temper. "Bringing a bloody lizard skull back." Mael turned to Arthur. "Where's Starkad?"

Arthur shrugged the question away. "He's here, he's fine. Did you bring the skull?"

"Where the hell is 'here'?" Mael shouted. "If anything happened to Starkad, I'll—" He remembered where he was and let the rest of the threat go unvoiced.

The king smiled and said very precisely, "Recruit, every one of the instructors placed over your friend has requested the Dane be discharged as unfit—too undisciplined to teach and too dangerous to have around. He hasn't gone anywhere, however. You'll find them, perfectly healthy, in his billet. As soon as you can give me the skull."

Mael pressed the latch of the casket and opened it. Merlin and the king crowded around. Cei and the other Companions hung back, curious but more afraid. The wizard traced around the small eyesockets with his left index finger, then ran down the line of the snout. "Yes. . . ." he said. "Tonight we can begin the work."

"Tonight?" Cei blurted.

"Can we start sooner?" Merlin sneered. He looked at Arthur. "I'll need a man to read the responses," he said. "One who won't run if something goes—"

"All right, I'll come myself," said the king with a nod. Arthur's attention was on the reliquary.

Impatience and the nearness of triumph drove Merlin to retort unthinkingly, "Come and read responses? Read? *Read?*"

Arthur went white. Maul, hearing the grating sound of drawn steel, looked up swiftly to see which guard would strike the blow. But the king took a deep breath and said, "Of course. I'll send for Lancelot, then. He can read."

"Mael will read your responses," said Veleda unexpectedly from behind the Irishman. Even Merlin had forgotten her after the casket was opened.

Mael twisted around to look at her, trying to discern in Veleda's placid expression what she meant to accomplish. There was nothing to be seen. Mael chuckled, acting on instinct. "I'll bet your Lancelot still has trouble talking through the teeth I broke for him before I left," he said. "I'll take care of your responses."

Merlin's gaze flickered from Veleda to Mael and back again. The wizard frowned. "You think I'd be afraid, don't you?" he asked the woman. "You don't think I'd dare display my powers in front of a—" his wand stroked—"a pawn of yours? We'll see." Merlin's eyes shifted back to Mael. "And you think you'd be able to read Latin letters, Irishman?"

To a British warrior, the question would have been no insult. The wizard might not even have meant it for one. Mael's head snapped back as if his face had been slapped. The Ard Ri's Guard had been an assemblage of scholars as surely as of athletes, ever since it was founded two centuries before by the great Cormac mac Airt. Mael reacted in much the same way as he would have to a suggestion that he could not out-wrestle an old woman. "My ancestors were kings in Miletos, Briton, when wolves chased your scampering forebears into the trees," he said. "I can read Ogam or Greek letters or Latin. If you British were civilized enough to have a script of your own, I would have learned to read that as well in the High King's school."

Cei grunted and started to raise his sword. Merlin laid his omnipresent willow switch across the seneschal's wrist without taking his eyes off Mael.

The angry Briton froze with a surprised look on his face. Merlin gave Mael an ugly grin. "You think you're a bold man, do you, Irishman?" he said. "You'll have had need to be before this night is out." He turned to Arthur. "We can finish this within the hour if you'll get us horses. I already have everything prepared at the cave in the bluff west of here."

"The old corral?" Arthur queried.

"That's right. And I intend to use it as a corral again—though for a very different sort of cattle."

The king shrugged and called to his guard officer. "Three horses. At once."

Merlin led, riding faster than the overcast night made safe, in Mael's opinion. The road was well defined but showed few signs of use in the recent past. Cei was stumbling directly behind the wizard, trying to light his king's path with the inadequate lantern. Mael checked to be sure Veleda rode comfortably. She grinned back at him, amused that he even thought she might be having trouble. Mael pressed his horse forward a little to put him alongside Arthur.

"Where is it we're going?" he asked.

Arthur's mouth quirked at the suggestion of equality in the question. "There's a row of limestone hills half a mile from the main building," he answered mildly enough. "One of them has a cave in it, a small entrance but a belly the size of a church. It used to be a stable."

"Umm. Then why don't you use it?"

The king's smile grew a little broader. "I said," he repeated, "there's one small entrance. I don't want my people to get in the habit of stabling their mounts in places they can't get out of fast. They only have to do that one night on patrol and I've lost a whole sector of border." He glanced back over his shoulder.

"Did you really think you had to bring your whore along?" he asked.

Mael laughed. "Didn't ask her to come," he said, "but I'm glad of her company." He dropped back and rode the rest of the short distance beside Veleda. Neither of them spoke, but Mael knew that he had not lied to Arthur about the companionship.

The cave was in a long bulk of stone, an outcrop thirty feet high rather than a water-carven bluff. It was not sheer, but its one-to-one slope was too sharp for a man to climb it easily without using his hands. The cave mouth was at ground level, an egg-shaped hole squared off by the addition of door posts and a great iron-strapped gate of hardwood. Merlin dismounted at some distance from the opening. He tied his horse to one of a small copse of poplars. "We'll leave our horses here," he said, explaining, "they don't like to feel—power being used."

Mael's chest tightened. He did not speak or look at Veleda.

They all trudged toward the gate in file. Merlin paused and took the reliquary from Mael before he entered the cave. The wizard's eyes met those of the witch woman. "You don't come inside," he snapped. "I know the kind of trouble you'd cause."

Veleda's hair twitched like the mane of a beast. "Be assured," she said. "that god watches you whether I do or not."

"God!" Merlin sneered. "God! You don't know— you can't imagine—what I'm about to do!"

"I suspect that you can't imagine the evil you're about to do," the woman said. "A little knowledge . . . but what will be, will be. Go raise your ravening monster, little man."

The wizard's eyes clouded. He passed his willow

wand between himself and Veleda three times. Without a word he touched the center of her tunic with the leafy end of the branch. Veleda laughed and reached up with her right hand. She broke the tip between her fingers, gripped the center of the wand and snapped it, too, and reached for Merlin's hand. He snatched himself away with a curse and flung the wand out into the darkness.

Still scowling, he took the lantern from Cei. "You," he said. "You stand out here and see that we aren't disturbed."

The seneschal stiffened at the tone. He looked doubtfully at Mael, even more doubtfully at the wizard himself. "Leader," he said, "I don't think you ought to go in there alone with—"

"Do as the man says, Cei," Arthur snapped. "Merlin's doing what I told him to do, and I can handle the Irishman—needs must." The king and Mael eyed each other appraisingly. Then, ducking their heads under the low lintel, they followed Merlin into the cave.

The single lantern could not illuminate the cavity within. From the opening it expanded so suddenly that Mael suspected parts of the hill face must be eaten almost through. It had been hollowed by water, not the hand of man; wherever the light shone, from the ceiling down the walls to shoulder height, the surface gleamed with the soft pearl of flow rock. Lower down, the dissolved and redeposited calcium carbonate had been worn away or fouled by the beasts stabled in the cave in past times. The air had a still, musty odor. Ancient dung covered the floor, trampled and compacted until it had become almost as dense as the limestone beneath. The cave was over twenty feet wide and its walls stretched back further than the light could follow, but there was no breeze to hint at a second opening to this bubble in the rock.

As Merlin had said, his paraphernalia was already ordered within. The wizard stepped first to a seven-branched lampstand and began to light the separate wicks with a spill of papyrus. Mael had first assumed the stand was Jewish. As it better illuminated itself, it became obvious that the object was not Jewish at all—not even as Judaism was misunderstood and libeled by gentile sources. Mael had seen worse things than that stand, but it did not mean that he cared for the lovingly crafted abomination.

The seven lamps displayed the rest of Merlin's gear clearly. Most striking was a brazier resting on a tripod and already laid with sticks of charcoal. A grill was mounted above the fire pan on narrow arms; it was raised more than a foot above the surface of the coals. The metal was black and without decoration, apparently wrought iron.

Two cases of sturdy wood stood nearby. One was a cylinder whose lid was askew to display a number of scrolls resting endwise within. The winding rods were tagged, but Mael could not read the titles without making an obvious effort to do so. He kept a rein on his curiosity. Scrolls of both papyrus and vellum were represented. One of the latter had a gilt fore-edge and a pattern of tiny agates set into the knobs of the winding rods.

The other case was of less common pattern. It was full of chemicals, each in a separate jar in one of the scores of pigeonholes into which the narrow chest was divided. The containers were generally pottery, but a few were stone and one was of glass so clear that a king would have been proud to sip his wine from it. A sliding lid could close the chest, but that had already been untied and leaned against the wall

Across the top of the chest was a silver scriber, an arthame, some two feet long. Mael at first mistook the instrument for the weapon it resembled. Then he noticed that the edges of the blade were blunt and that its rippled pattern was only a depiction of a flattened serpent's body. The tail tip, polished with wear, was the point. The head and neck straightened to form a guardless hilt.

Merlin set the lantern on the floor. His hands twitched absentmindedly. When he realized that they were playing with his missing wand, he cursed under his breath. The wizard plucked a shred of willow bark from under a thumbnail. Shooting a vicious glance at the Irishman, Merlin turned his face to the far end of the cave and muttered an incantation. The lamps cast on the wall the capering shadow of what Mael was blocked from seeing by the wizard's body. When Merlin faced around again, he was holding another willow switch. This one was thin and only a yard long. "The wood has eternal life," the wizard muttered to his audience in fuzzy explanation. He became more alert and looked again at Mael. Then he ran the tip of the wand across the sticks of charcoal in the brazier. Where the willow touched, the black turned white with ash. The brazier itself began to glow and stink of hot iron.

Mael grinned. His stomach was turning over with the memory of other magic he had watched. "You must be a delight on a winter bivouac," he said.

Merlin reached into the case of scrolls and took out one of the parchments. "Read this over," he directed Mael. "Not aloud! I have to ready the—rest of this." The wizard set his wand on the box of chemicals and picked up the arthame. Ignoring both men—he had not paid the king any attention since they entered the cave—Merlin began drawing lines and symbols in the lumpy floor. The design was centered on the lighted brazier.

Mael unrolled the first column-width of the scroll. He began to read. At first he thought there was something wrong with the letters. But no, they were plain enough. It was just that the words they formed made no sense at all. . . . "This isn't in Latin," the Irishman said aloud, thinking Merlin had given him the wrong scroll.

The wizard looked up from the pentacle he was scribing. He smirked. "I didn't say it was. The *letters* are Latin; the language itself is a good deal older than Rome, Irishman. Or Miletos."

Mael frowned but concentrated on the manuscript again. Its format puzzled him until he realized that what he held was a list of long antistrophes, each of them ten or more lines in length. Instead of copying out the strophes as well, the scribe had merely indicated the first speaker with the Greek letter "delta" wherever Mael's portion ended. None of the words made any sense, but Mael felt a compulsion to begin speaking them aloud. His frown deepened.

Merlin finished scratching on the floor. He set the arthame down and picked up the willow again. "Well," he demanded, "do you think you're ready, Irishman?"

Mael nodded, refusing to acknowledge either the challenge or the hostility in the wizard's tone. "Yes," he said.

"Believe me," Merlin went on, "this is no joke. If you start, you have to finish. If you panic, you'll be in worse danger than you can imagine."

Mael thought of violet serpents lighting the shadowed deck. "I can imagine a lot," he said. "And I don't panic."

"Then stand over there," Merlin directed, pointing

to one of the reentrant angles of the pentacle, "but don't scuff the line. Don't even lean over it after we start."

Mael obeyed. Heat thrown off by the brazier brushed his legs below the trousers.

The wizard carefully took the lough monster's skull out of the reliquary. Barehanded he set the yellowed bones on top of the grill. Then he bent over again and took a pinch of something from one of the opened jars of chemicals. When Merlin tossed the powder on the charcoal, orange smoke bloomed up and briefly hid the whole apparatus. The wizard coughed and swore under his breath. He took a pinch of white chemical from another jar. Nothing happened when he cast that as well into the fire. Nodding approval, the wizard plucked another scroll from the case. Finally he took up his position at the peak of the pentagram across the brazier from where Mael stood. He gave the Irishman a grin that was almost a rictus beneath his glazed eyes. Then he began to intone the spell.

Waiting made Mael nervous despite himself. The wizard's voice was higher than normal when he chanted. The timbre was not so much feminine as bestial, that of a small dog yapping something close to words. Mael shot a glance behind him at the king. Arthur was hunched against the wall of the cave. He had drawn his sword and was resting it point down in the gritty flooring. The king's hands lay on the cross guard and his long fingers were twined around the hilt. Arthur's face was as hard as the steel blade.

Merlin broke off at the end of the strophe. He dipped his wand at Mael like a choirmaster's baton. Mael gulped his throat clear and began to sound the unfamiliar syllables. At first the Irishman spoke slowly, afraid to misaccent or stumble over the gibberish. When he had begun, though, Mael found his mouth was shaping naturally to the words. They rolled out with a rightness not affected by the fact that they were still unintelligible. Even that was changing subtly. Though the words had no meaning, they left behind them an aura of purpose. When the passage ended, Mael stopped. He was breathing hard and listening with new ears to Merlin taking up the chant. It was only then that Mael realized that the last of the words he had "read" were on the next column of his scroll. He had not unrolled it. His fingers fumbled as he did so.

Merlin threw something more on the fire as the Irishman began his second passage. A thin, green tendril wound upward toward the ceiling. The smoke trembled like a lutestring at the impact of the readers' voices. The cave was getting colder. Mael thought for a time that the chill was in his imagination, but he noticed puffs of vapor from Merlin's mouth as he read.

The litany caromed back and forth between the speakers, proceeding toward the end of each scroll. Merlin dusted the fire with further chemicals without any significant effect on the flames or on the chill that utterly permeated the cave. Finally the wizard completed his last invocation and, beating the strokes with his wand, shouted the response aloud with Mael: "Sodaque! *Sodaque!* SODAQUE!"

The skull above the coals wavered and collapsed inward. The air was full of the stink of fresh blood. On the grill in place of the dead bones pranced a pigeon-sized creature with strong hams and a pair of wings instead of forelegs. The beast was covered all over with scales, black and with the suggestion of translucent depth that a block of smoky quartz gives. Its head and neck were serpentine. A long tail, thrust out stiffly to balance the weight of the forequarters, was the length of neck and torso together.

The creature's eyes were small and cruel and a red so intense that it seemed luminous. "My wyvern!" Merlin cried out joyfully. He dropped the scroll and began to dance with his hands clasped above his head. The wyvern launched itself from the grill and sailed around it in a tight circle. One of the scale-jeweled wings spread into the air above a sideline of the pentacle. The beast glanced away as though it had struck a solid wall. Shrieking with high-pitched anger, the wyvern opened its mouth and spurted a needle of azure flame as long as its whole body.

Mael looked at the capering wizard, then back at the dragon. He stepped away from the pentacle and began to laugh full-throatedly, clutching his sides. It was as much the anticlimax to his fear as the actual ludicrousness of the tiny monster that was working on the Irishman.

The chirping wyvern had had yet a third effect on the king. Arthur's face lost its death-mask placidity. He gaped. Then his expression began to contort with fury. "That?" he shouted. "*That* will lay the Saxons at my feet?" The king stepped around the pentagram with his sword raised. His eyes were fixed on Merlin.

The wizard was too caught up in his triumph even to hear the king's words, but the oil lamps threw multiple images of the sword past him to the cave wall. Merlin turned, suddenly sober. "Wait!" he cried. "Leader—it will grow!"

Mael had backed against the wall. He held his left

arm across his body where the tunic sleeve hid his
other hand's grip on his dagger hilt. Arthur had paused
an instant before striking. Merlin half crouched. His
wand was raised, but the fear in his eyes was certain.
Whatever the power was he had used to block Cei's
hand, the wizard did not care to chance it against
his king in a murderous rage. "Leader, this is what I
meant to do," he said. He stretched out his left hand
in supplication. "Other people have tried to raise
dragons full grown. That's dangerous, suicide—
nobody but a god, perhaps, can control something
that big from the first."

Arthur did not relax his stance or gaze, but he began
to lower his long sword to an on-guard position. The
wizard straightened, letting his wand tip fall in turn.
"This one—" he used his elbow to indicate the wyvern
so as not to break the lock his eyes had gained on
Arthur's—"is small and I can control it. It's going to
get bigger—very much bigger, you needn't fear. But
I'll still have power over it, because the power will
increase, too. You'll have your weapon in a few weeks,
and you'll have a weapon you can really direct instead
of being something all-devouring and masterless. A
less able student might have raised a real monster
in his ignorance."

The tension was gone. The wyvern squawked again
and perched on the grill. It was apparently oblivious
to the heat. Mael said, "You know, I've heard a notion
like that before. One of the lordlings in—where I
grew up. He decided he'd start lifting a newborn bull
calf once a day, so in a year he'd be strong enough
to lift a grown bull." Mael grinned at Arthur. "It wasn't
near that long before he'd broken his back trying,
of course. But it was an interesting notion."

"You can read, Irishman," Merlin snarled, "but don't

think you can teach me sorcery because of that! You know nothing. Nothing!" To Arthur the wizard added quickly, "Leader, in a few weeks you'll march beneath a power that no prince has ever equaled."

Arthur sheathed his sword. For a moment he watched first Mael, then the wyvern, askance. Then he said, "Explain the dragon to me, wizard. If I have to feed it to full size, I'll need to make plans."

"Oh, it won't need to eat at all," Merlin said, with a return of his giggly good humor. He began bustling about his paraphernalia, readying it to leave. "Not in this world at least. You see, what you think is a dragon, what looks like a dragon, is really thousands and thousands and uncounted thousands of dragons. Each of them for—well, not even an eyeblink. It's nowhere near that long a time. When the dragon seems to move—" he pointed with his wand. The wyvern reacted by screeching and throwing itself forward, to rebound again from the invisible wall— "it is really a series of dragons. A whole row of them moving each for an instant into this universe from one in which wyverns can exist."

"One exists right there," Arthur said irritably, pointing at the tiny creature. It was again swooping about its prison.

"But only because of my magic," Merlin replied, "and only for the briefest moment. Then it's back in the cosmos I drew it from and another—from a wholly separate existence—is there in its place for another hairsbreadth of time. Now, that's what others have done as well, yes, the ones who knew the path, the essence of power. But I—instead of having the same wyvern repeat itself from myriads of identical universes—I added a time gradient as well. This way each of the creatures is a little older, a little larger than the one before. And so on, forever, as long as I wish."

"As *I* wish, wizard," the king reminded him in no pleasant voice.

"As you wish, Leader," Merlin agreed obsequiously.

"If that's true," Mael interjected, "and I won't say that it can't be, I'm no sorcerer as you say . . . but why does the beast snap at you here in this world? You say it's only the moment's wraith from a world in which you aren't there to snap at."

"Yes, that's right," Merlin said, bobbing his head with enthusiasm at having an intelligent audience to display himself before. "But something's there, don't you see? There isn't any end of worlds, worlds with wyverns leaping and squalling and spitting flame. It's my control that chooses which world is plucked of which wyvern . . . that and a sort of . . ." The wizard frowned and sobered for the first time since Arthur had lowered his sword. "Well, a sort of inertia that the process itself gives it. I can't be ordering the creature to breathe or telling it which muscles to tense so that it can take a step. That sort of thing just—" he shrugged—"goes on. And with nothing else appearing, the . . . simulacrum . . . made from thousands of wyverns . . . will act by itself as though it were one real wyvern, here and now."

"And wyverns have nasty tempers," Mael concluded aloud. As if in response, the little creature sent another jet of flame toward the men. Mael's skin prickled even at a distance. He noticed that the fire crossed the wall of the pentagram easily, though the wyvern itself could not.

Arthur walked closer and stared at the details of the beast that leaped and scrabbled vainly to get at him. The king prodded at it with his sheathed sword, chuckling at the fury with which the wyvern's fangs and tiny claws attacked. Merlin tensed. The king tugged back his sword, stripping the dragon from it at the inscribed line. Still chuckling, Arthur twisted the scabbard on the baldric from which it hung. He saw the leather shredded where the beast had clawed it.

Then the king stopped laughing. With a muffled curse, he dropped the sheath and slid the blade free to examine it. The yellow light gleamed on deep scorings in the steel itself. Arthur grunted and shot the sword home again. "Stronger than I had thought," he said to Merlin in a neutral voice.

"They're not at all like things of this world," the wizard agreed. "They couldn't even breathe if they were here, if they had to stay. Things weigh much more in their worlds and the air is much thicker, besides being different. That's how they can fly, even though they're huge when they grow. They're like whales in the waves of our seas. And they're very strong, yes. . . ."

Merlin closed and thonged shut the case of scrolls. He fastened the chest of chemicals as well. Taking the books and his wand under his left arm, the wizard walked toward the cave mouth. Pausing to transfer the arthame to his free hand, he scribed a single line between the gateposts. He added symbols on the outer side of the line while he muttered the same half-sensed sounds he had used when drawing the pentacle. Finished, Merlin swung the door open. Cei, standing close beyond it, turned around with hope and concern limned on his face by the lamps still burning inside.

"Leader," Merlin directed, "if you'll pick up the lantern—the stand can stay here, I think."

Arthur nodded and obeyed. Mael picked up the

chest of chemicals without being asked and started to follow the king toward the gate.

"Don't touch the line or the words," Merlin warned. "Just step over them." To Mael he added, as if an afterthought, "Oh, Irishman—would you just smudge a side of the pentacle before we leave? There's no problem with the barrier drawn here."

Mael frowned. From the darkness behind the waiting seneschal came Veleda's shout of warning: "Mael! Use the silver!"

Mael reacted before rage had time to flush across the wizard's face, darting his hand out to pluck the arthame from the older man. Warrior and sorcerer stared at each other without speaking or needing to. Beyond stood Arthur, amused the way a certain type of dog owner can be as he watches a pair of his animals about to mix lethally. Cei's sword was drawn. The seneschal stood ready to slaughter both men if his Leader allowed him to. Cei did not understand the silent quarrel, but he abominated both participants.

Mael flipped the arthame so that he held it by the grip. He spat deliberately on the ground between him and Merlin; then he walked back to the pentacle. Under his left arm the Irishman still carried the box of chemicals. The angry wyvern watched his approach and redoubled its efforts to claw through the barrier. Mael slashed the air in front of it with the arthame. Screeching, the beast threw itself backwards. It rolled over as it tangled its tail and legs in its haste.

Mael knelt, eyeing the little monster. He drew the tip of the arthame through the inscribed pentagram. The wyvern spat fire in his direction but remained at a distance, curling and hunching itself. Mael straightened and backed away with quick, fluid steps. When the Irishman was halfway between the gate and the marred pentacle, the wyvern launched itself at his face like a bolt from a ballista.

The box of chemicals Mael held saved his left arm, for it was pure reflex that threw it up to block the sudden attack. The dragon's speed was beyond anything its swoops and caracoles within the pentagram had led Mael to expect. As it clung to the sturdy box, the wyvern lanced blue fire which danced over the edges of the wood. It seared Mael's forearm. The Irishman cut blindly with the arthame, the instantaneous sweeping reaction of a man who has felt a spider leap to the back of his neck.

The silver arthame caught the wyvern squarely and slapped the beast away. The creature bounced on the cave floor, knocking the lampstand over. The oil burst up in a flood of yellow light and a rush of heat. The dragon sat in the middle of the conflagration and yowled angrily. A long, red streak swelled where silver had touched the ebon scales. The wyvern bent and licked at the wound, oblivious of the pool of blazing oil surrounding it. Mael took two sliding steps and leaped the barrier drawn at the gate. The other three men gave back swiftly at his movement. The dragon, catching a peripheral glimpse of the motion, threw itself suddenly after Mael. The beast was an instant too slow, rebounding from the line just after the Irishman had crossed it. The creature sent a spiteful stylus of flame out into the night behind its intended victim.

Arthur still held the lantern. Mael turned the chest of chemicals to the light. The wood was blackened in a circle the size of a dinner plate. In the center, the panel was pierced by a hole large enough to pass a man's thumb. The ceramic jar of copper salts within had shattered. The fumes stank of hellfire. The flame had sprayed Mael's forearm with half-burned splinters blasted from the box and raised several blisters. Mael dropped the chemicals without a word. The chest jounced, breaking several of the containers from the sound it made when it hit. The Irishman flung the arthame to the ground at Merlin's feet. Its point sank several inches into the soil, making the metal ring with the shock. "Your beast has bad manners," Mael said. "It could be that I should've fed him the poker sideways, I am thinking. Or fed it to you, wizard."

If Merlin intended a retort, he swallowed it. From his other side, Veleda spoke. Her hair slithered as if in harmony with her words. "You're a man who rolls a rock down a mountainside and expects to run with it, Merlin. You can't control a landslide just because you had the power to begin it. There are no fools in the world so great as the ones who think themselves knowing."

Merlin snarled with the same frustrated rage that wracked the thing he had summoned. He turned and stalked to his horse, still holding the container of books. Arthur laughed. "You know, Irishman," he said, "I'm beginning to think you could be a credit to my Companions—if you lived long enough."

Mael still shook with anger and the shock of his near death at the wyvern's claws. "Maybe I don't shit well enough on command," he spat.

"Neither do my Huns," Arthur replied mildly. "Sometimes . . . but I think we've seen and done all we care to, here tonight. Yes . . . You'd better get to your billet. Tomorrow's a day of training, you know."

Mael laughed. He bowed to the king, then followed Veleda to the horses. Behind him he could faintly hear the dragon hiss and squall.

◆   ◆   ◆

Mael and Veleda slid from their mounts and unsaddled in front of the recruit lines. They lashed the beasts to the rail placed there, even though the recruits had not yet been issued horses. At the door to his and Starkad's dwelling, Mael paused and said to the woman, "Just a second. My friend sleeps light, and he tends to—react when he's suddenly—" Mael broke off because the door flew open. Starkad's huge right hand caught the Irishman by the throat.

"Wait a minute!" Mael gurgled, choked as much by his laughter as by the Dane's fingers. Starkad broke his grip and the two men began to hug and pummel each other's backs.

"Figured a dumb turd like you'd get back when any decent man'd be asleep!" the Dane thundered, while Mael was shouting, "You know, I met somebody even bigger than you in Ireland? And may the Dagda club me dead if he wasn't stupider, too!"

"Hey, quiet the hell down!" grumbled a voice in Gothic German from the billet beside them.

Starkad's face smoothed, his mouth dropping into a half grin. He loosed Mael and walked to the door of the other room. He was barefoot and wore only a tunic that fell midway on his hairy thighs. The Dane kicked flatfooted, his right heel catching the hinge side of the door and flinging the whole panel into the room. "Come on out," he invited pleasantly. No one stirred inside. Starkad walked back to Mael and Veleda. "And they say that Goths are tough," he muttered.

"Look," said Mael, "much as I'd like to help you mop up this whole army, I'm just about dead on my feet. I was, even before you started pounding on me. Suppose you can let me rack out and keep the damned cadre away when they come around in the morning?"

"Later in the morning," the Dane corrected him. "Yes, I think I can do that thing."

"Oh," Mael said. "Ah . . . this is Veleda." Starkad's expression changed, not exactly in the fashion Mael had expected. The Irishman misinterpreted the look of appraisal, none the less. He licked his lips and said, "Ah, Starkad, I know . . .Look, tomorrow they can issue me another room—"

"No problem," the Dane said, bursting into a smile again. "We've shared by threes and fours before. And you needn't worry, I like my women with a little more meat on their bones, you know." He clapped Mael on the shoulder. "Come on, get some sleep so you can wake up and tell me what's been going on."

Chapter Eight

From the angle of the sun, it was afternoon when Mael awakened. With his eyes still slitted the Irishman groaned and said, "Starkad, if I'd known how I was going to ache when I got up, I'd have just asked you to slit my throat in the dark."

"Up?" Starkad laughed, twitching the sheet down and slapping Mael's rump.

Mael swore and swung his legs over the side of the bed. "How'd I get in your bunk?" he asked.

"I picked you up and put you there when I saw you really weren't going to share the other one with your lady friend, that's how. You needed a mattress worse than I did."

"Oh," Mael said. Veleda's bed was empty. "Ah, where did she—"

"Out to the jakes," the Dane answered before the question was complete. Even as he spoke, the door

131

opened to readmit Veleda. She was beautiful and perfect in the sunlight.

"There're a lot of women in the camp," she said as she entered. She grinned brightly. "Families, I mean—I'd expected women around an army, but not wives."

"Yes, when we showed up, Cei—he took our names—told us it was fine to bring our families," Starkad said. "Of course, Mael and me were each other's family."

"It's useful to Arthur," Mael explained cynically, "for control. People think again about changing sides in a tight spot if they know it means their son gets used for a lance target."

"I need to find a place to, well . . . listen again," Veleda said in an abrupt change of subject. "I don't really understand what's happening—oh, not in the levels I see, that's obvious, but in the ones I feel. And things are moving, weaving, there at a rate that— that I don't like at all. There's a grove on the hill just north of here that should do for my purpose. I'll come back from there as soon as I can."

Starkad raised an eyebrow at the sober-faced woman, but it was to Mael that he spoke. "She going to be all right, wandering around alone?"

Mael hid his wince in a brief stiffness around his eyes. "She'll be all right," he said, turning to Veleda, "but I'd like to come anyway."

"No," she said with a smile. "This I really have to be alone to do. I'll be back soon."

She swung the door closed behind her. After a moment, Starkad threw it open to pass more of the sunlight into the room. "Well," he prodded, "what happened?"

"We got the skull at the shrine where I'd remembered

it," Mael said simply. "Had to kill a couple people, but we got out all right. And we came back on a ship from mBeal Liathain."

"Right," Starkad agreed. "We."

Mael looked up into the blue eyes of his friend. His own hands clenched, then reopened deliberately. "She met me in Ireland. She knew I'd be coming somehow," he said. "Starkad, she's a witch, and she scares me; scares me like nothing ever has. And dear god, I think I love her." Mael stretched out his hands toward his friend like a captive pleading. "What am I going to do?" he begged.

The Dane chuckled without particular humor. "I'd heard her name before," he said. "So she's a witch. So what?"

Haltingly, but with the fullness of detail he had denied before, Mael reported the events of the voyage from Ireland. "I'd thought she was so helpless," he concluded miserably, "but she killed them with her hands when I wouldn't have had a chance alone. And then when she touched me, I . . . What am I going to do, Starkad?"

Starkad remained silent for a moment after the Irishman had finished. The Dane's beard and moustache flowed back across his face to join the hair of his head. It was tangled and rudely cut, but fairly clean despite that. The individual hairs were golden and very fine, surprisingly fine on a man so gross in other respects. Starkad suddenly leaned forward and took each of Mael's hands, now lowered, in one of his. The Irishman's skin was in dark contrast to the Dane's. Mael's fingers were long and sinewed, but they were utterly dwarfed within the huge fists that held them.

Starkad squeezed gently. "You've touched my hands before, haven't you?" he asked.

Mael nodded, frowning. He tried to pull free and found that he could not.

"And once was at Massilia," the Dane continued inexorably. "I carried you out of a crib after the pimp had decked you with an iron bar. Do you remember what I did to the pimp first?"

"Starkad, that wasn't the—"

"Your bloody ass it wasn't the same!" Starkad roared. His face was inches away from the Irishman's. "I took his neck in one hand and an elbow in the other, and I pulled on the bastard until his arm came out of his shoulder. *That's* what I did to him. And if you're going to get all hateful about people saving your life, you can damned well start with me!" He let go of Mael and sat back, arms crossed against his chest.

"Yes, well . . ." Mael said. He tried a wan smile. "Guess I never thought I had to protect you and . . . all."

The Dane's black scowl softened. "Look," he said, "did she ever tell you she needed to be coddled like a nice glass trinket?"

"No."

"Then don't hold it against her that you're a lousy judge of people. Treat her like a woman and not a— a—I don't know what." Starkad paused. With a fleeting return of his previous seriousness, he added, "It doesn't sound like she—does what she did for fun. Remember, we've all of us done things we had to do but we'd rather not remember now. All of us."

"Except for you, Starkad," Mael said with more bitterness than he intended.

The Dane laughed. "You think I'm so wide open about everything I do that I couldn't be hiding anything? Sure I could. One thing."

Mael caught the tension underlying his friend's light

words. "Hey," he said falsely, "if something's eating at you, I don't want to hear it. I've got problems enough of my own." He was taut with fear that Starkad would blurt a secret and regret it immediately, shattering a decade's friendship.

"Balls," the Dane said, almost as if he were reading his companion's mind. "You've spilled your guts to me, don't know why I shouldn't do the same. It doesn't matter, anyway. . . . Ever wonder why I go by my mother's name, Thurid?"

Mael shrugged. "I've known other northerners who did. There was Odd Kari's son we met that night in Hippo. . . . I figured your mother raised you after your father died before you were born.

"Oh, he lived till I was ten," Starkad said. "Only thing is, he never married my mother. Ran off with her, took three months of her temper and her tongue—which wasn't a bad record; I had ten years of them but I made it a point never to see the bitch after I left home myself. But my father dumped her in Grobin among the Letts. He was a trader, you see."

"It's a better man who makes his own name than takes one left for him," Mael said, glad that Starkad's secret was nothing worse than bastardy.

Starkad laughed again. "You mean, I'm a bastard so many other ways it's no surprise to find I'm one in simple truth? Well, that's nothing that's ever bothered me—as many bastards as I've scattered around the world, I'll not fret to've been bred on the wrong side of the blanket myself.

"But you see, what happened is my mother went back to her father's house—I can guess now how she earned her passage. But she wouldn't tell anybody who the man had been, even when they tried to beat it out of her. They wanted a virgin's price out of whoever it was, for honor's sake, you know. They were respectable people. Except for mother. She was a strong-minded bitch, I give her that.

"I grew—fast," Starkad continued, spreading his big arms wide as much to display as to stretch the muscles. "When I was ten, I was as big as any sixteen-year-old. Any sixteen-year-old to come out of Ireland," he corrected himself with a grin. "And that summer I was in Hedeby with my mother, standing looking at the cutlery in a booth an Italian Jew ran. My mother grabbed me by the shoulder—have I said she was a big woman? She turned me to face down the boardwalk. 'D'ye see the man there?' she whispered. 'He's Steinthor Steingrim's son.'

"Well, I'd sooner have looked at knives and axes, but he was a striking fellow. Bigger than most. He looked old at the time, but I know he can't have been but thirty, thirty-five. He had a bright blue mantle with tassels down one side, and a belt of silver plates that he hung a sword from. And my mother said, 'He's your father, child. When you grow to be a man you must kill him for the dishonor he brought to both of us.' I reached out my hand and took a hatchet from in front of the Jew. He shouted but I was already running down the boardwalk. My father, that was Steinthor, saw me coming but he thought I was just a thief. He spread his arms to stop me and I put the axe to its haft in his forehead. I kept on running and at the docks I jumped aboard a freighter that had cast off. The owner signed me on to his crew. I was big, like I said, and—I still had the bloody hatchet in my hand."

Mael touched his tongue to his lips. He started to speak, realized that the sympathy he had been about to show would only have underscored the uncorrectable. Instead the Irishman said only, "I'm sorry."

Starkad lifted half his mouth in a wry smile. He said, "It's not that I killed him, or that there wasn't reason to have killed him—I've never needed much reason anyway, you know that. . . . But I've never killed another man just because some bitch of a woman told me to. And that won't go away, Mael, however long I live."

Mael leaned over and punched Starkad lightly in the chest. "Some day I'll tell you about the day I killed my sister's husband," the Irishman said. "But just for now I'd sooner leave confession to the Christians and talk about something that matters. Just what is Arthur trying to accomplish here? I haven't had a day awake in the camp, but you've been around long enough to notice things."

"Yes, I've talked to some of the long-service folks," Starkad agreed. "Come on, it's a pretty day. Let's take a walk outside and feel how nice it is not to be training some damn fool way or other."

The ground immediately around the recruit billets had been trampled bare. The men walked the fifty yards over into the shade of a small stand of poplars. Children played and called around the buildings, ignoring the pair of warriors. Starkad watched them with a mild affection sharply at variance with the way he looked at adults.

"He's building quite an army, Arthur is," the Dane said quietly. "They say he wants to conquer the world. He's bringing the whole world together under his banner to do it, too."

"Yes, there were men from at least half a dozen tribes in the group they stuck us in the other night," Mael remembered aloud. "And they were all fresh recruits like us."

"Anybody willing to make a business of war," Starkad said. "Didn't used to be that way, though. Arthur started with what troops he could raise from his own tribe. Most of the Britons, though—they're soft; their guts rotted away under Rome. Arthur got a few to join up besides his own tribesmen, the Votadini, but only a man here and a man there. Nothing that was going to stop the Saxons. The landowners and the bishops'd pay Arthur to fight for them, but they wouldn't give him men to fight with. He used their money at first to hire other Romans from the Continent, folk that had been beaten once by the Germans moving into the Empire. Some of them were willing to fight again. That was where Lancelot came from, and Lancelot was when the rest all changed."

"Lancelot," Mael repeated thoughtfully. "Sure, I know where I heard of him before. He was Syagrius' right-hand man."

"That's right," Starkad agreed. "The last Roman to think he was Emperor of Gaul. They tell me Lancelot got away from Vesantio with his life and a fast horse when Clovis mousetrapped the Roman army there. He got to Britain, anyway, and to Arthur . . . and Arthur started hiring anybody who'd sign on, leaving it to Lancelot to figure how to whip them into shape. Everybody gets a horse and a coat of mail if they don't have one. Everybody gets the same weapons and has to use them the same way— lance, sword, and bow. They thought they were going to make me leave my axe behind in a fight because they haven't issued one to everybody."

"Think they'll just ignore you?" Mael asked. "There're a couple thousand of them and two of us, you know."

Starkad nodded seriously. "Yeah, I thought about

that, figured if they were as stubborn as I was, they were going to kill me sure. But I looked around and there were the Huns—you know. Wear what they please, carry what they please, *do* damn near what they please, so long as they fight like Huns. So the first morning you were gone, the cadre took us out to practice with swords on six-inch posts they'd set up in a field. And I showed them why I carried an axe, not a sword—and I spent the afternoon hammering in new posts. But they stopped fucking with me about my axe.

"You just have to be good, is all," the Dane concluded complacently.

Mael laughed. Starkad had noted the same point that Arthur had mentioned to Mael at the cave—and made use of it. "Sure, if the Saxons'll just plant themselves ankle deep and wait, you'll play hell with them. But the sort of mix we trained with—that's normal for the Companions."

"For the last five years," the Dane said. "The old sweats, the Britons who've been with Arthur from the beginning—they complain and they don't care who's listening, Briton or German or Greek. They say Lancelot's doing the same thing the Vortigern"—Starkad used the British title for High King—"Vitalis did fifty years ago, hire Saxons to fight Picts, and hire more Saxons, until—bam! The Saxons cut everybody's throats one night and take over half the country."

The Irishman snorted. "Idiots. I'll call Lancelot a lot of things, but not stupid. Anybody can see the difference between this and what Vitalis did."

"Looks pretty much the same to me," Starkad said flatly.

Mael looked at him. "Hey," he said, "you're not

supposed to do the thinking, right? Mess with my job and I'll get mad and, oh, piss on your ankles or something." He punched Starkad's chest.

The Dane smiled. "Okay, so tell me, oh learned man."

"Vitalis hired groups," Mael explained. "He'd bring over a shipload of Saxons and settle them at a river mouth or a favorite landing spot of the Picts. They'd have their own government, their own thegn to lead them, and, after a little while, the kings followed the bulk of their tribes over. You don't come first if you've got a soft place at home, but when things seem settled in Britain and the land's so much better, you move in and be king there. And if there're locals there already who think they're in charge but they don't have any soldiers of their own—well, so much the worse for them.

"But Arthur isn't enlisting tribes, right?" Mael continued. "Just men. And they aren't from one tribe together and they aren't under their own leaders, they're under his. They don't even use their own weapons or their own language in his army—unless they're too good to waste, my heroic friend."

Starkad nodded in slow agreement. "Everyone who's been here any time calls him Leader," the Dane said. "And they don't have any ties but to him, you're right. I guess I could take any of the Companions—never met a man I couldn't—" Starkad paused, looked at Mael and rephrased his statement. "Never fought a man I couldn't take, some things I'll likely die without being sure. But even one at a time the Companions I've seen are good. And they don't fight one at a time, they move every man together, and I think maybe they could beat any army they didn't choose to get out of the way of."

The Dane fell silent and frowned. "I'm not much for following anybody," he continued at last. "I guess that's why you and I've knocked around so many places But I think most of the Companions I've met here—Goths and such-like as sure as the Britons, anybody who's been around him for a while—most of them would follow Arthur to hell if he wanted to lead them there. And they'd expect to ride back, too."

"He does things I wouldn't have expected," admitted Mael. "He got his dragon. Damned if I see what good it'll do him, but he wanted it and he got it. I'd sooner cuddle an asp, myself."

Starkad's eyes had been picking among the trees and fields around them. They focused. "Your—Veleda's coming," the Dane said.

Mael turned. Veleda had emerged from the wooded path a hundred yards away. Her hair was richly white in the sun's eye. Her face, never tanned, looked more gray than pale, and her expression was as tight and wasted as that of a day-old corpse. The Irishman stepped out of the shade toward her, got a better look, and began to run, with Starkad pounding a step behind him. Veleda fell into Mael's arms, trying to smile.

"What happened to you?" Mael demanded in a voice so calm that only Starkad could have heard the lethal threat underlying it. "Who did this?"

"No, no," the woman protested feebly. "Nobody did anything to me. Except myself. And I can walk."

Mael lifted her, his right arm supporting her thighs and his left hand her shoulders. "Sure," he said, "and I can carry you—which is how we're going to get back to the room. What did you do?" Veleda weighed only a hundred pounds or so, and the ordeal seemed to have drained away much of even that slight bulk. She lay supple in his arms, her hair brushing his knees as he walked.

"You've got enough of your own ways to tempt death," Veleda replied. "Leave me to mine. We all of us do what has to be done. There are things I'd never do for myself that I will for mankind and the earth."

Beside them Starkad grunted, a comment though wordless. Veleda raised her head from Mael's breast and said, "Yes, so urgent as that, Dane. There's a knot being tied in the fate of all the world, very soon in the future. Merlin's foolish toy is part of it, I'm certain. . . ." Her head fell back and she added in a whisper, "But those who speak to me aren't ones you can order to speak clearly, tell this and thus and why. They give answers as they please, and they care very little for men."

Mael turned sideways to fit Veleda through the doorway to their billet. He laid her down on the nearer bed. "Do you know a man named Biargram Grim's son?" the woman asked unexpectedly.

Mael frowned. "I do," said Starkad, seating himself carefully on the edge of the other bunk. "Biargram Ironhand, yes; a thegn of some note. He's a big man, big as me. I remember people guessing at which of us would win a catch-as-catch-can if we met—though we never did. But that was a long time ago. He must be fifty now and a graybeard."

"A Dane?" Mael questioned.

"A Saxon," Veleda corrected him. "He has a shield and a spear, and I need you to get them."

Starkad chuckled. "Biargram'll be as glad to give them up as he would be his left eye and both balls," the Dane said. "Besides which, we have a trip to make to Saxony and back. Want us to bring you the moon besides, along the way?"

"Starkad," the woman said wearily, "I mean it. And the weapons are here in Britain—that much I'm sure of."

"Why do you need them?" Mael asked.

"I don't know." Veleda saw the Irishman's face close and winced herself in frustration. She reached up and caught his hand, saying, "Mael, I don't know, but there's no doubt at all in my mind that I *do* need them, that I *will* need them soon, in a very few days or weeks—and that you and all the rest of the world besides depend on the weapons being in my hands when the need comes. But if you won't believe me, I can't make you believe."

After a moment, Mael's fingers closed on hers. "I believe you," he said.

"Sure, Biargram could've brought his folks across," Starkad agreed. "From what I hear, the country from the Bight to the Elbe's getting to be as empty as a vestal's cunt. Every Saxon and Jute's migrating to Britain. But I don't see how that puts us any forwarder. It's not just what the Saxons would do if we came skulking around—and believe me, Biargram's shield's been in his family more years than anybody can count—but besides the Saxons, neither you nor I can even get out of this damned camp without being used for archery practice."

"Umm," thought the Irishman aloud. He sat beside the woman, his hand still turned with hers. "I think we could arrange that. You know this Biargram—"

"A little. A damned little."

"—and nobody here is going to be able to prove it's only a nodding acquaintance if you say otherwise. Sure . . ."

"Could I have some water?" Veleda asked Starkad as Mael's mind clicked over plans that began to mesh like clockwork.

Mael's mouth dropped in embarrassment at not having offered something without being reminded. His hand snatched the drinking gourd from its peg on the wall. It was empty.

"There's a well at the south end of the buildings," Starkad said.

"Would you go get us a gourdful, then?" Mael asked, holding the container out to his friend.

Starkad did not reach for it as expected. "She's your woman," he said.

Mael blinked. All he said aloud was, "Yes, I guess that's true." He stood, adding to Veleda, "I'll be back in a bit."

When the Irishman was gone, Starkad said fondly—facing the open doorway rather than Veleda—"His mind works all the time. By the time he comes back, he'll have figured how to get the two of us away from Arthur and then back with the gear you want. Very bright fellow, very." The Dane switched his gaze straight at the woman. His blue eyes struck her like twin hammers. "But he's not German. He didn't sit by the fire when he was a little boy, listening to the women telling stories about the things they only said to each other. About the days when the spirits were all women and their priestesses ruled everywhere. And the most powerful of all the priestesses was the Veleda, in those days that are only dreams now.

"How old are you, Veleda?"

"You won't tell him," she said, not a threat or a question, only a statement of fact like the fact that his hair shaded from blond to red and that the vein in his neck pulsed as his heart beat.

"I wouldn't do anything to hurt him," Starkad agreed quietly. "He thinks you're a witch, and he's found he can live with that. The truth isn't so important to me that I'd hurt a friend for its sake." The Dane's voice changed. "But one more thing I'll tell you. You may be priestess or witch or goddess yourself; you may have any power you please and be able to live forever; but you'll live the rest of eternity in two parts if you harm a hair of that man's head. I don't doubt that you can kill me, but no power this side of hell or the other will stop me if I come after you with my axe."

"I won't hurt him," Veleda said. There was neither fear nor doubt in her voice. She smiled. "A man could have a worse friend than you, Starkad. Or a woman."

Mael strode through the doorway with the filled gourd in his hand. He gave it absently to Veleda. "Starkad," he began, his face vibrant, "this will work. There's not a man of Arthur's who could prove you're lying, and besides—they'll all believe it's true. You see—"

He bubbled on, too distracted by his coming triumph to notice the glance that Starkad exchanged with Veleda.

Chapter Nine

From the top of a low hillock Arthur and a dozen men of his staff and bodyguard watched two troops performing mounted evolutions in concert. Lances lowered, the hundred Companions advanced at a trot across the broken pasture in a double line abreast. As they approached the wooded margin of a stream, Arthur gave an order to his cornicine who then blew a three-note call on his silver-mounted cow horn. The horsemen raised their lance points and wheeled left in parallel files. One man fell off. In the center, the formation clotted awkwardly where a swale threw the timing askew.

Lancelot cursed. "Ragged, ragged. They do that in front of Saxons instead of willow trees, and there'll be a massacre."

"That's why we train them, isn't it?" the king retorted. On horseback his clubfoot was scarcely noticeable.

One of the bodyguards looked away from the maneuvering troops, back along the path that led to the villa. The man grunted. "Sir," he said, to Lancelot rather than the king. Arthur was too exalted to be bothered with details of intruders.

Lancelot turned, his eyes following the bodyguard's. "Face around, boys," he said in a flat voice which none the less carried to all the men around the king. To the cornicine Lancelot added, "Bring the troops in." Two notes and then two more sang out. The exercising Companions pivoted left again and rode toward their Leader.

"The Irishman, Mael, and his Dane friend," Arthur observed.

"So it seems," agreed the big Master of Soldiers. Lancelot unsocketed his lance, bringing it forward though still vertical. Its butt spike rested on his toes. The other Companions were also readying themselves unobtrusively, drawing swords and slipping their arms through shield loops. One of them, an Armenian, carried a bone-stiffened composite bow. He swung his horse sideways so that its body concealed his hands stringing the bow and nocking an arrow.

Mael and Starkad were on foot, fully armed but not actively threatening. Both wore their shields slung behind their backs. Mael's sword was sheathed and Starkad rested his axe helve in the palm of his hand. The bearded head was hooked over the Dane's shoulder. The rectangular peen of it facing forward was no reassurance to Lancelot who had seen it crush the stone from his hands, but it was as innocent a fashion as any in which the big weapon could be carried.

When they were twenty feet away, Lancelot

dropped his point at the men on foot and called, "That's far enough."

Neither Mael nor Starkad appeared concerned by the implied threat. Starkad even took another half step before halting. Unlike his guards, Arthur, too, appeared to be relaxed. He rested part of his weight on his hands crossed on his right front saddle horn.

"Leader," Starkad thundered at the king, "I claim the right to be freed from my oath to you so I may end a blood feud. That feud I swore long ago, so I must follow it now and leave you."

The berserker spoke clumsy Celtic, his inflections Danish and his idiom, such as it was, more Irish than British. Arthur frowned. Beside him the cornicine started to giggle. As if he had been ordered to explain, Starkad continued, "Kari, Tostig's daughter, married in her first youth the bonder Ulf Svertlief's son of Tollund and then, at his death, Asgrim Walleye, second son of—"

"Blood of God, Dane!" Arthur burst out. "If you've got to tell your story, tell it short or get your butt back to where it belongs. You're supposed to be training this afternoon, aren't you?"

Starkad blinked. He pursed his lips in concentration, then said, "Of this marriage—" he raised his voice as the troops of horsemen reined up noisily behind Arthur, awaiting further command —"was born Asa, niece to me through Tostig's line, who married the Saxon thegn Biargram—"

Arthur flushed and swung toward his Master of Soldiers, a furious command ready in his open mouth. Mael forestalled him, stepping forward with a hand laid on the Dane's shoulder to silence him. "Lord," he called in Latin. "Let me cut his tale down."

Arthur calmed slightly and turned. "Quickly then," he said.

Mael licked his lips. "My friend's niece wed a thegn named Biargram," he said, "a Saxon. He sent her home after a year but kept the dowry. The girl's family couldn't get it back since none of them wanted to take on Biargram. Starkad, here, had already been outlawed so there wasn't anything he could do, but he swore he'd kill Biargram if the two of them ever walked a land with no seas or mountains between them.

"And in mBeal Liathain last week, a Saxon sailor told me Biargram had brought his tribe here to Britain."

"That's right," said Arthur. As though his mind was riffling through a packet of military communiques, he continued, "He and his household, all told some two hundred, crossed over several years ago in four keels. They joined Cerdic—*the traitor!*" The king's face went momentarily bestial as he hissed the last words. Calmly he continued, "At last report they'd been settled near Clausentum and were doing quite well. But what is that to me?"

Mael was an educated man with an educated man's trick of assuming someone less well educated was also less intelligent. The Irishman kept his face smooth, but a clear sight of Arthur's mind at work frightened him in a way the flashes of bloodthirsty madness had not. "Lord," he said, "my friend is headstrong and worse, you know that. Once he gets a notion, you can't drag it away from him with a team of oxen. He's convinced now that he has to go track this Biargram down. We're brothers in a real way, he and I; we've mixed more blood on battlefields than ever womb-mates had in common. I have to go with him."

At the word "have," Arthur's eyes narrowed and a venomous smile spread across Lancelot's face. "Oh, aye," Mael snapped, the Celtic phrasing seeping through with emotion, "you can kill us, can you not? A pleasant time you'll have to do it, aye, but you can. And what will it gain you, to kill two men and save your enemies the labor of it?"

Arthur began to laugh. "And so I should send men on leave into the middle of the Saxons, because somebody diddled somebody's niece out of her dower share? No, I don't think I'll begin running my army that way, not just yet. Get back to your duties."

Behind Arthur, the cornicine added, "Sure, they're likely spies for Cerdic, Leader."

Unexpectedly, Lancelot reached over and laid his fingertips on the back of Arthur's hand. "No, Leader," he said. "Let them go."

Arthur looked at him dubiously. Lancelot continued, "They've asked your leave to go; your authority suffers nothing to grant the request, and your camp discipline, I understand—" he cocked a grim eye at Mael; the Gaul's speech was still slurred by thick lips and a swollen nose—"will improve. Let them go."

"And if they are returning spies?" the king asked, but as a genuine question.

"They'll leave the woman," Lancelot pointed out— that had been no intent of Mael's, but he dared not deny it—"and besides, if they are traitors, it's best we be shut of them."

"Leader," Mael put in, "I brought you—" he realized that Arthur might not want the skull and its purpose released to a hundred men, even his own men—"what you know of. I know you realize . . . how risky that job was. It was harder, perhaps, than even you fully understand. But I brought the thing back where scarcely another could have done; and if you give us leave now, I swear by whatever you wish that I'll come back myself and with my friend here, if there's life in either of us."

"Blood feud," Arthur repeated. He laughed again, loudly and without humor. "I have a blood feud, too . . . with the whole world, I sometimes think. It'll bow its neck to me some day, yes. . . . Go on, take this Saxon's head or leave your own, it's all the same to me. But if you enter the hall of Cerdic your master, tell him what you have seen here—and in the cave. And tell him that one day I will be coming to serve him in the fashion that traitors are served. It would be well for him if he had fallen on his sword before that day."

Mael dipped his head in acquiescence. Starkad, following the motion as he could not the words, nodded also. The two men turned and began walking back the way they had come, the Dane's axe-edge winking as it split sunbeams.

"Leader," they heard Lancelot say when he thought it was safe to speak to his king, "I'll ride back with them, arrange an escort to the Zone for them—and a guard for the woman."

Arthur nodded grimly. His mind was fixed on his memory of Cerdic, the British lordling who had weighed the danger of Saxon mercenaries against Arthur's growing tyranny—and had called in Saxons. The king's right hand twisted on the saddle horn as if it were a sword hilt, the knuckles as white as the skin across his cheekbones. Lancelot clucked to his horse and trotted toward the men on foot before they disappeared around a curve in the trail. Behind him, Arthur was giving orders in a normal voice to the exercising troops.

Mael and Starkad waited around the bend for the Master of Soldiers. The overt changes in their stances were slight but significant. Mael had thrust his left arm through his shield straps. Starkad's axe, though still on his shoulder, faced forward and was ready to strike. Both men were tense, certain that Lancelot would not have come alone to slay them, but knowing also how much the Gaul hated them both.

"Gently, heroes," Lancelot said. His grin had split a scab on his damaged face. A tiny runnel of blood streaked his chin. "I'm going back to make everything easy for you, to see that you're issued food and don't have any trouble with our own patrols."

"Why?" the Dane demanded bluntly.

"Oh, not because I like you," the big Gaul chuckled. "I've spent every day since—this—" he touched his swollen nose—"thinking about how I was going to kill you both. And it wasn't that easy, you know, because frankly, a duel didn't seem very practical. And though I certainly could have found a group of men to do what was needed, that would have been expensive in one way or another. Then there was always the uncertainty of how the Leader would react . . . ." Lancelot's voice dropped unintentionally as he thought about his king. "He's . . . one can't be sure with him, you know. No one can."

Lancelot cleared his throat, regaining his normal insouciance. The three men were walking down the trail, horseman in the center, like closest friends. "And of course I thought of poison," Lancelot continued, "but there was the problem of getting you both at the same time, and from what I hear of this woman you've brought back, Irishman, maybe poison wouldn't be a good bet so long as she's around.

"But you come and say that you want to walk into

Cerdic's kingdom and chop off the head of one of
his Saxon barons. That's fine, yes; I'll help you get
started any way I can. I never quarrel with the will
of God, Irishman."

Lancelot's mighty laughter boomed around them
as they trudged toward the villa.

⊕   ⊕   ⊕

The captain of the Cirencester Patrol was a Frank
named Theudas, no more of a natural horseman than
Starkad himself was. He dismounted with Mael and
the Dane at the furthest point of his patrol area, twelve
miles southeast of the walled town that was the pivot
of Arthur's domain. The score of men in the patrol
began nibbling bits of sausage and cheese in the
drizzle, talking in low voices and hugging their cloaks
tighter to their mail shirts.

"You're welcome to keep the horses, you know,"
Theudas said. "The warrant you brought from
Lancelot says to aid you in any way short of sending
men into the Zone."

The two friends continued to unlash their gear from
their mounts. "That bastard Lancelot probably hoped
this beast's spine'd open me up to the shoulders from
beneath," Starkad grumbled. He arched his back,
massaging his buttocks with both hands. "Don't know
that I'm sure that it hasn't already. No, I thank you,
but I'd just as soon walk some."

Both Mael and Starkad wore their body armor,
though their steel caps were lashed to their packs.
On their heads were droop-brimmed hats of leather,
protection against the traveler's twin foes: the sun
that might come out to bake them and the rain that
now collected in jeweled ropes sliding from the
leather. The packs themselves were thin rolls of oiled
canvas containing a week's rations and nothing else.

Grunting, the men slung their shields and then the packs over them. They carried spears in place of walking staves. Each spear had an oak shaft as tall as a man and as thick as a woman's forearm. Mael's sword and dagger were sheathed while Starkad's axe was slung under his right arm in its carrying loops, the head nodding free against the iron ringlets of his mail coat.

"Hell of a poor day to go off," Theudas said somberly.

"Not exactly a bloody social event," grunted Starkad in reply. To his companion he added, "Ready?"

"Half a sec." Mael shifted his target so that its lower edge no longer rubbed his hipbone. On an eighty-mile hike, the constant friction would raise a blister the size of a drinking cup, even through the iron mail.

"Don't know why the Leader wants to send spies into Venta anyhow," the Frank continued. "God knows, the Saxons aren't like us, running an army together on thirty minutes' notice. When they mount something it takes weeks, and Cerdic isn't planning anything of the sort. We know that, here with the Patrol. There's always somebody slipping into Glevum or Corinium to see a relative—or run away from their master, or maybe just to make a little by trading the part of their crop they hid from the thegn who owns the lands they farm. Sure, Saxons, too. We don't care, and Cerdic, he doesn't have the men to stop it, the cavalry. If he put his lumbering infantry out in little vedettes, the Leader'd ring the whole Southern Squadron out. We'd eat the Saxon patrols alive before they could do jack shit. Naw, this sector's quiet. It's Aelle who's about to raise hell in the North."

"Okay," said Mael. "Let's go, Starkad."

"There's going to be fighting, then?" the Dane

asked. He wasn't looking at Mael, but he held a hand toward the Irishman to indicate he had heard the request.

"Sure is," agreed Theudas. "Aelle—he calls himself king, has most a' the Saxons north of Londinum— he's raised his levies and must be ready to march by now. On Lindum, likely; he's got big eyes. Tried to get Cerdic and the rest to send some housecarls for the work. The good thing about the Saxons is they don't like each other a bit more than they do us." The Frank scowled. "Or than the North British bastards of the Reged like us, come to think."

"Mael," asked Starkad with a worried look on his face, "do you suppose we're going to miss the fighting?"

"We're going to root here in this goddamn place if we stand around talking much longer," the Irishman snapped.

"Umm," said Starkad. He waved to the Frank and said, "Well, we'll be seeing you again soon, you bet." Mael had already stumped off along the road. Grunting a little with effort, the Dane lengthened his own stride to catch up. The patrol of Companions vanished into the mist behind them, though the clink of their equipment sounded long after the horsemen were out of sight.

Mael's sandals clinked also. The drizzle irritated him. He knew he was in a bad mood, knew also that it was worse than foolish to let his friend's relative good humor irritate him still further. Mael kept his mouth shut and let an occasional remark by Starkad and the dull ringing of hobnails stand as the only sounds between him and the Dane for over a mile.

Finally Starkad said, "Hard damn road, isn't it?" The Irishman grunted. This time Starkad pursued the matter. "I mean, I think if I'd had to walk on this before, I'd have taken that Frank up on his offer of horses, huh?'"

Mael's anger swelled. Then the ridiculousness of it struck him. He began to laugh. "Hey," he said, "the least Lugh could have done for us is to give us decent weather to get killed in, don't you think?"

"Huh?"

"Look," Mael explained, relaxing and feeling as if chains had dropped away, "you know damn well what our chances of getting out of this in one piece are. Don't you?"

"Well," Starkad temporized, "we've gotten into some pretty tight places before, too. You always find ways out of them." He patted his axe. "You and this, hey?"

The Irishman snorted. "Sure, and that guarantees that any fool thing we get into is going to be fine, sure. And this August it's going to rain pieces of gold for my birthday. Well, right now I think I'm going to know you maybe three days longer, if we're lucky. I don't guess I want to spend that time pissed at you because I don't like the weather. Forgive me?"

Starkad cleared his throat. "Oh," he said, "that's okay. I don't much like the rain, either. And I sure wish we had something to ride on, now."

"Such chance as we've got," Mael explained, "pretty much makes us walk. On horses we'd get a lot of attention. The British were horsemen long before Arthur mounted his whole army, but on the eastern side of the Zone a horse marks you. I want us to blend in with the—human countryside."

Starkad looked doubtful. "I might pass for Saxon," he said. "Wotan's eye, I've got a cousin who wed one, though they both drowned. He was no kin to Biargram, either. But I don't see you, brother, looking

anything but a black-hearted, crop-haired Irishman
to anybody with eyes to see."

"Sure, but that's all right—now," Mael said. "You
know what happened when Hengst first made his
play against the Vortigern?"

Starkad nodded. "They cut and burned everything
British around that didn't have walls, until the British
got organized."

"Right. And what happened then?"

"They got their balls kicked between their ears,"
Starkad answered. "Got too confident. They found
the locals might not like to do their own fighting,
but if they had to . . . Horsa had his skull nailed to
the gates of Lindum; Hengst himself got shut up on
an island in the Thames, eating harness leather and
wondering if he was going to make it through the
winter. A damned near thing, from the stories I've
heard."

"Very near," Mael agreed. "And there wasn't a bit
of help coming from the Continent to get them out
of the hole, either. People don't pull up stakes to
migrate into the middle of a disaster. They stay home
and plow their own bit of dirt, even if it's sandy and
the weather'd make this wretchedness—" he shook
his head and scattered a coil of droplets from the
hat brim—"look like balmy summer or, if they've got
to move, they go south to Italy or east to try the Greek
emperor's pay for a while.

"And the Saxon kings have learned that. Arthur's
planning something. Maybe nobody knows just what
or just who's going to be first. But they damned well
know what'll happen to them if they wait till their
backs're to the wall before they go looking for help.
Aelle up north seems to be getting his punch in early,
but I'm betting that anybody who can handle a sword

can find a bunk in one thegn's house or another's. And I don't guess they'd much care what tongue his mother sang him lullabies in. Wandering housecarls don't ride horses, but looking Irish isn't going to call me to mind, particularly."

The rain was with them all day, and it was their only companion. The War Zone separating Saxon from Briton was a wasteland, proof that if neither side won a war, then both sides lost. Between the two races, across the center of the island, lay a no-man's-land that the British had given up but the Saxons could not hold. In the daytime, both sides might use the irregular ribbon for pasture. Their armed guards stayed nervous and watchful. Despite that, all too often they were unable to protect their herds or themselves against skulking bands of Saxons or a sudden brutal thrust by a troop of Companions.

Evening came late and almost indistinguishably from the wan daylight that preceded it. Although they were well within the territory that Cerdic claimed and taxed, the country to either side of the road was as barren as that of the Zone to the north. Cattle lowed in the near distance, however. Once the smell of wood smoke disclosed a cook fire whose plume was hidden in the mist.

To the left loomed a settlement, Saxon but burned out like the occasional Roman building Mael and Starkad had passed earlier. Mael pointed his thumb at the ruins. "They thought they were safe," he said. "There's no place safe within a half day's hard ride of Arthur's outposts. Straight down the road, torching everything that'll burn and slaughtering everything that's alive. No time for looting or prisoners, but sure, you can teach Saxons that civilized men are just as bloody-handed as the barbarians they despise. Any houses that stand, even this deep in toward Venta, are going to be far enough off the road that raiders won't chance ambush to hunt them out of the woods."

Starkad laughed. "Well, I wasn't raised to be a farmer, my friend. And if you were, you hid the fact well enough the time we tried our hands at it. . . . No doubt this destruction's very awful and I should feel miserable about it, but right now I'm a lot more concerned about whether there's a roof left to keep some of this damned rain off us for the night."

Mael squinted at the sky. "Yeah, well," he said. "Not likely we're going to find a better place."

One of the outbuildings had not been burned. Its door was wrenched off, and rotted grain floored the lightless interior. Mael settled himself glumly in a corner, deciding whether to strip off his armor for comfort or leave it on for safety. The metal creaked and galled him every time he moved. Cursing under his breath, the Irishman pulled the mail over his head and began to unlace his gambeson as well.

Starkad ducked back into the rain. Mael heard his axe *thock* loudly. Mael froze, then realized that the blade had rung on the wood, not metal or bone. He resumed undressing as the Dane continued to chop in the gloom. After a few minutes, Starkad returned. He was clutching an armload of wood lopped from the roof beam of one of the houses.

"You're not going to build a fire?" Mael grumbled.

"Sure I am," said Starkad. He dumped the billets and leaned his axe against the wall. Drawing his big dagger, he began to slice curls from a log.

"It's too wet to burn. And anyway, it's not safe. Even if you don't burn us both up, you'll call down some patrol of Cerdic's. Then it'll all be over."

"This is dry on the inside," the Dane said, pointing

to the billet he was shaving. "Go ahead, you light it. You're better at striking a spark than I am. And as for a smoke hole—" Starkad stood, his hair brushing the thatched roof even though he hunched. He raised his axe. With a single swift thrust, he straight-armed the head through the thatch in the corner diagonal to Mael. A quick twist enlarged the hole so it could pass enough smoke to keep the fire from smothering those it warmed. Water dripped in.

Mael scowled. "You think you can cure everything with your damned axe?" he demanded.

Starkad looked at him coolly. "Yes, pretty much. You think you're going to live forever?" The Irishman stayed silent. Starkad pressed, "I want to be warm and a little drier. This wood may smoke, but it's not going to toss any sparks into the thatch. And as for bringing Saxons down on us, we're going to meet Saxons anyway. Tyr's arm, Mael, that's what we're *here* for. We're going to have to talk our way out or fight our way out. We may as well be a little more comfortable tonight and meet 'em now, as meet 'em tomorrow in the rain."

Mael sighed and hitched around his wallet. With a pinch of dried moss from it and the shavings for a bed, he struck his firesteel on a flint until he had a small fire smoldering. "All yours," he said. "If it goes out, you light the next one."

Starkad, smiling, fed the fire with small doses of wood while he accomplished other domestic tasks. The Dane was generally cheerful on shipboard, too, Mael thought sourly to himself. That was because as a rule there would be killing at the other end of the voyage. Starkad covered the doorway with his cloak, pinning it to the withies supporting the thatch with his shoulder brooch and Mael's. The garment was of unbleached wool, so densely woven that it was virtually waterproof. A baulk of wood at the bottom kept the cloak firm against random gusts of wind. The shed began to warm at once. The stolid orange light of the fire did as much for Mael's disposition as the heat itself. He unlaced his sandals and began to strip the wool leggings from beneath them, humming under his breath. Smoke glazed the air. The odor of wool and bodies ripened as the shed heated. That was normal and inevitable; if Mael had a regret, it was that the fire lacked the peculiar pungency of peat-fueled ones like those with which he had been raised.

Starkad slid his own boots off. He cursed, but more in amazement than real anger. The condition of the ball of his foot would have justified a fiercer reaction. A blister three inches across had formed on the sole and burst. The skin hung in shreds. The cloth with which the Dane had packed his boot was glued to his foot by a film of pus and blood. Starkad dribbled a little beer from his canteen to loosen the fabric. "Told you that damned road wasn't fit for a man," he said.

Mael whistled in horror. "Are you going to be able to go on?" he asked. "That looks terrible."

"No problem, unless they get so slippery I keep falling down," Starkad joked. He was peering at his left sole where the callus seemed intact.

"Manannan, but you've got a nice mind," Mael muttered with a grimace.

"Don't see why you aren't having any problem, though," the Dane continued. "It's a damned hard road. I'd think it'd eat anybody's feet as fast as mine."

"No, I've got the gear for it," Mael explained, toeing one of his sandals over to his friend to examine. The sole was thick and multi-layered, studded on the bottom with a dozen hobnails. The iron was bright with recent wear, but a tracery of rust had already begun to hatch-mark the abrasions. The sandal was bound to the foot and high up the leg by straps that could be adjusted precisely. They gave a firm fit whether they were laced over cloth or leather against the cold, or bare skin in a hot climate. The footgear copied the Roman *caligae*, the sandals that had carried legionaries across the whole Mediterranean Basin and beyond. Mael had found it the most practical gear for a man who might have to walk far on a multitude of surfaces, so long as he was willing to accept weight in exchange for sturdiness. "Those buckets you wear," he said to Starkad, "may keep you dry and work well enough on dirt, but they let your foot slide around inside too much on a solid surface. And these roads were built solid."

"Damn well were," the Dane agreed, wriggling his toes toward the fire as he rummaged in his pack for a biscuit. "What'd they do, quarry 'em out of the bedrock? Must've been built a hundred years ago, too."

"Longer ago than that," Mael said. He leaned back against the wall, flexing his muscles so that the rough wattling would rub his shoulders. "I watched a slave gang trench through a road like this, digging a drainage ditch outside of Hispalia. . . ."

"Hispalia?" Starkad repeated. "Three years ago when the city senate was hiring to stiffen their militia against the Goths? We were both there, and I don't remember any road being cut."

"That's because you were in a whorehouse, as usual."

"Oh." Starkad frowned, then nodded. "You find the damndest things to do with your time when you could be screwing," he said. "What did the road look like?"

"Six feet thick and built like a fortress wall laid on its side," Mael said. He closed his eyes to remember. "Three and a half feet of rubble base. Six inches of rammed tufa to level it. Six inches of flints on top of that. Ten inches of pebble gravel set in loam. And then on top of everything, six-inch flagstones set in concrete. I tell you, they built roads to last, the Romans did. And they'll last a lot longer than the empire did that built them."

Starkad shrugged. He had taken a whetstone out of his pack and begun stroking the fine edge back onto his axe blade. Mael fell asleep with the gentle *skritch, skritch* of stone on steel sounding a warrior's lullaby in his ears.

Chapter Ten

The morning was dim but for a time the rain had stopped. Starkad walked without favoring his right foot. It would have amazed Mael had he not once seen the big man methodically hack apart an archer whose last shaft stuck out three inches on either side of the Dane's chest. Pain simply did not affect Starkad once he had decided to ignore it. Many a civilized warrior had discounted tales of berserkers—until one made for him, bloody but as inexorable as an earthquake. That had driven many a brave man to flight.

They passed near several openly sited villages and met a number of other travelers on the road the second day. Everyone left them alone. Even the six armed men heading north passed with hard glances but no direct comment. Mael and Starkad trudged forward purposefully, speaking to no one and in general projecting an aura of being busy but not too busy to cut throats if annoyed. They were not called on what was indeed no bluff.

That night they spent in the woods, wrapped in their cloaks under a fir tree. Its branches looked thick enough to protect them if the rain should resume— as it did near dawn. The tree was some help, but not enough to make it worth continuing to try to sleep. The tenth milepost from Winchester stared crookedly at them from the margin of the road, unnoticed the night before when they had stopped.

"We'd better cut west pretty quick," Mael said, his foot scraping morosely at the old marker. "Otherwise we'll be at Venta. It's got a wall and the guards there won't ignore us. Even if we just get close there's going to be somebody who'll wonder if we turn off. Besides, farther south is likely to be out of our way, anyhow."

Starkad nodded. "I'm not arguing," he said. "You're chief for this raid. Anyway, I don't mind walking on something softer than this rock, rock, rock."

Half a mile farther on, a track joined to the left through a line of poplars. It was narrow, a slick band of mud and trampled dung gleaming in the wider area cleared by the shoulders of driven cows. Mael pointed. Starkad nodded again, and they turned onto the local track.

It had a gloominess not wholly explained by the constant mist. The two men walked single file of necessity, and without speaking because they did not want to alarm villagers whom the rain might otherwise keep inside. The Roman road had not changed in four hundred years, but it had been built by strangers and for strangers. Even in the midst of Cerdic's dominions, Mael had not felt out of place on those stones. This track was newer in one sense but from an earlier age altogether, and there was nothing eclectic about it. An Irishman would be noticed and watched in silent hatred—perhaps even ganged by the village bravos. But the same would happen to a man from a neighboring village—who might steal a pig or a kiss from one of the womenfolk, and was in any case not "one of us." In armor and in company with a man as big as Starkad, Mael felt there was little actual danger, but it was as well to slip by in silence.

The path forked. The friends looked at each other. They took two steps on the right hand branch before a goat's bleating warned them of a village nearby. They turned left instead. Three miles further on and an hour later, they almost walked into the fenced garth of a house. Behind the fence in the drizzle bulked other buildings. The path led straight through the center of the village. No humans were visible, but Mael and Starkad faded quickly back into the trees beside the trail. There were murmurs from poultry and a whiff of wood smoke now that the dwellings had called it to the men's attention.

"Well, do we just walk through?" Starkad asked.

Mael thought a moment, visualizing the topography as best as he could from the glimpses the rain had vouchsafed him. "No," he said at last, "let's cut around here to the right. We can pick up the path again on the other side . . . and there ought to be a stream pretty near. I'd like to refill the water bottles."

He and Starkad turned into the brush and through it into the second-growth hardwoods. The area had been cleared for agriculture not too long in the past. Beeches and oaks had overgrown the fields, but pines had not yet started to drive the hardwoods out. There was a slight falling-off to the left. Mael thought he heard the purl of a stream and nodded to Starkad. They stepped between a pair of oak saplings and out into the misty drizzle of a swale too low-lying to support normal trees. A grove of silver birches straggled up at the very edge of the stream some thirty feet away.

Starkad's left hand gripped Mael's shoulder and stopped him as still as an altar stone. The whole population of the nearby village, some forty Saxons of mingled sex and age, was clustered among the birches.

Silently, backing the necessary step without breaking a stick or letting their equipment jingle, the friends eased into the added gloom of the trees they had just left. They might have been seen by someone looking for them, but the rain blurred outlines and washed colors away. Kneeling at the forest edge, their armor gleaming no more in the weak sunlight than the wet boles around them, there was nothing to call attention to the men.

In any case, the Saxons were wholly intent on what was going on in their own midst. At the back of the circle were children, naked or nearly so, clutching the skirts and hands of their mothers. The women wore either dresses, simple tubes pinned at the shoulders and tucked at the waist by belts, or skirts and shawls. Hoods or the shawls covered their heads. Their garments were woolen; some, where the weavers had chosen fleece of contrasting shades, were patterned attractively in soft, natural plaids.

Within the circle of women, nearer the snowy trunks which displayed the only primary color on a gray morning, were the men. Despite the chill and the rain, they were lightly clad in linen tunics and half-cloaks of skin or wool. Most of the Saxon males also wore tight-fitting leather caps, sewn with the hair side in, but these were less clothing than armor—and the only armor worn, save by one of the two men in the very center of the group.

The man in armor was clearly the chief. He was larger and at least as tall as the biggest of the men around him, despite the fact that he was slightly downslope of them. He wore ring mail and a horned helmet that must have been an heirloom from an age when warfare was less pragmatic. The other men carried spears or weapons which were obviously agricultural implements—axes and mattocks and, in one case, a flail. The armored thegn was the only one to have a long sword, besides the spear in his right hand. He faced a smaller, older man across what seemed to be a trench, listening to the other intone a prayer with arms uplifted: "Hear us, oh Lady Nairthus. Be near to us in our sowing and in our reaping, now in our Spring and in our Fall. . . ."

Starkad had slipped his pack off without a sound. His big fingers played over the slipknot that attached his helmet to the rest of his gear. The rawhide had swollen and would not give. Without hesitation or effort, the Dane pulled the thong in half.

Mael laid his lips close to Starkad's hair and whispered, "What's going on?"

Holding the iron cap in his hand rather than donning it at once—the neck flare would separate him from Mael by three inches and there was need for them to talk—Starkad said, "Oh, it's a sacrifice to Dame Nairthus . . . the earth goddess, the crop goddess. They're getting ready to butcher a man to her, I'd judge. In my tribe, we prayed to Thor in the Spring and made do with cutting a goat's throat—you can eat the goat afterwards, too. But some of these Saxons, they're so backward they come to war waving stone hammers. Besides, if you've had a bad harvest the past year you start thinking back to old ways—and you've got more useless mouths in the houses than you do in the fold."

The wizened old man facing the thegn continued to pray in a cracked voice. He sounded nervous. If what Starkad said was true, the priest probably wasn't used to human sacrifice either. His head was bare. Rain had plastered his white hair away from the bald spot at the peak of his skull.

The priest stopped speaking and lowered his hands. The thegn stepped forward, then down into the trench. The crowd murmured, shifting a little. Mael saw heels flash briefly above the lip of earth as the sacrifice kicked. Already the victim lay face down in the boggy ditch. The thegn had one foot planted on its back. Then the Saxon slid his other foot forward to force the victim's mouth and nose down into the ground water in the bottom of the trench. The sacrifice began to scream in a high-pitched, feminine voice. The big Saxon leaned his weight down on the outstretched foot. The screams gurgled to a halt.

Mael cursed quietly. He put his iron cap on and set the slouch traveling hat back atop it. Starkad touched his arm. "Shall we slaughter the whole village, then?" the Dane asked with no hint of emotion. "We'll need to, if we try and break up this ritual, you know. All we *need* to do now is slip back into the woods and get on with our own business."

The Irishman looked at him. Starkad shrugged and donned his helmet.

Mael stood and took two measured strides beyond the masking bulk of the trees. He did not draw his sword and his shield hung by its strap instead of being advanced toward the Saxons. "Hold!" he thundered in a huge voice, trained to bellow commands across the steel-shattered chaos of a battlefield. Starkad walked to the right, a half step behind Mael in the mist. His axe helve was balanced on his collarbone.

The pair of them loomed up above the startled Saxons, Mael a big man and Starkad a blurred giant in full armor. The leather hat brim flopped low over Mael's left eye as he had planned. The crowd's small noises were cut off by freezing panic as the Saxons stumbled away from the newcomers. The armored chieftain stepped quickly up from the pit. He unpinned his half-cloak and dropped it, then waited with rain dripping from the down-curved ends of his moustaches. He had not brought a shield, but he gripped his spear shaft with both hands.

Besides the thegn, only the Saxon elder stood his ground. As Mael strode closer, he could see that the old man's pupils were fully dilated and that the wizened face had blanched as pale as his hair. "Wh-what manner of men are you to interrupt the gift to Lady Nairthus?" the priest quavered.

"No men at all," Mael boomed back, walking steadily but slowly enough that the Saxons had plenty of time to give way.

It almost worked. The villagers were a dim semi-circle, some of them ankle-deep in the creek waiting for their thegn to act. The elder shuffled backward a step, slipped on the lip of the trench, and jumped across it away from Mael. When Mael was only three paces away, the Saxon chief trembled. Then he cursed and flung himself at the Irishman with his spear outstretched. Starkad had anticipated him. The Dane took a full stride, bringing his axe around as smoothly as a boy would a fly whisk.

The axe blade took the Saxon at a flat angle where the muscles of his left shoulder joined his neck. His head sprang off and the helmet flew loose from it. The two objects spun to the ground in opposite circles, thudding and clanging as they hit. Starkad's axe had continued, shearing the ring mail and separating the Saxon's right arm at the shoulder joint. The torso and the spear which the thegn's left hand still gripped pitched forward, but the impact of the Dane's blow had rotated the victim enough that the point did not even graze Mael's chest. The corpse struck the ground so near to the Irishman that the last spurt of blood from the severed neck covered his right sandal.

The village priest screamed like a pig with a knife through its throat. He ran, caroming off the trunk of one of the birches without slowing, then splashing across the creek. The old Saxon reached the other side without one of his boots. There he sucked in enough air to continue his screaming. He disappeared into the drizzle, again at a run. The rest of the villagers had already melted away, making less noise but with real terror. It was not death that seared their hearts—they had come to view a death. It was not even the loss of their thegn, but rather the way of his killing. Mael's bluff had raised the shadows of superstitious fear which were never far from the minds of barbarian peasants. Starkad had capped the bluff with a blow that appeared inhuman. It would have been spectacular enough to shock even spirits prepared for it.

For years after in that hamlet there would be no sacrifices save to Wotan and Thor, and the slaughter for those gods would keep the region poor.

Starkad levered his axe free of the boggy soil. It

had sunk helve-deep with his follow-through. Trying to halt the blow's inertia, even after its work was done, would have been useless and dangerous, likely to pop a cartilage in the Dane's back. Starkad grinned at Mael and began wiping the metal dry with the hem of the thegn's wool cloak. The air crawled with the stench of blood and the yellowish feces the Saxon had voided at the instant of his death.

Mael walked to the edge of the stream and stuck his right foot into the water. The blood washed quickly from the sandal straps but clung to the wool wrappings. From the ditch behind him wriggled the head and shoulders of the intended sacrifice.

"Get your feet soaked and it's going to be hell marching," Starkad said. "A little blood never hurt anybody."

Mael ignored the comment. He stamped his foot twice on the ground to squeeze out some of the water. "What do we do about the girl?" he asked.

"Uh? Leave her. Or do you need to get laid?"

The Saxon girl looked about seventeen, perhaps younger. It was hard to tell from a face so muddy and hunger-pinched. Her hair was a dirty blonde—the dirt might have been an overlay rather than the natural color—double-braided and coiled on top of her head, the braids caught by a bone pin. The men walked toward her from opposite sides. She shrank back down in the muddy ditch. All she wore was a linen singlet and some sort of armband of woven leather. She had been held by a heavy staff laid across her shoulders and pinned at either side by forked branches. Her struggles had dislodged that, but her knees were still pinioned by deep-driven forks.

Starkad tugged one stake free, then the other. The

girl did not move. Her face was turned upward and her eyes stared at the two men.

"Well, we can't leave her," Mael said. "Her people are just as apt as not to drown her when they come back again. Besides, she's seen us clearly; she knows we aren't gods. There're twenty men out there who'd be on us like flies on a turd if they got a notion of the truth. I don't fancy what they could do to us in this fog, even with sticks and manure forks."

"Well . . ." Starkad muttered. He raised his axe for another blow.

"MacLir take you, you butcher!" Mael shouted, reaching across the trench to grasp Starkad's wrist. "I didn't just save her so we could kill her ourselves!"

"Shall we carry her with us, then?" the Dane queried softly.

Mael grimaced and spat. "Yes, I guess we have to," he said.

Starkad laughed. He reached down into the trench. The girl squirmed to avoid his fingers.

They closed on her wrist anyway and the Dane hauled her upright. "Up we go, girlie," Starkad said. Beside his armored chest, she appeared a mud-stained wraith. She was thin except for her stomach which had been distended by long-term malnutrition. "What's your name, hey?" the Dane asked.

In panic or the belief that Starkad's grip had loosened, the girl tried to bolt. Mael thrust out an arm. Starkad had already jerked his prisoner back, throwing her feet out from under her on the lip of earth. The Dane straightened her up by the wrist until her toes scrabbled on the ground and her arm pointed straight up. She looked as though she were manacled to a high wall.

"Listen, girlie," the Dane said, without raising his

voice or needing to add that emphasis. "We've saved your life, and if you're good it can stay saved. If you aren't—well, you won't get away and you won't be the first Saxon I've killed, will you?" He laughed. "Or the fifty-first. Now, what's your name?"

Mael touched his friend's hand and guided it down so that the girl could stand comfortably. "We aren't going to hurt you," he said, half stooping to bring his face nearer a level with hers. "But we've got to get out of here. We're going to take you with us, as much for your sake as ours."

The girl looked at Mael, then down at the ditch in which she had almost been drowned. "I am Thorhild," she said sullenly. "Why is it you want to murder my people?"

"Look, we've got to get moving," Starkad said. He ignored the girl's question, but he did release her arm. The flesh was already starting to bruise.

"Yes," Mael agreed. He bent over and raised the half-cloak the chieftain had worn. The upper part of it was blood-sprayed, but the wool was dyed nearly black so the stain was not evident. "She can wear this," Mael said. "It's not much, but it's what we've got at hand."

Gingerly the girl wrapped the garment around her. It fell almost to her knees. Obeying Starkad's peremptory gesture, she followed the Dane. Mael brought up the rear of the file until they had again reached the beaten track. There was no sign of the other villagers or of anything at all human in the woods. As they stepped through the runaway privet which must once have been planted as a boundary hedge, Mael cursed. "Forgot to fill the damned water bottles," he explained.

Starkad was using both arms to force the locked

growth apart for his companions. He laughed. "Can't keep a thing in your head anymore, can you? Don't know what must be wrong with you."

They marched stolidly along the trail, Mael leading again. When he judged they had come farther than any of Thorhild's kinsmen were likely to have fled, the Irishman dropped back as nearly alongside the girl as the track allowed. "We didn't murder your folk," he said earnestly. "Only the one fellow there— and him we had to kill to save you."

The girl looked over at Mael with a blank expression. It slowly grew to distaste. "You ended the gift to Lady Nairthus," she said. "Now they'll all starve."

"Manannan MacLir, girl!" Mael exploded. "Did you want to smother in that ditch? You were sure fighting hard enough about it from what I saw." In his anger, Mael brushed against a beech tree. It flung him back onto the trail, cursing and using his palms to dampen the clangor the trunk had raised from his shield boss. Starkad snorted.

Thorhild ignored the Irishman's stumble. Her brow furrowed. "I thought I could give myself. But I didn't want to, not really, when the—time came. But that was me.

"It was—" she paused to count on her fingers— "five years that we sold everything to buy a ship so that Borgar could bring us to this land. We would be rich, he said—Borgar, your man—" she jerked a nervous thumb back at Starkad, afraid to turn her head in the slightest to face him—"killed him. Borgar said a great king of the British had called us over to guard him. He would give us fine land. But the first year and the second there was blight. We harvested little. The third, our harvest was good, but we owed the seed to rich folk in the city. Their interest rate

ate the corn as surely as the blight had before. Last year all was well, until the hail came just before the harvest. And if this Spring is so wet that the seed rots in the ground, we all . . ." Thorhild shrugged. "Lady Nairthus was angry with us. And now she'll kill all of them, all my family, my friends."

Again the girl glared straight at Mael. "What business of yours was it?" she demanded. "Why did you want to murder us?"

Mael shook his head and lengthened his stride instead of trying to answer. Behind him Starkad called, "Some day you'll learn, little brother. Stay away from any woman unless you want to screw her. And *especially* don't try to do one a favor."

They ate, completely enveloped by the branches of a weeping peach beside the ruins of a villa. The rain had finally ceased, but the tree's ground-touching tendrils were protection against eyes as well as rain. Within their cover, the earth was bare and fairly dry. The light that seeped through the foliage was pale green, insofar as there was any light at all. "We're going to need more food," said Starkad in Irish, popping the last of a cooked pork sausage into his mouth. Two of their bread loaves had been wetted through the Dane's pack. They had deliquesced into a gluey mass. Besides, the travelers had three mouths to feed now.

Mael shrugged agreement. The girl was watching them, but with no sign that she understood the Celtic tongue. In the same language Mael answered, "We needed directions, anyway. We've come about as far as we can on the little that Arthur mentioned. What I figured we'd do is find a lone hut towards evening— we've passed a few already. That'll be British. They won't dare refuse us whatever we ask—and they'll be enough afraid of the local Saxons, if they're smart at least, that they won't go running off to report us when we've gone. Anyway, we can leave them enough money that they won't take a chance of losing it. They'll know that sure as sin the Saxons'll strip them bare if they learn there's anything to strip."

"And the girl?"

Mael grimaced. "We'll figure out something. Maybe we'll let her go in the morning. She doesn't know what we're about, and she isn't too near her own people now. She'll be no real danger to us." He looked up at Starkad's smile, then added, "I do some stupid things, don't I?"

The Dane's smile broadened. "Oh, well," he said, "we all do."

By late evening the clouds had cleared and Mael could see the single finger of smoke etching the pale mauve sky. They had met several other travelers on the path by then. No one had spoken, letting a glance and a glower suffice to safeguard privacy. One old woman, alone save for the sow she drove in front of her, signed the Hammer at their backs. Starkad had turned and showed his teeth, thrusting the woman on like a blow.

Now the big Dane pointed at the smoke. "It's a ways off the trail," he said, "and there's only one, so it's not a village. Looks to me like what we're after—and none too soon for my feet."

A hundred yards farther on, another track joined the one they were following. Even the long twilight would be fading soon. There was little choice but to take the path to the dwelling. The building lay a quarter mile back from the main trail, surrounded by trees on one side and a small hand sown garden plot on the other. It was a rude hut, a dome like a

huge beehive. There was a cupola on the top to shield
the smokehole from the rain. The lowest two feet
of the walls were of wattle and daub on a frame of
bent saplings which provided the roof stingers as
well. Down to the wattling, the dome was thatched.
The low doorway was covered by a rush mat that
leaked light through its interstices. As the travelers
approached, the mat was flung open from the inside,
silhouetting a bent figure in the opening against the
dull glow of the fire inside the hut.

To the rear, Starkad swore under his breath. Metal
chimed as the Dane gripped his shield with a beringed
left hand. The stooping figure called to them in
British, "Welcome, travelers. I've waited for you."
The voice was high and feminine, the words so
reminiscent of Veleda's to Mael in the Laigin that
the Irishman froze. But this was an old voice, a
cracked one. As the travelers stepped closer, the
firelight showed them that the woman in the doorway
was as crabbed and sexless as an ancient fruit tree.
Mael's memory stayed with him, though, bursting
out of the scab laid over his longings by the chill
and the days of heels thudding on the ground.

The three of them ducked one at a time into the
hut. Mael went first, darting his head to either side
to be sure there was no one waiting flat against an
inner wall with a bludgeon raised. There was only
the woman. When Mael saw how the shawl of gray
homespun bulked about her body, he realized she
was even smaller than she had first seemed.

The interior of the dwelling was a single room,
dry and warm but thickened by the smoke that
swirled from the draft through the door curtain.
There was little furniture. To the left was a low
bedstead with a rush mattress and a covering of

cowhide. Surprisingly, it seemed clean. Across the hut from the bed were a half dozen large storage jars—the pantry, filled with grain and oil and beer, perhaps. A small ham, whittled far down on the shank, hung from a stringer above the jars. There were no chairs, but a three-legged stool stood near the tripod over the low fire. Suspended from the tripod was a covered bronze pot of something savory. There were no other furnishings or decorations in the hut, save the bundles of dried or drying herbs festooning the whole ceiling.

Starkad grunted as he entered the room. A bundle of dried parsley brushed his hair when he straightened up; his hand batted the herbs away reflexively; then he moved a step out of the way. "What do you mean, expect us?" he demanded bluntly. "Are you another of them?"

The woman smiled. It made her more attractive, though she was still neither young nor a beauty. Without pretending ignorance she said, "A wise woman? In a way. I'm not what the folk about here think I am, Saxon and Briton both . . . but I'm not the fraud they pretend to think when they talk in the daylight. 'Old Gwedda, too foolish to find her nose with both hands. For charity, we give her some bread and a flitch of bacon now and again.' I can't keep their lovers true to them, and I won't make their neighbor's cow go dry . . . but I can do more to cure them than anyone else in a day's ride, and I learn things from here and there. I learned that you—two of you, at least—would be coming, and that the world had need of your safety."

They were speaking in British. Thorhild looked from one face to another without comprehension. The girl was first sullen, then restive as her eyes took in the variety of gathered herbs and the paraphernalia half hidden at the head of the bed. The Saxon girl edged toward the door. Starkad's arm stopped her and walked her quickly back. The Dane's index finger curled beneath her shift, plucking one breast out to view. "Not so soon, little one," he said in German. "The party hasn't even started yet."

"You must be hungry," said Gwedda in a businesslike tone. "Sit down and we'll eat."

The two men stripped off their wet cloaks and formed them over their shields to dry a little in the warmth. Starkad leaned his axe against the corner of bed and wall, then hung his dagger belt over the upraised haft. Mael took off his body armor. This time the Dane continued to wear his mail shirt without commenting on his reasons.

Gwedda began dishing a stew of game and vegetables out of the hanging pot. She paused suddenly, realizing that she had only three plates.

"The girl and I'll share," said Starkad. His hand guided Thorhild to the bed where he sat down beside her. The three travelers set to work hungrily on the stew, round loaves of barley bread to sop the juices, and a handful of leeks. Gwedda ate also, with good appetite though she kept an eye out for her guests.

"Oh," she said. "Would you like some beer to drink? Or I even have a skin of mead. A Saxon gave it to me for setting his son's leg straight after a tree had broken it."

Mael grimaced. "Mead's too sweet to drink and too thick to piss," he said. "I leave the muck to Germans. Their tongues all froze in the cold so they don't taste it. But I'll take beer, indeed, and thank you for it."

"Never knew an Irishman with any sense about liquor or women," Starkad chortled happily. He reached for the tied-off goatskin Gwedda was handing him. "Come along, girlie, this'll put a little fire back in your guts." Thorhild twitched her head away from the Dane's caressing hand. Starkad appeared undisturbed by her attitude—unaware, in fact.

"Do you know whereabouts there's a village of Saxons under a thegn named Biargram?" Mael asked Gwedda. The Irishman leaned back against the wall with a pottery mug of cool ale in his hand. The room felt safe, cozy in a way that went far beyond its warmth and dryness. The smoke and dimness of the fire provided a curtain of sorts, dulling the images of Starkad and Thorhild across the room. It even seemed to mute the sound of the Dane's clumsy endearments.

"The village isn't that near," the old woman was answering with a frown, "though you can walk the distance in a day, I think. Now let me see. . . ." she closed her eyes and continued, "There are three, no, four forks in the road between here and where you want to go. You'll have to go around another village about a mile from here where two brothers rule together. First . . ."

The room and its sounds faded as Mael listened to Gwedda's words. The Irishman found a picture of the intended route forming in his mind. It could have been just careful description coupled with images formed from Mael's own years of travel; it could have been something more. Mael was never certain. But as the witch spoke, Mael seemed to walk the trails step by step. He saw the groves and the pattern of chalk cropping out on a hillside, the stream near a crossroad and even the fallen tree a hundred yards downstream from it where men could cross without wetting their feet.

Starkad lay back on the bed, continuing to swig the thick mead and trying to force some on Thorhild. The Dane was still drunkenly good-natured. Underlying his pleasantries, however, was the assurance that he was a stronger man than any other he knew, strong enough to take almost anything when he decided he had waited long enough for it to be offered freely. Thorhild had been edged against the wall. By turns she had been petulant, then taut and sullen. None of her moods made any useful impression on the big Dane, any more than her clenched hands could keep his fingers from prodding and fondling her at will.

Starkad leaned toward the girl to nuzzle her hair. Her singlet had been pawed free of her bosom. A fold of the Dane's chain mail caught her right nipple and pinched it. Thorhild shrieked and leaped away. Starkad shot his arm out to grab her, but the girl was already stumbling over the pile of his equipment. Metal crashed as Starkad threw himself to his feet. Then the girl's small hands were thrusting the point of his own dagger straight in the Dane's face.

Combat reflexes had kept Starkad alive a hundred times before, as they did now, but he flung himself back without thought of the fact that his right heel was under the bedstead. The dagger swept harmlessly in front of the fluff of his moustaches. The tendons of the Dane's ankle popped audibly, even against the din of the girl's screams.

Thorhild turned and ran for the door. Mael was on his feet now, eyes bright with the disoriented terror of a man roused to battle from dead sleep. Starkad was already striding for his prey, but his right leg folded beneath him. As Thorhild darted into the night, the Dane pitched forward helplessly. His forehead fetched up against the door-post. The ground-shaking thud that impact made stilled his roar of anger.

Mael tried to force his way past his friend's bulk. First, Starkad's prone body blocked him. The Dane rolled to his side. Shaking his head to clear it, Starkad put out a hand to bar the passage deliberately. "No," he said. "Let her go."

"What?"

Starkad's face was streaming blood from the pressure cut in his scalp. He lowered the hand he no longer needed to keep Mael away, trying to smear the runnels of blood from his eyes with the palm. Gwedda was there at once, interposing herself between the men and expertly daubing at the wound with her scarf.

"Let her go," Starkad repeated, "because she earned it." Before Mael could protest, the Dane added, "Look, we were going to let her loose in the morning, anyway, weren't we? We just did it a few hours early, think of it that way. That little hellcat's a real woman after all, by Frigga. I'll be damned if I'll have her carved up for it. After all this is over, I just might come back this way and see if I can't look her up. You know?"

"You damned fool," Mael breathed in wonderment. He shot his half-drawn sword back into its sheath. "And you say you like 'em better filled out than Veleda?"

"Don't stand!" Gwedda ordered sharply as the Dane started to get to his hands and knees.

"I can—" Starkad began, but the old woman cut him off.

"You can ruin your ankle forever, or you can stay off it for a few days now," she snapped. "Here, let me see." The shapeless boot slipped off easily, but

Starkad winced at even that slight friction. The ankle was red and angry already, so swollen that the big bones were hidden in puffy flesh. Gwedda probed the injury with her eyes.

"The shield and spear," Mael said slowly. "If we wait to get them for this to heal . . . Veleda said to hurry."

The witch's face paled even in the orange light. "The Veleda? *She* sent you after—"

"Shut up, woman," the Dane snarled, "or I'll shut you up."

Mael blinked in surprise at his friend, but Gwedda understood the reason for the threat. She said, "I can see there might be need for haste. If a—seeker of ability said to hasten, I would take her word for it, Irishman. I would take her word for anything."

"Look, I'll be ready to leave in the morning," Starkad said.

Mael caught the woman's grimace and demanded harshly, "Ready to go without slowing me down? Ready to hike twenty miles, to climb hills and ford streams without falling on your butt and pulling me down, too?" The Dane made a moue of frustration but said nothing. More gently Mael continued, "I know you're tough, old friend. And I know that even hurt you can do things that most people wouldn't be able to do healthy. But there're limits. You can't fly without wings, and you can't walk without two ankles to support you. Remember, we aren't here for any reasons of our own."

"Help me to the bed," Starkad said dejectedly. The ankle was sending jagged black pains up his whole side. "We'll see how it looks in the morning."

Chapter Eleven

It looked bad in the morning, as they all had known it would. There was no need for further argument, though. Starkad was delirious and mumbling demands to a chieftain Mael knew had been dead for twelve years.

The Irishman looked at Gwedda. "Look, take care of him," he said. "I'll be back as soon as I can be. If that's not in a week and Starkad can walk again, tell him to head back to where we came from and take care of Veleda. Until I get back."

The Briton nodded, catching at her lower lip with her teeth. "I've poulticed his forehead," she said. "The cut there won't get infected. But he's very strong. When he slips and turns that strength on himself, he's no less destructive than at other times. But I can lower the fever and the swelling soon, I'm sure."

With food in his pack again and his cloak spread

187

across his back to dry as the sun rose clear, Mael
strode along the path. The help Gwedda had given
him made his direction as certain as if he had walked
that way daily for a year. Mael was perversely sure,
however, that the wise woman herself almost never
left the narrow bounds of her clearing.

Mael had intended to let Starkad carry the burden
of entry into the closed society of a Saxon village.
The big Dane had a measure of fame, even though
he had never capitalized on it by welding masterless
men about him into a pirate band. Starkad could have
stalked into the village, roaring that he needed
protection during his outlawry and that, from what
he'd heard, Biargram was one of the few men big
enough for him to swear to. The thegn would have
been flattered, the men who had not heard of Starkad
might be doubtful but would keep silent because of
the Dane's size . . . and those who had heard stories
about Starkad would keep very silent indeed. Mael,
as a hanger-on and a foreign one at that, had hoped
to be lost in the impact of his friend's personality.
That would have given the two of them time to locate
the arms and remove them at leisure.

Without Starkad, the job became much harder. If
Mael were accepted at all, it would be with suspicion.
The women would shun him, the children spy on
his every movement, the men find his alien face
annoying and pick fights with the Irishman any time
they were drinking. It was quite possible that the
villagers would simply set on Mael and kill him out
of hand. But Veleda's urgency was still fresh in his
mind, and there seemed no way around it. Mael hadn't
really expected to come home from this one, anyway.

Well into the afternoon, the Irishman saw the first
signs of the village. A hillside, rolling up to the right

of the trail, had been cleared and recently plowed. No one was working in it at the moment, but the chink of tools could be heard in the near distance. There was an occasional soughing that was not the wind. Mael shrugged a little to settle his body in his armor. He went on at the same pace as before. As he expected, the village was over the rise.

There were a dozen buildings on either side of a small stream, laid out as haphazardly as if they had dropped from the sky. The settlement as a whole was not palisaded—it was too far back from the Zone to be threatened by Arthur save in event of a major disaster. Each of the houses, however, had a separate garth surrounded by a fence. The buildings had been dug down a foot or so and the turfs set around the excavations. These formed the foundations for the wall posts. The posts were joined with wattle and daub. The largest of the houses gleamed with plaster over the mud; its walls had been strengthened by cross-timbering. Like the rest, however, it was thatch-roofed and had no chimney. Smoke from the central hearth was expected to find its way out through the triangular openings at the peaks of the sidewalls. In the winter, their own fires were a worse enemy to the Saxons than Arthur more than dreamed of being. Now, in the spring, the heat of a score of bodies was enough to warm the houses without flames.

The first challenge to Mael's presence came from a pack of nondescript dogs. They had lain in pairs and triplets, sharing the shade of the houses with the village's chickens and hogs. When the dogs scented Mael, they leaped up and ran toward him yelping and snarling. The Irishman kept his stride steady. His lips were a little tighter. When the rangy, stiff-legged bitch who led the pack came close enough,

Mael swung his spear butt up from under her jaw
and cut the barking off within her teeth. The rest of
the pack gave back, prancing. Mael continued to
advance, using his spear butt freely on whichever
dog was the nearest or noisiest. He wetted the point
only once, on the shaggy brute who slipped up behind
him and snapped at his heel. The shock of that death
silenced the other dogs for a moment; then they were
yapping as enthusiastically as before.

The dogs had been the first to notice the intruder
because the Saxons were all at work in the fields.
The eyes of the laborers, men and women both, were
unable to reach beyond the plowshares or the wavering
stone fence at the field edge toward which they
dragged their equipment, staggering. The explosion
of barking drew their stares to the approaching
stranger in armor. Dropping their tools, the Saxons
began running down the hillsides toward the village.
Only a few small children stayed where they were,
freed from their own duties by their elders' rush to
arms. The children set down the long switches with
which they had been lashing birds away from the
seeds. Depending on their mood, they began either
to play or to watch the drama below.

Mael was a quarter mile from the village at the
time he was noticed. He made no attempt to hurry.
The Saxon warriors gathered in front of the nearest
house to await him. They were hastily equipped; at
every moment another man raced out of a building
to stand by his fellows. From the shuttered windows
peeped the women. The panic, Mael knew, was not
at what he was but for what he might be. He was
unexpected, inexplicable: a scout for an enemy, a
messenger from King Cerdic—who knew?

By the time Mael reached the band of warriors it

was some sixty strong. Half a dozen at most wore ring mail. Perhaps twice that number had leather jerkins, hardened with scales or at least metal studs. The rest, though the village was clearly much more prosperous than the one in which Thorhild had grown up, wore only boiled leather or no body armor at all. Almost all of the Saxons carried shields, round or kite-shaped and made of wood or oxhide. The fancier ones had iron rims and sometimes designs worked in their faces with metal. None of the shields looked out of the ordinary, the famous object Mael had come to steal.

Nor were the remaining arms exceptional. Most of the warriors carried spears six to eight feet long. A few made do with axes or agricultural implements, hoes or metalshod dibbles intended for planting. The wealthiest Saxons wore double-edged swords the length of a man's arm. More common were heavy fighting knives, scramasaxes, often thrust sheathless under a belt. The knives averaged a foot and a half long, sharpened only on the lightly curved inner edge.

The headgear was generally leather with a mixture of iron and bronze pots; it was here that the leader's equipment was most unlike that of the other Saxons. The apparent chief wore an iron helmet whose face was closed from nose to throat by a veil of fine ring mail. All the metal surfaces were silvered, and the cap itself was parcel gilt as well. Though striking, the helmet was not a modern design and probably had been handed down through several generations.

The thegn was as tall as Mael and broader. His face was unreadable for the veil and the bushy blond brows that twisted above his eyes. The Saxon took a step forward, his spear half poised, and called to the Irishman, "What's your business here?"

Mael halted within a spear length. He kept his own weapon upright. The dogs were backing away. Though Mael was well aware that the wings of the Saxon line were edging forward to encircle him, he ignored them. "I am Mael mac Ronan, of the Cenel Luigdech," he declaimed with deliberate formality. "Exiled from my own people for saving a Saxon trader's life, I have come among his folk to take the service of the thegn I am told is the greatest of them all. I come to join the chieftain Biargram Ironhand."

The intake of breath among the Saxons was swift and general. Many of the warriors signed Thor's Hammer at Mael, twisting their spears sideways in order to hold out their clenched fists palm upward. One man gasped, "A miracle!"

Even the thegn had started at the Irishman's words. Very carefully he asked, "What do you come here to do?"

Mael was uneasy. The Saxons were not reacting hostilely, but the reason for their religious awe was unclear; therefore, it was potentially dangerous. Had some priest foretold an outland savior appearing to aid Biargram at a crucial moment? If Mael's luck had been that good, then surely the gods were behind him in this mad quest! "I have come to join Biargram Grim's son," Mael repeated.

The Saxon chief clashed his spear against his shield boss in an access of joy. "And so you shall!" he thundered. "I'm Biarki, Biargram's son. My father died three days ago, but you'll join him tonight—in his barrow."

Mael's arm was quick, but a dozen Saxons had already launched themselves onto him. They pinioned and bound the Irishman before he could strike a blow.

"How far is it to this damned barrow?" grunted Mael to Biarki. The young thegn walked beside Mael in the midst of the procession of happy Saxons. They were keeping holiday. Some of the women had even bound flowers into their hair. As for Mael, he too was bound—by a pair of nooses held by three men each before and behind him. The cords were long and slack enough for comfort, but if Mael balked or ran, they would choke him at once. Mael was furious—with himself and his luck and his captors. He had cursed them all loudly from the beginning of the march. What could the Saxons do to him if his insults angered them, after all? Condemn him to death?

Little the Irishman said, however, could penetrate Biarki's buoyant mood, anyway. "Oh, well," the Saxon said, "a couple miles yet. We didn't want my father staying too close, you know . . . and not just any place would have done for his barrow. We needed a cave so that the walls would be solid and he couldn't . . . well, you know."

"Look," Mael snapped, "if you're going to kill me, you can at least tell me why. I don't know a *damn* thing."

Biarki laughed. "My father was murdered," he explained, "by magic. He had a spear and a shield you see, heirlooms of our house." Mael shot a side glance at the thegn but made no overt indication of his particular interest in the weapons—or of his surprise at Biarki's inappropriate good humor. "They were the arms made for the hero Achil by Wieland the Smith. That was long ago, at the Troy fight. No one ever had arms like those.

"We came here to take service with King Cerdic," continued Biarki. "He gave us good land and we were happy. Only, Cerdic has a councillor named Ceadwalla, a Briton who commands his housecarls. This Ceadwalla is a very great magician, and after a while he learned about my father's shield and spear. He came to my father and demanded them—a nasty little man with a birthmark like a spider on his right cheek. If Britons lived like men, they would have thrown Ceadwalla onto the kitchen midden the day he was born."

"Well, why didn't you do it yourself?" Mael asked. "You folk seem quick enough to murder strangers or do you do that just to people who come alone and friendly?"

"Ceadwalla was too powerful to kill," Biarki admitted easily. "He never came to us with less than a hundred men, and . . . we knew he was a magician, too, remember. But still my father held him off. Then last year, Biargram's head began to pain him both day and night. He called Ceadwalla to him and gave him the spear but kept the shield. And that was enough for one year, but last week Ceadwalla came back. My father refused him the shield again, and so my father—died."

Mael grimaced in utter bewilderment. The men at the head of the procession were singing a cheerful, bawdy song. Closer by, a group of women were chattering like daws in a cornfield. "If this is how your mourn your chiefs," the Irishman said, "you must dance yourselves to death at a marriage feast."

"Death isn't the worst that can come to a man," Biarki said, his smile wiped away as cleanly as smoke in a windstorm.

They marched along together in silence for a time, as if they were comrades. At that the two men were more similar than different to look at except for their hair color: two big fighting men in armor, young for any profession but the one they followed. "You've started your story," Mael said at last. "Now tell me the rest."

Biarki nodded. "You may as well know," he agreed. His expression became grim. It might better have suited the prisoner being led to death. "We held a wake for my father," he said, "laying his body out on a bier in his house garth. We feasted around him, lighting lamps after sunset. Each one of us told stories about how we'd ambush Ceadwalla and avenge Biargram. And then the moon rose, and so did my father, there in the midst of us."

Biarki swallowed thickly. Nobody looking at him could have doubted his sincerity. The Saxon went on, "He stood and tried to walk, but his legs didn't work and he fell. He was making sounds like a carp sucking air. His eyes had been closed. They opened again but I don't think he could see anything. He lay there on his belly, crawling with one hand and one foot. We all ran. We locked ourselves in our houses and didn't even look out at the garth until the morning. My—father—was still lying there, dead again. He had pulled the trestle out from under one of the tables and eaten most of the food there. He'd shit, too, great sloppy trails of it that stank like a bear's. . . ."

Biarki shuddered in a way that Mael could now appreciate. His own mind glanced back a few days to his horror in the ship, the purple hell-light writhing from Veleda's fingers. Mael trembled also. Magic was for those who understood it. And surely there were few human beings so evil that they understood it.

"We would have raised a true barrow," Biarki said "but there wasn't time and—maybe it wouldn't have

been strong enough. From the inside. So . . . there
was a cistern not far away, near where a villa had
stood. They'd cut it down into the rock, the Romans
had, and it was fifteen feet deep. Deep enough. So
we took m-my—" and this time the Saxon could not
get out the word "father," so he said, "Ironhand there,
with his shield and his horse and his dog. . . . And
we hoped that he could lie still now that he had his
grave goods, but we covered the cistern over and
put guards by it. And the guards heard Ironhand begin
to move when the moon rose again. They heard him
smack and slurp and eat.

"So we knew we would have to give his soul a human
before his body would lie still. Some said a slave would
do, and some said Thora, because she had been his
woman for a year before he died. And a few of them
said perhaps his son was the gift Ironhand sought,"
Biarki added with a fell smile, "but none of them
said so when they thought I might hear them. When
you came, there could be no doubt but that Wotan
had answered our prayers and sent us the sacrifice
he demanded."

Mael laughed. He could accept Biarki's story. He
could accept as well the Saxons' belief that their god
had listened to them and sent an Irish alien to take
the place of one of them—or a valuable slave. It just
seemed a pity that the best proof Mael had yet found
for gods taking interest in the lives of men was about
to end with him being eaten by an animate corpse.

The Saxons' destination was only a few minutes
further. The ruined villa was a jumble of masonry
overgrown with honeysuckle, recently disturbed by
the burial party removing stones to heap over their
chieftain's grave. Already the leaders of the procession
were beginning to scatter the low cairn to open the

cistern again. It lay some fifty feet from the other ruins, far enough that rain from the house gutters could be piped into it without being contaminated by surface runoff from the latrine and the stables to the rear.

"Just clear enough stone to lift one timber," Biarki ordered his men. "That's enough room to let him down." It was a low tumulus anyway, less a marker for posterity than an additional burden in case something from inside began to push up. The cistern had been a rectangular prism, six feet by twelve feet, cut into the rock. The original lid had been replaced for Biarki's purposes by a roof of logs. They were then covered with stone. The result was not airtight— the feed pipes would have allowed a prisoner to breathe, anyway—but it would be quite impossible to open from the inside without tools and a platform. The Saxons had left Mael his body armor, but nothing with an edge or a point or even a lip that could be used to dig. Mael greatly doubted that anything useful had been buried with Biargram, either. Grunting with effort, three of the Saxons tugged at the end log to pivot it away from the hole. "Enough?" one of them asked, wiping sweat from his lips with the back of his hand. The Saxons—the whole village was present, nearly two hundred of them—had grown silent. The six men holding Mael tensed for the first time.

Biarki strode to the edge of the cistern, motioning the guards to bring Mael along, too. "He'll fit," Biarki said, measuring the Irishman's chest against the opening. Then, after obvious hesitation, the thegn knelt to peer into his father's grave. Mael, shading his eyes, bent down also to take a first look at the barrow in which he was expected to die.

The walls were deep and sheer. The bar of sunlight through the opening fell across a low bier on which nothing lay. Instead there was a man in the far end of the chamber, slumped over the dim bulk of a horse. The stench of the pit was sickening, but it was not the effluvium of decay.

"You said you put his shield in with him?" Mael remarked, no longer concerned about what his captors would think of his interest.

Biarki nodded, pointing. The heirloom had presumably been leaned at the head of the bier. Now it lay half under the legs of the corpse, a circuit gleaming dimly in the light reflected from the plastered sides of the cistern. Another object on the floor among the disordered grave goods caught Biarki's eye: the head of a large hound, ripped or cut crudely away from its torso. The thegn gagged and turned back from the grave. Mael stared at him in surprise. Swallowing heavily, the Saxon explained, "Thunderer—his dog . . . we tied his feet, but he was alive when we put him in the barrow."

Mael straightened, looking with contempt at Biarki and the white-faced throng of Saxons waiting beyond. "Oh, you're fine brave men to do that to a dog," he said.

Biarki also stood. "Do you want us to kill you first?" he asked without meeting the Irishman's eyes.

Mael shook his head briefly. His limbs were weak with rage and fear. "No," he said, so that no one would think that he had been unable to speak Then he added, half in bravado, "You think you're going to lay a ghost this way. But keep your doors barred, Saxons—because I won't stay down there forever, and I don't think I'll forget you while there's a one of you alive." He glared like a demon at the men holding him. "Now, slack your god-damn ropes so that I can get down in there with your bogie."

One of the guards suddenly began to vomit on the ground. The others backed away, not actually releasing the ropes until Mael had lowered himself to full arms' length into the cistern. He clung to the stone lip for a moment. Just as the Irishman let go, a boot heel clunked down where his fingers had been. The rope ends writhed down into the pit beside him. Only seconds later, the men above had levered the heavy timber back into place. Mael was in darkness allayed only by chinks of light which dimmed as stones were piled back atop. The thud of rock against rock continued for what seemed an impossible length of time. When it ceased, the blackness within the tomb was unrelieved.

Mael sat on the edge of the bier and considered his situation. It was unpleasant and very probably hopeless, but it did not appear to be immediately desperate. The air stank, as was to be expected in an enclosed room fouled with liquescent feces. There was enough ventilation through the old pipes to keep it life-sustaining and, fortunately, his sense of smell was swiftly numbed. Mael had no way of getting himself out, though. By leaping from the top of the bier he could probably touch the roof, but that would not allow him to dislodge the tons of wood and stone above him. If he was to be released, it must be from outside—Starkad, searching for him in a week or a month, or perhaps Veleda, somehow learning of his plight and somehow aiding him. . . .

The thought of Veleda's witchcraft turned Mael's thoughts where he had not wanted them to go, to Ceadwalla's curse and the body with which the Irishman shared the grave. Sighing, Mael got up and shuffled carefully to the rear of the chamber in order to examine his companion.

Biargram Ironhand was as still and cold as any man dead three days could be. The Saxon had been a big man and seemed even bigger in the dark with only touch to guide Mael's judgment. Biarki's description of the corpse's rise had been so circumstantial, his terror so genuine, that Mael had not really doubted the account. Now, confronted with the flesh, the Irishman found death's reality more convincing than words ever could be. Muttering to himself, Mael felt over the grave goods to see if there was anything among them that could be useful to him.

As he had expected from the first, there were no tools or weapons. There was, however, food and a sealed cask of wine or beer. A few mouthfuls torn from a joint of boiled pork satisfied Mael's hunger. The meat was only a texture since his taste buds had been stunned by the fetor of the room, but it was no less nourishing for that. At first Mael could not decide how to open the cask without a point or blade. Finally he smashed in the top with a chunk of stone that had fallen down when the grave was reopened. The ale within was cool and sharp and satisfying.

After that, Mael waited. He had been a prisoner before, but never so thoroughly one or in such solitary fashion. There was probably no human being within a mile of him. For a while, Mael tried to concentrate on Veleda. No message of comfort or succor came to him, and besides, Kesair's thick black hair seemed to wave in front of his vision of the witch. At least, Mael told himself, he could ignore the false fear of Ironhand. It was certainly after sundown, and Biargram was no less a corpse now than he had been when the grave was opened.

Except that Biarki had been talking about moonrise, not sunset, hadn't he?

And then boots scraped in the corner by the dead man.

Had it not been repeated, the sound could have been Mael's fancy. It was followed by a thick, slobbering noise like that of a beast trying to drink with its nostrils under water. Then Biargram managed to tear the gobbet of horse meat loose with his teeth. The chunk was too big for a human throat, so more than a minute of wheezing and grunting followed before a smacking gurgle ended the process. Mael, who had remained as motionless as a fawn who scents the hunter, heard Ironhand pause and the leather of his harness creak as he turned from the horse. The dead Saxon stood up.

It was neither an easy process nor a swift one. Ironhand's fingers scrabbled on the wall for purchase. Mael could hear the nervous patter of bits of plaster falling away under the dead man's grip. From what Biarki had said, Mael had assumed the corpse was at least too discoordinated to move except by crawling. Now, one heavy step at a time, the thing was walking toward Mael. Very quietly, the Irishman eased himself to the far end of the bier. He could hear the breath whistling in and out of Biargram's mouth. Air did not seem to be sucked deeper into the dead man's lungs, however.

The low platform on which the body had been laid was over two feet wide. Mael had risen quietly on one side of it. Ironhand moved past on the other, a step, another step—he was parallel to Mael—*thick fingers brushed the Irishman's cheek*.

Mael screamed and flung himself back against the wall. The dead man lunged at him, tripped over the

bier, and crashed headlong. Mael ran to his right,
toward the end in which Biargram had lain. Mael's
first stride set his foot on the slimy dog's head and
he, too, skidded to the floor. His hands touched the
shield which he had come to take. The dead Saxon
was trying to regain his footing and was doing so more
easily than he had stood the first time. A detached
part of Mael's brain searched for a correlation. He
remembered that the moon was waxing toward full.
If the moon ruled this creature, than he would not
reach full strength for another day yet.

But that calculation was almost unconscious. Mael,
gripping the shield by the rim, was swinging it
edgewise like a great axe blade toward the wheezing
sound that marked the monster's face. The impact
felt like hitting a statue. The creature toppled, but
his flesh did not give the way a man's should have,
spattering fluids away from the blow. Even as the
corpse fell, his hands closed on the shield. Mael
pulled back to save his sole weapon. There was no
comparison between his strength and that of
Biargram. It was like tugging at a full-grown oak
tree, hoping to uproot it. Mael cursed and backed
away. The corpse came after him, dropping the
shield with a clang.

Those were the first moments. The creature's
coordination seemed to improve slightly as the hours
drew on, but still he stumbled like a two-year-old. A
two-year-old with the strength of Starkad's axe. In
one of their circlings, Ironhand snatched at Mael's
arm and touched the ale cask instead. In an onset
of rage or perhaps emotionless destructiveness, the
creature smashed the sturdy container to splinters.
He brought the cask down again and again on the
stone bier, spraying ale and ruptured oak across the

tomb. Then Ironhand began searching again for Mael. The tenor of his shallow, wheezing breaths never changed.

The monster, however slow and clumsy, was indefatigable. He could not see in the dark any better than Mael could, nor did he seem to hear Mael's breathing over the constant rasp of his own. His very motions appeared as mindless as those of a worm crawling back and forth across the bottom of a jewel box. But if the worm is ceaseless, it will cover every inch of the box a thousand times—and Ironhand was ceaseless.

The deep-dug cistern had felt cool when Mael first dropped into it. Now his exertions had heated the chamber into a steamy oven. The Irishman sucked in painful gulps of air through his open mouth. The ale was gone. Even if Mael had somehow saved it, there would have been no time to slurp a drink.

Mael was beginning to stagger as badly as the thing pursuing him. Once he horribly miscalculated in the narrow darkness and ran squarely into the creature's chest. As the Irishman ducked away, Biargram's hand flailed across his cheekbone and seized his right ear. Mael screamed and tore free. The pain was terrible, a dull ache like a hammer blow overlaid with piercing agony, but pain was a proof of life, and the pain would have stopped very suddenly had Mael hesitated in pulling away.

The Irishman's life depended on the bier. It was just wide enough that the monster could not reach across it to the far wall without overbalancing—yet. Had the corpse's motor control been a little better, had Biargram been able to step up onto the two-foot platform, he would have caught Mael at once. Instead, Biargram had to drive his prey into the arms of fatigue.

In all likelihood, another night would give Ironhand that needed agility, even if Mael survived this night.

At the end, Mael was so exhausted that he would have been blind with tears and sweat even had there been light in the tomb. He tripped and fell across the shield, then skidded to the floor again as he tried to rise. Mael lay there sobbing hopelessly for twenty long seconds before he realized he was no longer being pursued. The Irishman could hear the slow scratching of the corpse's fingers on the stone floor, but the breathing sounds had stopped. After a moment, the scratching ceased also.

The moon had set. Mael was to have peace until it rose again.

Mael stood with the metal shield of Achilles in his hands. Using his toes as antennae, he edged his way toward where the last sounds of the corpse had come. Biargram was there. Prodding from Mael's hobnails brought neither motion nor resilience. Mael had thought initially that the corpse was stiffened by rigor mortis; now he realized that the condition was more nearly akin to petrification. He brought the heavy shield edge down three times on the Saxon's skull, arm's-length cuts that would have sawn through a tree trunk.

Biargram was as unmarked after the third blow as before the first. Each hair was in place, and the teeth were still bared in a snarl.

Crying again, Mael dropped the useless shield and threw himself into the corner away from the dead horse. He was utterly wrecked by fatigue, physically and mentally. It was in abdication of his responsibilities, even for his own life, that he slept.

But there was nothing he could have done that would have been of more use that day, or of less.

Chapter Twelve

   Mael awakened to a sound. He lashed out with feet and hands in blind panic. He knew in instant terror that he had slept for hours, believed that the clinking against rock was the monster, moon-risen again and reaching for him. The sound came again. It was from above, from outside the tomb. Someone was clearing the stones away.

   Mael almost shouted. Instinct strangled the cry in his throat. It might be Starkad, might be Veleda or Gwedda, and any of them would continue with or without Mael's encouragement. Equally, it might be the Saxons returning for reasons of their own. If they thought Mael were dead, they might be relaxed enough to allow him to leap from the bier to the cistern's lip and squirm out. They might cut him apart on the surface, no doubt they would do so—but they would not return him alive to Ironhand's grave.

One of the logs stirred and fell back. The hands above that tried to remove it had proven too few for the job. A voice, harsh though muffled by the timbers, snarled in British, "Quickly, you idiots. We have less than an hour before moonrise, but I swear I'll send you into that pit whether you've got it open before then or not!"

The timbers shifted again, creaking as crowbars were levered under one in the middle. The log was prised upward. Light gleamed briefly through the crack before the same contemptuous voice ordered, "Close the lantern! Or do you want all the Saxons down on us to see what we're doing at their chieftain's barrow?" Metal clicked as the slide of a dark lantern shut again. Grunts and low-voiced curses were the only sounds for some minutes as the men above struggled to manhandle away the roof log.

As Mael listened silently to the grave robbers, his mind turned over the cramped layout of the tomb. There was no perfect hiding place, so he took the best he was offered. As swiftly as he could move without kicking any of the scattered grave goods, Mael stepped to the part-eaten carcass of the horse. He pressed himself against the wall in the angle it formed with the body. It was not truly concealing, but it blurred his outline. Mael did not think the Britons would look farther than Biargram's sprawled corpse at the other end of the chamber, anyway.

The log heaved up into the night, dropping a rain of rock fragments to the floor and bier as it swung away. Mael resisted the instinct to crouch lower. Movement would certainly have betrayed him. The lantern, a candle in a baffled canister with a shutter, thrust down into the opening and fanned light across the chamber. The illumination seemed much brighter to Mael's shrouded eyes than it really was. The quick sweep did not reveal him to the one directing the light. Rather, the lantern focused on the upturned shield, steadied, and winked out. There was muttered conversation above. Ropes slapped wood. A figure, swaying against the vaguely starlit opening, began to descend in a sling

When the Briton had been lowered shoulder-deep in the pit, he slid the lantern open again. The light flashed over the roof timbers. The commanding voice snarled through the opening, "Keep the bloody light down or keep it out!"

"Then keep this bloody rope still!" the man in the sling cried back. He trained his light on Biargram's glaring visage as if it fascinated him—or as if he expected it to move. The hot metal of the lantern stank in a different way from the fetid air of the tomb.

The sling dropped by jerks as the men above handed the rope down. When it touched the surface of the bier the man stepped off it, then down to the floor. The Briton's back was to Mael, his body silhouetted by the circumscribed candlelight. The man bent to pick up the shield. It was heavier than he suspected. He grunted in surprise and his thumb slipped off the slide of the lantern.

Mael swung to his feet at the moment of darkness. Like a dancer to his partner, he stepped to the grave robber just as the other began to stand up. The dim light through the roof was enough for Mael's eyes after their deprivation. He struck with the strength of frustration built up during his long pursuit by the monster.

The Briton's neck broke under the double-handed blow. The shield and the lantern clashed together against the stone. "Conbran!" someone demanded from the surface. "What's wrong?"

Mael tugged the shield out from under Conbran's body. Both the Irishman's hands were numb from the impact. "Just dropped the damn thing," he said hoarsely. He leaped to the top of the bier, holding the shield to mask his face against watchers above. "Pull me up," he ordered.

The rope swung upward more swiftly than it had lowered. The shield rim scraped against the logs. Hands reached to take it from Mael, but the shield was his only chance of survival and his fingers were locked on it. The sling drew Mael waist-high to the lip of the cistern and he stepped up to the ground. There were a dozen men around him, all armed, and a babble of muted questions. Suddenly one man cursed and threw back the velvet curtain shrouding a lighted oil lamp. The light flared across Mael's face.

"Lord Christ!" a Briton shouted. "It's not Conbran! The Saxon—"

The lamp fell to shatter on the rocky soil. Yellow light bloomed from the spreading oil like a beacon. The grave robbers were screaming, running, all but their harsh-voiced leader whose cheek crawled with a birthmark like a spider. Ceadwalla shouted another vain command, then turned to Mael. He carried a silver-chased spear which he raised to thrust.

Mael caught him across the bridge of the nose with the rim of the metal shield. The bones shattered like porcelain under a sledgehammer.

Ceadwalla's spear had a tubular socket and a blade as long as a man's forearm. The metal was iron or steel, but deeply incised and filled with silver. Mael hefted the weapon, then set it beside him as he fumbled with the dead Briton's sword belt.

There was a sound in the darkness, someone approaching. Mael tried to stare beyond the wavering circle which the oil flame illuminated. The belt buckle came loose. Mael rolled Ceadwalla's body aside. He tossed the ends of the freed belt around his own waist and snugged them before he rose. The shield was in his left hand and he balanced the spear on his right. The person coming toward him could be seen now. It was a man by his size, a big man porting an axe high so that its edge was a yellow crescent in the flames.

"Aye, come and be killed!" Mael shouted. He raised the long spear to hurl.

"Mael!" roared the figure. "It is you, you damn fool!" Starkad lowered his axe and bounded fully into the circle of light. He was not favoring his right leg. His arms opened to clasp his friend.

"Idiot!" Mael gasped as they pounded each others' backs. "You could see it was me, couldn't you? God knows I was so close to the fire that my bloody eyebrows were singeing."

Starkad took a step back, still clasping the Irishman's shoulders. "Oh, I could see you, all right," he agreed, "but—well, your mother wouldn't recognize you now at a glance."

Mael frowned. There was a dagger on the belt he had appropriated. The hilt was delicately jeweled and chased in gold. He was not surprised to find the blade had been silvered as well. It made a fair mirror, enough to test Starkad's statement. Mael's right cheek had been plowed with triple furrows. The blood that sheeted from those surface wounds had been runneled in turn by sweat. Far more blood had poured from the veins feeding the torn-off earlobe and the tuft of scalp that had been plucked

out at the same time. That gore had splashed on
Mael's shoulder and down the side of his armor.

"Oh, yes. . . ." the Irishman said. He touched the
throbbing remnants of his ear, grimaced, and
resheathed the dagger. "There're two things I still
regret about this business," he stated deliberately, "and
the first is that I killed this offal, this Ceadwalla—"
he toed the dead Briton contemptuously—"instead
of stunning him. I'd like very much to be able to drop
him down into that barrow alive."

"Sure," Starkad agreed, "but with all the commotion
we've set off up here, don't you think it's time we
moved on?"

"Right, before moonrise for sure," Mael said. He
picked up the weapons he had dropped. Pursued
by memories, he led the way north down a track
through the pine woods which had once been a
metaled road serving the villa. "The other thing I
regret is that we've got to get this gear back," the
Irishman continued, shaking the spear and shield
to identify them. "If we didn't have to do that, I
think I'd take a chance and give those Saxon swine
a better reason to remember me than some silly
threat I shouted as they dropped me into their
hole."

"Umm, you don't need to worry about that," the
Dane said.

"Sure," Mael agreed, "I know. There's no worse
waste of time and effort than worrying about revenge.
And hell, they didn't do anything that my own people
might not have done. If they'd run into the same
sort of—problem, that is."

Starkad began to laugh quietly. Mael glanced back
at him, but there was not enough light to catch the
Dane's expression. "You're sounding like a woman,"

Starkad said through his chuckles. "I'm ashamed of you, Irishman."

"Well, what the hell do you want me to say, learned one?" Mael blazed back.

"I just meant I burned the village last night," Starkad said. "They were all drunk and sleeping. I found the place late and lay around outside till near dawn when somebody came out to piss. He told me what they'd been celebrating, and I . . . well, I got a little pissed myself. If I'd been smarter, I'd have kept one of them as a guide and saved myself a day of stumbling around these hills till I saw the lights up here. But I just wedged the doors of all the houses shut and set torches in their thatch."

"My god," Mael murmured. He had spoken truthfully about how like his own people those of Biarki's village were. Now it was his own family which his mind saw screaming in the flames, children in the arms of women with their hair afire—

But what would he have done himself to folk who had sacrificed Starkad, though they were his own kin? "Hey," he said at last, punching the Dane's armored chest, "you shouldn't take chances like that, you hear me?"

Starkad guffawed. "Oh, well," he said, "maybe some day you'll do something for me, do you think?"

They walked on, chuckling without speaking further. When they crossed a north-leading trail, they followed it abreast with linked arms until, deciding they had come far enough from the tomb site for reasonable safety, they bedded down in a beech copse.

There was leisure in the morning to sort matters out before moving on again. Mael's pack, along with his own shield and weapons, lay somewhere in the ash of Biarki's village. Fortunately, Gwedda had restocked the Dane's store before sending him off.

"How in the Dagda's name did you get here?" Mael asked between mouthfuls of cheese. "You were supposed to be off your foot for a week, and here you are."

"The evening after you left," Starkad explained, "Gwedda dropped the bowl of soup she was handing me. Her face went white as the grime would let it, and she said that I had to get to you as soon as I could. Seems she'd gotten a message. She also got some help—somehow—that let her fix my ankle when she couldn't have done it herself. She put her fingers on the swollen part and didn't say anything, and she wasn't looking at anything either, not that I could see. And the pain left right away, and the swelling started to go down." The Dane frowned in apology for his weakness. "It wasn't that it hurt, you know," he said. "It was just that I couldn't walk without falling on my ass again."

Mael was still thinking about an earlier comment. "Help," he repeated.

"Yeah. I didn't ask who, but I wouldn't be surprised if she had white hair and was waiting for you when we get back to the barracks," Starkad said.

The trophies they had come for, the shield and spear of Biargram, presented a problem when the friends examined them by daylight. The intaglios of the spear head appeared to be of silver, but they showed no tendency to tarnish. The symbols etched and filled there were surely meaningful, but they were part of no script with which Mael was familiar.

But whatever the characters meant, they were certain to arouse attention as the two men trekked back to the British lines. Starkad suddenly guffawed, thrusting the spear head down into a puddle and smearing the mud carefully over the metal. The result looked slovenly, but it would be ignored by everyone they passed.

The shield was more difficult to deal with. It was about the size of the one Mael normally carried, a four-foot circle. At some sixty pounds, the trophy was much heavier than most shields. The man for whom it had been made must have been impressive if he could carry it through the course of a long battle. The man who had forged it had been impressive, too—if a man *had* forged the shield. Biarki's claim for Wieland seemed less foolish now that Mael had seen the object. The facing was without doubt the most exceptional work of art the Irishman had ever laid eyes on. It was of metal, laid out in concentric circles, each with its individual subject chased in reliefs of the utmost delicacy. Where humans were carved, they were so real that they seemed to speak and sing. Mael stared at the center where the boss was formed by the Earth encircled by the sun and planets. He had an eerie feeling that were his eyes good enough, he could even have seen men moving on the surface of the tiny world.

"Tyr's arm," Starkad muttered. "That damned thing'll shine a mile away. Mud'll just flake off a big surface like that when it dries, too." Without real hope, the Dane splashed muck across the shield anyway—and the two men watched in surprise as the dirt streamed away instantly, as if it were being hosed off under pressure. Not a fleck remained on the glistening metal.

"What would you say this was made of?" Mael asked suddenly, tapping the shield.

"The backing's hide, looks like oxhide," Starkad said.

"The rest, well, from the weight it's got to be metal all through. Iron, I'd guess, for the core. And the facing's silver, gold, looks like copper and tin and—and Surtr knows what all else."

"Not much doubt about the gold, is there?" Mael agreed. "Nice soft gold." He touched one of the golden figures with his dagger point, then forced his full strength against it. The steel skidded away. The gold remained unmarked. Starkad shrugged.

"I'll sling it on my back and wear my cloak over it," the Irishman decided "Makes me look like a fool, binding my shield up where I can't get to it if there's trouble. But hell, I feel like a fool a lot of the time, anyway. Let's get moving."

To avoid trouble, Mael and Starkad went thirty miles due north before heading west, instead of going back directly the way they had come. There was no telling what they had stirred up behind them. Although the return was no less dangerous than going among the Saxons had been to begin with, they both felt lighthearted. The sun was bright, and they had already been successful. Intellectually they knew that neither fact improved their chances of a safe return, but subconsciously there was an attitude of arrogant triumph that carried the friends well through one Saxon patrol.

They met Cerdic's men around a bend obstructed by hedgerows. There was no chance to hide. Mael simply snarled to the leader of the Saxons that they were a Dane and an Irishman landed at Portsmouth and headed north to join Aelle. Behind him Starkad thumbed his axe edge and muttered audibly that he'd as soon play hack-skull with mop-brained Saxons as he would with the British. There were a dozen of the Saxons, housecarls of Cerdic, but they looked

uneasily from one to another and back at the grim
men they had stopped. Mael had washed off the blood
and filth of the tomb. His cheek was still freshly
scabbed, and pus oozed from the swollen remainder
of his right ear. Starkad had never needed injuries
to look like a troll.

After some hand-muffled communication among
themselves, the patrol let Mael and Starkad continue.
It was the only significant encounter the friends had
until they came upon a group of Companion cavalry
near Cirencester, commanded by the same officer
who had seen them off a week and a half before. By
that chance, entry into Arthur's Britain was a matter
of hand-slapping congratulation instead of arrest for
investigation. The ride back to Moridunum was brutal,
but it was toward what was for the moment home
to Mael and the Dane.

❧   ❧   ❧

For most of the ride, Mael and Starkad straggled
behind the courier whom they accompanied from
Gloucester. Then Mael heeled his horse into a trot
when he saw the guard post, the westernmost of the
scattered structures of the villa. Starkad followed with
less enthusiasm.

The pickets, bored with inaction, rose and began
to peer toward the approaching riders. Then another
figure stood beside the Companions, shorter than
they by far. Her hair was a white fire in the breeze.
Mael whooped and kicked his tired beast into a full
gallop. Instead of reining up, he leaped from the
saddle and plunged into the group of guardsmen. It
was a technique which the Ard Ri's men were trained
to use against hostile infantry when their horses could
not be trusted to charge home. Surprised, the
Companions did not react quickly enough to cut the

newcomer apart. Mael came to a halt with his right leg braced against the wall of the guard post, Veleda in his arms, and a huge smile on his face. Witch and warrior kissed, oblivious of the half-drawn weapons of the startled men around them.

Veleda nuzzled the Irishman's ear, but instead of love the words she was whispering were, "Don't let anyone see what you brought back. You wouldn't be allowed to keep it."

Mael released her with a comfortable grin. The shield was still under his cloak, the spear head harmlessly mudstained. Mael had been a mercenary too long to flaunt extreme valuables. Circumstances change quickly. A wanderer with a golden sword hilt— or a silver shield—might find his skill of less interest to a lord than the goods he carried. With one hand, Mael unpinned his cloak and loosed the buckle of the shield strap beneath it. He offered both to Veleda as a package and its wrapping, saying, "You tie this to the saddle and mount my horse. I'll walk alongside."

"To the Leader," directed the captain of the guard. "Nobody comes in from the East without being taken to the Leader."

Escorted by two Companions who were by no means a guard of honor, Veleda, Mael, and the Dane went the half mile to the villa instead of forking off toward the barracks. Starkad, too, had dismounted, saying that he was not going to be on horseback if anybody had that choice. The transfer of the shield had gone unremarked. The camouflaged spear nodded innocently in the lance socket where it had ridden since Mael was issued a horse at Cirencester.

Arthur and Lancelot, Merlin, and several officers whom Mael knew only by appearance were drinking in the shade of the west portico of the building. Three tables had been set up in a squared-off U around which the captains reclined Roman-fashion. A score of servants and guards stood or squatted nearby. Mael unbelted his sword and handed it without comment to the guard who blocked his approach. Starkad scowled but followed suit with his axe. The discussion around the tables paused as the two men stepped into the hollow of the U, facing Arthur who lay alone at the center table.

The king set his cup down. He wiped his mouth and moustache with the back of his hand. "You returned, did you, Irishman?" he said in a voice half playful, half not. "That's a little surprising, isn't it?"

"That's bloody impossible if they'd tried to do what they said," snarled Lancelot from his position at the head of the right-hand table. "You're being played for a fool." The Gaul slurped down the rest of the drink in his cup and signaled peremptorily to a cupbearer for a refill.

"We were too late," Mael explained, speaking to Arthur and not his Master of Soldiers. Lancelot was wearing only an embroidered tunic and was unarmed, as were the other men at the table. There were, however, enough armed guards at hand to dice Starkad and Mael if the order were given. "Biargram had already died, so we just came back."

"Every word a lie," said Lancelot. The squat Briton beside him laid a restraining hand on the Gaul's ankle, but Lancelot kicked it away. "They went to carry word to Cerdic so he can plan to hit you—now. They came back because their oh-so-British traitor sent them to spy some more."

Arthur laughed. "Shall I have them both killed, then?" he asked.

Starkad growled. Mael clamped him by the elbow,

taut as a lutestring himself. He was looking for the
weapon handiest to seize if Arthur carried through
with his whimsy. Merlin grinned, the only man relaxed
in the sudden tension.

"Show him the spear, Mael, " Veleda called. "The
one you stole from Ironhand's barrow!"

Mael turned. Lancelot was rising. Veleda stood
beyond the pillars at the edge of the throng of guards.
She was holding the spear toward the Irishman, butt-
forward.

"No!" a Companion snarled, snatching the weapon
away. Mael had made no attempt to take it. Arthur
gestured. The guard, his eyes flashing sidelong toward
Mael and Starkad, scuttled around the table and
handed the spear to his Leader.

Arthur took it without speaking. He frowned at the
mud-smeared head, then dipped a napkin in his cup
and used it to rub the metal.

"We broke open the grave to make sure he was
dead," Mael lied. "That's proof we were doing what
we said—and didn't have time for anything more."

Merlin's face had lost its look of repose as he saw
the spear being carried forward. He stood, leaning
over Arthur's shoulder to get a closer look at the inlays
as they were cleared. "Leader," the wizard breathed,
reaching out with his index finger to trace the
markings, "I must have this. . . ."

Arthur twitched the metal away in irritation. "Don't
be silly," he said. "There's nothing here for you." Mael,
ready to protest if the spear were given to Merlin,
eased. "It's a royal weapon," the king continued. "I'll
keep it." Arthur looked up at Mael and Starkad,
holding the spear by the balance. "You two can go
back to your barracks now," the king said. "Be ready
to march in the morning. We're going to teach my

Saxon brother Aelle the lesson that Lindum is to remain a British city."

Mael licked his lips but did not try to claim the spear. He had seen the glitter in the king's eyes. Lancelot either missed that warning or was too drunk to care. The Gaul stood up, his anger so sharp that blood was spotting his face where tension had popped open the old scabs. He cried, "They're making a fool of you, I say, and everybody else knows it! You must *nail* them up, the both of them, or—"

"Must, Roman?" Arthur whispered, and there was suddenly no other sound in all the crowd. The king hurled the spear expertly, the motion smooth and backed by an arm as strong as that of any of his men. Lancelot moved at the same instant, tilting the heavy table up as he ducked his body into its shadow. The silvered spearhead smashed its full length through the parquetry, slamming the table back down onto all four legs The shaft stood quivering, an exclamation point between the king and his slowly straightening Master of Soldiers. No one else moved.

Arthur giggled. Turning to Mael and Starkad, he said, "I told you to leave, didn't I? We march in the morning." Then he looked back at Lancelot. "I think you'd better leave, too, Lancelot, and I'm for bed as well. We have a hard fight coming, and right now I seem to be too drunk to throw a spear straight."

Mael tugged circumspectly at the Dane's elbow. The two of them retrieved their weapons and stepped away with the quickly dispersing band of courtiers. Mael caught a final glimpse of Lancelot's face as the Gaul, too, strode toward his quarters. Lancelot's expression was as dead as a bowl of rendered fat.

Chapter Thirteen

"If we aren't going to do anything but stand here," Starkad complained, "I'm going to get some sleep." He threw his pack down for a pillow on a likely patch of turf and stretched out.

Before dawn the recruits had been roused and marched to a store shed. There they waited behind four troops of Companions also being issued rations for the campaign. After that they were marched back to the corral for horses. Now they waited again on one of the drill fields, trying to quiet their unfamiliar mounts. In the near distance were the lights and murmuring of one of the line troops, also awaiting the order to march. Down the road from the headquarters building clattered a messenger, one of the staff officers who had dined with Arthur the day before. Maglos, the aging Briton in charge of the recruit troop, waved the courier over with a torch.

221

"We're ready to mount," Maglos said.

"No, you're not," replied the courier without dismounting. He was the squat man who had tried to restrain Lancelot. "You've been moved back from third to ninth start, after Theudevald's troop over there. Run your men through another kit inspection and make sure none of them are trying to carry their gold around in their blanket roll."

"Second to the end?" Maglos shrieked. "Christ's bleeding wounds, you know how most of these sows ride! If you start me ninth, it'll be the bloody watch after midnight before I make camp!"

"Well, better you and not everybody behind you as well," the staff captain said unsympathetically. "Check 'em out good. If any of these oafs panics because the Saxons are in the baggage and they're afraid they'll lose their loot—well, it'd be better for them if they'd banked it here with the camp prefect, and it'd be better for you if you'd never been born."

Nodding, the courier rode off toward Theudevald's troop across the field. Maglos cursed and turned back to his own unit. The three other Companions of the cadre were murmuring among themselves. "Everybody on your goddamned feet for kit inspection," Maglos roared. Mael, already standing, pulled Veleda a little closer. His eyes were on the captain. Starkad, of course, ignored the shouting.

"Christ, what sorry whoresons," Maglos said. His frustration was real as he looked down the line of parti-equipped men, many of whom were not able to ride or speak a common language. "I'm going to tell you people something, and I don't want anybody to think it's a joke," the Briton continued. "You aren't being marched to Lindum to fight. You're going because there won't be enough trained men back

here to control you if somebody gets some smart-
ass ideas about desertion or looting. You're a burden
on the war, and we don't need any more burdens.
So if any one of you—or all of you together—steps
out of line for one instant you're dead. You're nailed
up to a tree in less time than it takes to shit. Do as
you're told, do *just* as you're told, and maybe some
of you can live long enough to be worth keeping."

Maglos and his men began working down the line
of recruits one by one. His voice blurred by his cloak,
Starkad said, "Why put so much of his army back
here where it's five days' march to any place the Saxons
are going to be? And five more damned days on
horseback for me."

"A safe place to train recruits," Mael guessed idly,
his attention still on Maglos.

"No," said Veleda unexpectedly. "One troop would
be enough for a cadre and a guard, love. Arthur
doesn't keep ten back here for training or for the
Saxons. They're to keep the landowners in support."

"Huh?" Mael said. "They do support him. They
always have."

"Together they *have* to support him," the woman
agreed, "or the only question is whether the Saxons
or your Irish kin will pick their bones first. But one
by one, it's different. They're self-willed men, these
magnates. They're powerful, each in his own right.
Who's to say that one's grain levy wasn't excessive,
or the weight of bronze for armor wasn't more than
another's smelters produced?"

"So if there's any trouble, Arthur sends in the troops
and burns their roofs over their heads," Starkad
chuckled, his eyes still closed. "Then the rest of them
ante up."

"He doesn't have to burn anything," Veleda protested.

"If a delivery's late or the weight is short, Gawain or one of the other captains takes a troop or two to the landowner's villa. He just stays for a while. After feeding a hundred men and horses for a month, the landowner makes his next tax payment on time even if his children may have to go hungry. Arthur's taught him that they most certainly *will* go hungry if he scrimps the levy again. And there's no fighting or need for it. No one magnate is so foolish as to think he can drive off a troop of Companions, and no group of magnates is so foolish as to think they'd live for long if they did all rise and defeat Arthur."

Maglos had reached them. Mael, knowing that Biargram's shield, the only thing of note he had, was hidden back in the barracks, was relaxed. Pointing at Veleda, the Briton snapped, "What's she doing here?"

"Waiting for the fools in charge of this botch to get moving," Starkad rumbled before Mael could get control of his tongue. "Then she'll tell us goodbye. And until you do get moving, just leave us alone. Neither I nor my friend ever left a fight for fear of losing our bedrolls."

The captain froze. He might in his frustration have carried the matter on, had not one of his cadre tugged at his arm. "Theudevald's troop's moving out," he reported, pointing.

Maglos sighed. "Prepare to mount and form column of fours," he ordered. "We won't get the word for another half hour—but it'll take that long for some of you hogs to get straight."

When the horn finally blew, Mael leaned over his saddle and kissed Veleda again. The Greek in the rank behind cursed as his horse balked to avoid the Irishman's. Starkad turned and stared back. The curses stopped as the Greek's throat froze.

"I'll think of you," Veleda said. "Of you both." Then she was gone and Mael and Starkad were headed into the first of five days of brutal route marching.

The ten troops of the Western Squadron were being sent off at half-hour intervals, interspersed with lightly escorted strings of remounts. There was no baggage train. Without fanfare, wagon loads of supplies had been sent forward weeks earlier to supplement the sparse forage available at the edge of the War Zone. The rations of biscuit, cheese, and dried meat which each man carried were for use after the battle, when the pace of flight or pursuit might not allow normal measures.

The squadron followed Roman roads for the most part. Cracked by subsidence, rutted by centuries of wheels gouging their surface, the roads were still straight and broad and as useful to Arthur's army as they had been to Hadrian's. The troops crowded civilians to the side and off onto muddy shoulders to curse at the miles-long road-block. Where the civilians were driving animals to market, the cursing became mutual. The column, regular enough at the start, began to bunch and straggle. One of the horses in Mael's troop found itself in the midst of a flock of sheep. It suddenly went into a whinnying funk. When the horse bucked him off, the rider broke his neck by landing on a milepost instead of the mud.

"First blood to Aelle," Starkad laughed. But the next time his own mount shied, the Dane sawed his reins as if he meant to pull the horse up on its hind legs.

Near noon the forlorn hope reached the prearranged bivouac site at Pen-y-Gar. In theory the rear guard should have joined them in three hours or so. Actually it was long after sundown that the hard-faced Companions chivvied in the last of the recruits. Streams to ford had caused confusion and delay. Hamlets along the route were built out onto the ancient roadway, narrowing it to the width of one horse and leaving the flagstones slimy with offal. All the recruits were fighting men, but a good number were not riders. Even the ones who were used to horses were unready for a regimen of fifty miles a day. Saddles became weapons which pounded and chafed. Toward the end, two of the recruits had to be tied to their pommels. When the cords were cut, the men fell as if heart-stabbed.

That first night the recruits were too late for a hot meal and too tired to care. If they had been less exhausted, they would have mutinied. As it was, even the failure to place guards as ordered was the response of inability rather than disaffection.

The next three days repeated the first. Mael had less trouble than most of the other recruits. He had ridden since childhood and was in as good condition as any man in the army. Starkad rode by dogged stubbornness. Others were able to make the journey; therefore he would. The Dane spoke very little after the first hours, dismounting mechanically at Mael's direction and swallowing food as if unaware of its taste or texture. Starkad was not a natural horseman, but his strength and sense of balance were enough to keep him mounted. Graceless, hulking, and silent, the Dane looked like a bear on horseback. Even in their most savage ill-tempers, none of the other men mocked the spectacle he made, however.

⊕　　　⊕　　　⊕

At twilight of the fourth day, the squadron entered the walled city of Leicester. The population was already swollen to triple its usual size by refugees, the troops of the Southern Squadron who had been pulled north for this thrust like those of the West, and the jackals who always batten on soldiers nearing combat. There were whores and their pimps, gamblers, ale merchants and silk sellers. Men need release as death approaches. Each has his own way of seeking that release, and the cost no longer matters.

There were no Saxons save prisoners within fifty miles of Leicester. That did not keep the farm families from pouring in to the protection of the walls. The civilians knew only generalities: Aelle was moving north—or was it west? Arthur was gathering his whole force to block the Saxons. To the households on lonely farms, there was little to choose between the two sides on the march. Either might loot and rape, would perhaps kill and burn. . . . Better to hide in a city where only one side was to be met, where the officer's eyes were sharper. At any rate, there were more potential victims and the resulting better chance of being overlooked. Leicester stank of excrement and animals sickened by hard driving and lack of fodder. The streets were choked with people, moving and eating and trying to sleep. The house-holders kept their doors locked and prayed for deliverance.

Like the stench, rumor was everywhere. The recruit troop dismounted in what had been the market square, now converted to their bivouac—the Southern Squadron had usurped all the permanent quarters available. Mael heard one well-dressed townsman saying to another, "Yes, they massacred every man of the Northern Squadron. Only half a dozen managed to get out with their skins. Geraint himself was captured. It won't take Aelle a day to storm Lindum, now—and how long do you think we can last in Ratae with Lindum gone?"

The speakers passed on, ignoring the hundreds of armed men around them. Mael grimaced and said to Starkad, "Just tents for us. Anything I can get you?"

"A drink and a cunt," the Dane replied with unexpected animation. The city—always a place of excitement to a countryman like Starkad—seemed to have revived his spirits. The Dane nodded at the warren of streets leading off the square. "Bet we can find both of them out there pretty quick."

Mael frowned. "How about the horses?" he asked.

"I can't drink 'em," Starkad grinned, "and I'm damned well not going to try to fuck 'em either if there's better stuff around. If somebody wants to steal mine, he's welcome to it."

Mael looked around the milling throng. Nearby was a Lombard recruit he knew slightly. "Vaces," the Irishman said, putting his hand on the Lombard's shoulder, "get my horse and my friend's here fed and stabled, will you? I'll make it worth your time."

"Hey, why me?" the other man yelped, but Mael could already see Starkad disappearing into an alley. The Irishman followed him with only a hand waved back at Vaces.

Leicester had inns, but they were stuffed with officers. There would always be entrepreneurs ready to care for the lower ranks, though. One of those benefactors had set up in what had been a fuller's shop before the influx of soldiers. The owner and his family now kept to their living quarters upstairs— the trap door in the ceiling was bolted. The ground floor was rented to a Moroccan at an exorbitant rate. The Moroccan, of course, was getting his profit quickly from watered beer and a percentage of the dice game in the corner, despite the expense of the three bouncers who kept a semblance of order.

Noise bloomed even out into the street, and within the big room it was at first hard to think. There was no furniture except the rough-sawn bar. Behind that barrier, the Moroccan and a vacant-faced girl dipped beer from open tuns. The bare walls echoed the din of a score of languages. Virtually all of the customers were armed; it was not a dive in which a civilian could have survived had one been foolish enough to enter. "I'll get it," Starkad rumbled to Mael as he eyed the press around the bar.

A blond veteran with bandages on his left foot stood near them. When his ear caught Starkad's accent, he brightened and said, "Hey! Danish?"

"Yeah, a long time ago," Starkad agreed watching the Companion sharply.

"Hel take it, we're next to brothers here in this snakepit," the blond man said. He thumbed coins out of his purse. "I'm Tostig Radbard's son, got a squad in the Northern Squadron. Geraint sent me back here when I got gimped up at Lindum." Tostig gestured at his injured foot. "Thing is, I can't even fight my way up to the bar with this. I'll buy if you'll bring me one back. No, two—stuff's so pissing thin it's not worth it to drink one at a time."

Starkad clapped the other Dane on the back. "Sure, I'll bring you beer and you don't need to worry about paying," the big man said, his momentary suspicion forgotten. He began to bull his way to the bar, ignoring the curses of the men he thrust aside.

"What *did* happen at Lindum?" Mael asked Tostig. The Irishman and the Dane were about of a size. The blond man had obviously seen his share of service.

"Same thing always happens when the Saxons come

play with us," Tostig chuckled. "We killed 'em by the shit-load and sent the rest off screaming for their mommies." The Companion was speaking loudly, but Mael had to strain to hear in the surrounding racket. "Two weeks ago, Aelle marched north with his whole levy. Must'a been ten thousand of 'em. We're based at Lindum, right? But we pulled back to Margidunum and the fort there. There's only five hundred of us and that makes the odds a little long, even for Geraint.

"So the Saxons throw up earthworks to blockade Lindum. And the people in Lindum don't do anything, and we don't do anything—and the Saxons get pretty damned hungry. There wasn't a goddamn thing to eat bigger than a field mouse left outside the city. You know the Saxons; they couldn't organize a supply train from the rear any better than they could've flown to Mikligard. So after a week, Aelle went back home with all but a couple thousand farmers. Them he left at Lindum to keep the place bottled up. He'd be ready to move the main body as soon as something happened on our side."

Tostig chuckled again. "Only what happened is, we caught the blockading force at dawn with their pants down. They hadn't even set up outposts, much less built a proper stockade against whoever might come up from the rear. We slaughtered Saxons from Lindum to the River Dubglas. I don't know half a dozen besides myself of our boys who aren't ready to ride again today. And I could if I had to."

Starkad, three mugs of beer in each hand, pushed his way back in time to catch the last of what Tostig was saying. "If you hadn't been in such a hurry to do it yourselves," he remarked as he handed the drinks around, "the bloody Saxons wouldn't have had time to get their shit straight again, like I hear they have now. The army together could've cleared Lindum and then gone through Aelle's whole kingdom before he got his breeches laced."

Starkad's tone was friendly, but the criticism made the Companion bridle. "Bloody general, have we here? Knows more'n Geraint or the Leader himself. Well, let me tell you what it's like, buddy. We can beat a Saxon army any goddamn time we like—you'll see that in a day or two or I'm no fucking squad leader. But there's a *lot* of them. Not just the soldiers, but back home. And we've got three squadrons, maybe fifteen hundred men counting every bugger and ass-wipe.

"We can beat 'em—" Tostig paused to slurp a long draft from one mug. The vessels were terra-cotta, unglazed and already dark with the brew oozing through the porous material—"because we're mounted, we're armed, and we're *trained*. And all the training in the world doesn't matter a fuck if you're trotting down a lane and some hick behind a hedgerow puts a pike through your back. Or you're riding some bitch in a stable and her husband cobs you with a wooden hay fork. *That's* why the Leader knows what he's doing."

Mael waited for Starkad's reaction. To his relief, the big Dane only laughed and downed his own beer. "Well, you've had your fun already," Starkad said to Tostig. "You ought to be willing for the rest of us to have some, too."

Relaxed, the three men finished the round. Starkad fetched another. As they drank he asked Tostig, "You want to come with us and find a whore?"

The Companion shook his head. "Hard enough to get a drink," he explained. "Damn if I'm going to try to get into a knock-shop. Not with a bum foot and a thousand extra troopers in town."

Bawling happy good-bye's, Starkad led Mael out into the street again. The night air was cool and the relative silence itself palpable. "You know, I'd just about settle for a bed to sleep in," the Irishman suggested.

"Balls," said his friend. "Now, if you were a whore, where would you be?"

They followed several narrow streets blindly, meeting other soldiers as drunken and confused as they were. All the doors were barred, the windows uncompromisingly shuttered. "Look," Mael protested, "this is a pretty good district and we sure as hell aren't supposed to be in it. If we run into the Watch—"

"Then we'll ask them where to find cunt," finished Starkad good-humoredly. "Anyway—"

There was a scream from the house beside them, a two-story structure of brick and tile. The front door flew open and a woman darted two paces into the street. The man chasing her seized her hair in his left hand and tugged her to a stop. He raised his bloodstained sword. Mael recognized his face in the moonlight; it was the Herulian recruit he had watched Lancelot pulp a few weeks before. Without thinking, Mael grabbed the raised sword arm and yanked the Herulian back into a knee in the kidneys. The weapon clanked to the cobblestones. Mael heard a grunt behind him. He turned. A second Herulian, this one wearing the medallion of a trained Companion, had started out of the house to his friend's assistance. Starkad hit him in the pit of the stomach with his axe helve. The struggle was over seconds from its start.

Starkad was holding the sobbing girl with his left hand. She was British, perhaps sixteen years old now that Mael had a chance to look at her closely. "Now, let's see," the Dane murmured, pushing past the Herulian he had disabled. An oil lamp was alight within. It shone on a room that seemed to have been painted scarlet. A middle-aged woman and a boy of about eight lay on the floor. They had been hacked at repeatedly. One of the child's hands had been flung separately onto the cold hearth. A balding, corpulent man in a night shift had fallen on the stairs and skidded face-downward almost to the bottom. Blood was oozing onto his body from above, down the treads from the upper floor.

Mael had followed Starkad through the doorway. There was a loud clatter and shouting behind them. Six Companions with drawn swords and the white armbands of the Watch burst in. The British girl looked up wildly. "Not these!" she cried, throwing her hands over the Dane who still supported her. "The others!"

"Check the upstairs," the squad leader snapped to one of his men. "And what were you doing here, buddy?" he asked Starkad.

Mael spoke before his friend could. "Got lost looking for the bivouac," he said. "We heard screams, and when those two—" the Herulians' hands were being bound expertly in front of them—"chased the girl out, we grabbed them."

The Watch leader grunted. "At least you didn't do all this," he agreed. "Not without getting more blood on you than you seem to have."

From above, his subordinate called in British, "Two more kids up here, sarge. The shutters're open on one of the back windows. Dunno if those fucking Germans were just drunk or if they planned to get in a little early looting."

"Christ," said the noncom. "You two," he added to

Mael and Starkad, "get the fuck back to where you belong. We'll get these slime off to where they belong."

The Watch filed out. Each of the prisoners was walking, secured by a baton thrust between his back and elbows and held on either end by a guard. Starkad followed them out and closed the door softly behind him. When he saw that the Watch had forgotten about him and Mael, he opened the latch again silently and tugged the Irishman inside with him. The bodies lay as they had. The girl, bent over a table weeping, looked up.

"What in hell are you doing?" Mael whispered hoarsely.

"Comforting the bereft," Starkad whispered back. Rising, the girl threw herself into the Dane's arms. She was sobbing uncontrollably.

Mael knuckled his lips in disbelief. Finally he started up the stairs, walking very carefully. "At least there'll be a softer bed here than back in the square," he muttered to himself.

⬧   ⬧   ⬧

The war horns aroused Mael and Starkad as surely as they did the troops billeted under canvas in the market. The two friends stumbled back to their unit, earning a black look but no comment from Maglos. Starkad had filched a skin of Spanish wine from the house in which they had slept. It was enough to square Vaces. "Her kin, her mother's folk'll be appointed guardians," the Dane said. "They'll strip the place. I figured we had as much need for the booze as they did. And she didn't mind. Her name was Luad."

The two Herulians had been crucified to either side of the North Gate, through which the combined squadrons rode on the final stage of their advance.

⬧   ⬧   ⬧

The way to Lincoln was deserted, stripped of all peaceful traffic by the threat of war. The Companions rode easily, four abreast. Even the lowering clouds were a boon for fending off the hammer of the sun. One brief shower set the cursing regulars to checking the fastenings of their bow cases, but few of the recruits were archers. Though their troop was near the end of the column as usual, the recruits reached Lincoln well before sundown. Geraint's force was in its normal barracks within the city, but they had palisaded a camp outside the walls for the two reinforcing squadrons.

Maglos and the rest of the captains attended a staff meeting at dusk. When the Briton returned, he summoned his motley troop together. The recruits stood around a cresset flaring in front of the four tents allotted to them. "Listen good," Maglos said in British. "You that can't understand, wait till I'm done and ask somebody who could." Realizing that what he had said made no sense, the captain scowled at himself and added, "Well, you know what I mean.

"Tomorrow's the real thing. Geraint left scouts across the Dubglas, that's the river just east. They rode back yesterday. Aelle's there and he's got a lot of men, maybe ten thousand. That's all of his own crew and anybody else who wanted to get in on the loot they're planning on. He's camped just across the river. We're going to meet him there in the morning."

The veteran Companion rubbed the knuckles of his hands together. "You guys aren't trained. You can't ride and you can't shoot, most of you. That doesn't mean you can't fight. It better not mean you can't fight. We'll be right in the center of the whole fucking line. The Leader'll be with us, *us*, and it'll be our job to protect him against any Saxons who get through. They'll be keying on him, don't kid yourself."

"If we're so goddamn worthless" demanded one of the Franks, "then why put us in the center?"

Maglos nodded as if unaware of the hostility of the question. "Everybody else'll have to ride or shoot," he said. "All you have to do is wait for the Saxons to run up to you. Then you spear them. Nobody who can't do that ought to 'a come looking for a berth with the Leader."

The grizzled Briton looked around the faces of his troop. "One more thing," he said. "You'll stand where you're put and wait. If anybody runs away, they'll be hunted down after the battle by whoever wins. You saw those two bastards at the gate this morning. That's not half what the Saxons like to do to Companions *they* capture. You're fighting men, that shouldn't be any problem.

"But none of you is going to leave your position and charge early, either. There's no glory in getting an arrow in your back, and that's just what you'll have before you've taken three steps. You don't know, you *can't* know, what the Leader's going to do. But he's got to know exactly what every man in his army does. That's how we've beat the Saxons before; that's how we'll beat 'em tomorrow. Anybody who doesn't think they can live with that had best consider falling on his sword. It's apt to be quicker than disobeying orders."

Maglos was breathing heavily with emotion. His eyes caught Starkad's. The Dane was as calm as a block of granite, impassive and untouched by anything that had been said. "Believe me or don't!" Maglos snarled. "But you'll learn tomorrow! Now get to bed!"

"When we get into line," Mael said very softly to

Starkad as they trudged to their tent, "let's just wait for the Saxons to come to us."

"Because that loudmouthed Briton tells us to?" the Dane snorted.

"Umm, " Mael temporized, "because Arthur plans his battles so he can win them. And I've got a taste for wanting to be on the winning side. More loot."

"You kill everybody on the other side, then you win," Starkad muttered, but Mael was no longer afraid of his friend deciding to break ranks. When the Dane went berserk he was beyond reason or argument, but Starkad could control the onset of the rage—and Mael was now sure he would do so.

Chapter Fourteen

The Northern Squadron marched out of Lincoln in the middle of the night. Mael heard the gates squeal, then the soft thudding of hooves. Geraint's men knew the terrain well enough to be able to take up their positions in the dark. They were reinforcing the troop left as pickets at the Dubglas ford when the rest of the squadron pulled back to await Arthur.

The two remaining squadrons rode at dawn. For the first time, Arthur's men left the network of wide, stone-dressed Roman thoroughfares. Their captains led them along narrow tracks in single file through woods and between tall hedges. The forks would have been bewildering had not Geraint left guides at each doubtful turn to direct the unfamiliar troops. When the rear guard came by, the guides would join it.

Near Lincoln, the dead Saxons had all been dragged into mass graves by conscripted civilians, but from a mile beyond the walls there were constant reminders of the rout. The bodies were bloated and so blackened by decay that their skins were indistinguishable from their leather garments. Perhaps the crows and the flies who lay across the corpses like sheets had risen when the first horsemen approached. By the time Mael and Starkad passed near the end of the column, they could ride within a foot of a cadaver rolled barely to the margin of the lane. The carrion eaters would still ignore them. The horses' hooves stirred up the scent of death along with the dust.

"None of them fought," Starkad noted idly as he and Mael rode side by side on a stretch wide enough to do so. "All the wounds are from behind."

"They were afraid," Mael said, realizing that the Dane's comment was accurate. Sometimes the stub of an arrow shaft protruded, broken when the archer tried to retrieve it; sometimes a diamond-shaped wound gaped between the shoulder blades where a lance had driven in with the stunning impact of a horse and armored man behind it. Less frequently, the victims had died when swords bit through skulls or collarbones in a huge, black fan of blood.

Starkad snorted in disgust. "You can't run away from a horseman," he said. "If you stand, you can maybe take a few of them with you to Hel."

The words were not braggadocio, Mael thought to himself. The big Dane really could not imagine panic, fear so great that a man would rather die than face it . . . though the fear itself was generally of death. Mael could not be like Starkad, but the Irishman knew from a hundred bloody fights that there was no fear so great that he could not function despite it. And invariably in the past, his opponents had proven to have had the greater reason for fear.

Forest opened onto plowed land, a narrow canal of sunlit ground between wooded dikes. In the cleared area, men and beasts were milling in disorder. Unarmed handlers from the support sections were leading clumps of riderless horses out of the way of the troops debouching from the woods to the west. Beyond the handlers, dismounted Companions were filing into the eastern woods, carrying all their equipment including the spears they seemed to be bearing instead of lances this day. The men in sight all appeared to be from British tribes, armed with long self bows instead of the more handy composite bows Arthur imported for the mercenaries of other nationalities. The western Britons had grown up with their highly effective weapon. Though the shorter bow of horn and sinew bonded to wood was more useful for a horseman, Arthur had not attempted to retrain his own countrymen.

Maglos rested his hands on his double pommels, counting his men as they appeared. "All right," he shouted. "Recruit Troop, dismount! Give your horses to the handlers, four to a man. Then follow me. And bring all your goddamned gear, especially your water skins, or by god you'll parch like raisins before this day is out."

Stumbling, his legs not working quite like legs after long days of gripping a horse, Mael followed Maglos up a recent slash in second-growth forest. Just behind him strode Starkad, bubblingly happy to be afoot again. The Dane's axe arced out in fun and nipped a two-inch branch from a pine tree. One of the cadre yelped a startled protest as the blade looped back at him. The Dane laughed and wiped sap from the steel.

A Companion stood at the head of the trail where

the slope flattened and occasional glints of armor
and sunlight could be seen through the trees. "Which
unit?" the guide snapped at Maglos, then noticed
the varied gear of the men beyond. "Oh, Christ, the
recruits," the Companion muttered. "Straight on
ahead and spread to the right, three feet between
men. And keep 'em the fuck back from the edge of
the trees. Every three feet, forming on the command
staff."

Ten yards further were knots of men and horses—
Arthur and a cornicine, Lancelot, and a blocky man
holding the red dragon standard. A fifth man walked
from behind a tree at the sound of the recruits
trampling through the brush. Mael recognized Cei
in a helmet whose long iron nose-strap seemed to
split his face. The four subordinates were on foot,
though their horses stood drop-reined just behind
them. The king himself was still mounted.

Mael took his position to Cei's immediate right
where Maglos motioned him. He met the seneschal's
eyes, then turned and knelt by a tree. Pretending
the command group was not present, the Irishman
slid forward to where he could look out over the east
slope of the hill. Maglos was spreading the rest of
the troop along the crest, man by man.

The valley below had the cross section of a shallow
U, half a mile from ridge to ridge. The floor was broad
and flat, marked with the darker green of reeds where
the Dubglas meandered down the middle. The slope
was slight but noticeable, grassy except for an
occasional outcropping of limestone. At the base of
the hill were a pair of incongruous pennons set on
staves some two hundred yards apart. They were
apparently centered on the command staff. Mael's
eyes narrowed as he saw the flags. To either side

the Dubglas glittered in a narrow band, but in front of Mael the water purled and whitened over shallows. Twenty of Geraint's horsemen, the only Companions in plain view, patrolled slowly up and down the meadow to the west of the ford.

Across the stream were the Saxons. The rumor that they were ten thousand strong might have been an underestimate. They were in such disorder that it was hard to say. The far side of the valley was covered with a litter of tents, cookfires, and wagons. Men sat or sprawled among draft animals and the sheep and swine driven along with the levy for food. The Saxons had built no palisade. The only guards apparent were the parties of housecarls formed in front of the largest tents around the war standards.

The Saxons were disorganized, but their numbers were stunning.

Many of the Saxons were awake and straggling down toward the stream in small groups, some to draw water but many to shout insults at the mounted vedettes on the other side. The Dubglas was no more than a hundred feet wide at the ford, though the current there was swift enough over the slick stones to make crossing an awkward business. Standing at the edge of the water, a few Saxon archers shot at the Companions. Their shafts wobbled harmlessly short. Arthur's men appeared to be paying no attention.

There was a bit of discussion among the vedettes. One of the horsemen, a Hun with a naked torso and hair streaming down his back like a horse's tail, uncased his bow and nocked an arrow. Lancelot caught the motion out of the corner of his eye. The Gaul broke off his conversation with the king. The Saxon archers began stumbling back away from the stream in sudden panic. The mud clutched at their feet. Several dropped their weapons to scrabble on all fours.

The Hun ignored them, arching his back and his bow together. He drew and loosed the arrow in a single motion. The nearby Saxons froze, but the arrow curved high beyond them. It plunged down into the group of armored housecarls in front of the largest tent, three hundred yards away. The high-pitched hiss of the dropping shaft was enough warning that the Saxons looked up from their banter in the instant before the arrow struck. Then the guards exploded apart. They left one of their number screaming on the ground with the arrow through the flesh of his right leg. The standard he had held, a boar's skull on a ten-foot pole, wobbled and dipped to the earth before any of the other housecarls could catch it. The Hun's laughter pealed into the sudden silence of the Saxon camp.

Lancelot was swearing in Celtic, his knuckles white on the hilt of his sword. "They were told not to shoot without orders, not to do *anything* without orders!" he snarled. "I'll have him flayed alive when he—"

"Be silent," said Arthur, without particular emphasis. The king was squinting for a better look at the archer. There was a slight smile on his face. "That was Edzil, was it not?" he asked, as much of Lancelot as of anyone. "One makes allowances for Huns, you know, Roman."

The tall Master of Soldiers said nothing, though his face grew pale. After a moment, Lancelot released his sword so that it could slip the six inches back to home in its scabbard.

Starkad nudged Mael and gestured to the left. An armored horseman from the flank was picking his way along the tree line toward Arthur's position. The rider was alone, but the gilt and silver of his arms suggested his rank. Lancelot noticed him, too, and said, "Here's Geraint. He'd better have everything in order or . . ."

Geraint nudged his horse into the command group. "Or what, Lancelot?" he asked. He was older than most of the Companions and rode with the stiffness of a man laced together with scar tissue. "Everything's fine. We set them between the two lances, from there up the slope to maybe forty yards from here. All of them you sent forward. They're waiting for the Saxons to come."

"Well, that's what they're doing now," said Cei expressionlessly. Every eye in Arthur's force riveted itself on the ford and the Saxons beginning to splash across it.

Not all of Aelle's army was advancing, nor were those who were crossing the Dubglas in as good an order as even the footing would allow. Bands of men, two or three or up to a score, plunged into the water, wearing long swords and full armor. The froth rose to their knees. They shouted, keeping their heavy shields raised to cover their faces and torsos against the expected sleet of arrows.

None of the patrolling Companions fired. Their officer gave a quick command. The squad rode north along the stream, then turned sharply away from the water and up the hill. The Saxon rabble on the other bank shrieked triumphantly and sent a useless volley of missiles after Arthur's men. Most of the arrows did not even reach the west side of the Dubglas. The last of the riders to disappear into the woods cloaking the British left flank was the Hun, Edzil. He turned toward the Saxons. They cried out in fear, but instead of firing again the Hun laughed and pumped his finger at the footmen unmistakably.

Cei and Lancelot had mounted their horses. Mael, who had been lying on his belly, rose and ran his left arm through the loops of his target. "Give me a minute, will you?" Geraint requested without concern. The squadron commander rode back toward his position at a canter.

The leading Saxons were berserkers and champions from among the housecarls, and thegns with a reputation for valor or the desire to gain one. When those leaders had waded ashore on the west bank, the mass of the army began to follow them across the ford in a brown wave. The Saxons slipped, spilling themselves and their neighbors in tangles of limbs and equipment. "Now!" Starkad shouted. The Dane had risen to his feet and slung his shield around to his back where it gave no protection but would not interfere with his axe.

Arthur gave his cornicine an order. Mael could not hear it in the din from the Saxons and the excited exclamations of the recruits nearby. The horn sounded a five-note series. Maglos and his cadre ran behind the untrained men shouting, "No farther than the standards!" as the whole British army shuddered forward into the sunlight.

The king was splendid at its head and center. He wore full mail, including chaps which covered his legs without preventing his inner thighs from gripping his horse firmly. All Arthur's armor had been silvered. The bronze wings flaring to either side of the helmet had been picked out in gold as well. The midmorning brightness made the king a lightning bolt rather than a man. The dragon standard borne at his side filled with the first breeze and unfurled its scarlet terror.

The scales of bronze and gold worked into the standard's fabric hissed as though the serpent were a living creature. The Saxons fell silent, save for a few shouts of bravado which rang more fearful than frightening.

Arthur drew up just clear of the trees. His armored squadrons, tightening ranks which the forest had disarrayed, halted to either flank. And the Saxon swarm which had stopped in fear, divided by the river at the king's appearance, raised a great shout and rushed to reunite on the west bank.

Whimpering with frustration but not quite mad enough to charge alone, Starkad turned from the enemy and hugged Mael to his breast. "What's he waiting for?" the Dane demanded in a voice that half the army could hear. "We could—while the river cut them—"

"Don't worry," Mael murmured, patting his friend's iron back like someone consoling a child on the death of a pet, "it'll be all right for us, yes. . . ." Mael's eye caught the glitter of the king's helm. He looked up at the monarch. Arthur, cold and remote as a statue from Karnak, was staring at the two of them. Mael stared back, repeating, "It'll be all right."

Starkad shuddered, regained control of himself. He gave the Irishman a final squeeze before loosing him.

Arthur's force, now that Mael could see it whole for the first time, was drawn up as a line of infantry between two solid masses of ranked horsemen. The center was made up of the native Britons and the recruits, dismounted to either side of the king. The Britons were setting their spears butt-first in the soil and propping their shields against them. That accomplished, the Companions strung their longbows and waited for orders.

The cavalry on the flanks was more restive. Mael noted that the mounted Companions, too, were handling their bows. Their lances pointed vertically upward—ready, but waiting.

Like a crystal with a core of glittering steel, the Saxon host grew by accretion. Men still wandered down the hillside to the ford, yawning and shifting their equipment into more comfortable postures. When they reached the river they paused, then splashed through it to find places among the thousands of warriors already knotted on the other side. In the center of the Saxon line, the nobles and their paid men were ranked ten deep around the standards. Those placed in the forefront were there of their own will. Already they stamped and clashed blades against their shield bosses. From the second rank rose Aelle's own standard, the Battle Swine, raised from the dirt to lower over the array

The men on the fringes of the formation, two-thirds or more of the Saxon force, were of another sort. These were the peasants who owed their thegns produce at harvest time and their bodies in war. It was men like these—freeborn and free-holders, but living at a subsistence level—whom Aelle had left as a tripwire at Lincoln. They had no mail coats nor even the long tunics of iron-studded leather which some of the housecarls wore. In linen and wool and occasionally a steer-hide jerkin, the peasants eyed the archers waiting on the hill before them. They shuddered, then edged a little closer inward toward their armored betters. The peasants' weapons were generally spears, leavened with a few axes and billhooks—tools on any day of the year save days of battle. There were a few men carrying bows. Since the bowmen generally lacked even the flimsy bucklers carried by most of the carls, they were especially determined to worm their way in from the exposed fringes where they might have been of some use.

In a clear, carrying voice, Arthur cried, "Now to grind the vermin away! Loose the horse!"

The cornicine lilted out a call that horns on both wings echoed instantly. The twenty troops of horsemen under Gawain and Geraint scissored down from the flanks at a fast walk rather than a gallop. The Companions began shooting at two hundred yards. Their targets, the mass of Saxon peasantry, crumpled like grass in a hailstorm. Each horseman carried two dozen arrows in his quiver. The front rank of nomad mercenaries, Huns and easterners to whom horses and horn bows were a way of life, spent their loads in less than a minute. The remaining Companions were mostly Germans of one nation or another who had been as innocent of archery as the Saxons until Arthur trained them. They were slower to fire, but there were eight hundred of them.

The Saxon wings disintegrated under the weight of fire. The carls had no protection but shields of wicker and unstrapped wood—and the bodies of the men dying in front of them. Arthur's men were using broadheads that slashed wounds as wide as paired thumbs. In the soft targets the arrows still penetrated completely and pinned men to their dying neighbors.

Without any defense or means to retaliate, without any stiffening from the chieftains who were concentrated in the center of the array, the surviving peasants broke and ran. The Dubglas, more an incident than an impediment when the Saxons advanced across it unopposed, became a bloody deathtrap. Men who slipped were trampled into the rocks. Disabling wounds left others to die, trying to scream in the frothing water that smothered them. The ford was only a hundred yards wide. It packed the thousands of fugitives into a still denser killing zone for the arrows that ripped among them. Fallen bodies dammed the water into a bloody pond. The surface foamed repeatedly as it broke through the obstruction, then stilled again when fresh corpses took the place of those washed downstream. Mael turned to speak to Starkad as the last rank of Companions wheeled their horses. Only then did the Irishman realize that he could not shout over the cries from the river a quarter mile away.

The cavalrymen were reforming and again filling their quivers from stores borne from Lincoln by mule train. A few horses had stumbled. Their riders had either remounted their own animals or swung up on the pillions of neighboring riders. Arthur's fighting strength was undiminished.

But so, despite the carnage, was that of the Saxons.

Aelle's thegns and housecarls had not been touched by the arrows. Their shields were broad and thick, wrapped and studded with iron. Raising them, chanting a war hymn, the Saxons began to plod forward toward the thin British line. Aelle's men still outnumbered their opponents two or three to one. Rightly, they feared neither lances nor the arrows with which the squadrons were being feverishly replenished. The Saxon formation was a wedge of interlocked shields, the inexorable swine-array whose invention had been Wotan's greatest gift to men of valor.

"Look there," Starkad said and pointed. Half a dozen horsemen still loitered near the Saxons. As the wedge began to advance, these Companions cantered even closer. Extra quivers were slung across the withers of their mounts and their bows seemed extensions of their arms. They were Huns.

Saxons in the center of the array raised their shields overhead; those on the left flank facing the horsemen crouched down so that their heads and torsos were covered by their shields. Completely protected, the Saxons waited for the arrows to come.

Come they did, stabbing into the bare calves and ankles of the outermost men of the swine-array. The screams and clash of falling armor masked the machine-like snap of bowstrings and the laughter of the Huns. Every time a Saxon fell or dropped his shield to clutch at his bleeding leg, a second arrow took him in the chest or belly.

"They aren't using broadheads any more," Mael muttered. "Those must be bodkin points to do that, I don't care how strong their bows are." At fifty yards the Hunnish arrows were driving through even good ring mail.

As if the sudden clutter of bodies were an anchor dragging it back, the whole formation faltered. Then, from the front where the boar's skull threatened, Aelle's deep voice boomed, "Wotan loves brave men! Forward!"

The bellow and the clashing of armor in answer to Aelle's shout startled even the seasoned war-horses of the Huns. The Saxon ranks closed; the swine-array resumed its advance upon eight thousand feet.

Hooting and yipping more to themselves than to frighten, the Huns guided their mounts with their knees to within ten yards of the Saxons. There the little men of the steppes opened fire again. They were so close that their shafts pierced even the sturdy shields raised against them, pinning the wood to the arms that held it or gouging deeper into faces.

Starkad's knuckles went white against the unyielding helve of his axe. The Dane was not an archer, and he could identify all too easily with the Saxons below.

One huge Saxon broke ranks and charged the tormentor whose arrow had lodged in his left eye-socket. The German was deaf to the shouts of those trying to bring him back. Iron medals cast in the shape of Roman horsetrappings glittered against his chest. The Hun who had pricked him wheeled his horse and retreated a dozen paces. The archers to either side waited until the footman had drawn abreast of them. They shot together. The goose-quill fletching of their arrows bloomed against the Saxon's rib cage without the hindrance of the heavy shield to penetrate. Dead on his feet, the warrior staggered on.

Shouting in high-pitched voices, the pair of Huns slapped six arrows apiece through the Saxon's cuirass. Each clump of feathers was so tight that a man's palm could cover the entry holes. The victim's arms slowly straightened so that his spear and shield were hanging as dead weights instead of weapons. Still the Saxon kept advancing.

When the dying warrior was within a yard of the Hun who was his quarry, that horseman shot once more. This time the shaft entered the right eye and clanked against the helmet at the base of the skull. The Saxon stiffened and fell backward like a tree sawn through at the roots. The Hun who had killed him bent without dismounting. He swung up again with the iron medallions in his hand.

Starkad cursed on the hill from which he watched the lethal toying. Beside him, Mael slapped his fist again and again upon his pelvis. The Irishman could see this game was almost over. It would be the Saxons' turn to strike next. Arthur's line overlapped the wedge to either side, but the Saxons were ten ranks deep and faced only a single row of longbowmen and recruits. Horns cried fierce, brassy commands from Arthur's wing squadrons. That was too late, Mael thought—the Saxons had reached the edge of the hill, only two hundred yards from the British. Aelle shouted and his men broke into a bellowing charge. Arrows could perhaps needle the margins of the swine-array, but missiles alone could never break it.

Then Mael gasped as the wedge disintegrated of its own accord at almost the instant the rush began. The whole Saxon front rank began to scream and stumble like their comrades who had been leg-pierced by the Hunnish arrows. The weight of the ranks behind the leaders pressed the charge onward. Men hopped and fell, shrieking as they stood one-legged and pulled black metal from the bare soles of their raised feet.

"Crows' feet!" Mael shouted, recognizing from the result what was breaking the Saxon line. The Irish used the devices, too, when time and location permitted. Crows' feet, caltrops, tetrahedrons—they were simply four iron nails welded with their heads together so that a spike was upward no matter how the object fell. Strewn in high grass, they were almost invisible. Their spikes ripped buskins or bare feet like so many two-inch spear blades.

The crows' feet were disabling but they could not kill. The arrows that now darted from three sides of the broken array accomplished the killing. Longbows from the hilltop thrummed as Saxons dropped their shields to pluck iron from their feet. From either flank rode three hundred archers, firing from refilled quivers. The Companions' fingers were bloody from earlier shooting and many riders were unable to draw their shafts to full nock. The body armor of the thegns was often able to turn a missile anyway, even when it missed the shields. Still, many arrows found targets and Saxons gurgled and fell.

Mael part drew and resheathed his sword a dozen times in nervous exultation. "If they run!" he was shouting. "If they run—"

Warriors in the rear of the array broke. That was their death, for the last two ranks of Arthur's horsemen whooped and charged with their lances couched. The wave of steel lance heads bit into the backs and necks of the running Saxons like saw-teeth in soft pine. The victims flew forward. Their arms windmilled; sometimes a bright froth of pulmonary blood sprayed from their nostrils. The killers rode over the fallen Saxons, pivoting their wrists at the balance of the lance shafts and dragging the points free. Then the Companions could strike again, either with butt spikes or the already bloodied heads.

As a week before at Lincoln, as other armies for a thousand years, the Saxons proved that to run from a lance was to die. The darting steel left them food for the battlefield crows, whether they were thegn or earl, naked or mailed.

Some of the Saxon peasants who had survived to recross the stream lay on the far bank watching. They were shivering spectators for whom the price of admission had been the death of the men to every side of them. Now, as their screaming superiors rushed toward the water to die, the carls turned again. They began to straggle off toward their homes as swiftly as exhaustion allowed their legs to move. War was coming too close again, and the peasants had had their bellies full of it for this day.

Not all the Saxons ran. The men in the front ranks

thrust forward and up the hill because it never occurred to them to go in any other direction. Some wore wooden-soled sandals which turned the points of the crows feet. Some were simply lucky, skipping across ground which, though thickly sown, was not interlocked with spikes. A few showed enough intelligence to shuffle forward instead of striding, scuffing the devices harmlessly out of their way. Most of the Saxon champions, however, twisted the bloody iron from their feet and walked on, treating the wound as one more incident of war like a bee sting or sunburn. Men who could not do that fled and died fleeing, but among warriors whose honor and livelihood was physical valor, it would have been surprising had there not been many who ignored injuries in order to close with the enemy.

The longbowmen, their quivers emptied, were snatching shields and spears. "All right, you bastards!" Maglos roared to his recruits. "Time to earn your pay!"

Mael shrugged once more to settle his armor comfortably. With a shout that tried to equal all the battle noise around him, Starkad bounded toward the nearest of the oncoming Saxons. Mael ran at the Dane's left and a step behind him. The Saxon, a great walleyed ruffian in chain mail, thrust his target forward to block Starkad's axe. The axe blade sheared the iron-bound linden wood from one rim to the other, gouging so deeply that it opened the Saxon's forearm as well. The Saxon screamed, spinning off balance from the torque of the blow he had received. Mael's sword tip laid the falling man's throat open, drowning his cries in a spray of blood.

Still bellowing his berserk challenge, Starkad met a clot of a dozen Saxons. They split apart at his fury.

Some of them were engaged by the other recruits and Britons following the Dane to battle. Starkad's axe was making broad figure-eight passes in the air before him. One housecarl counted on the pattern he imagined in the Dane's offense. Starkad, reversing the direction of the axe in mid-sweep, dashed the Saxon's brains out with the peen. A thegn to Starkad's left saw the Dane's back open, forgot Mael, and raised his spear. Mael thrust and the thegn took the Irishman's sword through the rib cage. The Saxon fell, his bones gripping the blade. Mael tried to tug his weapon clear as two of the dead man's housecarls pressed him. The blade bent as it came out, cocking up in the middle at a thirty-degree angle.

Cursing and suddenly in fear of death, the Irishman jumped back to avoid the spear which licked at his face. Mael's missing earlobe burned as if afire. The sword he carried was the one he had taken from Ceadwalla's body, a well-polished blade and solid to look on. But the metal was soft, and now it would be his death for not testing it earlier. . . . The Saxons struck together, both holding their spears overhand at the balance. Mael backed again, letting the points notch his shield facing. He set his blade under his right sandal and tried to straighten the weapon.

The leftward Saxon howled and thrust with both hands, driving his spear six inches deep in Mael's shield. The Irishman slashed from a crouch. The stroke severed the Saxon's wrists before he could step away from it. The dying man threw his spurting stumps in the air and turned, fouling his companion's blow so that the spear only ripped Mael's side instead of splitting his breastbone as intended. The Irishman's mail shirt was as good as could be forged, but its links parted before the spear head.

Mael countered with a backhanded slash at the remaining Saxon. Ceadwalla's blade had twisted axially under the stress of lopping through the previous opponent's wrists. The edge did not bite, but the effect on the Saxon was that of being slapped across the head with a long iron club. The man went down. Mael finished him with his shield edge. He dropped his useless sword so that he could use both hands to slam the iron rim down on the Saxon's neck.

Ignoring the swords sheathed at the dead men's belts, Mael worked the spear out of his shield to rearm himself. The weapon had a long, double-edged blade, and its shaft for several feet back was wrapped with iron wire. To free the spear, Mael pumped the shaft up and down. His eyes darted about the immediate battlefield to be sure that none of the men brawling nearby was about to stab him.

Lancelot's fine armor had drawn more than its share of attackers. The Gaul was handling them in easy—almost leisurely—fashion, striking with both the head and the butt spike of his lance. As Mael watched, Lancelot cleared a Saxon from his left side with a jolt from his buckler.

Arthur's own style was as lethal, though more frantic than that of his Master of Soldiers. The king was wheeling his horse in a tight caracole that intimidated footmen while he slashed at them to either side with his sword. Arthur's silvered armor danced as he moved. A blow of some sort had severed one wing from his helmet and scarred the plating beneath it. The war-horse foamed as it trampled over the bodies of two slain Saxons. Nearby lay the British standard bearer, his teeth locked in the throat of the berserker who had killed him. The red dragon lapped over both men like a shroud. Cei was nowhere to be seen, but his horse trotted riderless at the edge of the woods.

Below, the melee begun when Starkad had struck
the foremost Saxons had expanded into a full battle.
Men had flowed together from both sides. Now the
lines were beginning to disintegrate again from
attrition. Aelle, the Saxon king, traded spear thrusts
with two Companions. Twenty feet away, Starkad and
a Gothic swordsman fought a trio of Saxons. As Mael
wrenched his own weapon free, Starkad finished one
opponent by chopping through his left thigh. At
almost the same moment, the Gothic Companion
doubled over with a surprised expression and both
hands spread to catch the intestines spilling out of
his torn jerkin. Starkad turned to block the bloody
sword which had killed the Goth, leaving his right
side and the Saxon there unattended.

Mael took a step forward with his spear cocked
in his right hand. He loosed. The Irishman's legs
were rubbery from exertion and the heat, but they
held him. The shaft flew straight. The Saxon's
upraised sword glanced off Starkad's shoulder, but
dead fingers had released it even as the blow had
started. The impact of Mael's spear punching into
his chest drove the Saxon a step backward. He fell
there, hemorrhaging bright streams from mouth and
nose.

Mael knelt, panting hugely against the weight and
constriction of his armor. His eye settled on the Saxon
king. Aelle was not a young man; his beard was a
grizzled red like the fur of an old fox. But the Saxon
was as cunning as a fox as well, survivor of more battles
than most men could dream of fighting. Mael saw
him thrust one Briton through the thigh and drag
him like a harpooned fish into the path of the second.
When that Companion stumbled, Aelle's shield boss

laid him out as surely as a club to the head could have. Pulling his spear point free, the Saxon king stepped over the litter of bodies and hurled his spear at Arthur.

Arthur had just dispatched the last of his attackers. He was shouting with triumph when the Saxon spear took his horse in the right ham. The beast gave a whinny that was almost a scream. It reared. Arthur, terrified of being afoot, screamed himself. He dropped his sword and clutched his saddle with both hands.

Lancelot's eyes were as cold as the iron frame of his helmet. He spurred his horse from a walk to a gallop. His lance was couched under his arm, the point aimed at the center of Aelle's breastbone where the impact would knock the Saxon down even if he managed to interpose his shield to the blow. Aelle had drawn a hand axe from his belt. With a feral grin and the timing of a man who had seen thirty years of battle, Aelle brought his axe around in an overhand arc. It intersected the lance an inch behind the head. The wood sheared and the point flew away, its sharpened edges glistening like the facets of a gemstone. The shaft, swung downward by the blow, drove into the ground and lifted Lancelot by directing his own momentum onto the sudden fulcrum. With hideous perfection, Aelle made disaster certain by sweeping his target around. Its boss took the horse on the left eye as the beast drove past him. The horse shied. Its feet skidded out from under it, narrowly missing Aelle as the hindquarters slewed around. The beast's weight pinned the struggling Lancelot's right leg against the turf beneath it. The animal's rib cage thudded like a drum. Man and horse cried out together.

Aelle, midway between Arthur and Mael, regained his balance. He cried, "You at least will get your death this day, Unfoot!" As if in response, the legs of Arthur's wounded mount collapsed. The king slid to the ground despite his screams and his grasping at the mane and saddle. Brandishing his shield and hand axe, Aelle ran toward his fallen opponent thirty feet away.

To either flank, lancers were riding uphill to help finish the Saxons, but there was no Briton as close to the two kings as Mael was. The Irishman grunted and took a step toward Aelle. The Saxon was moving away from Mael, and besides, Mael had no weapon left but his target. He slipped his left arm out of the loops and gripped the rim with both hands. The shield was five layers of birch plywood, faced with leather and locked together by an edge band of iron. Slightly convex at the face, it weighed almost forty pounds. With all his remaining strength, Mael brought the shield up from his left side and released it. The target spun like a huge discus, curving uphill toward the point at which Aelle and Arthur were about to meet.

Aelle was raising his axe high overhead and shouting down at Arthur when the shield caught him in the back of the neck. It killed him instantly. The Saxon's cries snapped off as his spine parted. His head scissored back and met his shoulder blades while the target spun off to the side. Aelle's axe flew high over Arthur to stick in the ground near the fallen standard. Aelle's flaccid body slammed face-first at the feet of the British king.

Arthur stood up very slowly, bracing himself with a hand on the ground. His eyes were on Aelle, ignoring Mael and the riders spurring toward their Leader from both flanks. The Pendragon's face was white except for his moustache and the blood trailing from his bitten lip. With his twisted foot, Arthur kicked at Aelle's head. It lolled on the broken neck. The helmet rolled off and the sun gleamed on the Saxon's bare pate. Arthur kicked him again and spat. "Swine!" he shouted. "You Saxon swine will *all* kiss my feet or burn, *burn!*"

Arthur suddenly straightened and glared at the men around him. The Companions had paused when their Leader rose. Now the naked fury of the king's stare drove at them like a gust of chill wind. "Lancelot! Where are you, Lancelot?" the king shouted.

Mael turned. Lancelot's horse had scrambled to its feet. The Master of Soldiers raised himself to his left knee. Blood was dripping from the top of his other boot. Though Lancelot's leg had not been broken, its flesh, pinioned against the bone by the horse's half ton of weight, had been torn as if by an axe. When the Gaul tried to stand, his face went sallow and his right leg buckled under him.

"God damn you, Roman!" Arthur shouted. "You always fail when I need you!" Mael's own expression blanked. The Irishman had a momentary urge to put a sword through Lancelot's heart as a mercy, despite his hatred for the tall captain.

The king's eyes flicked aside. They focused for the first time on Mael. "You, Irishman, you'll not fail me. I need you to ride to Merlin. Tell him to loose the dragon now." Arthur's face was growing red. He paused, then the words began to spatter out again. "Tell him it must kill and burn and waste the whole land from here to the seacoast. Tell him to sear the Saxons until they either wade into the sea or beg me, *beg* me, for mercy! And that mercy I may grant or not grant!"

Mael licked at the sweat rimming his upper lip. "I—I'll need equipment—"

"Yes, yes," Arthur snapped, "anything, horses . . . Lancelot, write him out a warrant to take whatever he needs along the way. Hurry!"

Two men were helping Lancelot sit up. He had taken off his helmet and was sucking wine greedily from a skin bottle. He winced. "In my saddlebags," the Gaul muttered. "There's parchment there and an ink stick."

One of the pair holding the Master of Soldiers leaped up and caught the nearby horse before Arthur could flare again in rage. The Companion rummaged in the bag for the materials, then brought them back quickly. Lancelot spat on the ink and began to scratch words on the scroll with a reed pen.

Arthur had unlaced his helmet. He mopped his face with a towel soaked in water. There was a long welt on the left side where the cheek piece of his helmet had been driven into the skin. Otherwise, the king had his normal color back. "There'll be Saxons scattered from here to Glevum," he said to Mael.

The Irishman was examining the sword he had just taken from Aelle's body. It was a long horseman's blade of Roman pattern and Spanish manufacture, old and well cared for and deadly.

"Plenty of British cutthroats, too," Arthur was saying. "Battle draws them." He looked back down the slope. Some Saxons were still writhing amidst the crows' feet, trying to crawl away from the squads of Companions who carefully picked their way in to finish the wounded. Nearer the river, there was a denser carpet of men with arrows and sometimes broken lance heads protruding from their vitals. The Dubglas still choked on bodies. Its current had not yet washed all the blood away from them.

With unexpected insight, Arthur added, "Maybe

that's the only kind of men that battle does draw. But I'll send Gawain with you. I want the message to get through."

Mael looked up. "Leader," he said, "send Starkad along instead of Gawain."

The king glared at the Dane who was now shambling up the hill to his friend's side. Starkad's smile was contented. He had lost his steel cap somewhere, and blood, slung from his axe head after his first stroke, speckled him all over. He himself appeared to be uninjured. "The Dane?" Arthur said. "He rides a horse like a sack of grain."

"He fights like any three of your Companions," Mael said, with no attempt to keep the edge out of his voice. "Send him with me or send someone else in my place."

The good humor of victory held. Arthur shrugged and called, "Lancelot, add the Dane to the warrant."

The Gaul's face was impassive as he scratched a flourish on the parchment. He handed the document and pen to his Leader. Arthur signed his name laboriously, chewing at the corner of his lip as he formed each letter. He gave the result to Mael. "Don't fail me, Irishman," the king said. "Don't even think of failing me."

Chapter Fifteen

Mael led a pair of remounts while Starkad rode alongside him unencumbered. The two of them were on the best horses available after the battle, steeds which had carried longbowmen to the site and had seen no further use that day. It was late afternoon. Even with hard riding, it would be a full day before Mael and Starkad could reach Moridunum.

The pace that Mael set was jolting and would wreck the horses in thirty miles. That was expected, and the mounts were replaceable. Starkad was riding as clumsily as Arthur had suggested he would, clinging to the saddle as if it were a spar and he a shipwrecked sailor. Each step hammered the Dane's spine and the insides of his thighs. He treated the punishment as he had that which he had received in the battle: something to be ignored or, if it could not be ignored, endured. At some point, even Starkad's strength would fail him and he would roll out of the saddle like a bundle of scrap iron. Until then he would ride.

As when they hiked toward Winchester, the two men kept general silence. Hoofbeats sounded on the metaled highway and their harness creaked around them. At a patrol station west of Lincoln, they left the horses they had been riding. There were no mounts there to exchange for them because the stables had been stripped for the field army. Trusting that stations farther west would have a better selection remaining, they pushed on astride the remounts the Irishman had been leading.

Night fell. At the post at which Mael and Starkad next stopped, the keeper's wife—her husband had been carried along with the army as a horse holder—demanded to know how the battle went. "Dead Saxons," Mael said, thrusting his head in a horse trough to clear away some of the grogginess. "All shapes and sizes, all dead. I doubt thousand of them got away." The woman was chortling with joy as they remounted and rode away. Mael thought of the thousands of piled bodies, men he had never known and whose families would never know them again.

There were three more watch stations in the War Zone. Mael and Starkad changed horses at each of them. In the more settled country to the west, there were no longer military posts and stables to supply remounts, but the farms were more spacious. Privately owned horses were available. At a villa near Mancetter, they traded their blown army steeds for a pair of gangling bays, draft animals but the best that circumstances offered. They rode them twenty miles until they met a landowner rich enough to be accompanied on the rounds of his estate by a mounted bodyguard.

"Hold up," Mael called to the pair. He rode alongside the civilians and fumbled in his scrip for Arthur's warrant. Rubbing his eyes with his free hand, he held out the paper to the landowner.

While the bodyguard, a lanky man whose tunic half hid a mail corselet, lowered at his side, the magnate read the warrant. "We need your horses," Mael said. "Arthur will make it right in a few days."

"We'll exchange horses on Arthur's say-so?" the landowner asked, his eyebrows rising with his voice. He had a cultured Latin accent. "And what has that barbarian ever done for me?"

Behind Mael, Starkad grated out his first words in ten hours: "He left your head on your shoulders, scum. I won't, if I hear your voice again." Mael glanced back at his friend. The Dane was hunched forward in his saddle. The morning sun was low enough to throw his hulking shadow across both the Britons. Because Starkad had not taken time to clean it, the axe in his hand was crusted with dried blood.

The bodyguard was already swinging out of his saddle by the time his blanching master ordered him to dismount.

Starkad did not speak again until mid-afternoon of the day after the battle. They had exchanged horses for the tenth or twelfth time—Mael had lost count—and were on the last stage of their ride. Sounding surprisingly hoarse, the Dane croaked, "Brother, what do we do after we get where we're going?"

Mael opened his mouth. Though he tried to speak, his tongue did not want to bend. He spat toward the roadside and made another attempt. "We'll give Merlin the message. Bathe. Sleep. Drink. Drink first, yeah. Maybe Veleda will be waiting for me. . . ."

"Then let's stop here for a few hours."

"What?" Mael turned to stare at his friend. Starkad gripped both front pommels of his saddle. His legs hung straight down, toes pointing to the ground. The Dane's face and beard were white with dust except where tears had broken paths from the corner of each eye. "Are you all right?" Mael asked. He reined up sharply and reached out a hand to steady Starkad.

"I said these dwarf-begotten horses would have to kill me before I fell off," the Dane said very softly, "and neither thing has happened yet. But if we ride straight in there now, my friend, you won't have a man behind you. Only meat, raw and tender. And they'll see me like this, those women and the burned-out men we left behind. And I'll be no better than they, Mael, no better at all, and I don't . . . want that.

"Please."

"Manannan, you didn't have to ask," Mael lied in embarrassment. "I was going to suggest we lay up here myself. I figure there's a good chance they aren't going to believe us right off—Merlin or the rest of the crew, either. If I stumble all over my tongue and can't remember what day it is, which is the kind of shape I'm in right now, we'll be thrown in the hole as deserters until the rest of the army gets back."

The friends dismounted in a willow coppice near a stream which they muddied in washing themselves. Mael kept his back turned so as not to see the agony on the Dane's face as he forced his legs to move again. Mael's own thighs could not have been more painful had the femurs been broken. He could imagine how the less experienced Starkad felt. Stretched on the ground in front of their tethered horses, the men slept for five hours to the rim of twilight. Then Mael lifted his head from his pillowing saddle. Starkad, aroused by the creak of the leather, crawled to his feet as well.

"Feel okay?" the Irishman asked.

"Weak as a baby," grumbled Starkad. He grasped a two-inch willow beside him and tried to break it off with one hand. The supple trunk bent but would not part. Suddenly the root end flew up, spattering mud over both men. Mael cursed. "Maybe not quite as weak as a baby," said Starkad with a grin.

They rigged the horses and rode on at the same savage pace as before. The exercise loosened Mael's sleep-tightened muscles as lard loosens before a fire. The touch of the saddle was fire indeed to his bruised thighs.

With the sun low and in their faces, the riders approached the villa. The women in the enlisted lines high-built behind the main building, caught the glint and jingle of harness first. The watchers began to drift toward the flagged entranceway. The women had been sitting in little groups in the cool of the evening, talking and mending garments. A few of them ran inside, shouting on rising inflections to their friends within. Those, wives and mothers and daughters, tumbled downstairs and out of doors, stumbling in haste and pinning on their cloaks as they ran. The gentle motion became a rush akin to panic. A hundred yards from the doorway of the villa, the crowd struck Mael and Starkad like hens around a farm wife at feeding time. "Is my man—" "Tell me about—" A hundred variations on the theme sounded in as many languages.

Over the babel, using his spear shaft as a lever to thrust away the hands groping for his reins, Mael cried out, "We won! We won! But let us through, women. . . ." Then, "We don't know the names of anybody, *anybody*, and we've brought a message for Merlin."

The Irishman had to shout the same thing repeatedly since only the nearest of the crowd could hear in the clamor. As some melted back like ice in a torrent, other women as quickly took their places. Starkad was unexpectedly gentle himself. He said over and over, "Unless your man was a Saxon, he'll be back in a few days. It was no more trouble than a pig killing, it was."

The two spearmen at the door of the villa were a twenty-year-old with blond hair and one leg and an older veteran still weak with the dysentery that had kept him back from the campaign. The youth held out a flaring torch toward Mael to see him more clearly than the waning sun allowed. "Merlin," the Irishman demanded. "Where is he? We've got a message for him from the Leader."

The guards glanced quickly and oddly at one another.

"With the monster he raised," said Veleda from behind Mael. "With his dragon. Welcome back, my love."

Mael turned. Veleda was on horseback, as beautiful and free as the wash of her hair. The Irishman nudged his horse toward her. The press of clamoring women still separated them. Mael leaned sideways and Veleda caught his hands, bridging above the crowd for a moment. Starkad watched with an indecipherable expression.

Mael released Veleda. "Arthur sent us to tell Merlin to loose his beast," he said.

Veleda's laugh was real but harsh. "No," she said, "god sent you to destroy that dragon before it destroys the world and more. There is no limit to the number of universes, and there will be no limit to the size of the beast with all infinity to draw on . . . unless it can be killed while it is still able to die. If it is still able to die." Veleda stretched out her hands to touch Mael's, but she leaned away as he tried to gather her into his arms again. "Not now," she said. "It—it's at best very close to being too late. Did you bring the lance?"

Mael straightened and cursed sickly. "I could have," he said, remembering Arthur's dying horse and the spear still in its saddle scabbard. "I don't think."

Veleda smiled unexpectedly and kissed the Irishman's fingertips. "The time's here, and we're here, the three of us—and I brought the shield." She rang her knuckles on the cloaked circlet lashed again to her saddle. "Everything is the way god willed it to be. Let's see if he wills us to kill a dragon." Veleda clucked to her horse. It wheeled, picking its way through the clots of women still nearby. At the fringe of the crowd she turned north toward the cave.

Mael spurred after her. Starkad followed them with a wry grin and a curse as his mount jolted his bruises anew. "Well," Mael called to the witch-woman, "I'll learn never to take you for granted."

Veleda looked back at him. Her face was dim in the faded sunset. "I wouldn't ask you to do this if it weren't necessary," she said quietly. "If there were anyone else but you, you two . . . but there isn't, and things are as they are. If you're killed—and you may well be killed—I won't long survive you. And if you fail, the world itself won't long survive."

"Be the first wyvern we chopped, won't it, brother?" Starkad noted placidly. The Dane was polishing his axehead on his thigh as he rode. "Don't worry about us, Lady. This sort of thing may be all we're good for—this and women. But we're very good at this."

"And you'll not do anything stupid if something goes wrong," Mael added in real irritation. "I've enough on my conscience without adding your blood to it." After a moment, he frowned and added, "I thought that sound I was hearing was thunder. It isn't."

"No, that's the wyvern," Veleda agreed. "It roars as though the sound alone could bring down the walls that hold it. But the sound won't have to."

Blue-white fire stabbed suddenly from ahead of them. The hillside framing the jet was a dark blot against a sky which the thin moon lighted. The bellowing that followed the flame reminded Mael of the squeals of the tiny creature which he had slapped across the cave so recently—reminded him as the sun reminds a man of the stars its glare extinguishes. The vivid fire silhouetted the crabbed figure of Merlin near the clump of poplars. He was bent over a brazier like the one on which he had raised the creature. The jet of fire had come from the throat of the cave. The iron gate-posts still stood but they were red-hot. Only scraps remained of the panels themselves. Previous gouts of fire had burned away the oaken leaves entirely and had left only the hinges and reinforcing straps.

"The spell keeps it from crossing the doorway," Veleda explained. "It doesn't stop the flames, though. And it's only the cave mouth which the spell can block. No one, not even I, has the power to bind the whole hillside. Perhaps if I'd realized sooner what was happening . . . but . . ."

As Veleda's voice trailed off, flame exploded suddenly from the rock far above the doorway. That azure flare limned a narrow opening. It widened perceptibly as the limestone burned away. Mael frowned, trying to superimpose his memory of the cavern's interior against what he now saw of the cliff face. The stone at the top front of the cave must have been very thin, separating the hollow from the outside air by only a few inches. It was through that weakness that the fire had burst.

Briefly silent, the three newcomers dismounted beside Merlin. They lashed their horses to the poplars. Wheezing and the sound of crumbling stone were loud within the cave. Even through his thick sandals, Mael could feel the ground shaking.

"What in god's name have you done?" Veleda whispered to the wizard.

Merlin's face was as pale as the waning moon. "I don't know," he said simply. He still carried a willow wand, but his fingers had shredded it into little more than a belt of fabric. When Mael had last seen Merlin, the wizard had been as awesome to look upon as a Roman aqueduct: ancient and mighty and seemingly beyond human change. All that strength had wasted out of the man in a matter of weeks, leaving something pitiable in its disintegration. "Did Arthur learn?" the magician asked. "Did he send you to kill me?"

"What?" Mael said in surprise. "Kill you? He sent us to tell you to let the dragon loose against the Saxons."

Merlin burst into cackling laughter. "Let it loose? It's about to let itself loose, don't you see?"

Another jet of flame slashed through the hillside. A slab of rock collapsed with a roar which merged with that of the imprisoned beast. For an instant, the wyvern's head thrust through the opening high in the cliff. The shape of the head was the same as it had been when Mael first saw it. In size, however, it was now almost a yard from crest to muzzle. When the creature slipped back, its scales rasped more stone down into the cave with it. "It's grown large enough to tear its own exit," Veleda observed. "This one, this *magician*, depended on the rock to hold it forever if he couldn't control it himself. And it's grown too large already for anyone to control it through spells. Just as you told the fool it would."

Merlin shriveled away from the witch's scorn. He made no attempt to deny the statement.

Starkad shrugged. "We'll control it," he said. He loosed the strap of his buckler and gripped its double central handles with his left hand.

Veleda handed Mael the ancient target from Biargram's tomb. The Irishman took it by the rim. Its weight was a subconscious surprise. "Starkad—" he began uncertainly.

"Don't try to give me that thing," the Dane said. "You want to load yourself down like a mule, that's your business. This—" he gestured with his own buckler. It was also round, but it was less than a foot and a half in diameter—"is as much as I'm going to lug, dragon or no."

"Yeah, well . . ." Mael said. He turned away from Starkad as he slipped his arm through the loops of the target. He did not see Veleda's hand touch the Dane's and squeeze it briefly.

Veleda thrust a stick of brushwood into the brazier. After a moment, the end smouldered. It flared as she whipped it over her head. Answering flame cut deeper into the stone of the cliff thirty feet above the ground. The roar of the wyvern echoed again across the otherwise silent countryside.

Raising the torch so that it would not blaze in the eyes of the men following her, Veleda began to walk toward the bluff. Starkad and Mael were side by side.

The Dane carried his axe at high port across his shield face. The Irishman rested his lance on his right shoulder. None of the three bothered to look back at the huddled wizard.

Veleda skirted the original doorway at a safe distance. Though the wyvern was now concentrating on the vent in the roof of its cavern, it would have incinerated anyone passing the doorway within reach of its flame.

Mael used the butt of his lance to brace him as he began to climb the bluff which had been lifted out of the surrounding soil a million years before. Beside him, he heard Starkad twice slip clangingly onto his shield. The hole which the dragon had ripped stared darkly at the men as they approached it. It was an irregular oval, big enough now to drive an ox through. Its edges were thin where ground water had hollowed out the limestone to within inches of the outer surface of the hill. Mael edged forward the last sword's-length on his belly. The inner face of the cave showed deep gouges from the monster's claws. Rock near the opening had been burned to quicklime by the flame. The white caustic crumbled as Mael's shield brushed it.

Within the cave, the waiting dragon cocked an eye which reflected enough moonlight to glitter. Veleda cried a warning, but Mael was already twisting his head back. A gout of fire leaped thirty feet and tore the rock like a saw. A spatter of the flame heated Mael's whole shield by touching the rim.

The dragon's wings boomed as they flapped in the confined space. The beast heaved itself up on its left leg. Its right foot, triple claws extended, scrabbled a purchase on the lip of the opening. Its snout was braced against the upper edge of the hole. The dragon strained. The rock began to crack away. Mael had risen to his knees. The shifting surface flung him prone again. The wyvern flapped its wings and lunged upward, getting its head and neck completely through the opening. The tips of its left claws and the thunderous clapping of its vanes held the monster poised there although even its right leg must have been above the cave floor.

Starkad rose on the high side of the hill and chopped at the wyvern's neck. His axe glanced away from the dense, black scales in a shower of sparks. Mael shouted. The creature twisted more quickly than Starkad could recover. The jaws slammed. The Dane thrust out his shield more by reflex than by plan. It wedged at the hinge of the monster's jaw. The sturdy buckler was gripped top and bottom by the dragon's teeth, but it prevented them from closing on the man. Mael raised his lance as a furious snap of the beast's neck flung Starkad high in the air. When the Dane loosed the handles, he cartwheeled against the night sky. The buckler disintegrated in blue-white flame. The linden was blasted like thistle-down in the jet from the monster's throat while the iron boss scattered in a shower of burning gobbets.

Mael stabbed at the back of the wyvern's skull. His lance refused to bite. Sweat was washing the Irishman's body. His target glowed like the crown sheet of a boiler from its brush with the dragon's flame. The thicknesses of ox-hide backing the metal were barely enough insulation to permit him to carry the shield.

The wyvern strained upward again. The whole weakened cliff-face began to crumble down into the cavity. The ground dropped out from under Mael. He tried to stay upright, but the stone beneath him twisted and threw him on his back. Rocks as large as the Irishman's torso fell with him. Only his armor kept them from pounding him to death. Dust rose in a gray pall. It hid the walls of the trench which had been formed when the front of the cave collapsed. The dust hid also the jumble of rock that blurred and buried Merlin's blocking spell. The symbols were useless anyway, now that the cave gaped fully open to the sky.

Above everything, the dragon raised its mighty head and bellowed its victory to the moon.

The beast slammed the air with gem-scaled pinions which roiled the dust into ghost shapes.

Falling limestone had briefly bound the wyvern's left foot. The wingbeats now tore the claws free. Mael, stunned by the fall, lay on the rubble which covered what had been the cave entrance. Momentarily, the creature roaring above him was only a nightmare. Then the Irishman was alert once more, realizing that the dragon was growing as he watched it. In his mind echoed Veleda's voice saying, "There is no limit. . . ."

Mael fought upright, coughing from the dust. Splinters had cut his cheek and right thigh. His torn ear was draining down the side of his jaw again. The Irishman had not let go of his lance, and his shield was strapped firmly to his left arm. He gauged the wyvern's distance. With all his strength, and with both hands guiding the shaft, Mael drove the lance up against the creature's outthrust keel bone.

Sparks danced like fairy lights as the flint-hard scales shaved curls from the steel. The beast bent toward Mael and opened its jaws. Fire spurted. The air itself grunted as it flash-heated, making the powdered stone whiff away from the arm-thick jet of flame. The fire struck the center of the ancient shield, the silver-gleaming boss that was the world in every detail. The impact of the flame was like that of a battering ram. The metal glowed white and the hide backing stank like a slaughter-house as it charred. The facing did not melt. Though the iron core of the shield soaked up much of the blast, Mael burned as though he had strapped a lighted stove onto his arm.

Screaming with pain, the Irishman hurled his lance at the wyvern's sparkling eye. The weapon's point glanced off a bony scute and flickered into the night. Perhaps the silvered blade of Achil would have bitten, have penetrated, but honest steel was useless. The beast roared and rocked forward, reaching out with its right leg. The three toes were folded under for walking. As the foot glided toward Mael through the dust, its claws flared out like black horn scythes. Their thrust drove Mael backward. He fell into the crevice between two slabs of rock. The claws curled over the rim of his shield. Their needle points pricked the Irishman through his mail. The wyvern rolled its weight forward, crushing the unyielding circuit of the shield down on Mael and the tumbled stone beneath him. The metal sizzled where it touched the bare flesh of his thighs and the base of his throat. Mael could not fill his lungs to scream. Rocks were being driven through his back.

The wyvern cocked one eye down at the Irishman like a grackle studying a worm. The beast leaned forward, bending from the hip joint, and its jaws began to gape. One of its eyeteeth had cracked jaggedly; the other was a gleaming spearhead touched by the moon's cool light. Mael's right arm was caught under his shield. He had half-drawn the Spanish sword when the beast's weight crushed him against the rocks. Now he dragged the weapon an inch further from its sheath, feeling his skin tear and slip in his blood. The dragon's mouth stank like a furnace stoked with old bones. Mael whined curses into it. The blast of fire from the jaws would leave his helmet a pool of incandescent slag amid the ash of his head and shoulders.

Starkad leaped down from the hillside onto the dragon's withers. His beard and hair were tangled like a gorgon's locks. The shock of the Dane's mass was staggering, even to a monster fifteen yards long. The wyvern took three steps forward, all the weight of its first stride bearing on Mael's shield. The beast passed over the Irishman like the shadow of death. It was trying to twist its serpentine neck to the left to tear at the man on its back.

Starkad had locked his heels around the wyvern's throat, just ahead of the wings. The vanes crashed against the Dane, hiding him momentarily. When they lowered, Mael saw his friend still astride the monster.

Mael rolled to all fours "I'm coming, " he wheezed. His flesh had swollen cuttingly to the straps of the target. The circuit of burning metal tried to anchor him to the rubble, but he lurched upward and the shield came with him. Before him, earth spewed high as the wyvern pivoted. It was trying to turn more sharply than its bones allowed.

Starkad lifted his axe high over his head, peen forward. For a moment he was a bellowing statue against the night sky. Mael, staggering forward with his spatha out, raised his own banshee war cry, but the darkness drowned in the dragon's roars.

There was no sound and no movement. Starkad poised and Mael hung in the midst of his own attack.

The Irishman could see Veleda in the corner of his eye. Her arms were outstretched and her lips pursed in the middle of a chant. The woman's slim body was glowing violet. The cliff face brightened with the reflection.

Mael was cold. The ghastly color enveloped him and became a force created deep within his being. It was an amalgam of motion and fury and soul, all focused on Starkad's axe. Mael knew for an instant that there was something more dehumanizing than merely being the object of inhuman forces. Motionless himself, the Irishman strained toward the motionless tableau of dragon and axeman. The great axe began to shimmer violet.

The Dane brought his weapon down in an arc so perfect that it seemed the dragon was raising its skull to meet the blow. The stroke was swift enough that a line of steel hung in the air. Iron struck bone and rang and rebounded as it had when the axe head smashed the stone in Lancelot's hands. The dragon missed a half step, shaking its head. The eerie light had vanished. Starkad raised his humming weapon again, but the first blow had numbed his whole side. The creature's wings batted the Dane. His feet were no longer locked beneath its throat. Mael saw Starkad flung away, losing even his grip on his axe. Man and weapon struck the ground twenty feet apart.

The Irishman's legs drove him forward. The wyvern pivoted. Its head was twisting toward Starkad. The jaws were open. Mael howled and cut with his spatha at the beast's tail, the only portion of the dragon he could reach. The blade clanged and skittered away harmlessly. Mael raised his sword again, gripping the hilt with both hands. Through the rising arc of the blade, he saw the wyvern's head. The axe blow had caved it in. As the creature swung, its brains dripped from the open wound.

The beast turned further. Its jaws slammed shut and tore a huge gobbet out of its own left flank. The dragon screamed. It threw its head back, then forward and down with a gout of fire. The soil blew apart as moisture exploded into steam. Then the monster found its own right foot with the flame and sent itself sprawling like a broken-backed snake.

Starkad was crawling. Mael shouted to him. The Dane was not attempting to escape but rather to reach his axe. Beside Mael the wyvern began hammering the ground with its head and tail. The rocky soil shook in syncopated thunder. The dragon licked its side with another tongue of flame. One wing fell away. Scales, thrown high by the gases of their own destruction, spun back to the ground like dead leaves.

Mael shambled toward the Dane, letting his sword fall on the ground unnoticed. The shield was a fiery deformity which warped his body with its weight. He was past noticing even that. When it suddenly slipped off, the Irishman's back still bent to its imaginary burden.

Starkad looked up. With an effort that made his jaw sag open, the Dane rose to his feet. Some time during the night the left side of his beard had been scorched away. Blisters pocked his skin. He embraced Mael, each man cursing and praying in his own language.

Veleda stood beside them. Together, the knotted killers' arms reached out and drew her close. The blonde woman's touch was cool and clean in a way that nothing they could remember had ever been.

Mael croaked, "You said you couldn't kill it."

"Alone, I couldn't have," Veleda replied. She

nuzzled the bloody armor on the Irishman's chest. "I wasn't alone."

Starkad looked past her to the dragon. It was no longer thrashing. Scales were already sloughing away from the huge body. "What's happening to it?" the big man asked.

Veleda followed his eyes. "It grew on this earth a thousand times faster than was natural," she said. "Now that its reality is death, it decays the same way it grew. There won't be anything left by morning—except perhaps as much dust as a large salamander's skull would leave."

"We'd better get away now," Mael said. "Before Arthur learns what happened to his pet. Do you think you can ride as far as the nearest fishing village, friend?"

"Oh, I can do anything," Starkad grumbled. "Haven't I proved that already? But I don't see what you're worried about. We had to kill the thing, even Arthur's tame wizard—" the axe gestured toward where Merlin had been standing, but there was no one there now— "could tell hi—Oh. Yeah. Could tell him. But sure as Hel won't, not and admit how bad he'd fouled up. Hel and Loki, another damned ride."

"Well, maybe we can find a wagon at one of those farms," Mael said as they stumbled toward their mounts. "I've still got that warrant to commandeer anything in the kingdom. We can get a boat and sail for Ireland—"

"Spain, I remember the women."

"Well, wherever . . . ."

"Wherever god wills," said Veleda. She threw her arms about the waists of both men and began to laugh.

Epilogue

The war standard snapped in the breeze.

The walls of Arthur's tent had been rolled up, leaving its roof as an awning against the bright sunlight. Even after a week, smoke from the Saxon village tinged the air, though by now it was more an odor than a haze. Merlin lay in the dust between Gawain and the seated king. The lithe Companion toed the wizard, saying, "I brought this one back, but the others were gone. If there was ever a dragon, I couldn't find a sign of it. I'd have chased after the Irishman, but I figured the boat he and his friends stole would carry him farther than I wanted to go."

"So," Arthur said quietly. He stroked the arms of his high-backed throne. "Where is the dragon, wizard?"

Merlin raised his haggard face. "Gone. Dead. Finished."

"So," Arthur repeated.

He stood up, his scabbard knocking against the oak of the chair. The surrounding guards and courtiers stiffened. "But I haven't failed," the king said. His eyes were on nothing but the eastern horizon. "The Saxons, the world. They'll know me, *know me!*"

Men looked at their hands or at the ground or even, in horrified fascination, at their Leader. Only Merlin seemed oblivious of the king. The wizard was scratching at the dust with a fragment of willow twig.

"Do you hear me?" Arthur shouted to the world. "*I will not die!*"

Beneath the king, Merlin gestured and an image shimmered between his fingers. It was a silver chalice, jeweled about the rim. For a moment the sunlight haloed it.

Then the grail tumbled and fell back into the dust from which it had sprung.

operation is performed to save the uterus (and avoid an unnecessary hysterectomy).

It is very important for every woman to understand that all
visible fibroids can be removed from the uterus. Thereafter, a
doctor will perform a plastic reconstruction of the uterus so it
will heal and be like a completely normal uterus. Usually, a
woman experiences normal menstruation after this reconstruction, and often maintains the ability to bear children.

When Should Fibroid Tumors Be Taken Out?

Fibroid tumors are very complex and unpredictable. Accordingly, each case has to be determined on its own merits. There
are, though, some general guidelines which may help.

If the tumors are in the wall of the uterus, you will not need
to have them removed unless they are extremely painful, cause
infertility, or, as mentioned before, grow very rapidly.

When the fibroids are on the outside of the uterus, they can
twist, causing severe pain. They should immediately be removed if this happens. Fibroids can also degenerate, meaning
that if the blood supply to them decreases, they will begin to rot
and cause severe pain. In this instance, the fibroids should also
be removed.

During pregnancy, when the uterus starts to enlarge, the
blood supply to the fibroids often increases. This causes the
fibroids to grow. If these fibroids are subserous, they will generally be harmless. Many women deliver babies even though
they have enormous fibroids on the outsides of their uteri. At
other times, fibroids located on the lower part of the uterus can
occasionally grow to such an extent that they obstruct the birth
canal. Natural delivery would then be impossible and a Caesarean section would have to be performed.

Sometimes the fibroids on the outside of the uterus cause a
disturbance in the uterine wall which might cause an early or
premature delivery. For this reason, women with fibroids that
seem to be growing during their pregnancies should take it easy
during those pregnancies. Heavy lifting and energetic intercourse should be avoided in the later stages of pregnancy.

If a woman has experienced several miscarriages due to
fibroid tumors, she should have an operation to remove them.
She should, though, insist that her uterus be preserved and a
plastic reconstruction done.

When Is a Hysterectomy Indicated?

According to the American College of Obstetricians and
Gynecologists, a physician has the right to perform a hysterec-

tomy, the surgical removal of the uterus and cervix, when the uterus grows beyond the size of a twelve-week (or three-month) pregnancy from a fibroid tumor.

Unfortunately, many physicians abandon this rule. These doctors tell the patient her uterus has reached the twelve-week point of growth when, in fact, it hasn't.

Other doctors may perform an inadequate examination, and this results in your getting a less than accurate description of a fibroid condition. Sometimes physicians tend to exaggerate the seriousness of the condition, often leading to unnecessary surgery.

Some doctors will observe the growth of fibroid tumors for a long time, then suddenly tell the patient she needs a hysterectomy. Not only is this an example of bad medicine, the sudden change in the doctor's attitude could frighten any woman.

Without a doubt, there are too many hysterectomies performed without the proper indications. Hospitals are aware of this and try their best to control the situation. Each hospital has a committee that examines all tissue removed during surgery. This is done in an attempt to prevent unnecessary operations.

Malignant Fibroid Tumors

For the layperson, a malignant fibroid tumor is always associated with cancer; the medical profession will refer to this malignancy as *myosarcoma* (or *leiomyosarcoma*) of the uterus.

A malignancy goes through various stages. Like everything else, it is better to catch a malignancy in an earlier rather than a later stage. If a fibroid tumor is removed in an early stage of malignancy, it might not have spread. In such an instance, you might be completely cured. Because of this, it is important to remove malignant tumors as soon as they are diagnosed.

The incidence of sarcomatous changes in fibroid tumors is less than 0.5 percent, so when discussing malignancies, women should not get the idea that they are inevitable or common. Low-grade malignancies can even be removed by myomectomy alone. On the other hand, a more definitive treatment consists of a total hysterectomy and bilateral *salpingo-oophorectomy* (the removal of the entire reproductive system—the uterus, fallopian tubes, and ovaries). This is an extremely rare operation, and the likelihood of it happening to you is so slight that you shouldn't be needlessly concerned about it.

How Can You Protect Yourself?

In cases where you do not fully understand your doctor's explanation about why you need a hysterectomy, or in cases where a doctor's sudden change in attitude scares you, you should get a second, or even a third, opinion.

Many patients who are told by doctors that they need a hysterectomy go to other doctors for a second opinion and find that they do not, after all, need an operation.

It is important to realize that it is *your* uterus. You probably should not trust any doctor who does not make it exactly clear why you need the operation, or a doctor who seems to be *pushing* you into an operation without sufficient cause.

Of course, it is vital to your own protection that you understand the nature of fibroid tumors. If you do, it will be very difficult for a crooked or incompetent physician to talk you into an unnecessary hysterectomy. If you have any doubts whatsoever, get a second opinion.

There are good reasons for this.

The chance of malignancy in a fibroid tumor is extremely small. Usually a fibroid causes no harm, even if it has reached the size of a three-month pregnancy, the size at which your doctor can legally operate.

Also, if you are in your late forties, as you get closer to menopause, your hormone level will decrease. There will, therefore, be less stimulus of female hormones to the fibroids. At this point, the fibroids usually decrease in size and often disappear. Certainly, if this is the case with you, a hysterectomy would be unnecessary unless there were severe symptoms, even if the tumor was, again, of the three-month-pregnancy size. Of course, if the tumor does not shrink by itself after menopause, it might be advisable to have an operation.

At times, a fibroid tumor is mistaken for an ovarian tumor. The two often grow in the same region, and many excellent physicians have trouble distinguishing between them. If there is even the slightest chance that you have an ovarian tumor, an operation (maybe just a laparoscopy) must be performed, at the very least for diagnostic reasons. An ovarian tumor is much more serious than a fibroid tumor. The possibility of cancer is higher and it should be considered a dangerous condition. Still, if you have doubts, you should seek a second opinion before submitting to an operation.

Hysterectomy versus Myomectomy

If you are in your mid-thirties and have fibroid tumors which start to grow rapidly, your doctor might be right when recommending a hysterectomy. Still, if you have no problem with fertility and no heavy bleeding or abdominal pain, a hysterectomy might be unnecessary. Under those circumstances, a

myomectomy might be indicated, and you should ask your doctor to take out the fibroid tumors but to leave your uterus
intact. If your doctor refuses to do this, you should definitely
get a second opinion.

It must be remembered that in the majority of cases, if the
uterus is no more than four months' pregnancy in size and
there are no symptoms, a myomectomy will accomplish the
proper aims. You will then be left with a normally functioning
uterus and, as long as the fallopian tubes are not damaged and
you still have normal ovulation, you should be able to bear
children.

However, if you have a uterus that is more than three months
pregnancy in size, and you have decided not to have any more
children, you might *want* a hysterectomy. With a hysterectomy,
you will be sterile, but you will still have normal hormone production as long as the ovaries are not removed.

If the uterus is extremely large, say four or five months'
pregnancy in size, the uterus probably should be removed, because it might otherwise cause too much pressure and heaviness
on the adjacent internal organs. For instance, a uterus of this
size could push the bladder, which would either make urination
difficult or too frequent.

Unless you want a hysterectomy, and many women do, you
should always fight to keep your uterus. It is, after all, *your* body
and no one can force you to have any operation that you don't
want. A myomectomy often accomplishes the exact aim of a
hysterectomy, but without the result of permanent sterility.

Of course, if symptoms of heavy bleeding and pain are excessive, a hysterectomy is probably in order. But when faced with
an operation of this importance, especially if you don't want it,
you should *always* get a second opinion. Unfortunately, there
are always a few incompetent physicians in the medical profession, and you should watch out for them. Getting a second
opinion protects both you and your doctor, so no good doctor
will object.

Warning!

In the past few years, there has been much publicity about
unnecessary hysterectomies. Unfortunately, too much of this
publicity is true. There are irresponsible, incompetent, and
greedy people in every profession, and medicine is no exception.

It is important for you to understand that doctors make a
great deal of money through hysterectomies. Some unscrupu-

lous physicians could give patients high-estrogen birth-control pills just to speed the growth of fibroids.

Other doctors follow the progress of the fibroids while preparing you for a hysterectomy. Sometimes they wait as long as three or four years; by that time they have your trust. Then the day comes to scare you and they announce that the tumors have started to grow rapidly and you should have a hysterectomy, either immediately or in the near future.

At that point, you should get a second opinion. Remember, if the second doctor confirms the diagnosis of the first, it is a compliment to your original doctor.

It is vital that you realize that only *you* can decide if you should have a hysterectomy. Not that you should be your own doctor, but you should understand your body completely and have thorough biannual examinations. If your doctor does not make your condition clear to you, you should ask him to draw a sketch to further clarify the problem. Bring your husband or boyfriend, or even a close woman friend, and get a thorough explanation.

Once you have established the reliability of your doctor, and once you completely understand your condition, then you can make an intelligent decision with a clear conscience.

Sex and Hysterectomies

There are some very damaging myths concerning sexual enjoyment after hysterectomies. Some cultures, mostly black and Hispanic, believe a woman loses her sexual value and allure once this operation has been performed. This is a mostly male-dominated belief, probably springing from some misguided sense of *machismo*, and is sheer nonsense. This sort of stupid judgment has even caused many intelligent women to hide from their sex partners the fact that they have had hysterectomies.

Without a doubt, the removal of the uterus has little to do with sexual pleasure for either the woman or the man. During intercourse, the penis enters the vagina, not the uterus. The uterus is connected to the vagina by the cervix, and no penis can penetrate the cervix and enter the uterus. It stands to reason, then, that removal of your uterus will not interfere *in any way*, except perhaps psychologically, with your sex life.

PROLAPSE OF THE UTERUS

Prolapse of the uterus is a condition in which the muscles and ligaments holding the uterus weaken, causing the uterus to sag

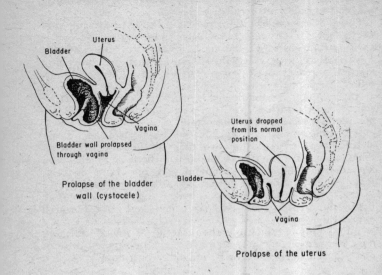

Bladder

Uterus

Vagina

Bladder wall prolapsed
through vagina

Prolapse of the bladder
wall (cystocele)

Uterus dropped
from its normal
position

Bladder

Vagina

Prolapse of the uterus

Fig. 13–4: Different types of uterine prolapse. Left, an example of a *cystocele,* where the bladder wall has prolapsed out through the vagina. A case like this can usually only be treated by surgery. Right, an example of a prolapsed uterus in which the uterus has dropped from its normal position and the cervix is almost at the level of the vulva. This almost eliminates the vagina, and the uterus, furthermore, pulls on both the bladder and the bowel. This can often be treated by a pessary.

into the vagina. This, in turn, shortens the vagina and sometimes pulls the bladder backward. Prolapse of the uterus is generally found in older women. It is more prevalent in women who have borne children, yet the condition is seen in women who have never been pregnant.

Prolapse of the uterus was seen much more often in the past, when women had several children and were often in labor for days. This was particularly true if the childbirth was difficult and a traumatic delivery of a very large child caused extensive tearing of the vagina and uterus. This condition is less frequent today, largely because many women limit their families to one to two children. Deliveries today are carried out under much supervision and Caesarean section is done if the delivery is judged too traumatic.

Prolapse of the uterus is more frequent in white women, particularly white women of East European background. It is rarely seen in black women, even if they have had several children.

In severe cases, a uterus can drop so far that it feels like something is falling out. This is caused by sagging of the uterus and is associated with prolapse of the bladder (cystocele). This condition causes problems of urinary control and frequency, and usually requires corrective surgery.

The bowel can also herniate (or sag) into the vagina. This is called a rectocele. The bowel may prolapse so far as to even be visible through the vagina. This, too, requires surgery.

Diagnosis of Prolapse

If a woman feels as if something is falling out of her vagina when she walks, urinates, defecates, or lifts a heavy object, she should consult a gynecologist immediately.

Although a prolapse is almost always a simple sagging of tired muscles and ligaments, cancer is sometimes associated with this syndrome. A physician should take X-rays to ensure that the kidneys, bladder, and rectum are intact. A cystoscopy should be performed to double-check the bladder for similar symptoms. Several other tests may be necessary to narrow down the diagnosis.

Treatment of Prolapse

A uterine prolapse is often treated with a pessary—a ring inserted into the vagina which keeps the uterus in the anatomically correct position. The difficulty with a pessary is that it needs to be removed for cleaning at least once a week. Furthermore, it causes a persistent vaginal irritation and discharge and it often erodes through the vaginal mucosa and causes an ulcer. Many women have no difficulty and are very happy with a pessary; however, others complain that it interferes with sexual intercourse.

If surgery is necessary, a hysterectomy is often performed through the vagina, and the muscles and ligaments surrounding the bladder are tightened. If a rectocele is present, it will be pushed back into position, and the hernia repaired.

Hysterectomy is not absolutely necessary in many cases, but since prolapse usually occurs in older women, removal of the

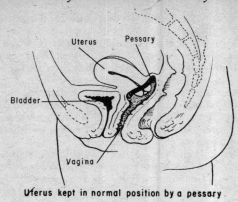

Uterus kept in normal position by a pessary

Fig. 13–5: A corrected uterine prolapse. The uterus has been moved back into its normal anatomical position and is held in place by a pessary.

uterus should not affect the woman in any way. This surgery is rather difficult and should be done only by gynecologists well trained in vaginal operations. If the surgery is not done perfectly, the bladder might prolapse again, or the surgery could leave symptoms such as inability to control urination. Difficulty of intercourse can also occur if the surgeon makes the vagina too tight.

During the operation, the gynecologist should pass a catheter from the abdomen to the bladder so the urine can drain into a bag, giving the vagina a chance for proper healing. Some surgeons place a catheter into the bladder via the urethra; this is no longer recommended since it causes discomfort and can result in infection. It is important to go only to the best hospital for this procedure, a hospital with competent anesthesiologists; since this procedure is usually performed on older women, anesthesia itself can cause serious problems. The hospital stay for this type of operation will usually be between six and ten days.

Posterior Repair of a "Too Large" Vagina —Increased Sex Life

The same operation that is usually performed for uterine prolapse can be done for women who do not have a complete prolapse but feel that childbirth and age have caused relaxation of the muscles which keep the vagina tight. These women feel their vaginas are getting too loose, and usually they lose some sexual pleasure.

Posterior repair of the vagina is performed by removing a portion of the vaginal mucosa and tightening the muscles. This can be done with or without hysterectomy. Most women want the vagina tightened, but want to keep their uterus because they feel it is important for sexual functioning. However, sexual pleasure can be as great after hysterectomy as before—even higher, in some instances. The uterus is not essential to achieving orgasm.

Still, a woman should not have an unnecessary hysterectomy. If a woman does have a hysterectomy, she should *insist* on keeping her ovaries under the age of fifty, if possible.

A posterior repair is recommended if a woman feels her vagina is becoming too large and is an increasing problem during sex. Her mate may also be getting older and intercourse may be becoming less frequent, resulting in a decrease in the size of the partner's penis. A posterior repair of the vagina tightens the vagina and sometimes relieves this problem by creating more friction during intercourse. Since it is done through the vagina, there are no scars on the abdomen, and the operation has often increased sexual pleasure.

ENDOMETRIOSIS

Normally, the *endometrium,* or uterine lining, becomes thick and spongy during ovulation to accommodate a fertilized egg. If conception does not occur, the excess endometrium is expelled during menstruation.

Endometriosis is a condition in which some of this endometrial buildup backs up through the fallopian tubes and into the pelvic cavity. Endometrial tissue is then mostly found on the ovaries, in back of the uterus, or on the bowel, but it has been known to spread throughout the body to the eyes, the lungs, and even the brain.

Although the exact mechanism for its spread is unknown, one of the most accepted theories was developed by Dr. Sampson in 1921. As the endometrial tissue backs into the pelvic cavity, he postulated, it implants and then reacts to hormonal changes just as it would in the uterus. Thus the tissue grows every month, but it is not expelled during menstruation. This growth causes problems as it spreads, creating adhesions (which can cause infertility) and pelvic pain. It might also spread through the body in the same manner as tumors.

Women who develop endometriosis are often tense, well-educated and prone to stress and menstrual cramps. Because of this profile, it is thought that endometriosis is caused by tension. Tension tightens the cervix to the extent that menstrual blood cannot get through. This, in itself, would force some of the menstrual wastes back into the fallopian tubes and into the abdomen.

Women with prior histories of *hysterotomy* (a procedure like a Caesarean section performed for late abortion, through an abdominal incision) often develop endometriosis in the abdominal scar.

The first symptom of endometriosis is increased pelvic pain prior to menstruation. This is often misdiagnosed as tilted uterus, polycystic ovaries, or pelvic infection, but a careful examination should reveal an irregular mass behind the uterus which characterizes the disease. This mass becomes more tender when progesterone and estrogen levels rise prior to menstruation. It can also create an adhesion between the uterus and the bowel, causing painful bowel movements. *Peristalsis* (waves of involuntary contractions of the bowel) can also cause pain in this condition. Similar adhesions between the ovaries and fallopian tubes can cause infertility.

It is thought that seven to eight million women in the United States suffer from this condition, but only ten to fifteen percent of the cases are diagnosed.

Treatment of Endometriosis

One of the best cures for endometriosis is, simply, childbearing. This halts ovulation for nine months, during which the endometriosis is not stimulated. Subsequently, delivery opens the cervix, causing less painful and more efficient menstruation.

Often surgery is necessary to determine whether the lump behind the uterus is, indeed, endometriosis, and not cancer. During surgery, the physician will remove most of the tissue, but because of the considerable spread of this condition, he cannot remove it all. Relapse is, therefore, common. Because of this, many women will have to undergo repeated surgery. For this condition, surgery is as much a diagnostic tool as it is a treatment.

Birth-control pills have been used effectively against endometriosis, since they, too, prevent ovulation. Some doctors have found that long-acting progesterone injections alleviate the symptoms, but the most promising drug treatment for endometriosis is Danazol. Danazol is a relatively new drug released by the Food and Drug Administration in July, 1976. It is closely related to the male hormone testosterone and inhibits the release of LH and FSH, therefore preventing ovulation. Danazol also prevents cyclic variation in estrogen and progesterone levels, so no stimulation of the endometrium or the endometriotic tissue can occur. The body subsequently absorbs the inactivated endometriotic tissue as if it were dead tissue. Some women who have had fertility problems stemming from endometriosis have been able to conceive after Danazol treatment. This drug seems to be a real breakthrough for treatment of endometriosis, and women should be placed on Danazol as soon as the diagnosis is made to prevent the spread of this condition. Women should also take Danazol after surgery to make certain that the tissue that was not removed during surgery is completely eroded. The suggested treatment is 400 to 800 milligrams of Danazol daily for at least six months, depending on the extent of the disease.

Danazol acts as a contraceptive during the treatment and has also been found effective in the treatment of chronic cystic mastitis, a very painful condition in which the breasts become cystic and painful. Women suffering from this condition can benefit from a Danazol treatment of 200 to 400 milligrams daily. This treatment also results in amenorrhea, becoming a safe and effective means of contraception.

Unfortunately, Danazol is rather expensive, but it is well worth the expense. Perhaps a discount drugstore can offer a bargain.

ADENOMYOSIS

Adenomyosis is a condition in which the endometrium, or the uterine lining, invades the myometrium, the uterine muscle fibers, causing an enlarged uterus and severe pain prior to menstruation. Abnormal uterine bleeding usually occurs. Most cases occur in women in their forties, but adenomyosis has been seen in fourteen-year-old girls. Most women, though, develop adenomyosis after childbearing.

There is some controversy over treatment of adenomyosis. It is sometimes treated with hormones, but hormone treatments have not proven successful all the time. Many physicians advocate hysterectomy. This seems to be the safest solution unless a woman is approaching menopause. After the change of life, the symptoms of adenomyosis generally disappear on their own.

chapter 14

OVARIAN ABNORMALITIES

Ovarian abnormalities are cysts or tumors of the ovaries. These abnormalities can be divided into benign, or noncancerous, and malignant, or cancerous. The words *cyst* and *tumor* are used synonymously by most physicians. A cyst means a fluid-filled enlargement and a tumor just means a growth or an enlargement. The word tumor, therefore, does not necessarily mean that the growth is malignant. If a physician finds an enlargement or a cyst on an ovary during a pelvic examination, there is no way he can determine immediately if the finding is malignant or benign.

The ovaries are very delicate and important organs. They store the potential eggs (oogonia) throughout a woman's life, and develop one each month into a mature egg or ovum. The ovaries also produce hormones such as estrogen and progesterone, which develop and maintain a woman's secondary sexual characteristics. These hormones prepare the uterus for pregnancy and regulate the menstrual cycle. The ovaries are very active organs undergoing constant internal changes. All these functions interrelate like biochemical clockwork, and a delicate balance is necessary for a woman's body to work correctly. If this mechanism is disturbed or fails to work correctly one month, ovulation might not occur and a cyst could develop.

The most common ovarian abnormalities are cysts. These fluid-filled growths that often enlarge the ovaries can be either benign or malignant. Most malignant ovarian cysts occur after menopause, though they may begin growing during the reproductive years. A cyst that does not disappear spontaneously may be malignant and should be removed surgically.

BENIGN OVARIAN CYSTS

By far the most frequent ovarian cysts are nonmalignant, particularly if they develop before menopause. The most common of these are called *functional cysts*, because they develop from tissue that functions, that actively changes every month with ovulation. These cysts are often larger than the ovary itself, though rarely more than three inches in diameter. If they are any larger, they are highly suspect in terms of malignancy and should be evaluated. Functional cysts can be divided into three types: *follicular cysts*, *corpus luteum* (or *lutein*) *cysts*, and *Stein-Leventhal cysts* (or *polycystic ovarian cysts*).

Follicular Cysts

Every woman is born with follicles, one of which develops into a Graafian follicle every month, producing an egg. This process depends on a fine chain of hormonal reactions. If, for some reason, there is a weak or missing link in this chain, the graafian follicle, instead of producing an egg, becomes a follicular cyst. Sometimes these cysts grow to the size of lemons.

Symptoms of follicular cysts are mild. Women may experience a feeling of fullness or heaviness, and there may be a dull ache in the side, but these symptoms subside as the cyst disappears. Usually the fluid is reabsorbed by the ovarian tissue, and after a month or two, the cyst shrinks away.

Follicular cysts can rupture spontaneously, causing internal or abdominal bleeding. There can even be cramps causing such severe pain that hospitalization is required. However, this type of bleeding generally stops by itself, and the lesion heals. Follicular cysts can also be ruptured during rough intercourse or a blow to the abdomen. These cysts have very thin walls, so care must be taken not to bump into anything that may break the cyst. Intercourse should be very gentle or avoided.

If the cyst does not disappear spontaneously within a few months, your physician may prescribe birth-control pills to depress the hormone level that may be stimulating the cyst. If this doesn't work, an exploratory laparotomy should be conducted and the cyst excised and examined for signs of malignancy.

Corpus Luteum Cysts

After the Graafian follicle ruptures to release a mature egg, a yellow body, or *corpus luteum*, forms within the ovary and begins to secrete progesterone. If there is bleeding into this corpus luteum, a cyst may form, filled by the blood. If the fluid is made up predominantly of blood, it is called a *corpus luteum hematoma*. The blood elements are usually reabsorbed gradually and replaced by a clear fluid. The cyst is then called a *corpus luteum cyst*. These cysts are rarely larger than three inches in diameter.

Because this type of cyst develops in the corpus luteum, which exists only after ovulation, corpus luteum cysts occur only in women during the reproductive years.

The symptoms are usually minor: a slight delay in menstruation, persistent or scant bleeding. Pain in one side can occur, giving symptoms resembling those of a tubal pregnancy. Immediate surgery is rarely necessary. If your physician is not secure in his diagnosis, it can be confirmed by a laparoscopy, a "Band-Aid" operation where a periscope device is inserted through the navel to inspect the ovaries, the uterus, and the fallopian tubes.

As with a follicular cyst, corpus luteum cysts can rupture easily, so intercourse must be gentle and heavy lifting avoided. If one ruptures, severe internal hermorrhaging may make surgery necessary. If not, the cyst usually disappears in a few months.

Stein-Leventhal Cysts

In 1928, Dr. Irving Stein described a list of characteristics he found in a certain group of patients who had come to him with infertility problems. These women had most or all of the same symptoms: irregular menstrual bleeding *(oligomenorrhea)*, often with months between periods; abnormal hair growth *(hirsutism)* on the face, arms, and legs; enlarged clitoris; and obesity. Years later, Dr. Leventhal conducted a hormone analysis on this type of patient and identified such patients as a special group. He subsequently called the syndrome *Stein-Leventhal disease*, or *polycystic ovarian syndrome*. This condition is characterized by enlarged ovaries caused by small cysts. The surface of the ovaries becomes hard and glistening white, probably too hard for the egg to break through, causing a new cyst to develop every month. If ovulation does not occur, infertility results.

No reason is known for the development of Stein-Leventhal cysts, but the syndrome is thought to be genetic. Since the ovaries are enlarged, they produce more of the male hormone testosterone, which leads to hirsutism. Not only will there be abnormal hair growth on the face and limbs, but the pubic hairline will tend to extend triangularly toward the navel.

The ovaries will also produce more estrogen, increasing the chances of developing cancer of the endometrium (uterine lining) or breast cancer. Cancer of the endometrium is always signaled by abnormal bleeding, and if it is caught early, it can almost always be cured. Breast cancer treatment is significantly easier and less drastic if the cancer is found early, so monthly self-examinations are extremely important for women with Stein-Leventhal disease. When a woman with this disease reaches her mid-forties, she should have a mammogram (breast X-ray) every year or two.

Treatment of Stein-Leventhal Syndrome

Treatment of polycystic ovaries varies with the symptoms. Some women require no treatment. In fact, the higher hormone levels often give women more energy and can even increase libido.

If the woman misses her period, she may think she is pregnant. If she is not, her physician can usually induce menstruation by prescribing progesterone tablets or an injection to slough off the uterine lining and cause bleeding. However, this sometimes causes heavy bleeding with cramps and clots because the lining has built up excessively. If this happens, a D&C might be necessary.

Infertility due to Stein-Leventhal disease occurs because the woman doesn't know when she ovulates, or if she ovulates at all. Fertility drugs such as Clomid may induce ovulation. If they do not work, a wedge resection of the ovaries might be required. This is an operation in which a portion of each ovary is removed to reduce the enlarged organs to normal size. This is done during an exploratory laparotomy. No one knows exactly why this operation works, but many women are able to conceive after undergoing it.

This operation reduces the testosterone level, at least temporarily, which helps reduce hirsutism, but the ovaries may enlarge again. If the patient takes daily estrogen, or high-estrogen-containing birth-control pills, it also reduces the testosterone level, again decreasing abnormal hair growth. However, the hair already grown does not disappear; electrolysis is, therefore, necessary to remove the hair. This can be done on the face, while the hair on the legs and arms can be shaved or removed by cosmetic hair remover. Women with too much hair on the abdomen should shave. Many women do this because they do not want the hair to show outside a bathing suit.

MALIGNANT OVARIAN CYSTS

If an ovarian cyst does not disappear after three months, you should consult a gynecologist, especially if it is larger than three inches in diameter. It should be examined carefully by X-rays and sonography. If it seems suspicious, an exploratory laparotomy might be required to remove the cyst. The cyst should then be sent for pathological analysis in a laboratory to determine whether it is malignant.

There are three basic types of potentially cancerous ovarian cysts: *serous cyst adenomas, mucinous cyst adenomas,* and *dermoid cysts.* The cyst adenomas are far more common than the dermoids, and are precursors of most ovarian cancers. They usually grow considerably larger than functional ovarian cysts, but can still be benign, no matter how large they become. Malignant ovarian tumors account for approximately 15 percent of all cancers of women's reproductive organs.

Serous Cyst Adenoma

Serous cyst adenomas occur in women of any age after puberty. They are called the fifty-percent tumors because they are malignant about half of the time and they are bilateral (occurring in both ovaries) about half of the time. They can be too small to be felt during internal examination, or so large that they fill the entire abdominal cavity. If an ovarian cyst is found which does not disappear spontaneously after a few months, it should be carefully investigated—it could be a serous cyst adenoma.

Since there is such a large chance of this type of cyst being bilateral, if a surgeon finds one on an ovary, he should always cut into the other ovary to ensure that there is no abnormal growth there, too. After surgery, the patient should be checked regularly for a few years for recurrence. If, during this period, the serous cyst adenoma does not return, it might never return, although there have been reports of malignancy many years later. If a cyst adenoma occurs after menopause, both ovaries should immediately be removed, since this type of cyst can develop into a very dangerous malignancy (see Chapter 20, Cancer).

Mucinous Cyst Adenoma

Of all potentially malignant ovarian cysts, only 10 to 15 percent are mucinous cyst adenomas, and of those, only 12 to 15 percent develop into malignancies. They tend to be found in only one side, and are often very large. This group of cysts causes the largest tumors in the body. The largest ever reported weighed 328 pounds!

These cysts have thin walls filled with a thick fluid. Like all other ovarian cysts, if they do not disappear spontaneously within a few months, they should be removed, and the woman should return for regular checkups.

This type of cyst can also develop after menopause. Since it can transform into malignant tumor, it should immediately be removed. Because ovarian malignancy tends to occur after age fifty, a woman should continue to have at least one pelvic examination a year.

Dermoid Cyst

Dermoid cysts are so named because they often contain tissue similar to skin, and in fact often have hair, skinlike tissue, and teeth in them. They can, however, contain elements that are developed from all three embryonic layers and can comprise all types of human cells. No one knows how these cysts originate. They represent between 10 and 20 percent of potentially malignant ovarian tumors. They are unilateral in three cases out of four, and the chance of a dermoid cyst becoming malignant is only *one percent*.

Occasionally these cysts contain thyroid tissue and produce thyroid hormone. This can cause a hormonal imbalance, possibly contributing to tumors of the thyroid.

Dermoid cysts are found most often in women in their twenties. They tend to weigh less than other tumors, since much of their mass is made of hair, sweat glands, skin, and other relatively light tissue. Because they are light, they "swim" inside the abdominal cavity, usually floating above the uterus. Therefore, during examination, if an ovarian cyst is higher than the uterus, it is usually a dermoid cyst. Since malignancy is rare, surgery can be postponed for several months to give the cyst a chance to disappear. If it proves to be a dermoid cyst, it will not disappear. If the cyst contains teeth, they will show up on an X-ray of the abdomen. If such a cyst is identified, surgery should be initiated to remove it.

Dermoid cysts tend to float, but they are usually attached to the ovary by a stalk. This attachment can cause them to twist, which stretches the nerves and can create extreme pain. Immediate surgery is then the only solution.

If a dermoid cyst should rupture, it can be highly dangerous, since it contains chemicals that can poison the abdomen. Even if there are no symptoms, these cysts must eventually be removed. Since they tend to be small, they can usually be removed through a bikini incision along the pubic hairline. Using that method, the scar is less visible. Future childbearing should be unaffected if the operation is performed by a competent surgeon.

RARE OVARIAN CYSTS

There are many other ovarian cysts, but their occurrence is very rare and need not be discussed in this book. Several of these cysts are hormone-producing: Some produce female hormones, others male hormones. Several of these rare ovarian tumors can become malignant, and they should be removed as soon as they are diagnosed. The behavior of these tumors is special and they should only be treated by a specialist.

chapter 15

SPECIAL TESTS

THE PAP TEST

The Pap test for early detection of cancer was described and developed by Dr. George Papanicolaou during the 1920s. The Pap test, originally limited to the early detection of uterine cancer, was acclaimed by the American Cancer Society as the most significant discovery in the field of cancer in our time. Later, Dr. Papanicolaou extended the application with his discovery of a diagnostic technique to include other areas of the body, such as the lungs, the stomach, the kidneys, and the bladder.

Dr. Papanicolaou was primarily interested in cytology, the discipline of cell studies. He discovered a special method by which he could stain cells in order to distinguish normal from abnormal cells more easily under the microscope. Using this staining technique, he was able to characterize cells taken from areas of inflammation and also to detect cells which indicated early cancer development. He could therefore describe normal cells, normal abnormalities of cells, early cancer and late cancer, as well as inflammation.

This unique staining method and description of cancer was initially researched at The New York Hospital, where *smears* were taken from the vagina. These smears contained cells shed from the cervical and vaginal areas. By microscopically examining these cells using this special staining technique, it could be determined whether they were normal or abnormal. This correlated with cases of diagnosed cancer, leading to a complete description and thesis by Dr. Papanicolaou. This test is now called the *Pap smear*.

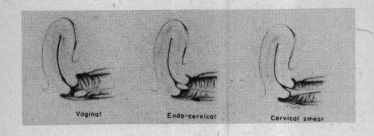

Fig. 15–1: The Pap Test.

The Pap Smear for Women

Twenty years elapsed from the time of Dr. Papanicolaou's earliest description of his method of cancer detection to its complete acceptance. At that time, scientists around the world discovered that Dr. Papanicolaou's staining method and description of early detection of cancer were indeed correct, and that by taking smears from the vagina and cervix, one could identify early and late cancer. The Pap smear became a worldwide technique.

The technique of the Pap smear is fairly simple and involves taking at least three smears, or samples. The first smear is generally obtained from the vaginal pool—the pool of cells which, immediately prior to the examination, have collected behind the cervix. This smear contains cells discharged from the fallopian tubes and the uterus, as well as the cervix and the vagina. This is the most important smear, since abnormal cells from cancer inside the uterus, and occasionally in the ovaries, can be detected through it.

The second smear is obtained from the endocervix. This is the area at which the lining from inside the uterus and outside the cervix usually join. The physician inserts the swab into the cervix and rotates it a few times so cells from the area will be taken.

The third slide, called a *cervical swab* (cervical scraping), is obtained by a special *spadle,* which is inserted and rotated around the cervix a few times.

After a swab has been obtained, the physician transfers it onto a slide. The slides are sprayed in order to fix the cells so they will not be destroyed during transport to the laboratory. When the cells reach the laboratory, they undergo the special Papanicolaou stain. A technician or physician examines the slide under the microscope to see if the cells are normal or abnormal. If the cells are abnormal, a clear description of the cells is carried out.

Essentially, this is the Pap smear. Many physicians take only two smears, a technique believed by many laboratories to be inadequate. The more smears taken, the more cells the technician will have to look at. This gives a clearer and more distinct diagnosis. In cases in which the patient earlier experienced slight abnormalities of the cervical cells, it is wise to take four or five smears, since this gives the cytologist or the physician more material to examine.

Can Anything Go Wrong?

There are two factors of error in the Pap smear: incorrectly obtained smears or smears sent to an incompetent laboratory.

If the smears are not obtained correctly, or if the smears are not sprayed immediately, the cells within the smears can be damaged. It is then impossible to study the cells under the microscope.

If the smears are not sent to a highly sophisticated laboratory, a correct reading might not be given. To save expense, and for other reasons, some laboratories employ younger, less experienced technicians who do not have long experience in reading Pap smears. For this reason, you should ask your doctor which laboratory he uses for the smears and do some checking on your own regarding the laboratory's reputation.

What Can a Pap Smear Determine?

A Pap smear can correctly evaluate the condition of the cells. In the cervix, the cells change throughout the month, depending on the hormonal level. Since estrogen influences the vaginal and cervical cells one way and progesterone another, physicians can determine the time of the cycle from which the smears have been obtained. A Pap smear can, therefore, indicate a woman's estrogen level. This level is important to a woman about to go into menopause, since her physician is then able to determine if she needs hormone-replacement treatment. Tangentially, it is also important to women who have irregular menstrual bleeding as an aid to which treatment should be instituted.

The description for abnormal cells is called *dysplasia* and is further divided into *mild* and *severe dysplasia*. Cervical dysplasia is a condition in which the cells of the cervix have become abnormal. In certain instances, severe dysplasia develops into early cancer, or *carcinoma in situ*. This is an early cancer which can be completely treated. From the time the severe abnormality, or early cancer (carcinoma in situ), is discovered to the time a fully developed cancer occurs, there might be a lapse of a few years. This depends on the individual. However, as soon as the suspicion of an early cancer arises, a patient must undergo treatment. Treatment might consist of a large biopsy performed during a so-called colposcopy, or the removal of a cone-shaped portion of the cervix. If it is not discovered and treated, the cancer might continue into *invasive carcinoma*, which can be fatal.

The development from dysplasia into invasive carcinoma might take several years. If a woman has a Pap smear at least once a year, she can detect the condition in time to obtain a 100 percent cure and ensure survival. If a woman has had an early abnormality such as dysplasia, it is advisable to have Pap smears two or three times a year.

The Pap smear further describes infections in the cervix, guiding the physician to treatment of the particular inflammation. In a like manner, trichomonas and fungal infections can be discovered in a Pap smear.

The Pap smear is a very important test for early detection of cancer, for description and detection of infection, and for determination of hormonal levels.

The Pap Smear—Not for Women Only

Despite the widely held belief that the Pap smear is used to detect cervical cancer only, the Pap test makes it possible to find and treat *many* cancers in the early, curable stages. The procedure is extensively used in both women and men to identify the cells which comprise the lining of an organ and are constantly being discarded. These exfoliated, or cast-off, cells can be removed from normal fluid and secretion, or scraped from the surface of accessible parts of the body. A small amount of this fluid or secretion is placed on glass slides, fixed, and stained so that cellular details will stand out when examined under the microscope. When malignant cells are present in a specimen, they can be identified with a high degree of accuracy.

For instance, cells are collected through sputum from areas of the respiratory tract, including the trachea, the bronchi, and the lungs. This sputum is sent to the laboratory; by detecting and examining the cells in the sputum, early or late lung cancer has been detected and many patients have been cured.

Aspiration of the stomach with a tube which collects cells from the stomach allows detection of cancer of the stomach or of the esophagus.

Cancer of the prostate gland, cancer of the kidney, and cancer of the bladder can all be detected by collecting urine and sending it to the laboratory. Although this test is used for both women and men, it has particular importance for men as one of the earliest and best methods for detecting cancer in the urinary tract.

Many *in situ cancers* (cancers still in an early stage of development which have not yet invaded the underlining tissue) have been detected cytologically by Pap smears in both women and men, as have other neoplasmas too tiny to otherwise be discovered on X-ray films.

Do Not Douche before a Pap Smear

The Pap smear taken from the vagina is a collection of cells that have been cast off from the lining of the vagina and cervix. This is a continuous process and it is, therefore, important not to douche at least twenty-four hours prior to going to the physician. In that way, the everyday vaginal flora is maintained. Douching washes away these cells and prevents the physician from obtaining enough cells for a correct analysis and diagnosis.

It is a normal human instinct to want to be clean, and everyone has been taught to be thoroughly washed before any medical examination. While this is generally appreciated, it can stand in the way of a proper examination. If you are going to the gynecologist for the detection of a vaginal infection or to have a Pap smear, do not douche before the examination. You can wash the outside of the vulva and perineum without interfering with a good Pap smear.

COLPOSCOPY—LOOKING AT THE CERVIX

Colposcopy is the examination of the cervix and the vagina through a colposcope, a binocular-stereoscopic instrument used to obtain a magnified visualization of the cervix and the vagina, enabling the physician to see clearly and diagnose any abnormality. If any abnormal tissue is present, the physician can obtain an adequate biopsy through the colposcope.

Colposcopy was developed in Germany in 1925 and is used extensively in Europe and South America to diagnose abnormalities, particularly cervical cancer. In the United States, the Pap smear replaced colposcopy, since the smear detects cells in precancerous states. Recently, however, colposcopy has been used along with the Pap smear. Any abnormality detected by a Pap smear is further investigated with the colposcope to identify the abnormality through magnification, determine its location, and obtain a better biopsy. It is even possible to remove any minor or early malignancy such as a carcinoma *in situ*.

Technique of Colposcopy

The colposcope is rather simple to use. However, it is expensive, so a hospital often has only one colposcope, or a group of physicians may have one in their office. During colposcopy, the patient lies on her back on the examining table with her legs in the stirrups. A speculum is inserted into the vagina to expose the cervix to the physician's view. The colposcope is then brought to the level of the vagina and a light source is attached so that the physician can easily see the cervix.

Various types of chemical agents can be used to improve the visibility of the cervix. A physician may apply acetic acid (which affects the cervical blood vessels) to the cervix to coagulate excessive mucus. If cervical abnormalities are present, the blood vessels form a specific pattern. The type of pattern helps determine the type of problem. Most colposcopes have cameras attached so the physician can obtain a picture and clearly demonstrate the position of the abnormality. If any abnormality exists, a biopsy can be obtained. Sometimes all the abnormal cells can be removed carefully through the colposcope.

Is Colposcopy Routine?

Some physicians who have colposcopes in their offices enthusiastically support their routine use on all patients. A Pap smear obtained by a competent physician and analyzed in a good laboratory is an adequate screening tool for most cervical abnormalities. However, if any abnormality is demonstrated by the Pap smear, it is advisable for a physician familiar with a colposcope to use this instrument as a diagnostic aid. Routine colposcopy has not been advocated except in a few institutions.

chapter 16

OPERATIONS

Surgery should be considered the last resort in the treatment of any condition, except in emergency situations such as to stop severe hemorrhage, repair lacerations and fractures, or remove an infected appendix. Surgery may be indicated in the treatment of certain cancers, although recent developments in chemotherapy and radiation therapy have proven that these methods can often replace some surgical treatments and limit the extent of surgery in other cases.

Any surgery entails a risk of complications or even death from anesthesia, infections, hemorrhaging, or misjudgment on the part of the surgeon. In gynecological surgery, there are added elements, which, though not making the procedures any more dangerous, do add to the strain of recovery. For example, removal of the ovaries causes a change in the body's hormonal balance, while removal of the uterus might have serious psychological effects.

Gynecological surgery is extremely sensitive, and it is imperative that it be performed by a specialist. That usually means a gynecologist, not a general surgeon. In the case of malignancy, the operation should be done by a gynecological oncologist.

IS SURGERY NECESSARY?

There are many reasons why too much unnecessary surgery is performed. It is partly because some physicians are not fit to practice medicine. Also, operations mean money to private physicians and training to interns and residents. Most physicians in this country are well qualified, but the Federation of State Medical Boards estimates that at least 5 percent, or 16,000 of the country's 320,000 medical doctors, are not conscientious or competent enough. Some physicians are mentally ill, and others are addicted to drugs. Some are too old and senile, while many are simply ignorant and do not care to educate themselves in modern medicine. Medical science is developing so fast that a treatment considered correct today may be outdated next year.

According to the National Center for Health Statistics, 250,000 of the 18 million Americans who underwent surgery in 1975 died either during or shortly after the operation. Many of these patients were very sick and might have died anyway, but some of the deaths could have been avoided if competent medical treatment had been available.

The main risk of surgery is general anesthesia; this is because very potent drugs are used to put a person to sleep. These drugs influence the heart, the lungs, the blood vessels, and the brain. If these drugs are not administered correctly by a well-trained anesthesiologist, they can easily result in death.

Other causes of death are postoperative blood clots, pneumonia, shock, bleeding, or infections. The incidence of these and other serious complications related to surgery varies from doctor to doctor, as well as from hospital to hospital. It is important that a person who needs surgery choose only the best doctor associated with the most competent hospital. Some smaller hospitals can be adequate if they have conscientious and competent staffs, but it is particularly important that the anesthesiologists are highly qualified.

According to a congressional subcommittee, at least 11,900 of the 250,000 surgery-related deaths in the United States in 1975 were totally avoidable, since surgery in all these cases was not indicated. Approximately 20 percent of all surgeries performed in America were, according to studies, not indicated. The rate of unnecessary surgery has not improved much since 1975. Approximately two million unnecessary operations were performed in 1978 with a loss of more than 10,000 lives and a cost of four billion dollars.

Get a Second Opinion

Dr. Eugene G. McCarthy of Cornell University Medical College in New York is presently studying the importance of second opinions before surgery. In a 1976 report, he found that 34 percent of 3,171 patients who were told they needed surgery, but voluntarily sought a second opinion, were found *not to need the operation*. In a second group, 17 percent of 1,094 patients who had mandatory second opinions were found not to need operations. Dr. McCarthy followed for three years patients who did not have surgery because of second opinions, and found that only a small percentage of these patients subsequently needed operations.

This high rate of unjustified surgery has been challenged as being non–representative. Nearly 5,000 operations performed at a group of Brooklyn and Long Island hospitals were recently evaluated and the rate of unnecessary surgery was determined to be less than 1%. However, these hospitals had stringent patient evaluation programs.

Studies have indicated that when a surgeon is paid for an operation, he is more apt to operate than if he works for a prepaid group health plan, where he is not paid extra for an operation. Furthermore, it is interesting to note that in Great Britain, where doctors are salaried, the rate of hysterectomies is 60 percent less than that in the United States.

Gynecological operations, like other operations, are performed in excess. When a woman's physician suggests an elective operation, she has the right to question the advisability of the procedure and should seek a second opinion. A woman should make sure that her physician is board eligible or certified and associated with a hospital with high standards.

Women should demand that none of their organs be removed unnecessarily. Ovaries, for example, might function until a woman is in her fifties, so should not be removed until later in life. A fibroid tumor can be removed without a hysterectomy (see myomectomy p. 365). The problem of unnecessary surgery has been recognized on a national level, and HEW is now recommending a second opinion program for surgery with its toll-free hotline, 800-325-6400 (in Missouri, 800-342-6600) to help patients find qualified consultants.

WHAT TO EXPECT AFTER SURGERY

Women who have surgery should not expect to get up immediately after the operation and drive home. After a D&C (dilatation and curettage), a patient stays in the hospital for six to twenty-four hours; older patients who require electrocardiograms or X-ray follow-up usually stay longer. For an operation that requires an exploratory laparotomy (an opening of the abdomen), a stay of six to eight days is indicated. Vaginal-surgery hospitalization may last seven to eight days. If there are urination problems, extend that to ten to twelve days. All this presupposes that there will be no complications. If any complications do arise, the hospital stay has to be extended until the problem is solved.

Regardless of what you are told, do not expect to go back to work following any major operation for three to six weeks. If you do, you are endangering normal recovery. You will be tired much of the time and will require plenty of inactivity and rest. You should be able to resume sexual intercourse after about five or six weeks. Don't be shy about asking your doctor specifically when sex will be allowed.

D&C

The most common operation of all, often called the bread and butter of gynecology, is the D&C. Though the letters stand for dilatation (opening of the cervix) and curettage (scraping the uterine wall), this operation is often jokingly referred to as a Dusting and Cleaning. The procedure is a minor one, and is carried out through the vagina so there are no scars.

There are two general reasons for a D&C: *diagnosis* and *therapy*. Many women feel that a periodic D&C cleans out potential infectious bacteria or precancerous growths. This is not true. If the uterus is normal and healthy, it cleans itself every month by menstruating. Prophylactic D&C is just asking for trouble; complications, though extremely rare, can sometimes occur. Unless your gynecologist suggests a D&C for a specific reason, don't ask for one.

For diagnostic purposes, a D&C is essentially a biopsy from the endometrium, or uterine lining. If any abnormality occurs that suggests symptoms of endometrial abnormalities, a gynecologist can, by performing a D&C, obtain enough endometrial tissue to have it analyzed in a pathology laboratory for potential malignancy.

If a minor abnormality exists in the uterus, such as a polyp, it can be removed during a D&C. This is one of the therapeutic applications of the procedure.

Indications for a D&C

The most common indication for a D&C is abnormal uterine bleeding. With younger women, many gynecologists first treat this problem with doses of progesterone to try to slough off the uterine lining and regulate accompanying abnormalities. This is especially indicated in women with high estrogen levels—for

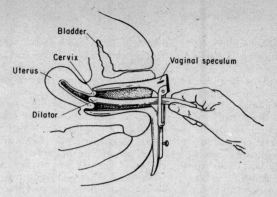

Fig. 16-1: Cervical Dilatation. Dilatation of the cervix is done in order to open the cervix so a physician is able to insert a curette during a D and C, or a suction tip in the case of a suction abortion. A speculum is inserted into the vagina to enable the physician a clear visualization of the cervix. The cervix is then dilated by using a series of dilators (special round-shaped metal instruments) with progressively increasing diameters.

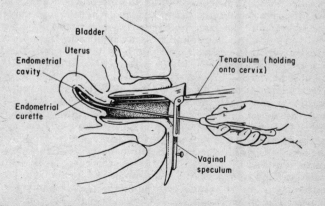

Fig. 16-2: Endometrial Curettage or Biopsy. After the cervix has been dilated, a curettage can be done. The vagina is opened by a vaginal speculum and a tenaculum (a special forceps) is placed on the lip of the cervix to stabilize the uterus. A curette is then inserted into the uterus and the physician gently scrapes the walls of the uterus in order to remove abnormal tissue, or obtain enough material for a biopsy of the lining of the uterus.

example, women with Stein-Leventhal disease—who develop too thick endometria. If drug treatment is unsuccessful, a D&C can remove the excess tissue or any abnormal growth.

In cases of a fibroid tumor breaking into the endometrium cavity (submucous fibroid), a D&C does not cure the condition, but it allows the gynecologist to diagnose the problem so that he can subsequently treat it properly. This is also true of cancer of the endometrium, whose first sign is irregular bleeding. A D&C can save your life by giving an early diagnosis of cancer.

If abnormal bleeding is the result of a misplaced or incompatible IUD, a D&C can remove the IUD and clean out the uterus.

In general, a D&C is a simple, fairly safe, multipurpose procedure that is extremely valuable when indicated. However, some women have a tendency to become D&C-happy and try to persuade their gynecologists to perform this operation regularly. Beware of this, since there could be complications and any anesthesia entails a potential risk.

The Technique of a D&C

A D&C is usually performed under general anesthesia, although it can be done with a local anesthetic injected around the cervix. After anesthesia has been administered, the vagina is washed with an antiseptic solution and the procedure begins. The physician should first take a scraping from the interior of the cervix. This can later be compared with tissue obtained from the uterus to determine if abnormalities in the uterus have spread to the cervix. The depth of the uterus is then measured with a uterine sound (see page 101). If the patient is diagnosed as having cancer, this measurement is important for determining the type of cancer treatment. It is also a useful measurement to have should the patient require an IUD (intrauterine device), since the size of the uterus determines which type of IUD a woman can have. The cervix then is dilated with a series of instruments that progressively increase in diameter. The process is gradual because the cervix has a very tight opening surrounded by strong tissue. When the cervix is opened widely enough, the *curette* (a small spoon) is inserted into the uterine cavity and scraping along the uterine wall is gently performed. The gynecologist's touch must be light so that any abnormalities inside the uterus can be felt. If too much tissue is removed, the physician can damage the endometrium, causing complications such as miscarriage and infertility in the future.

After the curettage is completed, the physician may take a biopsy from the outer edge of the cervix to send to the lab for analysis, but this is usually unnecessary since a good Pap smear renders almost the same information.

After discharge from the hospital following a D&C, a woman will usually experience slight bleeding and staining for five to seven days and on occasion up to two weeks. For the first three to four weeks following the procedure, she should avoid intercourse or the insertion of any foreign object, such as tampons, into the vagina, to prevent infection. The recovery period varies from person to person, but in general, a woman may return to work, if this does not involve physical work, in three to fourteen days.

CERVICAL BIOPSY

A biopsy, or a punch biopsy of the cervix, is a procedure by which a small piece of the cervical tissue is obtained for pathological examination in cases of suspected cervical cancer. This procedure is performed when the Pap smear is abnormal, or if an abnormal cervical lesion is seen during a pelvic examination. The cervical biopsy can be performed in the office, usually without any anesthesia since there are few nerves in the cervix. A woman usually feels only a small pinch during this procedure. This procedure can also be performed in combination with a dilatation and curettage (D&C) under general anesthesia in the hospital.

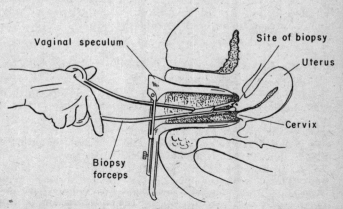

Fig. 16-3: Cervical Biopsy. Visualization of the cervix is obtained by insertion of a vaginal speculum. The biopsy is obtained with a special *biopsy forceps,* constructed so they will not damage the specimen.

The Technique of a Cervical Biopsy

When cervical biopsy is obtained in the office, the woman is placed on the examination table with her legs in the stirrups. A speculum is inserted into the vagina, and the physician uses a special biopsy forceps. The biopsy forceps is an instrument with a sharp edge and a spoonlike opening in the middle. The physician removes from the suspicious area a small amount of tissue, which is sent for pathological examination. If the cervical biopsy is performed on the basis of an abnormal Pap smear, a physician might perform Schiller's test, which involves staining the cervix with a special iodine solution prior to obtaining the tissue. This test is based on the fact that the glycogen in the normal cells of the cervix causes them to stain dark brown when painted with potassium iodine solution. However, if there are abnormal cells indicative of a premalignant lesion, they do not stain; thus it is easier for the physician to know which area to biopsy for the most accurate diagnosis.

A biopsy of the cervix is now often performed in combination with colposcopy, allowing the physician, through the colposcope, to get a clear, magnified view of any abnormality and to take a biopsy from any suspicious area (see Colposcopy).

Women usually experience slight staining for a few days after a cervical biopsy. Intercourse should not take place for two weeks or until the tissue has healed completely. Intercourse, or even the use of a tampon, might result in bleeding or cause infection in the biopsied area. Most women experience very little or no pain following cervical biopsy.

CONIZATION OR A CONE BIOPSY OF THE CERVIX

A conization is an extended biopsy of the cervix, with removal of a cone-shaped portion of the outer cervix. This is performed when an abnormality that may be precancerous shows up on a Pap smear or a punch biopsy of the cervix. The cone biopsy removes the tissue that is most susceptible to cancer and can even remove early cervical cancer. The operation should have no effect on a woman's sex life or ability to conceive.

The operation is usually performed under general anesthesia. The patient is then placed in the stirrups and the vagina is sterilely washed. A cone-shaped biopsy is then excised from the cervix. This can be associated with heavy bleeding, and several sutures must be placed to control the bleeding. The patient remains in the hospital for a few days and is then dis-

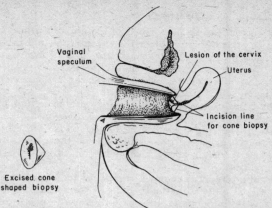

Fig. 16-4: Cone Biopsy of the Cervix. After the patient is anesthesized, the vagina is sterilely washed to prevent infection and proper visualization of the cervix is obtained by a vaginal speculum. A cone-shaped biopsy (shown to the left in the picture) is then obtained by cutting a cone-shaped portion of the outer cervix with a sharp knife. If there is any abnormality or lesion of the cervix, the physician must be sure to include that in the biopsy.

charged to rest at home. It is important not to have intercourse for five or six weeks, since this could break the sutures and result in heavy hemorrhaging. A woman should have a Pap smear after the operation, particularly if the operation was done for removal of a precancerous lesion.

CRYOSURGERY OF THE CERVIX

Cryosurgery, or freezing, of the cervix is a relatively new technique which is used to destroy any abnormal lesion by freezing. In gynecology, this procedure is mostly used for women who have chronic cervicitis. It has also been used in the treatment of early malignant lesions, but with questionable success.

Cryosurgery and electrocauterization, or burning, are used for the same indication. The reasoning behind both techniques is that both procedures kill abnormal cells. In cervicitis, where there has been a prolonged infection and cellular damage, the physician wishes to destroy the abnormal cells. This gives newer and healthier cells the opportunity to form and replace the old damaged cells.

Technique of Cryosurgery

Cryosurgery can be performed in the doctor's office. In this procedure, the woman is placed in the stirrups and the physician visualizes the cervix with the aid of a speculum. Cryosurgery is performed without the aid of anesthesia or analgesia because there are very few nerves in the cervix. The procedure itself is almost painless.

Many types of cryosurgery machines are now commercially available, and most physicians have machines in their offices. The actual freezing takes only a few seconds. The physician places a cryosurgery probe firmly against the cervix, making sure that a sufficient area is deeply frozen, thus destroying all abnormal cells.

After the physician removes the probe from the cervix, the cervix will be white from the freezing. A woman usually experiences few symptoms and little pain during the postprocedure period. A woman should not be disturbed if this procedure is suggested in well-indicated cases, where symptoms dictate that intervention is required.

What to Expect after Cryosurgery

A woman should not expect any serious problems after cryosurgery, although it will take up to four to six weeks before all the cells destroyed by freezing are replaced by new, healthy cells. During this time, she can usually expect a profuse, watery vaginal discharge caused by the sloughing off of the damaged cells, until the normal physiological balance of the vagina is restored. She will occasionally see a slight brownish discharge, which is caused by the shedding of the old, damaged, destroyed cells. A woman should usually refrain from intercourse for at least four weeks to prevent any infection or damage to the healing cervix. At the same time, she should not wear a tampon but use a sanitary napkin. She should see her physician four to six weeks after the procedure to make sure proper healing has occurred.

Cryosurgery is recommended in *indicated cases* if performed by physicians who are competent with the procedure.

ELECTROCAUTERIZATION OF THE CERVIX

Electrocauterization, or burning, is a procedure performed to destroy abnormal cells of the cervix due to chronic cervicitis.

This procedure has been performed for many years to destroy the infected and abnormal cells, giving new, healthy cells a chance to form, eventually changing all the cells on the surface of the cervix.

Technique of Electrocauterization

Electrocauterization is usually performed in a doctor's office and can be done without anesthesia or analgesia. The woman is placed on a gynecological table and a speculum is inserted into the vagina to visualize the cervix. The physician then carefully places a small probe on the area of the cervix to be cauterized. The amount of heat applied via the probe is easily controlled by a foot pedal. The cauterization causes an actual burning of the superficial layers of cells. This usually takes a few minutes; when the physician is satisfied that all damaged cells are destroyed, the procedure is over. Cauterization is usually associated with very little pain. In fact, the majority of women feel nothing during the operation.

What to Expect after Electrocauterization of the Cervix

After cauterization of the cervix, it usually takes four to six weeks before the destroyed cells are replaced by new, healthy cells. In the interim, a woman can anticipate a watery discharge and an occasional brownish discharge as the old cells are sloughed from the vagina. The insertion of any foreign object into the vagina might introduce new bacteria and cause another infection; therefore it is advisable not to have intercourse, to douche, or to use a tampon for four to six weeks. A physician should be seen approximately six weeks after the procedure to ensure that proper healing has occurred.

HYSTERECTOMY

The most common major gynecological operation is hysterectomy, or removal of the uterus through either the abdomen or the vagina. There are two basic types of hysterectomies about which there is considerable confusion among many women: *total hysterectomy* and *supracervical hysterectomy*. The confusion stems from the misconception that a total hysterectomy includes the removal of the ovaries. In fact, a total hysterectomy simply means that both the uterus and the cervix are removed. Removal of the ovaries, the fallopian tubes, and the uterus is called a total hysterectomy with a bilateral salpingo-oophorectomy.

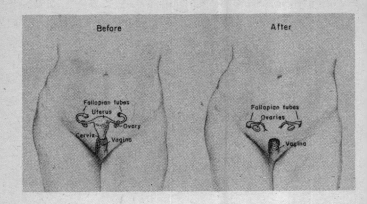

Fig. 16–5: Total Hysterectomy. A total hysterectomy is the removal of the uterus and the cervix, but *not* the ovaries or the fallopian tubes. The illustration demonstrates the anatomical position of the female genitalia before and after a total hysterectomy. When the uterus and the cervix is removed by a hysterectomy, a woman still has the same depth of the vagina and the operation should not interfere with sexual intercourse.

Supracervical hysterectomies are now not done very often. Years ago the cervix was not removed because it was a more difficult procedure and many physicians were not that well trained. The difficulties encountered in removal of the cervix are caused by its proximity to the bladder and the uterus. It can also cause severe bleeding. Today, however, with modern surgical techniques and better training, it is no longer considered dangerous or difficult to remove the cervix, and since this area is particularly cancer prone, most gynecologists feel the cervix should be removed with the uterus.

Many women have reservations about hysterectomies because they feel their female sexual characteristics will somehow be affected. Men, too, often feel a woman is desexed after hysterectomy. Nothing could be further from the truth. Masters and Johnson have shown that women have no orgasmic loss after hysterectomy. In some instances, the hysterectomy may even enhance sex, since the woman no longer has to worry about becoming pregnant. This does not, however, justify a hysterectomy.

Unnecessary Hysterectomies

Some physicians push women into unnecessary hysterectomies simply to earn fees. However, most unnecessary hysterectomies are performed for a less mercenary, but no less tragic, reason: namely, ignorance and incompetence on the part of the physician. Some physicians simply haven't kept up with the modern techniques or knowledge that render many hysterectomies unnecessary. They are not necessarily negligent, for there is more to keep up with in medicine than is possible for any one physician. That is the reason so many doctors specialize. Women should, therefore, make sure that their gynecologists are trained and are specialists in gynecology. A gynecologist should participate in postgraduate training and meetings to become familiar with the latest developments in the field. Some general practitioners and general surgeons call themselves gynecologists, but are not qualified. Some of these physicians, particularly general surgeons, have had minimal gynecological training and practice and tend to perform too many gynecologic operations, often not in accordance with the rules of the American College of Obstetricians and Gynecologists.

If your doctor suggests a hysterectomy and you have any reason to question this suggestion, especially if the doctor is not a gynecologist, you should seek a second opinion. Every woman has a right to this, particularly since so many unnecessary hysterectomies are performed. Every woman has the right to doubt her doctor, even if he is a trained and competent gynecologist. If you are still in doubt after a second opinion, a third opinion could solve the matter.

Unnecessary hysterectomies risk more than a woman's uterus; they can mean her life. This is one of the reasons the problem has received so much attention in the media. Of the 787,000 hysterectomies performed in the United States in 1975, 1,700 of the patients died as a result of complications, often from anesthesia-related causes. This is all the more reason to have a hysterectomy in a modern medical center where competent medical attention can be assured from both surgeons and anesthesiologists, and where consulting specialists are available if complications should occur. There is also a "tissue committee" in such hospitals, which reviews and questions the necessity of all surgical cases. This makes it more difficult for a doctor to perform unnecessary surgery.

Of course, it is unfair to say that doctors who don't work at large medical centers are not competent. Most women have seen one gynecologist for years, respect his advice, and know from experience that he is competent. Most physicians are worthy of that trust, but that does not mean you should not be aware of your options. Last year, *The New York Times* reported that up to 22 percent of all hysterectomies were unnecessary.

It's interesting to note that half of all physicians' wives in the United States have hysterectomies by the time they are sixty-five, compared to one third of the rest of American women. Both male and female physicians are themselves operated upon some 20 to 30 percent more than the rest of the population. All common operations are overperformed equally, but don't always blame the doctors. Sometimes a woman will push the physician to do an operation. It is estimated that there will be 3.2 million unnecessary operations of all kinds this year, resulting in some 16,000 deaths. Surgery not only carries physical threat, it often causes psychological trauma.

Surgery is also costly. It has been estimated that up to $4 billion was spent on unnecessary surgery in the United States in 1974. This money came not only from patients' pockets directly, but also from taxes and insurance (driving the rates up, costing the patient more in the future). Hysterectomies also mean money to the gynecologist. The average gynecologist performs about thirty hysterectomies yearly at a charge of between $500 and $1000 for each. This means an income of between $15,000 and $30,000 annually on hysterectomies alone.

Indications for Hysterectomy

One well-justified indication for hysterectomy is cancer or precancerous signs in the uterus. Approximately 8 percent of all hysterectomies are performed for this reason. The risk to a woman's life from cancer is too great to balance the benefits of leaving the uterus. This type of hysterectomy must be done through the abdomen rather than through the vagina, since the physician must be able to check the abdominal cavity visually for tumors, metastasis, or precancerous signs. This operation should always be performed in consultation with a cancer specialist, a gynecologist-oncologist.

Fibroid tumor is another indication for hysterectomy, but only if it is causing severe bleeding or pressing on other organs. In this case, too, abdominal hysterectomy is usually necessary, particularly if the uterus is too large to be removed through the vagina. Fibroid tumors are the most common indication for hysterectomies. However, many of these operations are unnecessary, since most fibroid tumors are asymptomatic and less than one percent ever become malignant. Most fibroid tumors start to shrink when a woman reaches menopause. According to the American College of Obstetricians and Gynecologists, a hysterectomy is indicated if the fibroid causes the uterus to enlarge beyond the size of a twelve-week pregnancy. Yet some physicians tell their patients that a fibroid is larger than it actually is, thus scaring women into having hysterectomies. Tissue committees find that many fibroids removed are of less than twelve-week size. Hysterectomies for fibroid tumors account for approximately 30 percent of all hysterectomies (see Fibroid Tumors).

It is often possible to carry out a myomectomy instead of a hysterectomy. This is recommended if further childbearing is desired, or if a woman does not want to lose her uterus. In the past, this has often been left up to the physician's discretion, but a woman has the right to a second opinion if she has any doubts, or if the doctor seems to be pushing a hysterectomy.

Hysterectomy is sometimes the only solution for chronic vaginal bleeding. If repeated D&Cs and hormone therapy prove unsuccessful, the uterus may have to be removed, especially if no further childbearing is desired. In these cases, vaginal hysterectomies are often possible. Chronic vaginal bleeding is the indication in about 10 percent of hysterectomies.

Endometriosis often causes such intense pain that if treatment with drugs such as Danazol does not solve the problem, hysterectomy is often required, particularly if the woman does not want to have any more children. Abdominal hysterectomy is usually the only possibility, since the physician must check the spread of endometriosis into the abdominal cavity. Also, there are generally many adhesions, making a vaginal hysterectomy very difficult.

Approximately 25 percent of all hysterectomies are done because of prolapsed uteri or dropped wombs. This operation is usually done through the vagina in combination with an A&P repair (see Anterior & Posterior Repair, page 370).

There are many other indications for hysterectomy, including severe menstrual cramps or chronic pelvic congestion, but these occur less frequently than those outlined above and vary so much from case to case that discussion here would serve no purpose.

Occasionally hysterectomy has been considered a means of sterilization, and about 9 percent of all hysterectomies are performed for this reason. If a woman has completed her family

and seeks sterilization, a hysterectomy, rather than a tubal ligation, ensures not only against future pregnancy, but eliminates
the possibility of uterine problems (including uterine cancer). A
hysterectomy for sterilization is often performed in conjunction
with an A&P repair, an operation which tightens the vaginal
muscles that become loose after several childbirths. An A&P
repair can often rejuvenate a couple's sex life, since the woman's vagina will be tighter and more responsive. A simple
vaginal hysterectomy is usually performed for sterilization.
However, women must realize that a hysterectomy is major
surgery—a much longer, more involved, and more dangerous
procedure than a tubal ligation, and one with many more possibilities for complications. The pros and cons of this procedure
must be discussed fully with your gynecologist.

Some hysterectomies are performed for the convenience of
the patient or because of the misjudgment of the physician.
Some women in their twenties ask for hysterectomies because
they are convinced they do not want children and do not want
to be bothered with menstruation. Some women request hysterectomies since they have heard that this procedure can improve their sex lives. Obviously these are not proper indications
for hysterectomy. Any of these operations involves a change of
life. A woman should never let any physician remove any organs except in well-indicated cases.

Surgical Technique of Hysterectomy

A hysterectomy can be done either through the abdomen or
through the vagina. These operations are usually done under
general anesthesia, but they can be done under spinal anesthesia.

The abdominal route is usually employed, since a vaginal
hysterectomy can only be employed in simple and easy cases.
The abdominal operation can be done either through a low,
horizontal incision—a Pfannenstiel incision—or with a so-called
bikini cut. This incision is made underneath the hairline and is
not visible. If a larger view is needed during the surgery or if
the operation is done because of cancer, a vertical incision between the pubis bone and the navel is performed. If the operation is less complicated, you should ask your physician to perform a bikini cut since the scar heals more strongly and is
hardly visible.

A vaginal hysterectomy is usually done as a sterilization procedure or if the uterus is not too large. Hospitalization after a

hysterectomy is about a week, but a woman cannot usually return to work until four to six weeks later. Sex can be resumed six to seven weeks after the operation.

MYOMECTOMY

A myomectomy is an operation in which a fibroid tumor is removed from the uterus without a hysterectomy. This is usually done through the abdomen. If a woman who has fibroid tumors wants to have children in the future or does not want the uterus removed, she should not have a hysterectomy; she should have a myomectomy.

During a myomectomy, each fibroid tumor is removed separately from the wall of the uterus and the incision in the uterus is then closed surgically by sutures. Afterward the uterus heals normally, relieving such previous symptoms as abnormal bleeding, pain, or pressure on the bladder that are typical of fibroid tumors. If this operation is done by a competent gynecologist, the uterus will look like a perfectly normal uterus a few months later. Women can often conceive after this procedure, even if they have not been able to conceive before, as long as the fallopian tubes and the ovaries are normal.

The alternative to myomectomy is hysterectomy. The myomectomy, of course, is less psychologically painful, because the woman's physiology remains intact. But a hysterectomy is better assurance of complete recovery. During myomectomy, the gynecologist should remove all fibroids (more than fifty have occasionally been removed). It is, however, possible to miss very tiny fibroids which have just started to develop in the uterine walls. Thus, the condition may return. However, if childbearing is desired, the recurrence may not be for several years, giving an interim during which a healthy child can be born. The choice is a personal one, but a younger woman is usually happier with a myomectomy. Hysterectomy at a young age often causes unhappiness, anger, and depression. If your doctor does not want to perform a myomectomy, find another doctor.

OOPHORECTOMY

Oophorectomy is an operative procedure by which one (unilateral oophorectomy) or both (bilateral oophorectomy) ovaries are surgically removed. The indications for unilateral oophorectomy are very few; they include precancerous ovarian cysts, twisted ovarian cysts, ovarian pregnancy, ovarian abscess, and damage to an ovary due to conditions such as severe endometriosis. Bilateral oophorectomy is performed if any of the above conditions has affected both ovaries. The vast majority of bilateral oophorectomies are performed in combination with total abdominal hysterectomy, and the main indication for this procedure is cancer of the ovaries.

Should Healthy Ovaries Be Removed?

The majority of oophorectomies are performed prophylactically as a routine part of a hysterectomy. The rationale behind removing the ovaries at the time of the removal of the uterus is to eliminate them as possible sources of cancer. Some physicians feel that once the uterus is removed, the major function of the ovaries, the production of eggs for possible fertilization and pregnancy, has been eliminated and they should, therefore, be removed. However, these doctors do not seem to appreciate fully the enormous shock to a woman's entire system that is produced by surgically inducing menopause at the age of forty. Healthy ovaries in some women can function into the fifties, and artificially administered hormones can never fully compensate for the delicate balance of natural hormones produced by a woman's own ovaries.

There has been a recent controversy over the association of artificial estrogen replacement and cancer. Because of this, it seems ludicrous to remove healthy ovaries simply because they might be possible targets for cancer and then to administer artificial hormones that could render a woman more susceptible to other forms of cancer. In Europe, the number of hysterectomies performed in relation to the population is much lower than in the United States, and similarly, the number of bilateral oophorectomies of healthy, functioning ovaries is a fraction of what it is in the United States.

Prophylactic bilateral oophorectomy in women under fifty during hysterectomy is advocated by a number of physicians as a method of preventing ovarian cancer. However, a recent study has shown that in order to prevent a single death from ovarian cancer, almost 7,500 healthy, functioning ovaries would have to be removed. In other words, only 2.7 of the 10,000 yearly deaths from ovarian cancer could be prevented if prophylactic oophorectomy was performed during hysterectomy in women under the age of fifty. Bilateral oophorectomy of healthy, functioning ovaries in premenopausal women *cannot* be recommended. After menopause, when the ovaries have ceased to function, prophylactic oophorectomy during hysterectomy would be advisable.

HYMENECTOMY

The hymen is not an important anatomical part from a medical standpoint, but from a historical, cultural, and religious standpoint, it has extraordinary importance. Throughout the ages, an intact hymen has been a symbol of virginity, a sign of purity.

A hymenectomy is an operation in which the hymen is surgically opened. This operation is performed only in rare instances, when the hymen is so strong that it cannot be broken and, therefore, does not permit intercourse.

Some hymens are so thin and fragile that they can easily break during a fall in childhood or accidentally rupture during bicycling or horseback riding. Other hymens permit intercourse without breaking. Thus a woman might not bleed during her first intercourse and still be a virgin. If a hymen is very thick and firm, and, furthermore, if the woman is tense, as many women are when they first have intercourse, the hymen can actually prevent penetration by the penis. In cases like this, the hymen can be cut surgically and the vagina dilated until the physician can easily admit two or three fingers (size of the normal penis) into the vagina. Intercourse then becomes possible, although a lubricant like Vaseline or saliva may be necessary at first.

Most hymens are broken before or during the first intercourse. Once the hymen is broken, it never grows back. Some women who have abstained from sex for prolonged periods may feel as if their hymens have returned, but this is actually a tightening of the vagina from disuse. This condition can lead to some pain during subsequent intercourse, but additional foreplay usually solves the problem.

Re-creation of Virginity

Though the hymen will not grow back, it can be surgically repaired. Such cases have been reported among women who belong to certain orthodox religious sects. An intact hymen is often a prerequisite for marriage among certain religious groups, and marriage is often the only decent life the woman can expect. Thus, if a hymen has been broken either accidentally or through illicit sex, it becomes essential to the woman's future to have it repaired. When the hymen is subsequently ripped a second time, the woman will experience the same pain and bleeding she might have at first. This operation was supposedly done two hundred years ago on prostitutes, since they were paid more if they were virgins. Some of these women had the procedure done several hundred times.

The operation is relatively simple and entails an approximation of the loose edges of the hymen with a few superficial sutures. This can be done so that it will be impossible for a layperson to detect it.

CUL-DE-CENTESIS

This is a procedure in which a needle is placed through the vagina into the cul-de-sac (the space behind the uterus) to determine if there is any intraabdominal bleeding or infection. The operation is done if a woman has symptoms of a ruptured ovarian cyst or an ectopic pregnancy; blood is found in the abdominal cavity in both cases. If the woman has ovarian cancer, this shows up in the aspirated abdominal fluid. This operation is usually done under local anesthesia. The procedure is very helpful for a physician in order to make a diagnosis.

CULDOSCOPY

Culdoscopy, a diagnostic and therapeutic procedure, has been used in the United States since the 1940s. During this procedure, a periscopelike instrument is inserted through a small incision in the vaginal wall into the abdominal cavity, providing the physician with a view of the uterus, the fallopian tubes, and the ovaries.

Culdoscopy is rarely performed at the present time, since it has been replaced in many instances by laparoscopy. Culdoscopy is a somewhat difficult procedure, since the woman has to kneel in the so-called knee-chest position and cannot be under general anesthesia. Furthermore, the physician must insert the culdoscope somewhat blindly and might damage the pelvic organs if the patient has adhesions. This procedure is, therefore, mostly performed by physicians who have years of experience with this technique.

The Technique of Culdoscopy

Culdoscopy is usually performed in a hospital under local anesthesia. The woman is placed in the knee-chest position—

Fig. 16–6: The "Knee-Chest" Position. The "knee-chest" position has a woman resting on her knees with her body bent forward resting the chest on the table. A pillow is usually placed underneath the chest and the head is rotated to one side.

kneeling, bent forward, head resting on her arms, with her chest lower than her bottom. Before the procedure, the vagina is washed sterilely. Since it is impossible to sterilize the vagina completely, some physicians are cautious about this procedure, because of the inherent risk of infection. After the vagina has been washed, a sterile drape is placed around the woman. A spinal or epidural anesthetic can then be administered or a woman can be given Demerol or other pain medication. The physician inserts a specialized speculum into the vagina to obtain an adequate visualization of the cervix and the area behind the cervix. Usually a local anesthetic is injected into the vaginal wall, and a small probe is then inserted blindly through the wall. When the position of this probe is determined, it is followed by the insertion of a larger probe containing the culdoscope. Through the culdoscope, the physician can visualize and inspect the area just behind the uterus, the ovaries, and the tubes. While a woman is kneeling in this position, her intestines usually fall forward, lessening the chance that the bowel will obstruct the physician's view. The physician can then observe if there is any abnormality in the area.

This procedure is often performed on women with fertility problems when the physician wants to determine if both fallopian tubes and ovaries, as well as the uterus, are completely normal.

In combination with this diagnostic procedure, minor operations can also be performed with fine operating instruments inserted through the culdoscope. The most common operation

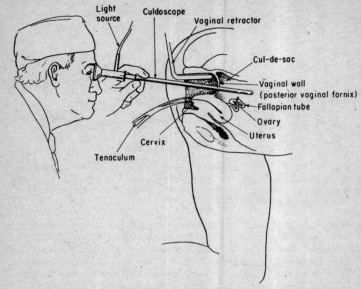

Fig. 16–7: Culdoscopy. Culdoscopy is often carried out under local anesthesia with the patient in a "knee-chest" position. The physician obtains good visualization of the cervix by vaginal retractors; the cervix is held by a tenaculum. A culdoscope is inserted in the posterior vaginal wall behind the cervix so the physician can, through this periscope type instrument, visualize the uterus, the ovaries and the fallopian tubes.

is tubal sterilization. The physician can sterilize the woman by picking up the fallopian tubes and either coagulating or dissecting a piece of the tubes. Other minor operations, such as the removal of small adhesions, can be performed with fine instruments through the culdoscope.

A woman usually experiences minimal pelvic pain for a day or so after the operation. Intercourse is not advised for three or four weeks, until complete healing has occurred. She should not return to work for at least a week, or maybe two weeks, after the operation.

ANTERIOR AND POSTERIOR REPAIR

This is an operation in which the vagina is tightened by a surgical procedure; often it is called an A&P repair.

After every childbirth, the ligaments that hold the uterus in place grow weaker, especially if the infant is large and stretches the tissue greatly. At the same time, the vaginal muscles stretch, making the vagina larger. Aside from the medical problems of sagging or prolapsed uterus (see Chapter 13, Uterine Abnormalities), the increased size of the vagina can make sex less enjoyable. This is especially true of middle-aged couples. As a man grows older and engages in sex less often, his penis tends not to become as large during erection as it might have when he was younger. The combination of the smaller penis and the loosened vagina can create sexual dissatisfaction.

Thus, for both medical and sexual reasons, many women undergo anterior and posterior repairs. Basically, this is plastic surgery to tighten the vagina. It is often done in conjunction with a vaginal hysterectomy. An anterior vaginal plastic operation is particularly indicated if the woman has urinary difficulties. If the only complaint is that the vagina is "too loose," only a posterior repair is needed. A hysterectomy is often not indicated, and the procedure can be done quite quickly. The operation entails excision of extra vaginal tissue and tightening of the muscles, making the vagina both tighter and longer. This operation can only be recommended if there is a sexual problem stemming from a vagina that is too loose. Do not be shy about this, but discuss it with your gynecologist.

The Technique of an A&P Repair

The operation is done under general anesthesia with the patient in the stirrups. The front of the vagina is opened, and if the patient has a prolapsed uterus and has opted for a hysterectomy, the sagging uterus is readily accessible for removal. This also makes it easier for the physician to tighten the muscles. By cutting out a piece of the vaginal mucosa from both the front and the back of the vagina and tightening the muscles with sutures, the vagina becomes both tighter and longer.

After surgery, the muscles tightened around the bladder will interfere with urination for the first week or so. The urine must, therefore, be drained out. The standard treatment for this used to be a urinary (Foley) catheter placed in the bladder via the urethra; this often caused bladder infection. A new procedure in which a hollow plastic tube is placed through the abdomen via an incision into the bladder to allow urine to drain has replaced the Foley catheter. This tube does not interfere with voluntary urination, and there are fewer complications and infections.

Women should expect to remain in the hospital for seven to

ten days following an A&P repair and should be extremely careful not to break the sutures loose by moving too much or even coughing violently. After release from the hospital, the patient should rest three or four weeks, being careful not to lift anything heavy. Sex can begin after complete recovery—about six to eight weeks later.

LAPAROSCOPY—THE BAND-AID PROCEDURE

The possibility of being able to observe the viscera of the human body directly through an instrument has motivated medical research for 170 years. In 1805, Dr. Bozzani constructed an apparatus in Frankfurt that used a series of mirrors and reflected candlelight to visualize the human urethra. In 1901, Dr. Kelling described a technique on dogs in which he observed the intraabdominal organs through a periscopelike instrument. In 1910, Dr. Jacobaeus of Stockholm described the first use of endoscopy in humans—he used a cystoscope-like instrument to look into the chest and abdomen. Still, it was only in the last decade that the development of fiber optics, or cold light, made it both practical and simple to develop instruments with which to peer inside the human body.

The result is the laparoscope. This instrument is quite new, but most competent gynecologists have learned its use. The laparoscope is compact, flexible, maneuverable, versatile, and extremely effective.

Indication for Laparoscopy

Laparoscopy can be performed either as a diagnostic or therapeutic procedure. The most frequent diagnostic indication for laparoscopy is to inspect the pelvic organs of women with fertility problems. In these cases, a dye is injected through the vagina and into the uterus. The dye will be passed out through the fallopian tubes if there are no obstructions. The passage of the dye can be observed through the laparoscope, and the physician can determine if the fallopian tubes are normal. The ovaries can be observed for signs of abnormality, and ovarian biopsies can be obtained to determine their functioning. Laparoscopy is also performed to determine the nature of pelvic masses or cysts. If any severe conditions that warrant immediate surgery (such as an ectopic pregnancy, a suspected malignancy, or a pelvic abscess), are discovered via the laparoscope, an exploratory laparotomy can be performed right away. The size and number of some uterine fibroid tumors can also be determined through the laparoscope, thus helping the physician in determining whether a hysterectomy or myomectomy is indicated.

The most common therapeutic use of the laparoscope is tubal sterilization. During this procedure, the fallopian tubes are picked up in the mid-portion and either coagulated or encircled by a fallopian ring. Other therapeutic indications are the cutting of small pelvic adhesions and biopsies of suspicious abnormalities.

Laparoscopy cannot be performed on extremely obese women or on women who have had previous extensive abdominal surgery, since numerous pelvic adhesions can exist and the bowel might be perforated during the insertion of the instrument.

The Technique of Laparoscopy

Laparoscopy can be carried out with either local or general anesthesia. An incision is made either in the navel or directly below it, and a small peritoneal needle is inserted into the abdomen to inflate it with four liters of carbon dioxide (CO_2) gas. The patient is tilted so her head is downward, causing the bowel to float upward toward the chest with the gas. This gives a better view of the pelvic organs (see Fig. 10–4). Because the abdomen is distended by the gas and the position of the bowel, the laparoscope has an unobstructed view of the organs. Not only does the laparoscope provide light and lens, but instruments can be introduced through it to move aside organs that block the view, or even to carry out minor surgery. Biopsies can be taken, the fallopian tubes can be grafted or cauterized (for sterilization), and dyes can be injected to see if the tubes are unobstructed. After the operation, the gas is let out and the patient usually goes home the following day. She will experience a dull pain for a week or two, but the only sign of surgery will be a small Band-Aid over the navel. That's why laparoscopy is often called the Band-Aid procedure.

HEMORRHOIDECTOMY

Hemorrhoids usually occur in women after childbirth, due to the pressure of the child restricting blood flow and causing varicose veins in the rectum. During the active phase of labor, these veins often pop up and become hermorrhoids. The problem becomes complicated if the woman suffers from constipation, and pain and infection can be extreme.

A hemorrhoidectomy to remove these veins is a relatively simple operation, usually performed by a general surgeon. Three incisions are made to remove a triangular piece of veined tissue: then the area is loosely sutured closed. The rectum is then packed, and since the patient had begun a liquid diet several days before the operation, there should be no bowel movements for a day or two to allow healing. Recovery is extremely painful, since there are extensive nerves in the rectum, and some patients are sick for several weeks. However, the benefits of the hemorrhoidectomy are easily worth a few weeks' suffering for a victim of chronic hemorrhoids.

MASTECTOMY

One of every fifteen women in the United States will develop breast cancer. Today the major therapeutic approach to this problem is mastectomy, the removal of the cancerous breast. The two major types of mastectomies are the *simple* mastectomy, the removal of the involved breast and the overlying skin, and the *radical* mastectomy, the removal of the involved breast, the overlying skin, and the muscles of the chest wall beneath the breast, as well as dissection and removal of the lymph nodes under the arm on the affected side.

History of Mastectomy

The technique of radical mastectomy for breast cancer was devised by Dr. Halsted of Johns Hopkins Medical School in Baltimore in 1882. There have been only minor changes in this procedure since then. Radical mastectomy is still the major treatment today of breast cancer in the United States, although in 1941, Dr. McWhirter, a physician of Edinburgh, proposed a so-called simple mastectomy for breast cancer. Dr. McWhirter found that there was the same five-year survival rate for simple as for radical mastectomy. Furthermore, there were fewer side effects and complications after simple mastectomy than after radical mastectomy. During a radical mastectomy, so much tissue is removed that there is a greater tendency for infection, and the tissues are stretched so much that healing is retarded. Radical mastectomy involves removal of the lymph glands in the armpit, thus there is a tendency for swelling (edema) of the arm, which can disturb the patient for a long time after surgery. Dr. McWhirter described much less swelling of the arm after simple mastectomy.

Simple mastectomy is the operation performed today for early breast cancer in Great Britain as well as the other European countries. In Germany, physicians find it difficult to secure permission for breast surgery unless a simple mastectomy is guaranteed. American physicians still prefer to perform radical mastectomies, because it is believed that a conservative attitude in the face of a killing disease is the best approach.

Breast Biopsy

If a woman is found to have an abnormal mass in the breast and there is a suspicion of malignancy, a breast biopsy must be performed. A breast biopsy can be performed either under local or general anesthesia. Some physicians prefer performing the biopsy under general anesthesia and having a diagnosis made immediately from frozen sections of the biopsy. If the mass is found to be malignant, they want to perform the mastectomy immediately because they believe the biopsy spreads the cancer. Other physicians do not hold to the theory that the biopsy stimulates the cancer. They feel that a mastectomy should not be performed on the basis of frozen sections alone, since this has led to the occasional unnecessary mastectomy. They often perform the biopsy under local anesthesia, and if the findings are malignant, the patient can at least prepare herself psychologically for the trauma of mastectomy. A breast biopsy usually consists of an incision right above the palpated tumor. The incision is usually carried out in a curved fashion so that it mimics the curve in the breast. If it is possible, the surgeon makes the incision in the edge of the areola, the pigmented area around the nipple. During this procedure, the physician excises the lump and sends it for pathological examination to determine whether it is malignant or benign. The breast is sutured up and closed, and the patient can usually go home the following day.

A needle biopsy of a breast mass is done in some institutions. A needle is placed into the mass, and part of the tumor is aspirated and sent to pathology. This can be recommended only in institutions where the pathologists are accustomed to looking at this type of biopsy, since the specimens are very small. Furthermore, if it is a negative biopsy, there is always some possibility that the surgeon did not aspirate the right area.

Radical Mastectomy

Most often in the United States, if the results of breast biopsy show a malignancy, a radical mastectomy will be performed. This procedure is performed under general anesthesia. The hair under the arm is shaved, the skin carefully washed with

Before Radical Mastectomy   After Radical Mastectomy

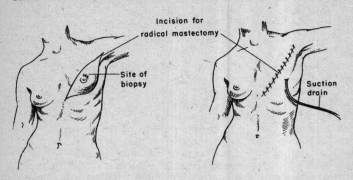

Fig. 16–8: Mastectomy. The incision line for a radical mastectomy, before and after surgery, is illustrated. In the illustration to the right, the placement of a suction drainage is shown.

antiseptic solution, and the area sterilely draped. The surgeon usually has one or two assistants for this major surgery, which occasionally requires a blood transfusion. The incision for a radical mastectomy is extensive and usually has an elliptical form, starting from the middle of the chest bone around the breast to the upper edge of the armpit. The surgeon first dissects the muscles and the arteries, veins, and nerves in the armpit. The insertions of the major chest muscles under the arm, the *pectoralis major* and *minor,* are freed. The surgeon carefully dissects and removes all the fatty tissue and the lymph glands in the armpit, hoping that if the cancer has spread to those areas, this procedure will eliminate further metastasis. All the breast tissue, the skin (including the nipple), and the pectoral muscles are removed inside the incision line shown in the illustration. The rib bones are completely exposed so that one can visualize the muscles between them. The incision is then closed by sutures. Usually a physician places a drain underneath the incision, because there tends to be a formation of blood and lymph which can disturb healing. A tight bandage is placed over the incision to prevent further bleeding. The patient is usually asked not to move the arm too much the first few days, or until good healing takes place. Special exercise is then recommended. Hospitalization usually lasts at least a week.

During this time, trained therapists instruct the patient as to the type of bra and clothing she can wear after the surgery. A patient is not able to work for four to six weeks after the operation, since there can be swelling of the arm and rest is required. There are very few deaths during the surgery itself. Most of the surgery-related deaths have been caused by anesthesia complications. The five-year survival rate depends on the extent of the cancer. If no cancer has spread to the lymph glands, the five-year survival rate might be close to 80 percent. If there is a sign that the cancer has spread to the lymph glands, the physician might advise radiation or cobalt therapy to kill the remaining tumor cells. A woman should only permit this procedure to be done in a hospital with competent physicians highly specialized in the treatment of breast cancer.

A few physicians in this country perform even more radical surgery. Some physicians even prefer to remove a few ribs because they are worried that some cancer might have spread into the lymph glands between the ribs. This very radical procedure is advocated only by a few physicians.

Modified Radical Mastectomy

There has been a trend in the last few years in the United States to perform a less radical mastectomy, the so-called modified radical mastectomy. The surgeon makes essentially the same incision as with the radical mastectomy. He removes the lymph glands in the armpit but does not remove the pectoral muscles. It is very rare that cancer spreads to the pectoral muscles, so it is unnecessary to remove them, at least in early breast cancer. The scar from a modified radical mastectomy is less extensive, and breast growth is more successful after this procedure. The survival rate has been as good with the modified radical as with the radical mastectomies.

Simple Mastectomy

A simple mastectomy is an operation in which an incision encircles the breast containing the malignancy. This procedure is also often performed immediately following a breast biopsy. Under general anesthesia, an incision somewhat smaller than the one seen on the right in Fig. 16–8 is made through the skin, and the breast is removed, leaving the pectoral muscles intact. With a simple mastectomy, there is no surgery performed under the arm, which means healing is usually more rapid and there is no swelling of the arm. After the breast has been removed, the skin is closed; because there is less tension on the skin, complications are rare. Women are able to return to work much more rapidly. The scar is less horrifying and breast augmentation is possible. Some physicians work directly with plastic surgeons and initiate augmentation surgery in combination with simple mastectomy, starting to rebuild the breast at the same time the cancer is removed. Women who have had only simple mastectomy seem, according to studies published throughout the world, to have the same survival rate as those with radical mastectomy, and have less psychological trauma.

Simple or Radical?

Today's woman is much more aware of her own body and, particularly, to the threat to life inherent in breast cancer. It is increased awareness and knowledge that have women examining their breasts on a regular basis. Ninety percent of all breast tumors are discovered by women themselves, and as women examine themselves with increasing regularity, breast cancers are being discovered in earlier, more treatable phases. If breast cancers are discovered early, either by regular breast examination or by mammography in high-risk cases, the indications for radical mastectomy are minimal.

The controversy over simple and radical mastectomy in the treatment of breast cancer continues in the United States. Most physicians in the United States today feel that until proven otherwise, it is better to overtreat breast cancer with a radical mastectomy rather than undertreat it with a simple mastectomy. They fail to realize that after a radical mastectomy, the psychological scars can be as extensive as the physical scars.

The survival rate for early breast cancer is the same for radical as for simple mastectomy. There is an important number that does not show up in the statistical tables, and that is the number of women who find and fail to report a breast tumor because of the fear of radical mastectomy. Perhaps many women die because of this.

Simple mastectomy may be the preferred treatment for even more advanced cancers, due to the advances in radiation and chemotherapy.

The majority of women with breast cancer in Europe are treated by simple mastectomy. Doctors in the United States have reserved judgment until a strict comparison study of the two methods has been performed. This study is now in progress, under the direction of Dr. Bernard Fisher of the University of Pittsburgh. At present, it involves 1,700 patients at thirty-four medical centers throughout the country. The study was begun in 1971, and although it is still too early for a judgment, which is usually based on five-year survival rates, there are strong indications that radical mastectomy offers *no* advantage over simple mastectomy.

One interesting study was performed in Illinois, where radical mastectomy was generally carried out before the war. During the war, most trained surgeons were drafted. Many of the remaining surgeons did not know how to perform radical mastectomies, so instead performed simple mastectomies. Statistics have shown that patients treated with simple mastectomy had the *same* survival rate as those who were treated with radical mastectomy before and after the war. All these indications point toward simple mastectomy as the treatment of choice in breast cancer. Hopefully, this point will one day be fully proved.

KELOIDS

No chapter on operations would be complete without some discussion of keloids. Keloids are ugly scars produced by a healing abnormality after surgery. The development of keloids has nothing to do with the surgical technique of the physician; it is probably genetic.

Though there is no known cure for keloids, plastic surgery techniques are being developed to remove them. Many patients go to surgeons to have keloids removed only to have them return immediately. It is essential that this type of procedure be performed by a surgeon with special training and expertise in keloids, to ensure that the operation is not futile.

One technique for dealing with keloids involves steroid injection combined with excision of the scars. This has been found to decrease the re-formation of the keloids in many cases.

If keloids are removed surgically, a rim of keloid tissue should be left beneath the epidermis. Since no new tissue has been cut into, this prevents the formation of new keloids; they will not form from an incision in the scar tissue. This process, combined with steroid administration, is often very effective.

chapter 17

CIRCUMCISION

MALE CIRCUMCISION

Between the time a boy is born and the time of his first locker-room shower, he might never question the physical normalcy of his penis gland. It's there, it functions, it's even fun to play with, but it must be kept faithfully behind a zipper. Yet as soon as he walks into that shower uncircumcised and confronts a mass of ten or fifteen circumcised boys, he may be in for a shock. It is exactly this type of psychological trauma which constitutes the major arguments, pro and con, surrounding circumcision.

Throughout the history of circumcision (literally meaning "to cut around"), the operation has been performed more as a ritual or duty than for medical reasons. In the Old Testament, it was deemed as a "blood for life" sacrifice. It was feared, by mothers, especially, that the gods would take revenge on an uncircumcised baby. In certain Middle Eastern tribes, as stated in the Bible, the newborn boy was a threat to the father's prominence in the hierarchy of the family, and circumcision became a jealous act of revenge, a "taking away."

Even in the Hebrew religion, where circumcision as a practice still prevails, the ceremony derives from religious beliefs rather than from any untoward hygienic concern. The Jewish *briss* of today, a circumcision on the eighth day of life, dates back to the Mesopotamian practice thousands of years ago. Today circumcision is practiced by Europeans and Americans, independent of religion.

Procedure

Basically, the operation is simple. A *gomko* clamp is secured around the tip of the infant's penis gland. The foreskin is cut after it is stretched and tightened over the gland to prevent blood from reaching the area. The incision is then covered with a Vaseline gauze, and the cut is completely healed seven to eight days later. It is rare for infection to invade the area, but when it does, it can be serious because the baby is sometimes too weak to fight back. There have even been cases when a child has died from just such an infection.

If a male has a circumcision later in life (usually stemming from insecurity at being different), the operation is more complex. An anesthetic is needed, and the healing may take weeks, not days. Still, the surgical procedure is basically the same.

Side Effects

In terms of the physiological side effects of circumcision, there are two major considerations: (1) the relationship to cancer in women; and (2) the effect on the man's sexual ability.

It was first believed that circumcision was a link to cancer in women, especially after several reports emerged claiming that Jewish women had fewer cases of cancer because their men were circumcised. It was felt that *smegma* (the secretion of the sebaceous glands) which developed beneath the foreskin would damage the woman's cervix during intercourse.

However, recent research has denied this association. Rather, it is generally agreed that cancer of the cervix is connected to women who are more sexually active and who began having intercourse at an early age. Also, the earlier a woman bears a child, the greater her susceptibility.

The low rate of cervical cancer among Jewish women with circumcised mates might merely reflect marriage later in life. According to Orthodox customs which demanded virgin brides, this would indicate coitus later in life. It also indicates a limited number of sexual partners for the woman—another factor in cervical cancer.

The second myth regarding the circumcised man is that he is sexually superior to the uncircumcised man. After circumcision, the glands become firmer and, therefore, are not so easily stimulated. The correlation, of course, is that it takes longer to ejaculate a circumcised organ, and this accounts for the prevalence of this myth. Not true! There are no medical indications that this is fact. Many circumcised men have problems with premature ejaculation. It is interesting to note that in Europe, where the majority of men are not circumcised, there are generally fewer sexual problems. Most sexual problems, though, originate in the mind, not the genitals.

Women, for the most part, don't seem to care if their men are circumcised. In fact, a recent survey showed that most women could not even tell if their men were circumcised. On an erect penis, the foreskin usually pulls over the gland, making circumcision difficult to determine.

Still, the sexual-superiority myth continues. It must be said time and again that there is no association between circumcision and sexual prowess. If there is an association, it is psychological, not physiological.

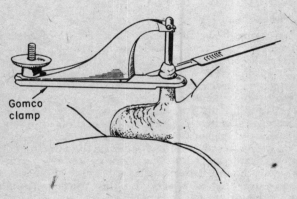

Gomco
clamp

ABOVE
Fig. 17–1: The physician places the base of the Gomco clamp at exactly the level at which he wants to perform the circumcision. If the doctor wants to remove a small amount of foreskin, less tissue is pulled up through the clamp. When the Gomco clamp is properly placed, the foreskin is squeezed at the area where the cut will be carried out by tightening the screw on the Gomco clamp.

RIGHT
Fig. 17–2: Degrees of Circumcision. The drawing to the right shows a penis that could either be semi-circumcised or an uncircumcised penis with a natural shortening of the foreskin. An uncircumcised penis is shown in the upper left corner and a typical circumcised penis is shown below.

When to Circumcise

When confronting the decision of circumcision for the new-born boy, parents should consider the community in which he will be raised. If he is to be reared in a place where most of the men are circumcised, then the child should probably be circumcised. Conversely, if he is to grow up in a European culture, he should probably be left uncircumcised.

Semi-Circumcision

There are alternatives to full circumcision. Essentially, these are described by the amount of foreskin removed. In Europe before the war, Jews concerned with recognition often underwent this half-circumcision. In this procedure, only half of the foreskin is removed. The procedure is enough to satisfy the religion, but equally important, the skin can be pulled over the gland without risk of an infection underneath. This enabled

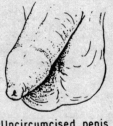

Uncircumcised penis

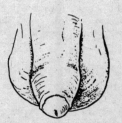

Semi-circumcised or uncircumcised penis with natural shortening of the foreskin

Circumcised penis

many Jews to escape detection at a time when their religion brought them much persecution.

Today, Orthodox parents who don't want their sons to feel embarrassed, yet who want to complement community standards, may choose a semi-circumcision.

Prevalence of Circumcision

Years ago, only Jews and a few other groups performed circumcision with any regularity. Nowadays, circumcision is common not only to Jews but to all Americans—Catholics, Protestants, blacks, Chinese, and so on.

In Europe, most men are still uncircumcised, but the procedure is catching on. It is estimated that within twenty years, most European men will also be circumcised.

Circumcision, as you can see, is a matter of community standards and practice, and not a gravely important medical issue.

Tissue Research

Unfortunately, it has been the practice, up to now, to discard the foreskin removed during circumcision. This has been an enormous waste, since it is all fresh tissue. Only recently, researchers have found that this tissue can be used in laboratory analysis. Hopefully, new means of treatment will be aided by studying this all too often discarded yet plentiful tissue.

FEMALE CIRCUMCISION

Although most men are unaware of the fact, a woman can also be circumcised.

There are several types of women, unable to achieve orgasm during intercourse, who feel that the foreskins, or hoods, over their clitorises are too large. In the instance of a woman who rarely masturbates, the hood may cover the clitoris in the same way the foreskin covers the male penis gland.

Many women decide to have this hood surgically removed. This operation is also performed with the aid of the small *gomko* clamp. Yet even after removal of the hood, the problem of difficult orgasm remains. These women probably need more stimulation in order to achieve orgasm, and circumcision will *not* usually help.

Sex researchers have found that many women do not directly stimulate the clitoris while masturbating. The women still achieve orgasm, though, because the surrounding tissue is high in nerve supply. These nerves usually lead to arousal of the clitoris. Because of this, female circumcision is not advocated by many doctors.

In Western cultures, most female circumcisions are performed exclusively for sexual reasons. This is not the case in parts of Africa, including Egypt, where circumcision of a woman is part of a religious custom. In many of these cultures, circumcision qualifies a woman to act as a temporary man while the men are away from the family, either foraging or at war. It is a circumcision based on a supposedly practical need rather than a sexual consideration.

Clitoridectomy

There is an operation performed, mostly in North Africa, that is called a *clitoridectomy*. This is, simply, removal of the clitoris.

When the North African man goes to a war, he performs a clitoridectomy on his mate, thinking it is then safe to leave her alone. The only problem with this is that nerve sensations remain even after the clitoris is removed. These nerves lead directly to the sex centers in the brain and do not stop the woman from having, or enjoying, intercourse.

Justice, it seems, sometimes triumphs in these backwardly chauvinistic societies.

chapter 18

BREAST EXAMINATION

Many observers feel that the most profound economic, religious, ethical, and personal symbolism revolves around the female breast. From the minute we are born until the second we die, we are confronted with the symbolism of the breast. Madison Avenue uses the breast to sell a wide variety of products—from toothpaste to motorcycles. Society implies that a "real" woman is one who has a perfectly proportioned body, one with relatively large breasts. Breasts signify femininity, motherhood, sexuality, the girl next door, beauty, wealth, power, and fame, among many other positive attributes.

Is it any wonder that most women are absolutely traumatized with the thought of one day losing one or both of their breasts? For years, women have been taught that their worth resides, in large part, with their breasts. One day, these women are told they have cancer and a breast must be removed. The women lose not only the breast; they often lose their sense of self-worth and of their place in the world.

Ironically, it often is just the fear of losing the breast that ultimately causes the trouble. Many women are so frightened by the thought of breast cancer that they hide from it in hopes that the threat will go away. In so doing, they completely fail to provide themselves with adequate protection, protection that has been proven time and again to thwart the invading cancer.

That protection is *self-examination,* and if you don't think it is important, consider this: Breast cancer, which, if detected early enough, can be completely cured, is the leading cause of cancer death in women and the leading cause of death in women between the ages of thirty-nine and forty-four. If it is discovered very early, the breast can even be saved, but this can only happen if a woman sees her doctor for a regular checkup, if she uses the available diagnostic techniques at suggested intervals, and if she employs *monthly* self-examination.

THE IMPORTANCE OF SELF-EXAMINATION

Obtaining a complete cure depends heavily on finding the cancer in time—while it is still treatable. Over the past twenty years, diagnostic techniques have improved greatly, making early diagnosis much more possible. But, even more important, in recent years women are becoming much more aware of self-examination, which makes early diagnosis much more probable. Still, there are too many women who rely solely on yearly or six-month checkups for breast cancer detection. That is a great mistake. A doctor may discover the disease at that time, but it might be too late. Instead of removing a very small tumor with almost assured success, the surgeon will have to operate more widely and the patient will have to wait . . . and hope. Interestingly, most breast lumps *are* discovered by women, themselves.

High-Risk Women

While self-examination for every woman cannot be overemphasized, it is especially important for women who fall into a high-risk category. Generally speaking, a woman has a higher than average risk of developing breast cancer if she has a strong family history of breast cancer, a chronic cystic breast condition, a history of premalignant breast lesions, a history of breast cancer, a late menopause, previous exposure to high doses of X-rays, or various conditions such as Stein-Leventhal disease, in which high estrogen levels are produced.

Women who are obese tend to produce high levels of estrogen; this, in turn, causes greater stimulation of the breast glands, thereby placing obese women in the high-risk category. And finally, women who take hormone replacement or estrogen hormones after the change of life might fit into the high-risk category. Of course, being in a high-risk group does not necessarily mean that a woman will develop cancer. It means only that her chance is greater than those not in the group.

Feeling the Cancer

Many women think that it isn't necessary to examine their breasts. They reason that if they had cancer, they'd feel it.

Nothing could be further from the truth. When a woman has a tender lump in a breast, it is quite often not cancer, but a cyst or a breast gland that is developing and stretching the tissue. Since breast cancer grows slowly, it usually does not pull on the nerves; it therefore causes little pain. In other words, breast cancer does not hurt.

What to Look For

Of course, examining your breasts is not particularly helpful unless you know what you're looking for. Basically, you should notice any dimple on the skin, any nipple discharge, any nipple that was previously normal and has suddenly started to become inverted (or pulled in), any discoloration or abnormality of the breast tissue or the nipples, any type of ulceration of the skin, or any persistent lumps, either in the breast area or in the armpits. These symptoms warrant immediate attention and further examination by a physician. Remember, they do not mean that you definitely have cancer—they mean only that you might. The sooner a doctor can diagnose the abnormality, the sooner proper treatment can be carried out.

PROCEDURE FOR SELF-EXAMINATION

Every woman should understand how her breasts are affected by the natural functions of the female body. While she is in the fertile age and having menstrual periods, her breasts undergo natural hormonal changes throughout the month. The feel of her breasts, therefore, changes during the course of the cycle.

Immediately after the menstrual period, the hormone level is at its lowest. This is the ideal time for a self-examination, because there is usually less tension and swelling in the breasts. Later in the month, the estrogen level begins to increase. By the end of the month, both estrogen and progesterone reach their highest levels. This, in turn, causes tension in the breasts as they prepare for possible conception. All the milk glands enlarge, sometimes creating pain and tenderness. For some women, the breasts become more cystic as the body becomes more edematous (swollen with water). Since hormonal influence is high, this is the worst time for self-examination.

Consequently, women are advised to examine their breasts once a month, after each menstrual period.

Technique of Self-Examination of the Breast

The procedure for self-examination has two parts. Both are easy to follow and neither takes a great deal of time.

Fig. 18–2: In order to examine the armpit properly, the arm should
be lowered and placed along side the body.

A positive answer to any question is a warning sign, and you
should see your doctor as soon as possible. The abnormality
may not be serious, but only a physician can diagnose with
certainty.

The purpose of the second part of the exam is to find any
new lumps or thickening in the breast. You should lie flat on
the floor, or on a bed, placing a pillow or folded bath towel
under your left shoulder. Place your left hand under your head
and the palm of your right hand over your left breast. With the
right palm, move the breast around. This is done to ensure that
the whole breast can move freely around the chest wall.

Then, keeping the fingers of your right hand flat and together, gently place them at the twelve o'clock position on your
left breast. Using small circular motions, rotate your hand
gently over the area—this is to feel any abnormal lumps that
may be present. Once you have determined that there is or is
not a problem, move your fingers a few inches clockwise and
repeat the circular motion. Be sure that each new position over-
laps the old, so no area is missed.

When you have completed the circuit, returning to the twelve
o'clock position, move your fingers slightly closer to the nipple

Fig. 18–1: Breast examination should be done both lying down and sitting up. When lying down, a pillow should be placed underneath the shoulder of the breast being examined. When the left breast is examined, the left arm should be placed behind the head. The right hand should examine the left breast and visa versa. The fingers of the examining hand should be kept flat and touch each area of the breast gently.

In the first part, you are looking for any changes in appearance that your breasts may have undergone since the last time you examined them. You should sit or stand in front of a mirror, with your hands at your sides, and take a few minutes to look at your breasts. Become familiar with their appearance. Is there any unusual dimpling or puckering of the skin? Have the superficial blood vessels gotten larger, or have they increased in number? Has the shape, size, or contour of your breasts changed?

Next, raise your hands over your head. Ask yourself the same questions. Then, observe your breasts with your hands on your hips.

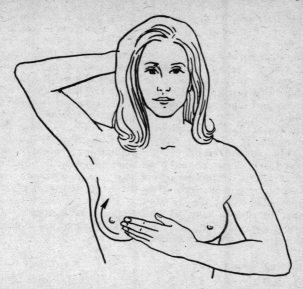

Fig. 18-3: In the sitting position, if the right breast is examined, the right arm should be placed behind the head. The arm should then be lowered down along side the body and the armpit thoroughly examined for any enlargement of the lymph glands.

and begin again. In other words, you are now moving in a circle within the circle you just made. Continue this pattern until the entire breast, including the nipple, has been examined. When you finish with the left breast, follow the same procedure on the right breast, placing your right hand behind your head and using your left hand to examine the breast.

After each breast has been covered thoroughly, the armpit areas should be examined. The lymph glands are located here, and sometimes cancer spreads through the lymph channels into the glands. The procedure is similar to that for breast examination. Lie down and put your left arm alongside your body. Then place the fingers of your right hand on your left breast at the three o'clock position. With the same circular motion, rotate your hand as you move toward the left armpit. When you reach the armpit, be sure to press the entire area against the chest wall, using flattened fingers. Remember, you are feeling for abnormalities, just as when you examined your breasts.

After the left armpit has been checked, follow the same procedure for the right side, using the nine o'clock position instead of the three o'clock. Make sure you put your right arm alongside your body, using the left hand to examine the area.

There are some women who have breast tissue that spreads into the armpit area. This is called *accessory breast tissue,* and it is a perfectly normal condition. The best way to know if you have this condition is to check with your doctor. This tissue is more enlarged and tender immediately prior to menstruation. You shouldn't worry about this; it is not a sign of cancer.

When you have finished the entire procedure, the self-examination is complete. Any abnormalities that you find should be reexamined daily. If they continue to persist beyond several days, a doctor should be seen immediately. If, however, the breasts and armpits are completely normal, a woman need only examine herself again after the next menstrual period. Every woman should also be examined by her doctor every six months, or once a year, whichever her doctor suggests. Of course, if a woman falls into the high-risk category, she might need to see her physician more frequently.

Building Your Confidence

Too many women secretly believe they cannot give themselves adequate examinations. If you are one of these women, there are two steps you can take to build confidence in your ability.

First, the next time you see your doctor, ask him to observe you as you perform a self-examination. A physician is in the best position to see if you are doing it right and to correct any faults. A doctor who is truly concerned about the health of a patient should be happy to do this.

Secondly, give yourself an examination several times a month over the first two or three months. As you do this, try to develop a sense of how your breasts and your entire body change from the beginning of your menstrual cycle to the end. Although some of the changes are very subtle, many women become surprisingly sensitive to them. They soon know how the feel of their breasts fluctuates naturally during the course of their cycles. This kind of familiarity enables a woman to distinguish more easily between a normal and an abnormal change. Becoming an expert on the subject of your own breasts should build confidence in your ability to perform regular self-examinations.

BREAST EXAMINATION PLUS

The importance of self-examination should be emphasized over and over again. Most breast tumors are found by women themselves, yet if the cancer could be detected even sooner, chances of recovery would be greater.

It is now known that cancer of the breast starts as a so-called *in situ* cancer. It may take years before it develops into a tumor or spreads to the lymph glands. While in the *in situ* stage, the cancer is usually not large enough to be detected by a physical examination alone. Yet this is the ideal time to find it. Consequently, researchers have been developing and improving several diagnostic tools and techniques geared specifically toward the earliest possible detection of breast cancer. These techniques include *mammography, xeroradiography, sonography,* and *thermography.* Because a woman will probably be exposed to one or more of these new detection methods, she should understand and be familiar with each of them.

Mammography

Perhaps the best known of all the new techniques is mammography. A *mammogram* is a soft-tissue X-ray of the breast. Screening women this way has proven effective in finding breast cancers before they are large enough to be felt. Some physicians consider this method the closest thing to a PAP smear for breast cancer.

The mammogram gives a picture of the breasts. This picture shows the location and extent of any suspicious lesions. The physician can, if necessary, perform a biopsy to confirm any suspicion and base treatment on these findings. Early cancers found using this procedure are curable in 85 to 95 percent of the cases. If the cancer is found in a more developed stage, but while it is still confined to the breast, the five-year survival rate (the number of patients still alive five years after discovery of the cancer) is 84 percent. If, however, cancer is discovered after it has spread to the lymph nodes, the five-year survival rate is only 55 percent. Obviously, the benefit of mammography is that it enables the physician to detect cancer while it is still small. The smaller the growth the less radical the surgery, and the better the chance a woman has to recover fully.

Unfortunately, mammography has one major drawback. The procedure exposes breasts to radiation. While the amount of radiation received during one mammogram is low and not itself considered dangerous, the effect is cumulative—if a woman is exposed to a small dose of radiation every year for ten years, at the end of those ten years, her breast tissue reacts as if it has been exposed to the *sum* of all the small doses. Some people fear that the total amount of exposure could cause cancer in yet another ten years or so. This does not mean that a woman will necessarily develop radiation-induced cancer if she is regularly

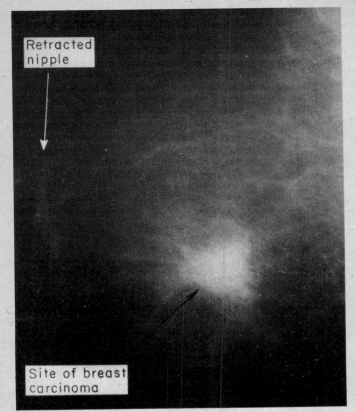

Retracted
nipple

Site of breast
carcinoma

Fig. 18–4: Mammography. It is easy to see how cancer shows a completely different configuration from the surrounding breast tissue. Cancer of the breast causes tissue changes which often pulls the skin of the breast to an extent that the skin becomes retracted. In this X-ray, the nipple is retracted.

screened by the mammogram. It only means that she increases her chance of developing such a cancer. Because of this, a woman and her doctor must weigh the possible benefit against the possible risk before deciding on mammography.

Is the choice haphazard?

No. A woman falling into the high-risk group is advised to get a mammogram on a routine basis, the frequency of which should be determined by her doctor. Since she runs a greater chance of developing cancer, the opportunity of finding it in time, if in fact it does develop, far outweighs the possible danger that could occur ten or twenty years later.

For the average woman not in the high-risk category, the use of the mammogram should be governed by her age. As a rule, it is rare for a woman to develop breast cancer before the age of thirty-five. At thirty-five, the risk increases. The older she gets, the greater the risk. Statistically, women between the ages of thirty-five and fifty account for approximately 25 percent of the cases of breast cancer that occur each year. The other 75 percent occurs in women over fifty. When you relate those statistics to the risk of getting radiation-induced cancer, a logical course of action emerges.

Generally speaking, the under-thirty-five woman not in the high-risk cancer group does not need to be routinely screened by a mammogram. It may be advisable for women over thirty-five but only if the benefits of the examination outweigh the risks of the radiation. Finally, some women over fifty should probably have mammography done every year. Remember, as a woman gets older, her chance of developing breast cancer increases. Because of this, the risk of having a cancer that needs to be detected is greater than the risk of getting cancer from mammogram radiation.

In other words, mammography is simply a matter of playing the odds that are in your favor.

Xeroradiography

Another technique beginning to gain as much popularity as mammography is called *xeroradiography*. Developed by Xerox, this diagnostic tool combines X-ray with the Xerox copying technique. Recent studies have shown that diagnoses made from xeroradiography closely correspond to follow-up biopsy diagnosis in determining the difference between malignant and benign lesions of the breast. In other words, xeroradiography is an extremely effective diagnostic tool.

The pictures produced by the *xeroradiogram* are clearer than those produced by the mammogram, and the edges of lesions are much more distinct. For this reason, many researchers believe that xeroradiography is superior to mammography. However, other specialists contend that there is no difference between the readings each method provides, claiming that while xeroradiography may provide a clearer picture, anyone properly trained to read mammography will find that it records the same information.

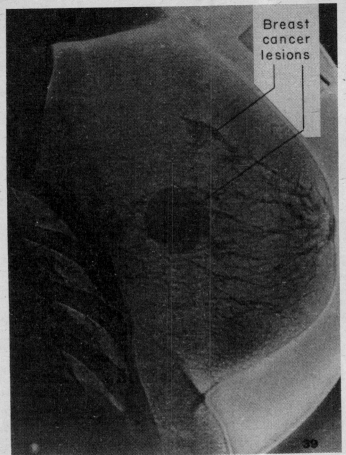

Fig. 18–5: Xeroradiography. The picture illustrates two cancer lesions, clearly separated from the other breast tissues. One can see tissue bands between the breast cancer lesions and the nipple, which is slightly retracted. (Reproduced by permission of Daniel S. Cukier, M.D.; Sharlin Radiological Associates, P.S., Hackensack, N.J.; and Xerox Corporation, Xeroradiography, Pasadena, California.)

It is still unclear whether one method is superior to the other, but development of the xeroradiogram has created a much-needed atmosphere of competition. As a result, manufacturers of each method are doing more research to improve their respective techniques, each trying to get better readings while utilizing less radiation. This research should provide superior X-ray type diagnostic devices within the next few years.

Sonogram

Other researchers are trying to develop diagnostic devices which do not involve the use of radiation. One such device is the *sonogram*. This method uses sound as the determinant agent. Several studies done in Great Britain and Japan suggest that sonography might be a very effective way to detect breast cancer in the future. (Sonography is described in greater detail in the fibroid tumor section in Chapter 13, Uterine Abnormalities.)

Thermography

Another relatively new method of diagnosing breast cancer is *thermography*, which operates on the theory that all objects give off infrared energy. A *thermogram* takes a picture of these infrared emissions, which vary depending on the temperature of the body from which they come. Since cancer is comprised of rapidly dividing cells requiring a greater blood supply than normal, a cancerous area generates more energy and heat than surrounding tissue. Therefore, when thermography is used to screen the breasts, any cancerous area appears hotter than normal.

Thermography gives physicians a greater indication of where to look for abnormalities, but it cannot pick up very early *in situ* cancer, as can mammography and xeroradiography. For that reason, it should not be used alone, but rather as a supplementary diagnostic tool.

Blood Sample Diagnosis

Besides trying to improve already existing diagnostic techniques, researchers are always looking for new and better methods. Several studies are presently being done to see if cancer can be diagnosed from blood samples. These studies are still in a preliminary stage and are not yet of any clinical value.

Fig. 18–6: Thermography. The picture illustrates a normal thermography; the darker area shows higher temperatures.

Government Projects

In 1972, the National Cancer Institute and the American Cancer Society, in conjunction with the United States government, set up twenty-seven screening centers throughout the country. These screening centers are participating in the National Breast Cancer Detection Demonstration Project. Mammography, xeroradiography, and thermography are among the many diagnostic tools that are being tested for effectiveness. From 1972 to 1978, 270,000 women in the over-thirty-five age range will take part in the program. At the end of 1978, a more definitive choice between the methods should be available.

Biopsies

Many women want to know what happens if an unusual mass is discovered during examination. There are several different, though related, procedures that can be followed. If the abnormality is slight and the physician doubts malignancy, the patient is usually sent for an X-ray, or maybe an X-ray in combination with thermography, for further analysis. However, if the mass is distinctly abnormal, a physician may feel that a biopsy is in order. In such a case, mammography may or may not be used to help define the area on which the biopsy will be performed.

A biopsy is a medical technique used to examine body tissue. In cases of possible breast cancer, an extremely small piece of the suspicious tissue is removed and sent to a pathological laboratory. The tissue is then cut into extremely thin layers, and various dyes are applied to stain the cells of each section. These dyes show whether cysts or cancerous growths are present. By examining the various dyed sections under a microscope, the nature of the growths can be diagnosed. Biopsy is at present considered the only definite way to determine whether a growth is cancerous.

If the mass appears highly suspicious and possibly malignant during an examination or X-ray, a biopsy is performed in a hospital. In this country, it is normal for the surgeon to send a sample of the suspicious tissue to the hospital's pathological laboratory during the course of the operation. The tissue will be examined in the lab, and the physician will know if the mass is malignant within a few minutes. If it is, the patient usually has an immediate mastectomy—the breast with the malignant tissue is removed.

Although it has been the standard for years, this procedure has recently come under attack. Some people believe a less extensive operation with postoperative chemotherapy would be just as effective as mastectomy. However, if the mass is so large that it can be felt and it is suspected of having spread to the lymph glands, a mastectomy is in order. If the operation is very extensive, radiation and chemotherapy may still be needed afterward to obtain a complete cure.

CYSTIC DISEASE

There are several disorders beside cancer which affect the breasts. Cystic disease is one of the most common of these, occurring in approximately 15 to 20 percent of women between the ages of twenty and fifty. There are several varieties of cystic disease, each with a different name and somewhat different symptoms. Among the various types are *cystic mastitis, chronic cystic mastitis,* and *fibrocystic disease.*

The exact cause of cystic disorders is unknown, but they usually occur during a woman's reproductive or estrogen-producing years. Some women develop a chronic cystic condition, while others experience cystic conditions only just prior to menstruation. While some women suffer slight discomfort, others experience extreme pain. The pain can be so severe that a woman can hardly wear a bra or other clothing on the breasts, particularly just prior to menstruation, when the hormone level is highest. Sometimes a cystic condition makes a breast feel very granular. At other times, as in the case of fibrocystic disease, the masses tend to be more solid (a woman with this type of cystic disease runs a higher risk of developing breast cancer. Therefore she should examine herself more often and more carefully. After the age of thirty-five, she should have a biyearly X-ray of the breast in combination with thermography).

Aspiration

If a patient has a tendency toward cystic breasts, she may occasionally feel the development of a cystic mass that causes extreme pain. In these cases, the mass can be *aspirated* (drawn out) by a needle. This is usually done in a doctor's office.

The procedure is quite simple. A needle is inserted into the cyst, and the fluid is drawn out or aspirated. If it is suspect, the fluid drawn from the cyst is sent to a cytology laboratory to be analyzed for cancer cells. If cancer lines the cyst, the cancer cells expel into the cyst fluid. Therefore, they are present in the aspirated matter. Aspiration is, in fact, a sort of needle biopsy.

Many physicians prefer not to perform needle biopsies and will only aspirate an area if they are certain the patient forms cystic masses. In these cases, aspiration takes pressure off the breast and alleviates pain. Although aspiration can provide a rough screening for cancer, most doctors continue to perform surgical biopsies for cancer diagnosis.

Treatment of Cystic Breasts

A number of treatments other than aspiration have been suggested for cystic conditions. Some physicians feel that since water retention causes tenderness in the breasts, women with cystic tendencies should take diuretics. Diuretics cause the body to lose water, thereby reducing tenderness. Other physicians believe a woman with cystic tendencies should be placed on a low-dose hormone pill. This keeps the hormone balance at a steady level throughout the month, rather than allowing it to fluctuate naturally. For a woman with cystic disease, this can alleviate some problems. Yet, while low-dose hormone pills are prescribed for some women, others are treated with Enovid, a birth-control pill containing a rather high amount of estrogen. Women on Enovid also experience improvement of their conditions. Most doctors will not recommend this treatment because of the dangers of the high estrogen content in these pills.

Danazol in the Treatment of Cystic Breasts

Recently a new antigonadotrophic hormone called Danazol has been developed. An antigonadotrophic hormone stops stimulation of the ovaries and is usually used to treat endometriosis. Aside from its intended use, though, Danazol, in doses of 200 or 400 milligrams daily, has been proved effective in relieving cystic mastitis. The reason is simple: Danazol decreases FSH and LH in the pituitary gland. FSH sends the signals which cause an egg to be produced in the ovaries. Once the egg has been produced, LH signals the release of that egg. When a woman takes Danazol, her ovaries receive less stimulation as a result of the decreased levels of FSH and LH. As a consequence, there is less estrogen production and no cyclic variation in the hormone level. This causes a decrease of the breast's cystic glands. However, although Danazol has in some cases cured cystic mastitis, it has not yet been approved by the Food and Drug Administration for use in treating cystic diseases. That approval will doubtless arrive soon, and many women with cystic tendencies will enjoy the benefits of Danazol.

OTHER BREAST ABNORMALITIES

Of course, not every irregularity in breast appearance means that something is wrong. Breasts come in different shapes and sizes and, for peace of mind, women should know some of the more interesting variations.

Some women have unevenly sized breasts, a condition similar to men who have one testicle larger than the other. This characteristic is usually hereditary. Such women are completely normal and function every bit as well as women with evenly matched breasts. As a matter of fact, their breasts are just like other women's; they're just not evenly matched. This difference hardly needs to be corrected surgically.

It is also considered normal for some women to have inverted nipples. Generally if a woman is born with an inverted nipple, it is a genetic factor, and should not cause concern. It does not change sex characteristics or affect pleasure.

However, if a woman has had a converted nipple that *becomes* inverted, she should see her doctor. It could be a sign of some abnormality developing inside the breast. Such a condition should be examined and treated accordingly.

Other women are born with several nipples. In such cases, the nipples start where the breasts are usually located, and two or three additional nipples are located on each side of the abdomen, going down toward the pubic hair. The condition seems to be a throwback to our evolutionary predecessors, but it is not rare or dangerous. However, if one or more of the extra nipples is large and causes psychological trauma, it can be removed by a plastic surgeon. Still, such an operation is not considered necessary for good health.

MAINTENANCE OF HEALTHY BREASTS

Good health care should be constant practice for everyone. Ultimately we are all responsible for ourselves; we can't rely on doctors to provide miracle cures when we notify them too late about specific abnormalities or diseases.

Concern for health is the most important weapon in the fight against disease. Monthly self-examination of the breasts and regular checkups with your physician should be routine parts of your life. It is important not to allow fear to get in the way of common sense. Remember, what you don't know can hurt you, especially if you neglect it. Cancer of the breast is cured every day of the year, and it is beaten by those women who discover and recognize the disease while it is still in its early stages.

chapter 19

CORRECTIVE BREAST SURGERY

Many women are unhappy about the appearance of their breasts. Some who feel their breasts are too small undergo all forms of exercise and/or hormone treatments to enlarge the breasts and often finally decide that such efforts yield no results. Some of these women decide to have silicone injections or implantations, only to find that the silicone injections are frequently harmful. In some instances, the breasts become very hard and lumpy, resulting in fear of having them touched or caressed.

Other women, who consider their breasts to be great beauty assets, find that after childbearing, their breasts often become softer and start to sag. This often causes unhappiness. Some women feel they are not as attractive as before, and so decide to have corrective breast surgery.

Quite a few women have been happy with the results of corrective breast surgery. It should be emphasized, however, that if you decide to have breast augmentation surgery, you should be sure you choose a very competent surgeon, one familiar with the latest developments in this field.

In the last few years, surgical corrective procedures of the breast have developed into a fine art. Pendulous breasts can be made smaller; sagging breasts can be elevated; ugly scars can be excised, and small breasts can be enlarged. Most of these operations must be considered major procedures, but not in the risk-to-life category. Nevertheless, because these major procedures require general anesthesia, which in itself entails a certain risk to life, breast surgery should not be performed on every woman wishing a correction for minor abnormalities or a reduction of slightly large breasts. Nor should it be performed to enlarge breasts that can be considered normal. However, a great number of women can and have benefited from the techniques of corrective breast surgery.

Today the desire to beautify the breasts is not limited to any particular age group. Young and old alike display great interest in the possibility of help through plastic surgery, and such help should not be denied any woman on the basis of age. On the other hand, the general state of a woman's health should be considered before any final decision is made. The most important consideration is the type and extent of the breast deformity. Remember, one should never undergo breast surgery for a minor defect.

Another equally important consideration is the emotional stability of the woman. It has been found that insecure, maladjusted, and unstable women are usually poor candidates for corrective breast surgery. Such women tend to expect the operation to cure emotional ills unrelated to the shape or size of their breasts. It should be pointed out that no plastic surgeon, no matter how good he is, can change your life. Only you can do that. Many plastic surgeons, especially if they are honest and competent, soon become familiar with the psychological problems of their patients and know beforehand who should or should not be subjected to breast reduction or augmentation surgery. When in doubt, many plastic surgeons refer patients for psychiatric evaluation prior to any surgery.

Finally, this type of surgery should only be performed by very skilled plastic surgeons—surgeons who are highly specialized in these procedures. Women should seek a physician who wants to do a good job, who carefully evaluates his patients, and who tries not only to increase the beauty of the breast, but who also takes into account the psychological stability of the woman. Obviously, plastic surgeons who are just looking to make money should be avoided.

It is, of course, difficult to find the right and most competent plastic surgeon. Referrals from friends who have had plastic surgery performed and were satisfied with the results could be good leads. It is probably a good idea to try to find a plastic surgeon who is associated with a teaching institution, since they are generally familiar with the most up-to-date procedures and also are not likely to recommend unnecessary surgery. For more concrete guidance, a woman considering corrective breast surgery can write to the American Society of Plastic and Reconstructive Surgeons (29 East Madison, Suite 807, Chicago, Illinois 60602) and request a list of qualified plastic surgeons in her area.

UNDERDEVELOPED BREASTS

Usually a woman's breasts are fully developed by the time she is sixteen or seventeen years old. Of course, some women's breasts develop later in life, and this is usually determined genetically. In other words, if your mother developed late, you might also develop late. Sometimes, however, the estrogen hormone, which gives the secondary sex characteristics in women and is the stimulus to breast growth, is not released normally, and therefore does not trigger the development of the breast or the growth of pubic hair. If this is the case, a physician can administer hormone treatments, which sometimes help trigger the growth and development of the breast and other secondary sex characteristics. Birth-control pills containing a high level of estrogen usually increase the size of the breasts. When this type of birth control is discontinued, the breasts generally return to their original size. Pregnancy also stimulates hormone production, causing the breasts to increase in size. Again, the breast size usually decreases after pregnancy, or after a woman has finished breast-feeding.

Breast Exercises

Advertisements for various types of breast-development techniques and exercise programs erroneously lead many women to believe that it is relatively easy to increase breast size through these methods. As a result of these advertisements, many women spend a great deal of money only to discover that the promised results are never achieved. There is no exercise that will increase the actual amount of breast tissue. All exercise and breast-development techniques can do is strengthen and firm the pectoral muscles, which support the breasts. Good posture, with the back straight and the shoulders back and down, also greatly improves the breast contours by giving them better lift.

Many women wonder what breast developers actually are. They are merely exercise props. Many consist of a strong rubber band with two handles; others consist of an exercise bar which is held with both hands to stimulate the movements of isometric exercises for strengthening the pectoral muscles. Some breast-development courses include additional devices, such as plastic cups containing tiny jets through which water is emitted in order to massage the breasts, and various kinds of moisturizing and massage creams for the breasts. Needless to say, these extras are completely useless as far as increasing the size of the breasts is concerned. Most breast-development programs include a booklet illustrating various exercise movements which should be performed with the aid of the rubber band or the exercise bar. Many also contain a nutritional guide, since proper nutrition may affect the fatty deposits in the breast tissue. Once again, it should be pointed out that no breast-development technique or exercise program can actually increase the amount of fatty tissue in a woman's breasts. This is a genetically determined characteristic.

Instead of spending money on these so-called breast-development programs, it would be much more reasonable for a woman to do some isometric exercises especially geared to developing the pectoral muscles and strengthening the back muscles for good posture. These exercises are often featured in various fashion and other women's magazines. Isometric exercises work on the principle of opposing muscles which are so contracted that there is little shortening but great increase in the tone of the muscle fibers involved. Pushups are another way of strengthening muscles in the back, chest wall, and upper arms. Swimming is also an excellent all-purpose exercise which improves the tone of the muscles that support the breasts. Remember, though, there is only so much that exercise can do to change the size of the breasts, since it can only firm the muscles which support the breasts.

Who Should Have Breast Augmentation?

As the saying goes, it is not how much you have, but how you use it that counts. It is time for women to start looking at themselves in a more positive light and not allow their self-esteem to be unduly influenced by the male fetish of large breasts, an attitude prevalent in the United States. It is perfectly understandable that a woman wants to be attractive and feel good about her appearance. This can, however, often be achieved through dieting and proper exercise. Also, the right clothes can do a great deal to enhance a woman's figure. Unfortunately, many women go to great lengths to appear younger and more attractive to men. For this reason, many women resort to all kinds of breast-development courses, exercise programs, and even plastic surgery to achieve this goal. It should be pointed out, however, that a majority of men do not look at a woman's breast size when they first meet and are attracted to her. They are usually more interested in the qualities that make up the total person. A woman should try to be pleased with herself as she is, and not necessarily look to a plastic surgeon as soon as she notices minor wrinkles or sagging.

If you are extremely unhappy with the size of your breasts, try to delay any surgical procedures until you have finished childbearing, since too many women who have breast augmentation before they become pregnant find that they need additional surgery after childbearing. Breast size has nothing to do with erotic sensitivity or pleasure. Only those women who feel their breast size has become a burden to them should consider breast augmentation, and then these women should realize that the results of breast augmentation are not always what they expect them to be.

Silicone

One of the first methods of breast augmentation was the injection of liquid silicone into the breast. This created a cystic mass inside the breast, which enlarged the breast and kept its contour up. Some of the first women to have this procedure performed were go-go dancers, belly dancers, stripteasers, and others whose livelihood depended on their physical assets. However, by looking closely at these women, one could see that the breasts did not move naturally, and furthermore, they were as hard as rocks when touched. Many of these women did not want anyone to touch their breasts for fear of being ridiculed.

Worse still, when examined under research conditions, the injected silicone was found to be very dangerous. It formed a hard mass encapsuled inside the breast tissue, making it impossible for a physician to examine the breast or to determine if cancer was present.

Even though they were widely used for mammary augmentation, liquid silicone injections involved several other serious hazards. Since liquid silicone is really a foreign substance injected into the tissue, all types of foreign-tissue reactions could occur. There was a fear that it could even cause cancer, and if cancer did occur, that it could not be detected. Often a solid tumor developed around the injected silicone and created a nodule so painful that surgery for removal of the mass was necessary. The silicone often migrated into the lymphatic tissue and bloodstream, and from there to other parts of the body, where it could also form tumors. Liquid silicone has, by mistake, been injected into blood vessels, and in some instances, it has even traveled to the heart. There was a recent report of a nightclub dancer who died a few hours after a silicone injection. For a variety of reasons, silicone was found to be dangerous in an injected form and was finally taken off the market by the Food and Drug Administration. Silicone injections are now illegal.

However, silicone itself is a substance which is extremely body friendly—if it is put into the body, there is usually no body reaction against it. Silicone does not react completely like another foreign body, and it has many advantages over other substances, such as plastic, since it can be implanted into the body for longer periods of time. Silicone is now used as a prosthesis in the replacement of hardened arteries, as well as for other types of corrective surgery.

Eventually breast implants of a hard, silastic material (also called silicone) were developed in the shape of a cup. A surgeon could perform an incision underneath the breast and implant these cups in such a way that they would not move around in the body. These cups would then stretch out the breasts, thereby uplifting them and giving them better contour. This operation was performed on many thousands of women throughout the United States and Europe, particularly on well-to-do women or those in the public eye. These women found that such silastic implants improved their appearance and also uplifted their self-image.

A major problem, however, was that these implanted masses were very hard. Although thousands of women who had these hard silastic implants found pleasure and happiness after the surgical procedure, many were afraid that as soon as a man would touch them, even while dancing, he would feel the hard cup. Subsequently, there was a great deal of psychological trauma for some of these women. Although many women felt improvement in their appearance, they were often afraid to tell a man, particularly a new boyfriend, that they had silicone implants in their breast—justifiably so, it seems, since many men were repelled by the new breasts and felt as if they were making love to a rubber doll, not to a woman. This caused uneasiness for both the men and the women involved.

Soft Silicone Implants: A Real Improvement

A new type of silicone has recently been developed by the Dow Corning Corporation. This silastic is made of low-viscous silicone gel which is so soft that it approximates normal breast tissue. This gel is poured into a very strong, thin cover, which prevents it from leaking out. It is then implanted into the breast, where it will stay *in situ* (i.e., it will not leak into other areas or be absorbed by the bloodstream and then transported to other parts of the body).

This new type of soft silicone is available in different shapes (including round) and sizes, all approximating various breast shapes. This soft silastic has been used by certain specialists for

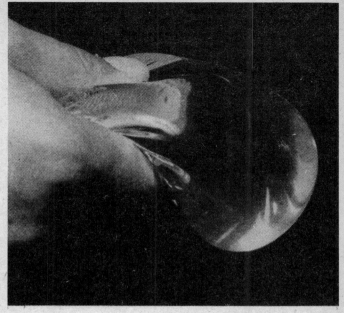

ABOVE
Fig. 19-1: A soft silicone breast implant. The silicone is smooth and easily conforms to the pressure of the hands. This implant comes in many various sizes and shapes.

BELOW
Fig. 19-2: The position of a soft silicone implant inserted through an incision in the inframammary fold underneath the breast. (Courtesy of Dow Corning Corporation.)

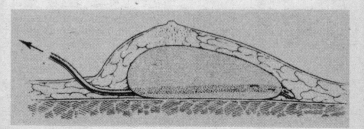

several years and has been very successful. Since it is implanted underneath the breast next to the chest wall and is completely surrounded by breast tissue, it is impossible for a layman to feel any difference between the implanted soft silastic and normal breast tissue.

Still, many institutions and clinics do not use the soft silicone extensively, and many physicians are still inserting the hard silicone. Women should be alerted to the fact that soft silicone is now available, and many specialists, particularly plastic surgeons specializing in soft-silicone breast implantations, have gained great knowledge and skill in the implantation of the soft material. Further, these specialists have become very knowledgeable in using the right size and shape implants so as to create the most natural look for each woman.

If you are planning to have a silastic implantation, you should ask for the soft silicone. It is ideal for breast augmentation if the breast sags too much or if it is too small, or after breast surgery, biopsy, or maybe even after mastectomies. The hard implant should only be used in very special cases. It can cause great unhappiness, and you should refuse to have the hard silicone implanted unless it is absolutely necessary.

Implanting the Soft Silastic

The implantation of the soft silastic is essentially performed in one of two ways. The silastic can be inserted through an incision underneath the breast, in the so-called inframammary fold (the fold between the chest wall and the breast). This incision is usually not seen, because the breasts tend to fold in that area. The operation is performed under either general or local anesthesia. Under a local anesthetic, you normally receive premedication, such as morphine or Demerol, and thereafter, local injections of Novocaine. The physician then makes an incision in the inframammary fold, inserts the silicone prosthesis underneath the breast tissue at the chest wall, and closes the incision with a few sutures. He then places a tight bandage around the breast to prevent bleeding and to insure that the implants remain in the right position. A small tube is often placed through the incision in order to drain off any blood which otherwise could form a hematoma. The new, soft silastics do not tend to slide once they are placed in the proper position.

The majority of physicians prefer to perform this procedure in a hospital under general anesthesia. By doing this, a physician can better determine correct size and can more easily mold the breast, placing the silastic implant in exactly the right position, without causing unnecessary harm or pain to the patient.

Usually the patient is released from the hospital one to two days later. The patient is asked not to move around too much during the first week, giving the implantation time to rest and heal inside the breast without causing any harm, unnecessary bleeding, or damage to the tissue.

If a woman has a large enough areola (the pigmented area around the nipple), plastic surgeons often make a circular incision on the edge of the pigmented area and insert the silicone through this incision. A small pocket is made from the incision into the chest wall so the silicone implant is placed right at the chest wall, underneath the milk glands. The incision usually heals well and is hardly visible after the operation.

Many women have been pleased with the results of the soft silastic implants; however, it must be noted that the results are not always satisfactory. Many other women have had to undergo repeated operations because they were dissatisfied with the appearance and size of their silastic implants, or because of complications, such as hardening of the silicone or scar tissue which subsequently developed around the implant. In order to ensure the best possible results, a woman should try to find the most competent and experienced plastic surgeon she can. The final result of a soft silastic implantation will depend upon the original size of your breasts, areola, and nipple, and upon the extent of enlargement that you desire.

Replacing Hard Silicone Implants with Soft Ones

Any type of silastic that has been inserted into the breast can usually be fairly easily removed and replaced by another type. Many women have already had the hard silicone replaced by the soft gel. The results have often been excellent. Furthermore, if a woman has already had implantation of either the hard or soft silastic and feels that the size is not right, the implants can usually be removed and replaced.

One such patient recently came to my office. Before the examination she told me she had had the hard silicone removed and the soft inserted, and was very pleased with the results since her breasts now felt completely normal. I asked two nurses to examine her, pretending that I thought the patient had a breast tumor. Both nurses examined the patient's breasts thoroughly, and could not feel a tumor. Later on, when I told them the woman had had soft silicone implanted, they could not believe it, because to them, the breasts felt perfectly normal. Several other patients have also said that after they had soft silicone implanted by specialists, even their own gynecologists could not detect that they had implants.

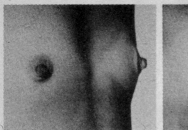
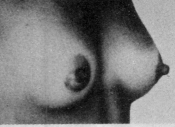

ABOVE

Fig. 19-3: A woman before and after soft silicone implantation. This woman had almost no breast tissue prior to surgery, but by implantation of a small cup, the breast is given sufficient enlargement to create a natural look. (Courtesy of Robert G. Schwager, M.D., attending plastic surgeon at New York Hospital, New York City.)

BELOW

Fig. 19-4: A woman before and after a breast augmentation with implantation of soft silicone. The silicone was inserted underneath the breast, in the inframammary fold, and a smooth, natural curve has been achieved. (Courtesy of Robert G. Schwager, M.D., attending plastic surgeon at New York Hospital, New York City.)

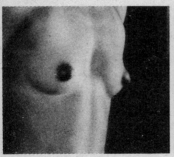
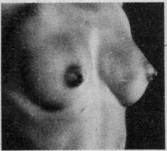

Is the Silastic Implantation Dangerous?

The soft silastic has not been found to be dangerous. It is a product which does not give a foreign-body reaction, and it can be easily implanted into the breast. If the soft silicone is implanted in a lower incision, in the inframammary fold, it is put underneath the breast tissue so that the tissue completely surrounds it. A physician examining the breast can still detect cancer, either manually or by mammography. Soft silastic implants have never been shown to cause cancer in any laboratory studies. If the implantation is done by a qualified and experienced physician, there should be no major complications. For these reasons, it can be safely stated that the new silastic should not be dangerous to women.

Breast-Feeding after a Silastic Implant

A woman who has a silastic implantation performed through an incision in the inframammary fold underneath the breast will still have normal breast tissue and can, therefore, breast-feed, since such an incision leaves the milk gland intact. Normal breast examinations and mammography are also the rule. On the other hand, a woman who has an implantation through an incision in the nipple might have difficulty breast-feeding, since some of the ducts leading the milk to the nipple might have been cut during this procedure.

BREAST REDUCTION

For every woman who is unhappy because she feels that her breasts are underdeveloped, there is another woman who is burdened by overdeveloped breasts. There are numerous reasons why women with very large breasts are unhappy, and each individual case is different. Many problems which women with overdeveloped breasts face can be attributed to the trauma which our breast-oriented society imposes upon women in general.

Many women become so concerned with breast size that they diet extensively, hoping that a drastic weight loss will also reduce the size of their breasts. Unfortunately, this doesn't happen consistently. Girls in their teens are often alarmed at the rate at which their breasts develop, because the breasts undergo continuous growth during this period. This growth is accompanied by increased vascularity, which, in turn, can make the breasts feel very heavy. Naturally, this feeling is quite different from what a young girl experiences in her early teens. A woman's breasts do not reach their maturation until she is about twenty years old.

Because of the breast-oriented society in which we live, many women become so concerned and emotionally upset about the size of their breasts that they decide to have reduction surgery at an early age. These women often feel very uncomfortable, since they think people are always staring at them. Instead of being known for their personality, intelligence, and other qualities, such women feel that they are only known as "the girl with

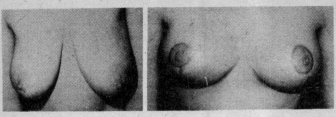

Fig. 19–5: Breast reduction. The picture to the left is before and to the right is after breast reduction, *mammaplasty*. This woman complained of heavy, large breasts which became increasingly troublesome after childbirth. She also developed large stretch marks in the breasts. She underwent breast reduction surgery by a modification of the *dermal mastopexy* operation. This is a procedure developed by Dr. Dicran Goulian, Jr., professor and chairman of the department of plastic surgery at the New York Hospital–Cornell University Medical Center, New York City.

Dermal mastopexy is a procedure in which the areola and the nipple are moved upward on the breast and excessive skin tissue is excised. This procedure stretches the skin on the breasts and makes the breasts look healthier and younger without damaging the milk glands. This procedure has been referred to in lay terms as a "breast lift." The patient in the illustration had a modest breast reduction in association with the mastopexy. The breast tissue removed is usually a small part of the mass. Most of the resected tissue is excessive fat. The scars had not completely healed when this picture was taken a few weeks after the procedure. The scars subsequently become lighter and more difficult to notice. The milk glands have not been damaged during this procedure and the patient will be able to breast-feed if she has a child. The stretch marks which were seen before the procedure have become less conspicuous because of the tightening process. (Courtesy of Dicran Goulian, Jr., M.D., chairman of the department of plastic surgery, New York Hospital, New York City.)

the big breasts." Most girls are aware that breast size is genetically determined, so if their mothers and grandmothers have very large breasts, this is often an additional incentive to seek breast-reduction surgery at an early age.

Aside from the emotional discomfort which hypertrophic breasts may inflict upon a woman, there can also be considerable physical discomfort. Pendulous breasts can be so heavy as to cause strain on the back muscles by pulling the shoulders forward, thus contributing to poor posture. Also, many women have complained that the weight of their breasts causes their brassiere straps to cut into their flesh. This, too, can be very disagreeable. Furthermore, some women with pendulous breasts tend to adopt poor posture in an effort to minimize the size of their breasts.

Most women have some slight variation in the size of their breasts, with the left breast tending to be somewhat larger than the right. Although this slight variation is perfectly normal and usually goes unnoticed, some women have a very marked asymmetry of the two breasts. Again, if a woman is emotionally mature and has a healthy amount of self-confidence, this asymmetry should not be a source of concern, although it does cause psychological trauma in some women. Women should not be too concerned about a slight variation in the size of their breasts, since this is much more common than most people realize. However, if the asymmetry becomes too great a problem, plastic surgery to even out the two breasts through reduction of the larger breast might be warranted.

Before making a definite decision regarding breast reduction, women should remember that this type of surgery does not always produce satisfactory results. Since the breast is composed of fatty tissue, any reduction in its size often entails the removal and replacement of the nipple. This means that several incisions must be made in the breast. Although the breast might have a better overall appearance, upon close examination, there will often be scars, because fatty tissues tend not to heal well. These scars can be very ugly and can cause unhappiness, despite the fact that a woman can be pleased with her improved overall appearance.

Sadly, breast-reduction surgery is often performed very early in a woman's life, sometimes while she is still in her teens. This is a time when most people have not yet found themselves emotionally. Physiologically, although a girl may be fully grown by the time she reaches her teens, she might still have baby fat. Frequently when a woman reaches her twenties, she loses this baby fat and her body assumes its normal size and proportions. If breast-reduction surgery has been performed while a girl is still in her teens, she might find later that, as she loses weight, her once overly large breasts become too small. There are even cases in which women who have had breast-reduction surgery in their teens have subsequently undergone silastic implantation to increase the size of their breasts. For this reason, breast-reduction surgery should not usually be performed until after a woman has borne children. Following childbearing, the tissues are more relaxed, especially when the breasts are large, and the breasts might then start to sag. If the breasts sag after bearing children, corrective surgery might be in order.

Is Breast-Reduction Surgery Necessary?

The possibility of breast-reduction surgery should be very carefully evaluated. If a woman feels that her breasts are too large or asymmetrical, she should try to focus on the other beauty in her life instead of letting this bother her unduly. Furthermore, large breasts should not usually cause a woman to suffer from poor posture if she has the discipline and determination to exercise in order to strenghten her back and to correct her posture.

Some women have been conditioned by religious upbringing to feel ashamed of their large breasts. This is strictly a matter of cultural conditioning. In some countries—for example, in France—women have not been negatively conditioned in this manner, and every Frenchwoman is generally happy to show how well endowed she is by maintaining erect and good posture.

Before deciding to undergo breast-reduction surgery, a woman should first carefully evaluate the reasons she feels such an operation is necessary. She should also be well aware of the fact that she will most likely be left with many scars in the breast after such an operation. Also, a woman should first try to camouflage her breasts with the right kind of clothes.

A woman should not have any kind of corrective surgery performed on her breasts unless they really are damagingly large. If she does decide to have such an operation performed, she should go only to the very best plastic surgeon she can find—to a physician very experienced in this specific procedure.

It is only after a woman has been married and has had at least one child that she should consider breast-reduction surgery, and then only if the breasts begin to sag to such an extent that they cause the woman psychological trauma. At this time, a woman might have a breast-reduction operation, or perhaps a breast lifting. In any event, a woman should not have either of these operations performed while she is in her teens unless her breasts are unusually hypertrophic or asymmetrical.

Does Breast Sensitivity Decrease after Breast-Reduction Surgery?

Breast-reduction surgery is a procedure in which most of the fatty tissue and all of the nerve endings in the breast are removed. The nipple is also generally removed and replaced. Consequently, some women do not have any feeling or sensation of sexual arousal in their breasts following surgery. This deprives these women of so much sexual pleasure that they find

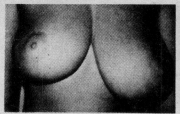 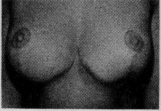

Fig. 19–6: Breast reduction in a patient with marked breast asymmetry. The picture illustrates the breasts of an eighteen-year-old woman who complained of breast hypertrophy and marked asymmetry, the left breast being much larger than the right. Her breasts were very heavy and the veins very visible; the veins can just be seen on the picture before surgery. The picture to the right shows the results after breast reduction surgery. Both breasts were reduced in size; they are now equal in size and have a natural look. The fresh scars are still visible beneath the left breast. The patient has subsequently undergone further correction of these scars — and is very pleased with the operation, claiming both physical and emotional satisfaction. (Courtesy of Dicran Goulian, Jr., M.D., chairman of the department of plastic surgery, New York Hospital, New York City.)

it more difficult to achieve orgasm, or orgasm must be reached without breast stimulation and satisfaction.

Also, some women become so emotionally upset following breast-reduction surgery that they feel they can no longer show their scarred breasts to a man, and therefore have turned to lesbian relationships. It must be made clear, however, that this usually happens only to women who have always attached too much importance to the appearance and/or sexual appeal of their breasts.

If a woman feels the need for any correction of her breasts, especially if she is still in her teens, it might be wise to try to accomplish this through exercise rather than with an operation which could leave her with unattractive scars, and which could also cause a possible loss of much sexual pleasure by desensitization.

CAN STRETCH MARKS BE REMOVED?

Many women find that as the milk glands grow during pregnancy, the breasts enlarge so much that stretch marks appear. This is more likely to happen to girls who become pregnant in their teens. When a woman has reached her twenties and her body is fully grown, there seems to be a lessened risk of stretch marks. Nevertheless, many women who become pregnant in their teens and early adult lives find that their breasts have been disfigured by stretch marks. This may cause problems with their sexual partners.

There is presently no medication to prevent or remove stretch marks. Many women apply vitamin E cream, other creams, baby lotions, and a wide variety of other products to their breasts during pregnancy to prevent stretch marks, but this has never been scientifically proven to be effective. The best way to avoid stretch marks is to wait until you are in your twenties to have children. If you already have stretch marks, there is no way, surgically or otherwise, that they can be removed. If the stretch marks bother you, you might try getting a light suntan on your breasts. When the skin is lightly pigmented, these marks are less visible.

REMOVING SCARS OR BURN MARKS

Some women, particularly those who have undergone breast-reduction surgery, find the surgical scars so unattractive that they cause great unhappiness. Such women return time and time again to plastic surgeons for removal of the scars. If a surgical scar is really wide and disfiguring, a competent plastic surgeon can usually minimize it. Still, as the doctor is again making an incision and suturing the skin, there will be one remaining scar. By closure with finer sutures resulting from modern plastic-surgery techniques, though, the final scar should have a much better appearance. If a woman has problems with scars, she should make sure that she goes only to the best plastic surgeon. It is generally better to go to plastic surgeons associated with large medical institutions, since they know about the latest developments in this area. In this way, a woman can usually be assured of excellent results. Remember, though, there will always be one remaining scar.

RECONSTRUCTION AFTER A MASTECTOMY

Much research has been done to develop implants for women who have undergone mastectomy. Some women who have undergone radical mastectomies, entailing the removal of all of the muscle under the chest wall and in the armpit, have so little tissue left underneath the breast that it is very difficult to insert any kind of silicone. Women who have undergone such major surgery have usually had a very extensive type of cancer, and in such cases, the woman's health is undoubtedly more important than aesthetic considerations.

Nonetheless, as newer developments and understanding of cancer progress, there is hope of finding new ways to cure breast cancer. Perhaps by removing a lesser amount of breast tissue and at the same time giving chemical or radiation therapy, breast implants could be cosmetically utilized. In fact, research centers are now developing varying types of breast-augmentation techniques in combination with mastectomy to rebuild the removed breast.

Reconstructing the Nipple Following Mastectomy

One of the major difficulties in breast augmentation after or in combination with mastectomy is the nipple. The nipple is usually removed along with the excised breast, and to rebuild a new nipple is virtually impossible. However, a nipple can be reconstructed using tissue from the vulva, and occasionally a new breast can be built using tissue from a woman's own body or through augmentation with soft Silastic. A breast can occasionally be built up after mastectomy so it has approximately the same size as the other breast when a bra is worn. It is, however, impossible to rebuild a breast that is exactly like a woman's own breast and that will look the same in the nude. Most breast reconstructions involve several surgical procedures. If there is some tissue left underneath the mastectomy scar, a small silastic implant can possibly be inserted, and this can subsequently be replaced with larger implants until the right size is achieved. A nipple can then be constructed from genital tissue. Since it is often difficult to achieve the same size breast, though, plastic surgeons often perform a reduction on the woman's other breast to equalize more or less the size of the two breasts.

Several European surgeons who have been performing less extensive mastectomies are saving sufficient skin tissue to enable them to reconstruct a new breast. They are creating a nipple by placing sutures underneath the skin in a circular mode to form a nipplelike protrusion. They then simulate the areola by tattooing this area in the same color as the other side.

Future Developments for Breast Reconstruction Following Mastectomy

More than a thousand women in the United States, and many more worldwide, have already undergone breast augmentation after mastectomy, and almost 90 percent of these women have been satisfied with the results. However, in order to achieve the most satisfactory results with breast-reconstruction surgery, it is crucial to save the woman's own nipple during mastectomy, if it is at all possible. Since cancer involves the nipple in only about 10 percent of all breast cancer cases, it is often possible to save the woman's nipple.

In order to obtain optimum results from both cancer treatment and breast reconstruction, during mastectomy it is important for the cancer surgeon and the plastic surgeon to work as a team. Usually when a woman discovers she has breast cancer, she becomes so frightened that her first reaction is to go to a surgeon and have a mastectomy performed as quickly as possible, so as to safeguard her health. This is a perfectly normal reaction.

However, after such women have fully recovered from cancer surgery and look every day at the resultant scars, they become concerned with the appearance of their bodies and wonder whether it would be possible to have reconstructive plastic surgery to minimize the mastectomy scars. They also wonder if the excised breast can be reconstructed.

Unfortunately, it is very difficult to achieve satisfactory results in breast reconstruction following mastectomy if the woman and her doctors have not planned on this possibility before performing the mastectomy. Because of this, it is strongly suggested that whenever a woman is confronted with the dilemma of breast cancer, she should concern herself not only with the mastectomy procedure, but should also investigate the possibility of having reconstructive breast surgery performed concurrently. Several medical centers are presently investigating various types of combination mastectomy/reconstructive surgery procedures, but such centers are few and far between, since this possibility is still in the very early stages of development. At the present time, most doctors are not likely even to consider the possibility of breast reconstruction in combination with mastectomy. Still, these new developments hold great promise for the future.

Some experimental techniques of reconstructive plastic surgery following mastectomy involve the removal of the nipple and the areola (the pigmented area surrounding the nipple) during the actual mastectomy. A piece of this tissue is then checked for cancer. If it is free of cancer, the nipple can be temporarily grafted onto other parts of the patient's body, such as the abdomen or the buttock, where it would remain to draw nourishment until such time as it can be transferred back onto the newly reconstructed breast. When the mastectomy scar is completely healed and there is no more sign of cancer, the breast reconstruction could be initiated.

This type of breast-reconstruction plastic surgery involves several stages of surgical intervention. First a roll of skin and fatty tissue must be obtained by making a transverse incision in the lower part of the abdomen, where it remains until the scar has healed. The next step involves freeing a part of this roll of skin and fatty tissue from the lower part of the abdomen and swinging it into the position of the mastectomy scar, where it remains as a tube of tissue connecting the abdomen, from which it draws nourishment, to the mastectomy scar, where hopefully it will "take." When good vascularity between the mastectomy area and the skin and fatty tissue roll has occurred, the skin and fatty tissue can be detached from the abdomen and then, in the next operation, rolled up and formed like a breast. The final stage in this type of breast-reconstruction plastic surgery is to move the nipple back from the area where it has been receiving nourishment to the newly reconstructed breast. This particular technique looks promising, but several other ideas for breast reconstruction are also presently being developed.

Several European centers, in order to reconstruct more natural-appearing breasts, perform less radical surgery than in the United States. They rarely remove the pectoral muscles, which United States surgeons often do. Therefore, they have much greater success then their United States counterparts in breast augmentation.

There is much hope that in the future, women will be able to achieve satisfactory cosmetic results following mastectomy.

CANCER

Cancer is a frightening, costly, and painful disease which strikes indiscriminately. Medical researchers are now stating that we are in the midst of a cancer epidemic. The cancer rate in America has almost tripled since the turn of the century, and what had been a one-percent yearly increase since 1933 jumped to a five-percent increase in 1975. Approximately 650,000 new cases of cancer are discovered each year, and about 365,000 (over half) of them are fatal. Cancer strikes one out of every four people today, touching two out of every three families. More than 1,000 people die every day from cancer—more than one every minute and a half. As you can see, the chances are that *you* will not get cancer, but the odds are extremely slim.

On the other hand, some 222,000 Americans are cured of cancer every year because of early detection and improved treatment techniques. Cancer is no longer the certain death it was only a few years back, but it still sends a deserved chill through us when we encounter it. Probably because of the quickened pace and complexity of modern life, which affect our environment, eating habits, and life-styles—all of which may contribute to cancer—cancer is definitely on the rise. The only method to guard against it is *constant vigilance* and *early detection*.

WHAT IS CANCER?

Cancer is a disease in which normal cells start to grow uncontrollably. There are more than one hundred different forms of cancer; it is found in all the organs, as well as in the bones and in the blood. The disease is older than man. Evidence of this disease has been found in dinosaur fossils. The Egyptians wrote about it in their papyrus scrolls, and Hippocratic surgeons studied it in Greece.

The causes of cancer have baffled scientists through the ages and even today are only scarcely understood. For instance, we know that cigarette smoking contributes to lung cancer, but we still don't know exactly why. The first documented indirect cause of cancer was discovered by Sir Percival Pott in 1775. He noted a high incidence of cancer of the scrotum in chimney sweeps who had undergone prolonged exposure to soot. Soot is closely related to tar, and the sweeps were suffering from the same type of cancer that afflicts the lungs of smokers today.

Any cell in the body has the capacity to become cancerous, but once it does, its descendants exhibit some of the normal functions of the cell from which they originated. Thus if cancer begins in the liver and spreads to the kidneys, the tumors in the kidney will have liver characteristics, and doctors will be able to determine where the disease originated.

WHAT CAUSES CANCER?

It is possible to be exposed to a carcinogenic, or cancer-causing agent, and not develop the cancer for twenty or thirty years. Obviously this makes it extremely difficult to isolate the causes of cancer. Researchers are often criticized for introducing absurdly large amounts of questionable substances into laboratory animals to see if cancer develops. The resultant data are thought by some to be irrelevant because of these distorted quantities. But researchers have no choice. A well-controlled experiment over a period of twenty years is not feasible. In the face of the rush to add more and more preservatives and additives to our food and to stretch the limits to which we can pollute our air and water, criticism of these experiments is not completely valid. There is growing concern nationwide, however, that these critics (who themselves can offer no conclusive data to refute opposing research) are quick to criticize on the side of danger rather than safety—and when you're dealing with the environment, mistakes are irreversible.

So the debate rages. Some researchers are trying to find psychosomatic causes for cancer. Others look into cyclamates and other artificial sweeteners. Still others suspect the key will be found in the genetic code. A few causes have been positively identified, like the chimney sweeps' soot, radiation following

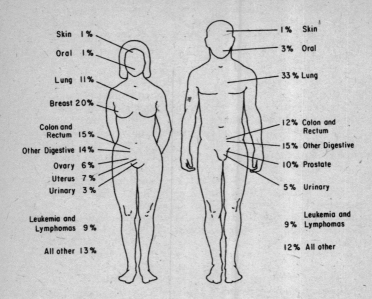

Fig. 20-1:   Cause of Cancer Deaths in 1976.

the bombings of Hiroshima and Nagasaki, prolonged exposure to the sun, and, most conclusively, cigarette smoking.

The effects of these agents on tissue are not fully understood, but the mechanism is usually described as *irritation.* Cigarette tar clings to the lungs and irritates the cells. A chronic inflammation may occur and persist for as many years as you smoke, until one day the cells begin to transform into abnormal cells— the start of cancer. The ultraviolet rays of the sun irritate the skin, and the same process may occur. Certain industrial pollutants carcinogenically irritate the liver, while others cause cancer of the kidneys.

Of course, with over a hundred varieties of cancer, all of them may not stem from the same cause. Some scientists believe cancer is a virus that can be cured as soon as an effective vaccine is developed. Others believe it is a physical reaction to emotional stress. These theories are not mutually exclusive.

Still, even though the *how* of cancer is unknown, the *what* is becoming clearer every day. Because of this, cancer prevention is probably far ahead of cancer treatment, or could be if people would heed the warnings. Unfortunately, they generally do not, endangering not only themselves, but whomever else they may expose to their carcinogens. One of the major causes of cancer today is human indifference and irresponsibility, as well as ignorance.

Tobacco

Sixty million Americans still smoke cigarettes. Considering its proven and well-publicized links to cancer, emphysema, and heart disease, the popularity of cigarette smoking is baffling. True, nicotine is physically addicting, but that didn't stop almost half the doctors who smoked from quitting when they first learned that smoking caused cancer. As the militancy of nonsmokers increases and they realize that smokers are giving them cancer and causing them physical discomfort, which is a violation of their natural right to breathe clean air, smoking may undergo a cultural transformation and become less fashionable, less accepted, and less appealing to children.

Unfortunately, this process has not yet begun. Today, 33 percent of all cancers in men are lung cancers, while 11 percent in women are lung cancers. It is feared that since more women are smoking tobacco today, the incidence of cancer in women will increase.

It seems peculiarly ironic that while science has finally made steps to solve this centuries-old puzzle, at the same time the problem increases because the facts are being ignored.

Cigarettes are especially toxic in an urban environment, where the air is already filled with potential carcinogens. In conjunction with alcohol, the chance of getting cancer is up to 1,500 percent greater for someone who drinks and smokes as for someone who neither drinks nor smokes. Too much liquor alone is related to cancer of the mouth, throat, esophagus, larynyx, and liver. When liquor is linked with tobacco, the danger expands to many other types of malignancies. The agents goad each other on to progressively more destructive acts.

Pipe and cigar smoking are less harmful if the smoke is not inhaled, though the danger to nearby nonsmokers is as great. However, pipes lead to higher incidences of cancer of the mouth and lower lip, while cigars have been linked to cancer of the bladder.

Stress

Though there is no conclusive evidence to prove it, stress is thought by many physicians to be a key factor in the development of cancer. Stress is known to stimulate the body's production of steroids, particularly cortisone. These chemicals inhibit the functioning of the body's immunity system. If cancer is a virus or some other entity that can be fought by the body's immune system, stress clearly can open the door for the development of tumors by stripping the body of its protective antibodies. The solution to this threat is simply to relax. Sleep more, cut down your work regime, and act decisively to clear up personal problems. However, if you find this difficult, *learn* to relax through such techniques as yoga or transcendental meditation. Try to organize your life so that it will become more enjoyable.

The Cancer-Prone Personality

Although there is no conclusive proof, many studies have found that certain personality types are more prone to cancer than others. Women who cannot cope with stress and who suppress extreme feelings of anger and other deep emotions were found in one study to have a high susceptibility to cancer of the breast, while women who expressed their emotions freely, were more assertive and spontaneous and generally more relaxed were less likely to develop the different types of gynecologic cancers. It is interesting to note here that many women develop cancer during periods of severe life stress such as divorce, separation, or the death of a loved one. It is the cancer patient's inability to deal with her personal problems successfully that, many times, triggers a malignancy. Therefore, if there is such a thing as a cancer-prone personality, and evidence is pointing in this direction, women should make every effort *not* to bottle up any strong feelings. There are books and training courses now available that teach people how to be more assertive. There are different techniques for achieving deep relaxation.

Good nutrition is an important factor that is very often forgotten in fighting stress. Perhaps in the future, doctors will give immediate attention to a patient's psychosocial problems, thus creating another means of early detection and a more favorable prognosis.

Genetic Factors

Cancer can run in families. This does not mean that if someone in your family has it you are going to get it, but your chances are greater. It is estimated that there is a 15 to 20 percent genetic factor in breast cancer, which means if a relative has it, 15 to 20 percent of your chances of getting it are genetic. Of course, this factor is not fully understood. The cancer could actually be in your genes, or there could simply be a genetic weakness in your immune system. The problem could even be in the traditional eating habits of your family.

Some cases, however, have definitely been related to genetic, rather than cultural (eating habits, sleeping patterns, etc.) factors. Patients suffering from Down's syndrome or mongolism (a condition of mental retardation caused by chromosome abnormalities) have been found to exhibit at least eleven times the normal risk of developing leukemia, a cancer of the blood.

Two or more first-degree relatives with the same or related kinds of cancer (cancer of the breast, for example, is related to cancer of the colon or the uterus), can be considered evidence of inherited cancer or susceptibility to cancer.

Diet

In the past decade or so, there has arisen in our culture a stereotype known as the health-food nut. She is generally considered to be a fanatic with a make-believe cause. Ironically, as so many people ignore science's warning about tobacco, so do they ignore the warnings about diet. In fact, animal fats, additives, preservatives, and overprocessed foods like white bread may contribute, directly and indirectly, to half the cancers in women and almost a third of those in men.

Dietary causes of cancer are especially acute in countries like the United States, where the diet is rich in soft foods such as meat, white bread, and all white-flour products, refined sugar, and related overprocessed foods without roughage. These factors are related to cancer of the colon, stomach, esophagus, breast, liver, and uterus.

The Western world is especially afflicted by cancer of the colon, due to a lack of fiber in its diet. Until recently, fiber was largely ignored as a nutritional requirement because it provides no nourishment—it does not contain protein, sugar, starch, fat, vitamins, or minerals, it is simply roughage, the plant food we do not digest. A person living in the West consumes four to six grams of fiber daily, while his or her African counterpart consumes five times that much. In fact, Africans very rarely developed any type of cancer until they started to eat the Western diet; then cancer began to appear where it had been virtually unknown. Experiments have shown that this Western diet results in more than twice as long a transit time for stool—about seventy hours as compared to thirty—which means bacteria have more time to multiply and harmful substances are held against the intestinal wall for a longer period. This leads not only to cancer, but possibly also to benign tumors, polyps, and appendicitis. The easiest way to get more fiber in your diet is to eat fresh fruits, vegetables, and raw salads and substitute whole-grain flour, cereals, and bread for refined flour, processed cereals, and white bread. Whole bran is especially high in fiber content if it has not been ground and reconstituted, as it is in many of the popular bran breakfast cereals. Your local health-food store is the best source for obtaining raw, unrefined bran.

Fatty diets have been linked to cancer of the breast and of the bowel. This is evident when you compare the high rate of bowel cancer in the United States, with its meat-oriented diet, with the low rate in Japan, with its staple diet of fish. The Scots, who consume 20 percent more beef than the neighboring English, have one of the highest bowel-cancer rates in the world. The current suspicion is that fats overstimulate hormone production, causing unrestrained growth of some cells, especially of the breast, prostate, and uterus. Throughout the world, there is a five to ten times difference in the death rate from breast cancer between countries with low-fat diets and those with high-fat diets. The solution here is to eat less meat and saturated fats and more fish, fowl, and polyunsaturated fats. At the same time as we cut down our use of saturated fats, we should also curb our intake of protein. We are too obsessed with eating large amounts of protein, thinking it will improve our health, when just the opposite may be happening. It has been found that overeating of protein causes deficiencies of vitamins B_6 and B_3 and magnesium, as well as pancreatic enzymes—deficiencies which are considered among the reasons for cancer development. It is this overindulgence in protein and the body's inability to digest and utilize it that may cause cancer.

Overeating has also been related to the increase in the occurrence of cancer, as well as heart disease and diabetes. Statistics from the Metropolitan Life Insurance Company have shown that the prevalence of these conditions is much higher among the overweight than among those of normal weight. This fact was clearly demonstrated in the hunger years during and after the world wars, when there was a sharp decrease in cancer. However, when food rationing ended and people again started to overeat, the incidence of cancer started to increase sharply, going back to the prewar levels. Smaller, more frequent meals would be a healthier way to live rather than our standard three-meals-a-day routine. In Europe, the main meal or course is served in the afternoon, in a leisurely fashion, allowing plenty of time for rest, relaxation, and good digestion.

Americans might learn something from this—with our fast-food restaurants, we often eat not only in fifteen minutes, but many times, standing up! To make matters worse, we eat our main meal in the evening and then most likely retire for the night. This is the typical pattern of eating for the American people. The results can only be tragic, as we are surely starting to learn.

Preservatives and Dyes

To add insult to injury, the meats of which we are so fond—and which probably are giving us cancer—are impregnated with dyes, growth hormones, additives, and preservatives which are also probably giving us cancer. A controversy surrounding the chemical preservatives and dyes known as sodium nitrite and sodium nitrate, has developed. You will find these two in most processed meats—salami, bologna, bacon, ham, smoked meats, corned beef, pastrami, hot dogs—to enhance their color and inhibit the growth of the deadly bacteria that cause botulism. Although not carcinogens by themselves, sodium nitrite and sodium nitrate combine with *amines* which are found in the body to form *nitrosamines,* which have proven to be highly potent carcinogens in animals. Food processors complain that the threat of cancer is minimal compared to insurance against botulism, but consumer advocates insist that no one knows just how serious the cancer threat is, since the incubation period is so long, and that we are better off safe than sorry.

Interestingly, we swallow as many natural nitrites daily in our saliva as are found in a pound of bacon, but they are combatted by vitamin C, an important intake. Both vitamins C and A are known to reduce various cancer risks.

There is a continuing controversy over the Food and Drug Administration's ban on cyclamates and red dye #2, once one of the most prominent dyes in our diet. Though there have been conflicting studies over cyclamates, red dye #2 was shown to be carcinogenic after having been in our food for decades. Other dyes have yet to be properly tested. In the case of some preservatives, processors argue that the choice is between the lesser of two evils; in the case of mere colorings, this argument is hardly relevant. In essence, we are exposed daily to various possible carcinogens for the sake of marketing techniques.

It is interesting to note that diethystilbestrol (DES) is one of the hormones injected into cattle to fatten them up. Traces of this hormone are found in all beef products that reach the market. This hormone is banned in twenty-one countries, and eleven European countries refuse to import our meat as long as DES is used. Young girls reach puberty at a much earlier age than they used to, and many young men are becoming increasingly more feminine. Several scientists now wonder if this could be due to the DES found in meat, considering that Americans are big meat-eaters. This is presently under further scientific investigation. In Europe, the grave consequences of DES have already been considered. Why have we closed our eyes to the danger to the American public?

Health-food stores are still too expensive and offer too limited a selection for many people, but by carefully reading labels in your supermarket, it is often possible to choose between two products that are almost identical except for their chemical additives. This is especially true of bread, cereal, canned goods, cheese, frozen goods, condiments, snacks, pastries, and salad dressing.

In addition to these chemicals, some foods contain known carcinogens in the forms of pesticide residues, trace elements picked up from the soil, and a poison called *afflatoxin* produced by mold. Washing all fruits and vegetables carefully, while not completely purging them of these chemicals, at least gets rid of those that are not ingrown.

Excessive alcoholic intake is associated with an increased risk of cancer of the esophagus. This is especially acute if the drinking is mixed with smoking. In general, moderation is wise not only in drinking but in all food consumption. The body reacts differently to all vitamins and minerals, fats, starches, and sugars. If our hormonal balance is to be maintained, these nutritional elements should remain relatively well balanced. A moderate diet and plenty of exercise will keep the body working properly and strengthen the immune system which helps prevent cancer.

Drugs

Many experts consider carcinogenic drugs far more dangerous than the carcinogenic chemicals we find in our food, mainly because the drugs are ingested in larger doses. But the drugs, despite the risk of cancer, are often necessary to treat some other disorder. Your doctor must carefully balance the various dangers in such cases and should warn you about any risks you may be taking.

More frightening is the case where the drug is not essential, and is found, in retrospect, to cause cancer. This happened in 1971, when it was discovered that the daughters of women who had taken synthetic estrogen diethylstilbestrol (DES) during early pregnancy were more susceptible to an often-fatal vaginal cancer. A few decades ago obstetricians felt that DES was a cure for women who repeatedly miscarried. The treatment is no longer prescribed, but women who were given DES during pregnancy should be aware that their daughters should be checked frequently for carcinoma of the vagina.

Recent studies have suggested that the use of estrogen by middle-age women to alleviate the symptoms of menopause increases the risk of uterine cancer. It might also be linked to breast cancer. Women who have undergone hysterectomies need not worry about uterine cancer, but other women should be aware of the danger because this treatment is still widely prescribed. Estrogen helps maintain the hormonal balance, which some researchers feel helps prevent cancer of the ovary, a far more serious disease then cancer of the uterus. The estrogen treatment keeps a woman's skin, vagina, bones, and organs healthier, slowing the deterioration of the aging process somewhat. The first symptom of uterine cancer is bleeding, so if a woman is aware of this and watches for it, early treatment is almost always successful. Again, careful weighing of risks and benefits must be made, and the patient should be able to make a well-informed choice. Many doctors suggest that women who take hormone replacements should have biopsies taken from their uteri to detect any abnormalities about once a year when they have their Pap smears.

There have also been reports linking certain birth-control pills to uterine cancer. However, only ten to twenty such reports have been confirmed out of fifty million women who use the pill. Still, these reports generally stem from high-estrogen-containing pills. Most of these brands have been taken off the market. Women on the minipill, which contains low hormone levels, have never been shown to develop increased risk of cancer.

Drugs used to prevent rejection of organ transplants have also been found to cause cancer. Among more than six thousand kidney-transplant recipients, the risk of lymphatic cancer was found to be thirty-five times greater than normal. These drugs are designed to counteract the body's immune system, a system thought to be a key element in cancer prevention. In these cases, there is usually no choice but to use these drugs, but your physician should watch carefully for any signs of tumor development.

Before any drug goes on the market, it is first tested on animals, then on a controlled group of human beings. The U.S. Food and Drug Administration is responsible for evaluating and licensing drugs for general or prescription use on the basis of these tests. Unfortunately, the agency cannot possibly keep up with the hundreds of drugs introduced every year, and must often rely at least in part on data supplied by the manufacturer. Because it can take so long for cancer to develop, the carcinogenic implications of any new drug are never completely understood until the drug has been in use for several decades. Thus no drug should be considered entirely cancer-safe, and no drug should be taken unless its use is specifically indicated by symptoms.

X-Rays

Are X-rays miracle viewers or zap guns? This question has plagued the scientific community since Roentgen first discovered X-rays in 1895, but only recently have the negative charges been substantiated. There is no longer any doubt that X-rays and similar forms of radiation can cause leukemia and other cancers if received in high enough doses. Survivors of Hiroshima and Nagasaki have shown significantly high incidence of leukemia and cancer of the breast, bowel, and brain. The radiation from an atomic explosion and that from an X-ray machine are fundamentally the same.

Recently researchers have found that children in the 1940s and 1950s who were treated with radiation for tonsillitis, enlarged thymus glands, and skin conditions such as acne have increased risks of thyroid and skin cancer. The threat is real, but no one knows yet how dangerous it is. There is no doubt that X-rays are one of the physician's most valuable tools for diagnosing and treating a vast range of diseases, disorders, and traumatic injuries. Are they worth the risk?

Some researchers feel that a single dose of X-rays will age the cells it hits by a year. Others feel that routine X-rays are perfectly harmless as long as they are spaced sufficiently to give the body a chance to recover. Many physicians frown on X-rays of men and women during the reproductive years because of the increased chance of leukemia in the offspring. For this same reason, and because of the danger of damage to your own reproductive system, you should have a shield over your abdomen whenever you have X-rays taken, even by a dentist.

Surely, no matter how slight the danger may turn out to be, caution is indicated. Your physician should not order any routine X-rays, including chest X-rays, unless you have symptoms that require X-rays for diagnosis. If he does prescribe X-rays, you should question him about their necessity.

The Environment

In the air we breathe, the water we drink, the food we eat, the products we use, and the materials with which we work, there are about 1,400 chemicals that are now suspected of causing cancer. Many experts link these substances to the five-fold increase in the cancer rate in 1975. Previous years had registered increases of only about one percent.

The dangers of pollution are impossible to escape, although they can be controlled to an extent. Country air is safer than city air, for example. Choosing not to smoke cigarettes, not to live near a fume-infested freeway, or not to use aerosol sprays all help.

Perhaps the most susceptible to environmental dangers are certain industrial workers who must work in atmospheres thick with carcinogenic dust and gas. The list of these occupations grows every day. Painters are exposed to chromates that are linked to lung cancer. Rubber workers have a risk of leukemia from exposure to benzene. Lung cancer and lymphoma occur in high rates among workers exposed to inorganic arsenic, a major chemical in over forty processes from tinting windshields to spraying roses. Like vinyl chloride, found in many plastics, arsenic has been linked to liver cancer. For eighty years, benzidine, which is used in dye making, has been known to cause bladder cancer. Benzidine has been withdrawn from the market in Great Britain, the Soviet Union, and several other countries because of its carcinogenic properties, but it is still widely used in the United States.

Many occupational carcinogens work in concert with other agents—asbestos workers radically increase their chances of getting lung cancer if they smoke.

These industrial pollutants make their way into surrounding communities all too easily. Epidemiologists in South Africa and England have found *mesothelioma* (cancer of certain abdominal linings) in a number of men and women who had never been inside an asbestos plant, although asbestos was indicated as the cause. In the United States, people living in communities with smelting facilities have higher-than-average lung-cancer rates. In three Ohio towns where vinyl chloride was used in industries, researchers found a mysterious series of deaths from cancer of the central nervous system in adults and numerous birth defects in children.

Employers should be aware of these dangers and should be legally bound to minimize them as much as possible. Unfortunately, enforcement of such safety regulations is almost impossible, so employers must police themselves. This is not a question of expense, it is a question of human life. Employees should also be aware of the chemicals with which they work and should see a doctor regularly to check for signs of any cancer that those chemicals may be suspected of causing.

The Sun

One of those things we all know but which we all hate to think about is that the sun causes skin cancer. A committee of the National Academies of Science recently estimated that among white people living along the fortieth parallel, 40 percent of all melanomas and 80 percent of all other types of skin cancer could be attributed to ultraviolet rays. Most skin cancer is slow-growing and has a low mortality, but not all. *Melanoma,* one of the deadliest, kills 75 percent more people in the span of states running from Louisiana to South Carolina than it does in the northern latitudes from Washington to Minnesota.

It is possible that ultraviolet light interferes with the body's defense system against cancer, a system still unknown to immunologists. This theory would explain why the worst form of human skin cancer, malignant melanoma, shows up as often on unexposed skin as on exposed, yet the source is probably the sun. On the other hand, other forms of skin cancer affect only the areas exposed to the sun. Perhaps the rays initiate cancer by various means.

The danger of skin cancer from the sun is real, but you don't have to stay indoors for the rest of your days. Unless you work in the sun (in which case you should shade your face with a hat), normal outdoor activities should not expose you to a dangerous extent. Excessive sunbathing, however, may do more to your skin than add color.

TYPES OF GYNECOLOGICAL CANCER

Breast Cancer

Breast cancer accounts for 20 percent of cancer deaths in women. This is the most common form of cancer among women, especially those over forty-five years of age. It has been linked to various causes, from obesity to not breast-feeding, but very little progress has been made in the understanding of the causes of breast cancer. It is generally considered a disease of various origins. Breast cancer will kill approximately thirty-three thousand Americans this year. One of every fifteen women will develop breast cancer during her lifetime, but usually not before age thirty-five. In 1975, about ninety thousand new cases were diagnosed in the United States.

Causes

Though the causes of breast cancer are elusive, it is known that a history of the disease in the family not only increases a woman's possibility of getting cancer, but also of developing it earlier and in both breasts instead of one.

Other women in the high-risk group include those with polycystic ovaries (Stein-Leventhal disease). In this condition, the ovaries become enlarged, producing a higher amount of estrogen than normal. It is possible that because the hormone levels with this condition are high throughout these women's lives, this overstimulation of the breasts can subsequently lead to the development of cancer. By the same token, estrogen-replacement therapy for menopausal women might increase their risks of developing breast cancer. Obesity and heavy fat intake can also increase the risk of developing breast cancer. The explanation is that fats overstimulate estrogen production and that the prolonged effects of hormones cause an irritation of the breast tissue which subsequently can lead to cancer. In animals used in experiments, fats have been found to be directly related to development of breast cancer.

There have been studies that maintain that breast-feeding lowers the incidence of breast cancer, though other studies have contradicted these findings. The theory here is that the milk glands, if not used as nature intended, can cause an irritation leading to cancer. Recent studies have shown that the incidence of breast cancer is more common in the United States and the United Kingdom than in developing countries. These studies concluded that these differences were not related to the number of children or the length of breast-feeding, but rather to the age of a woman at her first childbirth. Women who have their first child at age thirty-five or later have a risk of developing breast cancer three times higher than that of women who have a first child before their eighteenth birthdays. This is why some researchers believe that oral contraceptives, which simulate pregnancy to a certain degree, might protect a woman from developing breast cancer. The birth-control pills result in a steady hormone level and prevent the natural hormone fluctuation with the cyclic breast stimulation.

Stress can also increase the chances of breast cancer by overproducing steroids which depress the body's immune system. This overproduction has led some researchers to recommend treatment with vitamin A or bacillus Calmette-Guerin (BCG) injections, both of which can increase immune responses.

Symptoms and Diagnosis

The best way to detect breast cancer in its early stages is by conducting regular self-examinations. If a woman is in a high-risk category, she should see a gynecologist twice a year. A breast tumor most frequently begins as a *painless* lump in the upper outside quadrant of the breast (see chart in Chapter 18, Breast Examination). As the lump grows, the overlying skin tends to be pulled inward and eventually dimples. Skin discoloration can occur when the cancer is more advanced, and the nipple sometimes retracts. Any of these signs should prompt an immediate examination by an expert. The fact that the lump is usually painless leads many women to ignore the problem until it is too late. Breast cancer grows slowly, so it does not pull unduly on the nerves. Small, painful lumps are usually harmless cystic milk glands, common in many women in their fertile years and especially before menstruation.

Women with cancer in the family and who are overweight or over forty years old should have yearly or biyearly mammography or thermography exams in combination with breast palpation. Early discovery almost always leads to successful treatment. More than 90 percent of all breast cancers are discovered by women themselves. If a suspicious breast lump is found, a breast biopsy is indicated to confirm the diagnosis (see section on Breast Biopsy).

Treatment

There are three basic treatments for breast cancer—surgery, radiation, and chemotherapy. The correct treatment, or combination of treatments, depends on the spread of the cancer. If the disease is caught in the early stages, the tumor can usually be removed surgically. If during surgery cancer is found in the lymph glands, it may have spread even farther, and surgical removal is not enough. Then radiation or cobalt therapy is needed to kill the cancer throughout the lymphatic system around the breast. Occasionally chemotherapy is also added to the treatment schedule.

There is considerable controversy about the various cancer treatments, none more heated than that about radical or simple mastectomy (surgical removal of the breast). If cancer is suspected, a biopsy should be performed. This is often done in conjunction with preparations for mastectomy. If the tumor is benign, the operation is over. If it is malignant, the surgeon may perform an immediate mastectomy. At this point, the surgeon must decide whether to remove the bulk of the breast in a simple mastectomy, or the entire breast with its underlying muscles and the lymph nodes in the armpit by a radical mastectomy (see Chapter 19, Corrective Breast Surgery).

The radical mastectomy allows a pathological examination of the entire breast area to determine the extent to which the cancer has spread. This gives the physician data to use in prescribing further treatment. Many doctors believe, however, that once the main tumor is removed by a simple mastectomy, the body's natural antibodies can effectively fight the remaining cancer. The debate continues, and worldwide research is being conducted in an attempt to settle the question. A woman can be sure of getting the best treatment by choosing a physician or medical center that is thoroughly up to date on the latest research. There are only three centers in the United States with facilities and staff capable of treating every form of cancer as proficiently as possible: the Anderson Hospital and Tumor Institute in Houston, Texas; the Roswell Park Memorial Institute in Buffalo, New York; and the Memorial Sloan-Kettering Cancer Center in New York City. If it is impractical to visit one of these centers, they can probably direct you to the best facilities in your area.

If the breast cancer is localized without any sign of spread when it is removed, the five-year survival rate is between 75 and 80 percent. If it has spread to the lymph nodes, the cure rate is somewhat lower. Some physicians have suggested removing the ovaries in women under fifty to decrease estrogen stimulation which could promote cancer in the remaining breast, but most breast-cancer specialists do not recommend this anymore.

Some researchers recommend radiation therapy *instead* of mastectomy in treating localized breast cancer. In one study, more than one hundred patients with localized tumors who either were too old or who refused surgery were followed for more than two years. Every patient was given an average dose (5000 rad) of radiation over a period of five weeks. The results showed that the cure rate for radiation alone was as high as the best rate obtained by radical surgery. A group of French physicians has also reported the same successful cure rate with radiation therapy alone in a large group of patients which has been followed for many years. Of course, the danger here is that the physician may underestimate the extent of the tumor. If the tumor has spread and a radical mastectomy is performed, followed by radiation therapy, a New York study found the cure rate to exceed 90 percent. Some experts support radiation therapy as a means of preventing recurrence of the cancer, but chemotherapy is generally considered more effective.

According to Italian researchers, a new three-drug treatment
—*cyclophosphamide*, *methotrexate*, and *5-fluorouracil*—after surgery has produced a great reduction in breast cancer recurrence. However, doctors in the United States who have been
using this treatment caution that the Italian tests were limited to
207 cases, and that the results are not yet conclusive. Without
chemotherapy, the recurrence rate when there are no cancerous lymph nodes found is 24 percent within ten years; with
cancerous nodes, the rate jumps to 86 percent. The Italian
study noted a recurrence rate of only 5.3 percent with the
treatment, compared to 24 percent recurrence in a similar
group who did not receive the three-drug chemotherapy, but
these statistics were collected after only twenty-seven months.
Further testing is being conducted in the United States now,
and a four-drug program is also being studied.

The drug BCG (bacillus Calmette-Guerin) has shown spectacular results when used in combination with a three-drug
chemotherapy program for recurrent breast cancer. In a study
group of twenty-one patients in the United States who received
three-drug therapy alone, three died and six relapsed. But of
fourteen patients who received the three-drug therapy plus
BCG injections, there were no deaths and only one relapse.
BCG is thought to build up the body's immune system.

Chemotherapy may be an unpleasant experience. The
treatment often causes vomiting, gastrointestinal pain, and loss
of hair. But it is certainly preferable to the alternative of recurring tumor.

Cancer of the Cervix

In the past decade, deaths from cancer of the cervix have
decreased from approximately eighteen thousand to nine
thousand per year. Epidemiologists have ascribed this reduction to two causes—a greater awareness among women, and the
Pap smear, which detects the cancer very early. This is the only
cancer with a decreasing death rate.

There are great disparities in the cervical cancer rates of
various ethnic groups. For example, 3.6 Jewish women per
100,000 suffer this disease, whereas for Puerto Rican women
the rate is 98 per 100,000. Black women have a rate of 48 per
100,000, as opposed to 14 per 100,000 white women. No one
knows why these differences exist. Some experts contend that
the factor is cultural—some races traditionally have children
earlier, for example, which increases their chances for cancer of
the cervix. Others believe that the problem is a genetic weak-

ness in the immune system. The mean age for development of cervical cancer is between the ages of forty and fifty. This type of cancer, however, is not uncommon in women under the age of thirty-five.

Causes

Though not much is known about the causes of cervical cancer, there are numerous indications linking it to sexual intercourse. Prostitutes have an extremely high incidence of cervical cancer, while nuns have an extremely low incidence. It has been shown that cervical cancer is more prevalent in women who experience early sexual activity, childbirth at an early age, and/or numerous sex partners. It is possible that the penis secretes an inflammatory substance. The longer that sex has been engaged in, the more this irritant has been working on the cervix. Just as the irritation of the sun causes skin cancer and the irritation of tobacco causes lung cancer, so might the irritation of this still-unidentified penile factor cause cancer of the cervix. In the past, this irritant was thought to be *smegma*, a whitish, cheesy secretion from the penis which collects under the foreskin. Circumcision prevents this accumulation of smegma. Since Jewish men are circumcised, this seemed to be the logical explanation for the lower incidence of cervical cancer among Jewish women. However, even though a large number of men in the United States are circumcised today, there has not been the expected decline in cervical cancer. In fact, studies have been performed comparing the incidence of cervical cancer among women with circumcised mates to the incidence among women with uncircumcised partners, and when the groups were matched for age, initiation of sexual activity, childbirths, and number of sexual partners, there were no significant differences between the two groups. Circumcision in the male does not appear to protect his sexual partner from cervical cancer. In retrospect, it was felt that the low incidence of cervical cancer among Jewish women was due to infrequent premarital sex, later marriage, and having a single sexual partner.

The irritant might be directly related to the sperm itself or to sexually transmitted diseases such as herpes simplex Type II (see Chapter 7, Venereal Disease). During pregnancy, there is an increase in the vascularity of the cervix, often leading to the development of cervicitis, which can reoccur with each pregnancy. Chronic cervicitis may predispose a woman to cervical cancer, and this could be the reason for the higher incidence of cervical cancer among women with many children.

If a woman leads an active sex life or began having sex at an early age, she needn't change her life-style, but she should have regular Pap smears at least once a year.

Symptoms and Diagnosis

Early cervical cancer is asymptomatic and can only be detected by a Pap smear. Cancer of the cervix usually starts as an inflammatory reaction which, over the years, develops into a slight abnormality of the cells in the cervix. This abnormality, called *dysplasia,* can either heal spontaneously or develop into cancer. The development of the cancer usually takes several years and the Pap smear, analyzed in a competent laboratory, can detect dysplasia before it develops into cancer. This very early detection in the precancerous state should lead to colposcopy or biopsy of the cervix to verify the diagnosis, so that appropriate treatment can be instituted even before the cancer develops. If cervical cancer is detected in the precancerous state or in the cancerous state, but before it has had a chance to spread, a well-trained specialist will be able to remove the cancer surgically with an almost 100 percent cure rate.

In 1975, forty-six thousand new cases of cervical cancer were diagnosed. There were nine thousand deaths reported to have stemmed from the disease. Many researchers agree that no one should die from cancer of the cervix, especially since modern techniques are effective in diagnosing and treating this type of cancer. Deaths from cervical cancer are almost always the results of diagnoses made too late. Your only insurance is to see a specialist who keeps up with the latest research in the field, and to see him regularly. A woman must have Pap smears at least yearly as soon as she becomes sexually active. Women in high-risk groups should consider having Pap smears every six months.

Treatment

If cervical cancer is detected in its *in situ* state, it is usually removed with a *cone biopsy,* in which a wide, cone-shaped piece of the cervix is excised. If the patient has had children and intends to have no more, some physicians advise removing the uterus to ensure that the cancer will not spread.

If the cancer is more advanced, it can be treated by an extensive hysterectomy, either alone or with the addition of radiation or cobalt therapy. Cobalt treatment must be performed by a specialist. If it is not properly administered, cobalt can cause extensive tissue damage of the bowels, the vagina, or the bladder. The American Cancer Society can recommend a suitable treatment center or specialist.

Cancer of the Uterus

Uterine cancer is on the rise. In 1975, there were 3,300 deaths from this disease, predominantly in the white population (as opposed to cervical cancer, which appears more often in black and Puerto Rican populations). The average age of development is fifty-seven, with 75 percent of all cases occurring after fifty and only 4 percent occurring before forty.

Causes

The incidence of cancer of the uterus is higher in women who have not borne children and in obese women (especially those with hypertension and diabetes). No one knows the link between the absence of children and uterine cancer (nuns have a high rate of occurrence of this disease), but obesity is linked to high estrogen production, which is thought to overstimulate the uterus, becoming a carcinogenic irritant.

A woman who is twenty to fifty pounds overweight increases her chances of developing a uterine tumor by 300 percent, while a woman who is more than fifty pounds overweight increases her chances by 900 percent.

The racial differences in the uterine cancer rate (or endometrial cancer, cancer of the uterine lining) are now thought to be largely a matter of diet. Asian women, who have a relatively low incidence of endometrial cancer and a high incidence of stomach cancer while living in their native countries, tend to have a higher incidence of endometrial cancer, consistent with the American norm, after one or two generations in the United States. This could be due to the high caloric and cholesterol intake in the American diet, which, again, affects estrogen production.

Women with Stein-Leventhal disease (polycystic ovaries), who have higher estrogen levels, also run an unusually high risk of having endometrial cancer. Women with polycystic ovaries should be aware of this threat and respond to any abnormal bleeding by seeing a doctor for an endometrial biopsy.

Millions of American women have been taking estrogen for years to prevent such menopausal symptoms as drying of the skin, backaches, or fatigue. Naturally, since various cancers (including that of the uterus) have been linked to estrogen, this treatment increases the risk of tumor growth. This is a calculated risk that you and your doctor must ponder carefully.

Again, if you are undergoing estrogen treatment, you should have any abnormal bleeding checked out immediately. When endometrial cancer is diagnosed early, the cure rate is almost 100 percent.

Symptoms and Diagnosis

If abnormal bleeding occurs in any of the instances already discussed, or anytime after menopause, a biopsy of the endometrium or a D&C should be conducted to investigate the cause. Pap smears are adequate for cervical cancer but detect uterine cancer in less than half the cases. Endometrial biopsies can occasionally be performed in the doctor's office, but many physicians prefer to conduct a D&C in a hospital with the patient under general anesthesia. This gives the doctor an opportunity to check the uterus for any abnormality or enlargement. If there is a cancer development but the uterine cavity is less than eight centimeters deep, the cancer is usually in the early stages and can be fairly easily treated by hysterectomy.

Treatment

In general, to treat endometrial cancer, surgery is combined with radiation therapy. This varies from case to case and from institution to institution. The aim of the radiation is to shrink the uterus and block the lymphatic system to prevent the tumor from spreading. An abdominal hysterectomy and bilateral oophorectomy, in which the uterus and both ovaries are removed, is then performed. This is usually accompanied by radiation treatment of the vagina to prevent the cancer from spreading there.

If the tumor has already spread deep into the uterine wall or to the lymphatic system, it is very difficult to cure, since it may have spread into surrounding organs as well. This situation would call for chemotherapy in the hope of eliminating the cancer wherever it has spread. The treatment of endometrial cancer should be guided by a cancer specialist.

Cancer of the Ovaries

Although the incidence of carcinoma of the ovaries is lower than the incidence of cervical and endometrial cancer, there are almost as many deaths from ovarian cancer as from uterine malignancies. The reason for its unusually high mortality rate is simple. There are no early symptoms, so early detection is rare. By the time cancer of the ovaries is discovered, it has often spread too far to be contained.

Causes

Unlike most other gynecological cancers, ovarian cancer is probably not influenced by estrogen. There are no known high-risk groups for this type of cancer, either, and it seems unaffected by diet. Some researchers suspect that the gonadotrophins LH and FSH irritate the ovaries, causing them to become cancerous. If this is true, estrogen might very well inhibit ovarian cancer, but there is no conclusive evidence to back this up yet. Tests are presently being conducted.

Symptoms and Diagnosis

Cancer of the ovaries is estimated to be responsible for 6 percent of all cancer deaths in women. Ovarian cancer seems to be more prevalent after menopause, although it can occur during the childbearing years. The disease is varied, with different types of tumors causing different types of symptoms, but usually it starts with gas pain and abdominal distention. The ovaries are aligned very closely with the intestines, so that, when cancer inflames the ovaries, the intestines are disturbed. Any continuing, unusual gas pains should be checked by a *gynecologist;* an internist might evaluate the symptoms without a diagnosis for months. Following gas pains, weight loss and fatigue occur, all relatively vague symptoms. Unless the physician is specifically looking for ovarian cancer, it will often go undiagnosed.

After menopause, many experts believe the ovaries shrink because they are no longer needed. They should be difficult to palpate (hard to feel during a pelvic exam). If a postmenopausal woman comes to her gynecologist with gas pains and her ovaries are easy to palpate, an *exploratory laparotomy* should be conducted to examine the ovaries for possible cancer. Many deaths from ovarian cancer could have been avoided if the patient had visited her gynecologist more often. After menopause, a pelvic exam should be conducted at least once a year, perhaps even twice a year if gas pains are felt, since ovarian cancer develops quite rapidly.

Scientists are presently working on blood tests (similar to the CEA [carcino embryonic antigen] test for cancer of the colon) and urine analyses to detect ovarian cancer. Development of these tests is especially critical for this disease, since early detection is so difficult. At the moment, an ovarian biopsy is the major diagnostic tool, and that is performed only if ovarian cancer is suspected.

Treatment

Carcinoma of the ovaries is generally treated by a *total hysterectomy* and *bilateral salpingo-oophorectomy* (removal of the ovaries and fallopian tubes). Removal of the omentum (a fatty fold of abdominal lining attached to the stomach) is also recommended, since it is often a site for cancer spread. Total abdominal radiation should follow surgery, often accompanied by chemotherapy.

Cancer of the Vulva

Cancer of the vulva accounts for about 5 percent of all gynecological cancers. The prognosis is relatively good once the diagnosis has been made.

Causes

As with most cancers, the cause of cancer of the vulva is unknown. It strikes most often in postmenopausal women, who are susceptible to basal cell carcinoma, or skin cancer, which is what cancer of the vulva actually is. The average age for contraction is fifty-nine.

Symptoms and Diagnosis

Cancer of the vulva frequently starts with white lesions or other abnormalities and itching of the vulva. If a woman experiences these symptoms, she should consult a gynecologist. The diagnosis can only be verified by pathological examination of a biopsy from the vulva.

Treatment

Surgery is generally required to treat cancer of the vulva, but in the early stages, a wide excision is almost always successful. When the cancer is more developed, there is some controversy about whether the lymph nodes in the groin should be removed during a *radical vulvectomy* (removal of the entire vulva), but this question must be evaluated in every individual case. Chemotherapy has also successfully effected cure in some cases.

Cancer of the Vagina

Vaginal cancer is rare; it accounts for less than 2 percent of all genital cancer in women. This type of cancer is most common after menopause. It is often an epidermoid cancer, developing in the outer skin layer of the vagina, though it can also spread from the uterus and other areas. Of particular concern is the incidence of this cancer in children. In 1974, an estimated 3,600 deaths were reported in the United States from cancer in children under fifteen. Though most of these deaths were caused by leukemia or neoplasm of the brain and central nervous system, up to 5 percent were due to cancers of the female genitalia.

Causes

The cause of vaginal cancer in adults is unknown. The cause of vaginal cancer in children might be linked to genetic abnormalities, though no one knows exactly how or why. These cancers may develop while the child is still in the uterus (when the child's immune system is not yet fully developed) or might be related to complications during pregnancy or drugs taken by the mother.

Diethylstilbestrol (DES) is an estrogen-type hormone that was used years ago to treat repeated miscarriages. It was later found to cause *cancer* of the vagina in the daughters of women who took DES during pregnancy. If a woman was given DES during pregnancy, her daughters should be considered to have a high risk of vaginal cancer and should have regular gynecological checkups twice a year with Pap smears and possible colposcopy.

Symptoms and Diagnosis

Early cancer of the vagina is asymptomatic but can be detected by a Pap smear. Thus, Pap smears should be performed even in women who have had hysterectomies. If a young girl experiences any abnormal vaginal bleeding, she should be taken to a pediatrician immediately for further investigation. This is especially crucial if the child's mother was given DES during pregnancy. Clear-cell carcinoma can be detected either in a Pap smear or a colposcopy, followed by a biopsy if any abnormalities are found.

Treatment

If vaginal cancer is discovered early, it can be removed by local excision. More extensive cancer requires more extensive surgery, though some vaginal carcinomas also respond to radiation therapy. Clear-cell carcinoma of the vagina usually requires extensive surgery and should only be treated by a cancer specialist.

CANCER PREVENTION

The National Cancer Institute estimates that 25 to 30 percent of all cancer deaths in the United States could be prevented through more conscientious use of early detection techniques and changes in the American life-style. Many of the 80,000 lung cancer deaths every year could be prevented by putting an end to cigarette smoking. This would also tremendously reduce the 13,500 deaths annually from cancer of the mouth and the esophagus. Of these 13,500 deaths, 5,000 could be prevented by a reduction of alcoholism. Almost a third of the 30,000 colon and rectum cancer deaths could be prevented by switching to a diet lower in animal fats. And 5,000 of the 18,000 bladder and liver cancer deaths could be prevented by better controls over industrial pollution. Obviously, we are not going out of our way to protect ourselves against this group of diseases. Cancer is still on the increase, despite constantly improving detection techniques and treatments. Cancer claims over 1,000 lives daily.

How to Prevent Cancer

The future is promising for progressively more effective cancer treatment, and there are certain steps you can take today to lessen your chances of developing the disease. There are numerous substances in our world that are known to be cancer producing. You are probably familiar with at least a few—industrial pollutants, many food additives and preservatives, animal fats, talc, and so on. By limiting your voluntary exposure to these carcinogens, you improve the odds against getting cancer. The key here is the use of the word *limiting*, not *avoiding*. Animal fat probably does not cause cancer, but *excess* animal fat does.

Tobacco is another story. There is *no* safe amount of tobacco. Every cigarette is carcinogenic, not only to you, but to your children, to your friends, or to strangers near you. If you must smoke, don't mix tobacco and alcohol.

If you live near an industrial area, there's not much you can do about the air, but you can drink bottled water to protect yourself against potentially polluted municipal water supplies.

Excessive radiation is known to predispose a person to the development of cancer; therefore, overexposure to the sun and to unnecessary X-rays should be avoided.

It is fairly well known that if a close member of your family has developed a particular type of cancer, your chances of developing this cancer are increased, and you should take particular precautions. For example, if your mother or aunt had breast cancer, you should be especially faithful in performing breast self-examinations every month, keeping your weight within reasonable limits, taking oral contraceptives with low levels of estrogen, and being cautious about postmenopausal estrogen-replacement therapy.

Anticancer Diet

The anticancer diet is simply a well-balanced diet—balanced not only among the four food groups (meat, dairy foods, fruits and vegetables, and grain), but balanced within each group. As a general rule, don't eat red meat any more than you eat chicken or fish. Enjoy a vegetarian meal once in a while. Most people use approximately half of their food calories on fats, both animal and vegetable. Beneficial effects could be expected if the fat calories were reduced to one third. In general, polyunsaturated oils and margarines should be substituted for saturated fats whenever it is possible to do so. A link has recently been established between nitrosamines, which are present in all processed meats, and the development of cancer. Therefore, nitrosamines should be avoided. Avoid cholesterol-rich foods such as organ meats, liver, and egg yolks, particularly if you have a high level of cholesterol in your blood. Increase the amount of fibrous food in your diet by eating more raw fruit and vegetables, as well as more dry cereals and un-adulterated whole grains. A bran supplement can be added to the diet, but if bran is added, be sure to increase water consumption to prevent bowel problems. Substitute brown rice for processed rice and whole-grain breads and flour for white bread and processed flour. If it is possible, reduce sugar intake. Yogurt, but only yogurt with live cultures, may be an important source of protein in the diet. A study of mice showed that yogurt had some effect in the prevention of the growth of cancer tumors in mice. The intake of all vitamins should be watched, but particular attention should be paid to vitamins A and C, which appear to have some anticancer properties. Try to buy food with the fewest additives and preservatives. Whenever possible, buy fresh food without any artificial ingredients. And remember, drink plenty of water. Watch not only what you eat but how much you eat. Obesity results in excessive estrogen production, which predisposes a person to the development of breast and uterine cancer.

Early Diagnosis of Cancer

You may have noticed a common phrase in the treatment of every form of cancer mentioned in this chapter (and in every form of cancer not mentioned): early diagnosis. This is the determinant between life and death in many cases. Early diagnosis can mean the difference between a simple procedure and major surgery. It means shorter recovery time, less expensive treatment, less psychological trauma. It is the strongest weapon in the war against cancer.

The seven warning signs of cancer listed by the American Cancer Society are:

1. a change in bowel or bladder habits
2. a sore that does not heal
3. unusual bleeding or discharge
4. a thickening or lump in the breast or elsewhere
5. indigestion or difficulty in swallowing
6. obvious change in a wart or mole
7. nagging cough or hoarseness

These should be memorized, and at the appearance of any of these signs, a physician should be consulted.

Women must become aware of their bodies and heed the warning signs. Any abnormalities should be questioned, and most should be looked into by a gynecologist. Routine checkups should be scheduled at least once a year, and self-examination should become a frequent habit. If you've but one life to live, you should live it in health.

The Future—Cancer-Preventing Agents?

Researchers at the National Cancer Institute and elsewhere are looking into the possibility of vaccinations against cancer and of pills that can be taken daily to prevent cancer. The main thrust of the research is aimed at three chemical agents: vitamin A, Laetrile (vitamin B_{17}), and a compound called 13-CIS-retinoic acid.

Vitamin A

Vitamin A has been proven to stimulate greatly the immune response in doses of more than ten times the daily requirement. These extremely high doses of vitamin A have been successfully used as an anticancer agent in about 1,100 German patients. Not only did the vitamin A seem to prevent tumors, but those patients who had developed cancer before being treated showed a much higher survival rate. Unfortunately, high doses of vitamin A cause hypervitaminosis, which can result in headaches, dizziness, diarrhea, change in skin coloring, edema behind the eyes, and liver damage. Because of this, the dosage must be carefully controlled by a physician. Large amounts of cod liver oil containing vitamin A might diminish the problem of toxicity.

13-CIS-Retinoic Acid

This chemical compound is a member of the chemical family of *retinoids*. Retinoids, although they show no effect on cancer that has already developed, appear to regulate cell growth in the epithelial (lining) tissue of organs such as the lungs, the breasts, the bladder, and the prostate gland. These organs are the site for development of 70 percent of all human cancer. The specific retinoid—13-CIS-retinoic acid—is the only one of these compounds considered safe for human use. By regulating this tissue growth, retinoids have reduced cancer development in laboratory animals. The prophylactic effects of this drug are presently being investigated in humans.

Laetrile–Vitamin B $_{17}$

Laetrile, the controversial anticancer substance, has received a great deal of recent publicity. There have been tests with this drug for more than twenty-five years and no valid scientific evidence yet exists to prove its value in the treatment of cancer. However, there have been reports in the media and publications on cancer cures and remissions following treatment with Laetrile. There are a number of organizations attempting to have Laetrile made generally available in the United States. The Food and Drug Administration has not legalized Laetrile since it feels that there is no dependable scientific evidence of the efficacy of this drug and its release might prevent some people suffering from cancer from receiving the necessary, early, effective treatment.

Laetrile is available in Mexico (and a growing number of states) and people have gone there to receive the drug. At the present time the proponents of Laetrile have shifted the emphasis from Laetrile as a cancer cure to Laetrile as a cancer preventative and/or a means for slowing the growth of the cancer.

The Food and Drug Administration will probably not release Laetrile without documented proof of its effectiveness.

BCG (Bacillus Calmette-Guerin)

One of the most promising anticancer treatments is the injection of BCG, an antituberculosis agent. BCG strengthens the immune response. When it is used in conjunction with chemotherapy, BCG has drastically reduced the death rate in cancer patients. Research is presently being conducted to determine the possible prophylactic properties of BCG. If cancer is caused by a virus—herpes II has been linked to cancer of the cervix—BCG could turn out to be an essential component of a cancer vaccine.

Vaccination

When you receive a vaccination against a disease like polio or smallpox, you are actually being given a small dose of that disease. Your body reacts by producing antibodies to fight whatever you've been infected with. These antibodies, once in the bloodstream, protect you against the disease, sometimes temporarily and sometimes for life. The chances of developing such a vaccine for cancer are encouraging. The field of immunology is progressing by leaps and bounds, and some experts believe certain types of cancer will eventually be as rare as polio. Anticancer vaccines would be especially valuable for the elderly, who are highly susceptible to cancer, since the immune system deteriorates with age.

Whether the answer is BCG, vaccination, pills, or vitamins, cancer prevention is certainly in its infancy. The prognosis for the future, based on the successes of medicine in the past, is good. The answer may be a long time in coming. Still, it will come.

chapter 21

SEX

WHAT IS NORMAL SEX?

People have sex for one or more of three simple reasons: to have children, to express their love, and to have fun and relax. The variety of ways in which sex can fulfill these needs is astonishing.

No one can define *normality* with exact precision, especially when dealing with a sociopsychological phenomenon such as sex. Still, the lesson of history is clear: Sex has always existed, and so has almost every imaginable sexual act. For example, group sex was a normal feature of life in the days of Imperial Rome, incest has been a traditional practice of royalty since the Egyptian pharaohs (Cleopatra was a descendant of six generations of brother-sister marriages), sadism and masochism were common in early religions and familiar fairy tales (such as Cinderella, who willingly suffered torment and humiliation from her step-mother and step-sisters). Homosexuality has been common in tribal societies around the world. Homosexuality was also common in Greek mythology; even Zeus was so inclined. Indeed, in ancient Greece, a homosexual relationship was a standard, respected part of the total education of any well-bred young man.

The lesson of nature is equally clear: There is nothing "unnatural" about any of this. Whales and porpoises enjoy group sex. Homosexuality is everywhere in the animal kingdom; monkeys are the gayest. Zebras and wild horses kick and bite each other bloody as a prelude to sex. And in the Vienna zoo, a white peacock and a Galapagos turtle were observed trying to mate.

So what is "normal"?

The answer is that normal sex is any kind of sex that is felt to be normal by the participants. Oral sex and masturbation are criminal acts (sometimes even for married couples) in more than forty states, yet the Kinsey Report found that 95 percent of American men and 85 percent of American women qualify for a prison sentence under these laws. It could be normal for a couple to enjoy group sex, as long as neither partner is *forced* to participate. Homosexuality is normal sex for homosexuals but not for heterosexuals.

Anything can be normal sex if there is love and understanding between the partners. When it is abnormal to one of the partners, it becomes abnormal sex. Unfortunately the Judeo-Christian morality of Western society—and particularly our own American Puritan heritage—has rigidly opposed the enjoyment of human bodily functions and sensations. This narrow attitude has influenced every area of our modern lives. Our schools, churches, laws, manners, and dress all inhibit us. It is no surprise that our beliefs are in confusion between what we are told and how we feel.

PSYCHO-SEXUAL PROBLEMS

Masters and Johnson, the leading sex therapists in America today, have stated that approximately half of the marriages in this country have or will have sexual problems.

And the fact is, *most sexual problems start above the waist.* That is, most sexual problems are not physical, but psychological. Our upbringing has taught us to feel guilty about sex. Now, in our sex-oriented world, we feel anxious about meeting our own and our partner's sexual expectations. Evidence shows that sexual problems are not usually manifestations of profound emotional disturbance. To the contrary, they occur regularly in people who function normally in all other psychological aspects.

The cause of many sexual problems is simply lack of information. With sex as highly visible in our society as it is today in books, magazines, movies, plays, songs, on TV, and right there on the street, it's hard to believe anyone could still be handicapped by an ignorance of basic anatomical facts. Yet doctors and sex therapists see couples who have been married several years and have never had intercourse because they don't know how. More commonly, a man might not know that it takes a woman much longer to become sexually aroused than it does himself; a woman might not know that a man's sexual abilities change throughout his life. Lack of information—

lack of sex education—works differently in different people, and can cause problems in a number of different areas.

Guilt

Sex therapists treat many patients who are inhibited by guilt and who never suspect it as the root of their problem. Moreover, they are surprised when the therapist points it out. One of the most frequently observed sexual dysfunctions in men, for example, is premature ejaculation, which often originates in guilt feelings. Guilt is both a cause and an effect of lack of information; a misunderstanding that produces a sexual problem which is itself misunderstood.

Frustration

A lack of information can obviously frustrate a couple who want a full and fulfilling sex life. Gaining knowledge can bring a second frustration—the sense of having missed something—which may lead the woman or man or both to blame their relationship and look elsewhere for a second youth.

Overexpectation

Many women are looking for the perfect, sublime orgasm that everyone is talking about. These women often feel cheated when they don't achieve it. Many women react to their first sexual experiences by thinking, "Is that all?" They wonder if they have an average amount of sex. Yet studies consistently show that how often people have intercourse has nothing to do with how much they enjoy it. Like sexual problems, sexual pleasure also starts above the waist—with an open, understanding attitude between the partners. This is a statistical fact. People often expect too much of sex because they don't know what to expect.

Insecurity

Many couples are so anxious to please each other sexually that each member will ignore her or his own enjoyment to concentrate on the other's. Men worry about achieving an instant erection. Women worry about faking orgasm. It's unfortunate when sex becomes a theatrical performance striving to attain a glossy ideal, with an audience of two critics who don't know any better.

Hidden Problems

Many people are unaware that certain diseases (like diabetes), medications (such as those used for hypertension), and alcohol abuse can seriously impair sexual pleasure. The first step in treating any sexual problem is a complete physical examination, to determine if the problem stems from physiological causes.

Embarrassment

Many sexual problems could be avoided if the couple openly discussed their attitudes and preferences, learned about each other's bodies, considered new ideas—in short, exchanged information about themselves. Too often, embarrassment prevents this. People are ashamed to reveal their ignorance. Or they are confused about what they do know. This embarrassment complicates old problems, creating new ones.

The First Step to Solving a Problem

A lot of sexual problems can be cured simply by education. This education should start at an early age and continue until death. Parents should be open and honest with their children, explaining to them what happens in sex and what doesn't, what to expect and what not to expect. Schools should supplement and reinforce parental teachings, supplying, perhaps, facts which are not within parental grasp. As an adult, it is vital to continue seeking information—from lovers, friends, books, or anything else. There is nothing you shouldn't know about sex, and no information you should greet with a less-than-open attitude. After all, how can anyone enjoy sex before knowing what is possible and what isn't? In the limited space of this chapter, we will offer a closer look at the exotic cornucopia of sex and the basics, too—what happens and what doesn't, what's possible and what isn't.

One thing that isn't possible is for a peacock and a turtle to mate. What's important, and perfectly normal, is that they tried. All the information in the world will be useless if your mind isn't open to receive it. Relax, feel good, and expand. Learn to enjoy sex for the beautiful experience it is.

YOUR BODY

It's sexy, all right . . . but what, exactly, *is* sexy about it? And why?

People are different and fashions change, in sex as in any other preference. Ancient religious cults featured vaginas and penises as powerful symbols and images. In eighteenth-century Europe, women's ball gowns were tailored to extreme décolletage in order to display their powdered nipples. In the Roaring Twenties, women bound their breasts and men ogled their "gams" instead. Modern American men seem to admire most a woman's breasts. The girl from Ipanema, or anywhere else in South America, wears a *tonga*—a string bikini—when she walks down the beach because Latin men are more stimulated by a woman's buttocks than by any other part of her body. Turnabout is fair play, and a majority of young American women who were questioned in a recent survey agreed that they liked *men* with trim buttocks.

Fads and fancies come and go; the truth is, as the old saying goes: What you have isn't as important as how you use it.

The Vagina

People come in all sizes, and so do their sexual organs. In general, the larger a woman is, the deeper her vagina will be; the important fact, however, is that most women, large or small, can usually accommodate any size penis.

After all, the vagina is an amazing organ. Its ability to stretch and then return to its normal size is astonishing. One month it can accommodate a baby's passage. The next month it is large enough to accommodate only a penis.

The vagina's ability to stretch is always present. Because of this, if a woman complains that she has difficulty accepting a very large penis, it may be simply that she needs a greater amount of stimulation, since the vagina actually increases in size the more excited a woman becomes. More frequent intercourse will also cause a woman's vagina to enlarge.

When a woman first starts having intercourse, she might face a different problem—the size and type of her hymen. Since, like everything else, the hymen ring inside the opening of the vagina varies from woman to woman—from a tight, thick membrane to an open, thin one—some women will be more stretched than others, will experience greater pain, and will be harder to penetrate. If a woman is young and just beginning to have sex, then some sort of external lubrication (with, for example, K-Y lubricant or baby oil) should help the immediate problem, and intercourse will probably become easier with the passage of time. In more serious cases, where penetration may be impossible, the surgical procedure called hymenectomy is advisable. This is merely a matter of surgically opening the hymen ring, requiring a short hospital stay.

Often the complaint is just the opposite. A woman, especially after bearing several children, will feel stretched to such a degree that she is unable to squeeze tightly around a man's penis and has less pleasure during intercourse. Sometimes this is the result of a traumatic or prolonged childbirth, and the solution lies only in a surgical procedure (a posterior repair) which tightens the vaginal muscles, returning the vagina to normal size. If, though, a delivery has been uncomplicated, with good obstetrical care, the vagina usually returns to its normal size by itself. A simple exercise can help most women keep their vaginas in tone.

The Kegel Exercise

Today many people are concerned with physical fitness. They jog, visit health clubs, or do exercises at home to keep healthy. A woman's vagina is an opening covered with muscles that respond to exercise like other muscles and should be kept in as good condition. The Kegel exercise was developed by the late Arnold Kegel, a California gynecologist. Dr. Kegel initially used his technique for older patients who couldn't retain their urine. The purpose of the exercise was to strengthen the muscles around the vagina. Dr. Kegel found that after doing the exercise for a while, women experienced a greater capacity for orgasm, even when they were previously unable to achieve one.

The Kegel exercise is easy. Squeeze your buttocks together and draw in your pelvis: the contraction you feel is the *pubococcygeus* muscle. Try to keep this muscle contracted for three seconds, then relax for three seconds, then squeeze again. Women sometimes have trouble contracting the muscle for three full seconds in the beginning. The Kegel exercise starts with three three-second contractions at three different times during the day and increases up to twenty three-second contractions at a time. The Kegel exercise can be done while you're walking, riding the subway, or sitting in a car, and the improved vaginal control it brings means better sex for you and your partner. To check the progress of this exercise, you should occasionally insert a finger into your vagina and squeeze, determining if you are exercising the right muscles and monitoring the increased pressure on your finger. The same exercise can be used to great benefit during intercourse. All you do is replace your finger with a penis. Some stripteasers have gained such control that they can pick up dollar bills with their vaginal lips.

Vaginal Malformations

All kinds of malformations can exist in the vagina, as in any organ. In rare cases, a woman may even be born *without* a vagina or uterus, and yet possess other normal sex characteristics such as breast development and pubic hair. In these cases, doctors can create an artificial vagina with skin taken from the inside thigh. If the uterus is absent, the woman is not able to have children, but the artificial vagina will respond sexually like a normal vagina, with normal secretion, orgasmic contractions, and pleasure during intercourse. This is the same type of vagina that is created in men who undergo sex-change operations.

The Clitoris

From various specific research, including the implantation of electrodes in the vagina, modern sexologists have determined that the crucial factor in producing female orgasm is stimulation of the clitoris. The clitoris is a tiny vestigial penis, a bundle of nerves with a head and shaft which gathers and transmits impulses to the sex centers of the brain, where orgasmic responses are controlled. The clitoris has six to ten times more nerve endings than the tissue which surrounds it. It is so sensitive that some women find direct touch painful, preferring to masturbate or be stroked around or near the clitoris instead.

The in and out movements of a man's penis during intercourse pull the vaginal lips and tissue around the clitoris, and a woman may therefore conclude that her arousal is linked to the penetration of her vagina rather than, as is the case, to the stimulation of her clitoris. Also, a woman will feel a pleasurable sensation deep in her vagina as it secretes and enlarges with her excitement, and may identify this as the source of her orgasm, although the transmitter and pacemaker of her sexual response is really the nerve center of the clitoris.

The Penis

There is no connection between a man's race or body size and the size of his penis. It's like his nose—it all depends on genetics. Large and small penises seem to run in families. A large unerected penis may give a man a psychological boost, but what counts is, of course, the size of the erected penis, and this does only vary slightly from man to man. Studies have shown that a large flaccid penis may only increase slightly to its erected state, while a small flaccid penis often can more than double its size to an approximately equal erection. The average size of an erect penis is between six and seven inches, regardless of its size when it is flaccid.

The more sexual stimulation and intercourse a man has, the larger his penis will become. Mood and health also affect a man's sexual response; a man's erection can increase or decrease by an inch from day to day. Finally, a whole group of devices guaranteed to increase penis size is available in sex shops and through magazine advertisements. While these devices may be pleasurable to use, they are only a gadgety excuse to stimulate the penis, and this stimulation can be achieved more simply and economically by masturbation and intercourse.

Men worry about these things, but women seem to agree that the size of a man's penis has little to do with his ability to be sexually satisfying. A man can best satisfy a woman by understanding a woman sexually and preparing her for intercourse.

Silicone Implantation in the Penis

As is the case with the vagina, there are surgical procedures available to correct or rebuild the penis. Silicone implantations have been performed, mostly in urology departments for patients whose penises were partly excised due to cancer. In order to allow the patients sexual satisfaction, doctors will implant silicone rods in the penis to produce a permanent stiffness (although true erection, a raising of the penis, will not usually occur). Men with small penises sometimes inquire about this operation, but urologists are reluctant to perform it except where severe corrective surgery has been necessary.

The Breasts

A woman's breasts are a very sensitive erogenous area for the woman and an important sexual attraction for many men. Some women feel such excitement having their breasts stimulated that they can reach orgasm; some women actively dislike it. In either case, a woman's breasts will swell and become fuller, and the nipples will become erect during arousal.

The size of a woman's breasts has as little importance as the size of a man's penis. A woman may worry that her breasts are too small, or too large, or different sizes, instead of simply enjoying them for the pleasure they can give. In fact, the erogenous focus of the breast is the nipple and surrounding area, which is equally sensitive no matter what the size of the breast.

A common complaint of women is inverted nipples, which they fear may be a deformity or a block to sexual pleasure. Not true. Inverted nipples are considered to be well within the limits of normal breast variation, and in no way affect the quality of sensation a woman feels in her breasts.

The breasts are among the most blatantly obvious sex characteristics, which certainly accounts for much of their attractiveness to men. Furthermore, the mother's breast means warmth, nourishment, and safety to the infant. This sensual bond can easily carry into adulthood on a subconscious level. For whatever reason, many men substitute the part for the whole, and respond to the woman in terms of her breasts. Some men prefer women with big breasts, on the theory that quantity means quality, while others always want small-breasted women, expecting them to be more sexually diverse. Both attitudes miss the point completely.

As women and their sexual partners mature, and sex becomes a regular feature of their lives, the emphasis on breasts, big or small, seems to fade. The entire range of sexual experience becomes available, and a woman's breasts are only one of many means of enjoyment.

The Buttocks

One recent theory has proposed that as human beings evolved into using a face-to-face position in intercourse, women's breasts grew larger and rounder to replace the twin globes of her buttocks as a sexual lure. This may be only anthropological speculation, but the sexual function of the buttocks (the rump of animals) is undeniable. Almost all male animals approach and mount the female from the rear. The persistence of the hourglass shape as an ideal woman's figure suggests the strong sexual power not only of the breasts but of the buttocks as well among human beings since antiquity. Clothing from bustles to bikinis has served to accentuate the appeal of the buttocks.

The buttocks are a sexual feature of both women and men, which seems to clarify and confuse their function. Much of the enjoyment of anal sex, which is practiced by heterosexuals and homosexuals alike, is undoubtedly provided by the visual and tactile stimulation of the buttocks. The confusion of gender may add to the excitement for some people, but the simpler truth is that the anus and buttocks are an extremely sensitive area for everyone.

THE ORGASM

Our present knowledge of human sexual orgasm comes largely from the excellent and extensive research carried out by Masters and Johnson during the past two decades. These two pioneers investigated the physiological functions of orgasm in more than six hundred women and men from eighteen to ninety years of age.

Masters and Johnson divided the orgasm response into four phases: the excitement, the plateau, the orgasm, and the resolution.

The Excitement Phase

This is the initial phase of sexual response, characterized in the woman by vaginal and clitoral response. Lubrication or wetness and enlargement of the vaginal lips occur within thirty seconds after the initiation of any form of effective physical and/or psychological stimulation. This stimulation can be caused by anything from erotic fantasies to direct sexual contact. In some, but not all, women, there is an increase in the size and hardness of the clitoris. These changes are partly caused by vasoconstriction (a narrowing of the blood vessels), which holds blood in the vulvar area.

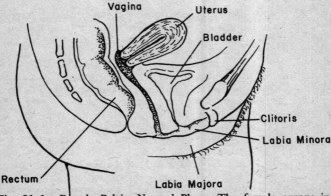

Fig. 21–1: Female Pelvis: Normal Phase. The female organs in cross-section, in a normal resting phase before sexual stimulation. The uterus is in the anteverted position. The vagina is relaxed.

Blood continues to be pumped into the vulvar area and causes a swelling of the vulva and the lower part of the vagina. There is also an enlargement and lengthening of the upper part of the vagina. Uterine contractions increase. All these changes enable easier penetration, since the vagina is now opened, softer, wetter, and lengthened to accommodate a fully erect penis. These changes take place even in women who have had hysterectomies, in women after menopause, and in women with artificial vaginas. There is also often a noticeable increase in the size of the nipples as the breasts become aroused in this first phase.

The initial physiological response to sexual stimulation in a man is the erection. Younger men can achieve an erection from fantasy or other indirect causes, while older men need more direct stimulation, such as masturbation or oral sex. Blood is pumped into the penis and held there by vasoconstriction, and the penis erects as it fills with blood. At this time, the man's scrotum contracts and elevates. There is an increase in his heart rate and breathing, which also occurs in women. Although direct manipulation can make a man's nipples harden, there is no consistent breast response in men during intercourse.

The Plateau Phase

The bodily changes already begun continue in this phase to their most advanced state in both women and men. Vasoconstriction further swells the outer third of the vagina. This results in increased wetness of the labia, allowing easier penetration and a firmer grip on the penis. The upper two thirds of the vagina continue to balloon out and lengthen. The uterus elevates, and contractions occur with greater frequency, which the woman experiences as a pleasurable sensation. The clitoris retracts and rotates upward. The significance of this is not clearly understood. The labia will change in color from light pink to red to deep purple as they engorge with blood. Heightened blood pressure causes the vessels on the neck to stand out noticeably. The breasts continue to swell, becoming largest immediately prior to orgasm. The areolas around the nipples also swell so that the nipples appear to retract. Breathing pattern and blood pressure increases in both women and men.

During the plateau phase in men, the erection is complete and the penis extended to its maximum size. The testes are elevated and engorged with blood and about 50 percent larger than in their resting state. A few drops of clear fluid, probably expelled as a lubricant by the Cowper's gland, may appear on

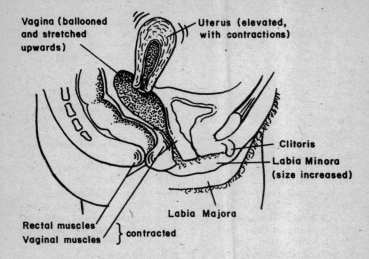

Fig. 21-2: Female Pelvis: Orgasmic Phase. The upper portion of the vagina balloons out during orgasm, and the uterus has risen from its resting position to an upright position. The vaginal muscles which surround the lower portion of the vagina contract, and both the uterus and the vagina have rhythmic contractions occurring every .8 seconds. The labia minora swell and increase in size; the labia majora spread slightly apart. The clitoris rotates and retracts upward and the rectal sphincter muscles contract. During sexual intercourse, a man can usually recognize the orgasmic phase, since the upper part of the vagina usually becomes larger, and he should be able to recognize the squeezing of the lower vagina.

the head of the penis. There may be some darkening in color of the penis corresponding to the darkening of the vaginal labia. The pupils dilate and the nostrils flare in both sexes. Light-headedness frequently occurs in both partners during this phase.

The Orgasm Phase

The characteristics of orgasm are identical in all women and are always triggered by direct or indirect stimulation of the clitoris. The variety of ways this may be achieved probably explains the different abilities to reach orgasm in various women.

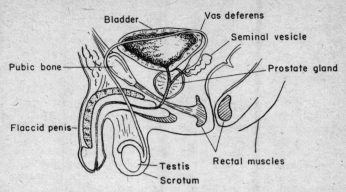

Fig. 21–3: Male Genitals: Normal Phase. The anatomical relationship of the male genitalia is shown, in cross-section, in the normal resting stage. The scrotum in this stage is usually relaxed and the testes hang low. The picture clearly demonstrates the vas deferens, which leads the sperm from the testes to the prostate gland, where both urine and sperm pass through the penis via the urethra.

Fig. 21–4: Male Genitals: Orgasmic Phase. The penis is erect and the muscles of the scrotum are contracting, which lifts the testes during the preorgasmic and orgasmic phase. The rectal muscle is contracted and the urethral bulb dilated.

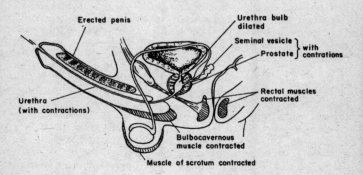

The uterus rises and regular contractions occur every 0.8 second, which is the same rhythmic frequency as the ejaculations of the man's orgasm. These contractions may create a suction in the vagina, and a woman may feel air being drawn into her during this phase. The woman's anal sphincter tightens. Her toes curl, as do the man's. In women just prior to or after childbirth, there may be a small secretion of milk from the breasts due to their enlarged state at orgasm. Pulse rate and breathing are elevated. The clitoris retracts further under the foreskin. Maximum sensation and intensive pleasure occur at orgasm, which rarely lasts longer than ten or fifteen seconds.

During orgasm, the man ejaculates semen in regular spurts every 0.8 second. These contractions are so strong that semen can be ejaculated a distance of several feet from the penis. The scrotum contracts and the testes elevate. His anal sphincter tightens. Pulse rate and breathing are elevated and blood pressure increases to its highest level. There is a necessary interval between orgasms for all men, which is brief in the prime of adolescence and becomes greater as the man ages.

The Resolution Phase

This final phase begins with the fading of the woman's uterine contractions and release of the vasoconstriction, draining blood from the pelvic area. This phase continues until the pelvic organs return to their resting state, and heart rate, breathing, blood pressure, and skin vascularity are again at normal levels. This takes up to a half an hour. The drop in blood pressure initiates a sense of easeful fatigue and relaxation.

Corresponding changes occur in the man. The erection fades, the testes relax, and the bodily rhythms slow until functions return to normal and the man grows drowsy.

COMMON VARIATIONS IN SEXUAL RESPONSE

A significant number of women do not reach orgasm during intercourse. They can reach the plateau phase and are not able to relieve the tension created in their bodies. In many such cases, a woman needs longer or greater or more direct clitoral stimulation. It is not possible for all women to achieve an orgasm by intercourse alone, and masturbation, the use of a vibrator, or other means of additional manipulation of the clitoris might be necessary.

A woman must be frank with her partner if she needs extra or special attention. All too often a woman fakes orgasm rather than suggesting her particular needs, thus depriving herself of the profound delight of a successful orgasm, and depriving her partner as well of the opportunity to enjoy further sex play with her.

Pelvic Congestion

A woman who remains too long in the plateau phase, or who cannot go beyond it to orgasm, often experiences restlessness, the inability to sleep, and severe backaches from pelvic congestion. In the plateau phase, blood is pumped into the vagina and uterus. This causes a swelling (or *edema*) of the pelvic organs—a pelvic congestion. The rhythmic contractions during orgasm, as well as the cessation of the vasoconstriction, relieve tension by pumping the blood out of the pelvic tissues and allowing fresh oxygenated blood to reach the area. When this buildup of fluid, or *edema*, is unrelieved, it creates a physical tension in the body which quickly becomes a psychological tension, too. In many cases of pelvic congestion, researchers have found a woman's uterus can be enlarged to twice its normal size by fluid. Clearly, the woman's body is in a state of stress. A woman may complain of pains, discomfort, or exhaustion and blame it on family, friends, or work, and not realize her tension has this sexual basis. Pelvic congestion is both unpleasant and unhealthy—and it's unnecessary, too, considering the simple remedy, which is orgasm, either through intercourse or masturbation.

Frequent intercourse without orgasm results in a greater incidence and more severe symptoms of pelvic congestion. Because of this, prostitutes are especially vulnerable to this malady.

Multiple Orgasm

Once a woman has achieved one orgasm she has a good chance to enjoy multiple orgasms—a whole series of successive orgasms during a single act of intercourse. For men, as mentioned, the interval in the resolution phase between one arousal and another becomes longer as they age, and many older men are only able to reach one orgasm during a session of sex. A woman, though, does not descend from her orgasm directly into the resolution phase the way a man does. A woman goes to the plateau phase first. So, by continuing stimulation, she can be brought rapidly back to the orgasm phase. This can be repeated many times. Five or six orgasms are common and ten to fifteen are possible. There have been occasional reports regarding women who have reached up to a hundred orgasms. Needless to say, the validity of such reports is difficult to confirm. The ability to achieve multiple orgasms continues in women throughout their lives.

Status Orgasmus

Sadly, there can be too much of a good thing. *Status orgasmus,* or persistent orgasm, is a physiological state caused by rapidly reoccurring orgasms between which there is no relaxation or plateau phase. This results in a sharply increased heart rate (often over 180 beats per minute) and a sharp, cramplike pain in the vagina caused by a lack of relaxation and a lessened supply of oxygen. A woman may feel this painful sensation during prolonged intercourse and think she is being hurt by the size of the man's penis, when in fact her vagina is cramping from status orgasmus.

Can Orgasm Initiate Labor?

Since orgasm involves multiple contractions of the vagina and uterus, it is similar to, and can in fact initiate, labor. Also, the semen ejaculated by the man during intercourse contains hormones called *prostaglandins,* which are known to cause uterine contractions, reinforcing the woman's natural response. Therefore, doctors often tell patients who have a tendency toward premature labor to avoid masturbation and intercourse in the last weeks of pregnancy. On the other hand, midwives in certain countries traditionally urge pregnant women to have sex if their babies are past term, as a way to induce labor.

Does a Hysterectomy Affect Sexual Response?

Many women who undergo hysterectomy at first feel "de-sexed" by the operation. Many men wrongly think that the penis enters the uterus in intercourse, and that a hysterectomy removes the "pleasure zone" from a woman's body. As has been shown, orgasm depends on the clitoris, not the uterus. Once a woman realizes that her sexual satisfaction is unimpaired by a hysterectomy, she may even discover that her sex life has improved. This is particularly true of women who have experienced uterine problems and are now free of them.

SEX AND APHRODISIACS

Hormones and drugs are agents that act on the chemical balance of the body in many ways, one of which is to influence sexual ability and pleasure.

The so-called sex hormones are secreted by the sexual organs and by the adrenal cortex. Under normal circumstances, men and women will have some amount of hormones of the opposite sex in their bodies. Transsexuals (people who have undergone sex-change operations) are administered a large dose of the hormones of their adopted sex over a period of time in order to complete their conversions, and hormones are regularly used by doctors to treat lesser sexual deficiencies.

Female Hormones—Are They Aphrodisiacs?

The female hormones, *estrogen* and *progesterone*, control the regular menstrual cycle and stimulate the secondary sex characteristics in women. The influence of these hormones on behavior varies from woman to woman.

The first female hormone, estrogen, has some aphrodisiac effect, but not to the extent of the male hormones. Immediately prior to menstruation, when hormone levels are at their highest, most women experience heightened sexual desire and can achieve orgasm more easily. The same effects are reported in women taking birth-control pills containing high amounts of estrogen. After menopause, when the estrogen level decreases, so does sexual desire. At this time, if estrogen replacement is administered, it usually increases desire.

The second female hormone, progesterone, has a lesser aphrodisiac effect and, in some cases, can even inhibit sexual arousal. This has been found true in some women who take the minipill, which contains progesterone alone.

Male Hormones—An Effective Sexual Stimulant

Male hormones, known generically as *androgens*, are the most potent hormonal aphrodisiac for women as well as men. Androgens control the development of the secondary sex characteristics in men and maintain sperm production. They affect appetite and metabolism, as well as behavioral patterns like dominance and vigor. Every woman produces a small amount of male hormones in her ovaries. Women with large or polycystic ovaries produce more, which increases energy and sexual desire, but can cause side effects such as heavy facial-hair growth, low voice register, or more developed muscles. This last characteristic explains the furious controversy in athletics concerning the permissible level of hormone injections given a woman contestant.

It is known that women who, after menopause or after removal of their ovaries, subsequently lose all production of *testosterone* (the most common androgen) will lose some of their sexual drive as well. When women receive hormone replacement treatment after menopause, they're usually better able to reach sexual fulfillment, particularly if they also receive testosterone.

Aside from being the strongest aphrodisiac in women, testosterone also strengthens bones and muscles and aids in the ever-constant battle against fatigue.

In men, the androgens again act as aphrodisiacs, and testosterone is employed in the treatment of male impotence.

Drugs and Sex

People use a variety of drugs to enhance their sexual performance or pleasure, from aphrodisiacs considered to have specifically sexual purposes to substances such as marijuana and alcohol, which seem to have a generally more pleasurable effect on all activities. The inclusion of the use of drugs in this chapter is intended to be informative only. It is not the authors' intention to recommend the use of such drugs.

Lovers in every society throughout history have sought the perfect aphrodisiac, a guaranteed stimulus to the sex drive. From *abelmosk, burra gokeroo,* and *cubeb peppers* right on through the alphabet to *rhinocerous horn, serpelot,* and *yohimbe,* everything has been tried by someone somewhere, including *strychnine.* Many of these substances do have some sexual effect (including strychnine). They also may have other, unpleasant effects (ditto). Most aphrodisiacs, however, are inert at best. The only boost they generally give the user is a psychological one—but that can be enough, since so many sexual problems are psychological in origin. Other aphrodisiacs produce a state of sexual stimulation by means that are distinctly harmful to the body, such as the most famous aphrodisiac of all, *Spanish fly.*

Spanish fly is not a medicine; it is used solely as an aphrodisiac. It is a toxic substance which causes sexual stimulation by creating an irritation and inflammation of the genitals and bladder. Unfortunately, this irritation and inflammation is as dangerous as it is stimulating, since it can result in permanent damage to the genitalia and kidneys. This damage can even cause death. Today there are many drugs which are being advertised and sold as Spanish fly. Most of them are not Spanish fly but substances such as cayenne pepper, which cause minor urethal irritation and mild sexual irritation. In most instances, these imitations are not dangerous.

As you can see, though, the quest for an ideal love potion should be pursued very carefully. Drugs which are used for an overall "high" will affect people sexually in different ways: What turns you on can turn someone else right off. A person can respond differently at different times to the same drug. A discussion of a number of popular drug substances in terms of their possible sexual effects follows. These drugs are *not*

SEX 469

aphrodisiacs, because they are not used for strictly erotic stimulation, but in certain circumstances they may have sex-enhancing properties.

Alcohol

Alcohol is not a stimulant, but a depressant. However, it does not depress all parts of the brain equally and simultaneously. Rather, it produces a specific sequence of effects. First, it depresses the brain center which controls fear, and thus releases anxiety and inhibition. It is at this point that alcohol seems to cause sexual desire. While alcohol in small amounts can have a stimulating effect on both women and men, the borderline between freedom and intoxication is very fine. Higher doses of alcohol depress the brain completely and bring sedation and sleep instead of arousal. Chronic intake of alcohol decreases the hormone level and reduces sexual ability considerably; in men, it often leads to impotence.

Amphetamines

Amphetamines ("speed") are agents which stimulate the central brain. The claims as to the sexual effect of amphetamines vary from person to person. Some people report that amphetamines heighten their sexual desire and performance, and that they have trouble functioning without these agents. Other sources suggest that amphetamine users experience a diminishing of their sexual ability as their dependency grows, until finally they become too ill to have any interest in sex. The danger of amphetamines should be emphasized, since they have a debilitating, addictive effect.

Amyl Nitrite

Amyl nitrite is a *vasodilator* (an agent which opens the blood vessels) sold by prescription to relieve the pain of angina, or heart spasms. It comes in small glass capsules which are broken (or popped open, hence the popular nickname, poppers) and inhaled through the nose. Popped just before orgasm, amyl nitrite causes dilation of the blood vessels in the brain and intensifies all sensations, particularly sexual ones. The increased blood supply causes a hot feeling, which directly heightens erotic sensation for the few minutes the drug is effective. It also relaxes the vaginal and anal openings and permits easier penetration. There are usually no negative side effects from the use of this agent, although it is extremely dangerous for persons with low blood pressure and certain heart conditions. In high or frequent doses, it has caused several deaths.

Barbiturates

The so-called downers (sedatives, sleeping pills, and insomnia tablets) have an effect on sex somewhat similar to that of alcohol. At first and when taken in small amounts, these agents relax inhibitions for about an hour. During this time, sexual interest increases while a generally mellow feeling occurs. After a while, the entire body is relaxed—sexual desire diminishes, and sleep, or at least fatigue, comes. Another type of downer, chemically unrelated to barbiturates, is *methaqualone*, commonly available by prescription as Quaalude. Although many people have found that this drug can stimulate sexual desire and prolong intercourse, its long-term effects are similar to those of barbiturates. Addiction to downers of any form is not unusual, and chronic abuse is harmful to sexual functioning. Cases of death from downers mostly involve a combination of excessive drug use and alcohol intake.

Cocaine

Cocaine, a derivative of the coca shrub of South America and once the effective ingredient in Coca-Cola, is today the prestige item of the drug elite, no doubt in part because of its extremely high price. (Its use is, however, illegal in the United States.) Cocaine comes in the form of a white powder which is "snorted," or sniffed, up the nose; the more fashionable coke users snort the ingredient from miniature spoons—gold or silver—which have become a symbol of the user's membership in the drug community.

Cocaine has a vasoconstricting effect and is said to get rid of a cold in no time. The drug is not always effective as an aphrodisiac, but when it is, it stimulates the higher brain centers, the nervous system, and the musculature, giving a feeling of enormous energy (a "rush") which the user may wish to express sexually. A couple using cocaine can enjoy much prolonged intercourse. Cocaine may also be used as a surface anesthetic, applied to the head of the penis or clitoris, to decrease sensation (sometimes preventing premature ejaculation) and permit longer and more varied sexual activity. Chronic use of cocaine is not addicting, but can lead to psychological dependence, and will certainly damage the mucous membranes and olfactory nerves in the nose. There is also increasing evidence of other damaging side effects from cocaine and its use is not recommended.

Heroin and Methadone

Heroin users report that in the beginning, they experience exquisite sensation during intercourse. As they become hooked on the drug, however, they develop other needs, mainly the need to find enough money to support their habits. At first, heroin produces a "high." Later, an addict must continue and increase the dosage just to feel normal. If this is impossible, the addict will be subjected to debilitating physical anguish. Methadone, which is administered to heroin addicts as a replacement drug on the way to complete withdrawal, usually decreases sexual appetite in men. For this reason, many heroin addicts are reluctant to enter methadone programs. Women who take methadone do not report this sexual decline.

LSD

The effects of LSD vary tremendously from person to person and from experience to experience. LSD is a hallucinogen which has a centrally stimulating effect, and in erotic circumstances sexual activity can be, literally, fantastically enhanced; the user's experience becomes not simply more intense but of a different quality—a cataclysmic, cosmic, spiritual coupling. In less successful situations, this chemical substance can produce an equally cataclysmic feeling of terror, paranoia, and hysteria—the typical "bad trip." The after effects can be so horrendous, that the use of LSD should be condemned.

Marijuana

Marijuana is the dried flowers and leaves of the cannabis plant, from which is also derived the similar, but more potent, drug—hashish. Marijuana is a mild psychedelic with some history as a sex stimulant (aphrodisiac sweetmeats are made in India from cannabis seeds, musk, and honey). The drug combines the freedom from inhibition that alcohol offers with the exciting properties of amphetamines. While some users feel more sensuous, erotic, and aroused after smoking or eating marijuana, others feel no sexual enhancement or sometimes even a depression of sexual interest. Many studies of this substance have been prejudiced by official disapproval of marijuana, so scientific findings about its true effects are contradictory at best, and often useless. It seems to increase sexual enjoyment in most users, but this may well depend on prevailing psychological factors at the time it is used.

Tobacco

It is well known that smoking cigarettes will increase the risk of lung cancer, heart trouble, stomach ulcers, and other diseases. There have recently been further findings that smoking tobacco reduces sexual desire, probably because tobacco is a vasoconstricting agent and decreases the amount of blood reaching the sex center in the brain. Some smokers claim that after they stopped smoking they have noticed, among other benefits, a greater sexual arousal.

WHAT ARE THE BEST APHRODISIACS?

Nothing can replace, or be more effective, than the natural aphrodisiacs: health, happiness, love, and caring.

Love and Caring

One of the nicest ways to express love and caring is to approach them honestly. Unfortunately, this approach is often lost in modern society, where many feelings are measured only by the frequency and quality of intercourse. Intercourse (a longer discussion of which follows) is great—it is healthy and fun. But it is not the total expression of love.

Touching, for instance, is always a beautiful and effective means of expressing feelings. It can surpass intercourse in its emotional, if not physical, intimacy. An affectionate hug or a kiss on the cheek can be just as pleasing as intercourse—often more so. Too often, couples feel they must jump directly into bed and perform sexually dizzying feats to express their affection. This should not be so.

People should understand each other, should be open to each other, and should care for each other in all aspects of life—not just intercourse. By doing this, each partner can discover the most satisfying way of expressing his or her love at any given moment—whether it is a soft caress, a gentle word, or imaginative intercourse. Orgasm is not the best response; loving is, however it is attained.

Imagination

The more love and caring there is in a relationship, the freer each partner becomes. Each can discuss her or his individual responses to different stimulants, fantasies, or sexual techniques. This openness frees the imagination and better sex and a closer relationship result.

THE POSITIONS

For many couples, sex has become all too routine, with intercourse occurring at the same time of day or night and always in the same position. Here, freedom and imagination can certainly enhance the couple's sex life by breaking the monotony.

There are literally hundreds of positions for sexual intercourse. One new publication described a different position for each of the 365 days of the year. This might be a little too much variety for the average couple, but it is useful information because it provokes the imagination. It is easy for a couple to fall into a particular pattern of sexual behavior which might once have been exciting, but which over a period of time becomes dull. Their sexual pleasure fades, perhaps so slowly that they are unaware of it. They think this eventually happens to every couple, or perhaps they are too embarrassed to talk about it. What is important is not how many positions you regularly use in intercourse, but how willing you are to experiment.

However many positions there are, most couples will usually find a few that they most enjoy at any one time. They may have sex simply in a single position, or sample several positions before orgasm. There are plenty of illustrated sex manuals around that you can use to get ideas for new positions. First and most important, though, use your imagination.

The Missionary Position

There's nothing wrong with the good old missionary position (face to face, male superior); in fact, it has a lot to recommend it. Lying together this way, a couple has intimate visual contact. They can kiss and touch each other easily. They can speak directly to each other. This position offers many variations—the woman can squeeze her legs together or put them on his shoulders or around his waist. Despite its advantages, though, it need not be the only mode of lovemaking.

The Female Superior Position

As a woman's pleasure mounts, she may prefer to change places with the man and take the superior position. The woman, kneeling on top, positions herself and moves her body as she wishes to bring herself the most fulfilling sensation. By

Fig. 21–5: The Missionary Position.

bending forward slightly, she can increase the direct stimulation of her clitoris for more intense pleasure; by sitting back she can moderate the stimulation and prolong the act of intercourse. The woman can control how much she is penetrated by the man's penis. She has the freedom to move up and down or circularly on the penis, at her own rate, at the angle she wants. For the same reasons, sex therapists often recommend this position to women whose partners are impotent or ejaculate prematurely.

The Sitting Position

Sex in a sitting position has many variables. A woman can either sit on top of the man, facing him in the riding position, or she can place her feet or knees on either side of the man, and her arms around his shoulders, giving her great freedom of movement in the squatting or kneeling position. The couple face each other, so all visual and psychological stimulations are in play. In either of these positions, the woman's back can be toward the man. This allows greater freedom of movement, but less visual contact. She can use the arms of a chair to push herself up and down.

A woman can also be penetrated by the man while she is in a sitting position—either in a chair or on the edge of a bed. The man can penetrate by kneeling on the floor when her knees are bent, sometimes even extending her legs over his shoulders.

This last position favors deeper and harder thrusts since the man can balance his power by grasping the back of the chair.

Of course, what you sit on is important, too. A sofa is good, so is a small chair without arms—anything that allows a natural position for the woman and supports the man upright. Armchairs are generally unsuccessful for women unless the arms are low and padded, to reduce the pressure on the woman's legs, or so wide that the woman can keep her knees inside the arms. If a chair is placed in front of a mirror the woman may wish to sit facing away from the man so that both partners can see each other in the mirror.

The Kneeling Position

A kneeling position, with the man entering the woman's vagina from the rear, brings the woman's buttocks into view as a sexual stimulant to the man. This position allows the man to drive into the woman with some force, which may be an exciting mode of indirect stimulation to her clitoris. If still greater stimulation is desired by the woman, she can kneel against one or two pillows and her clitoris will be rubbed against them by the man's thrusts. In this position, the woman can reach between her legs and touch the man's scrotum to excite him.

The Standing Position

Some difficulty may occur with standing intercourse, since the man is often taller than the woman and must crouch slightly to enter her. The woman can assist by raising one leg and placing it around the man, thus changing the angle of her vagina and making it more accessible. Or the man may lift her off the floor by her thighs and move her on his penis as she holds him around the neck. This variation is fairly strenuous for both partners and is usually of short duration. If this becomes too strenuous, he can rest the woman on an edge of a table, continuing his standing position. When a woman is wearing shoes or boots—which excites many men—she will minimize the difference of height. This is especially true if she turns and bends over to be entered from the rear, a standing position which is most comfortable for both partners. In order to keep her balance, it may be necessary for the woman to rest her arms or upper part of her body on a table, counter, or chair. As with the similar kneeling position of rear entry, the woman can easily reach the man's scrotum and arouse him by gently fondling it.

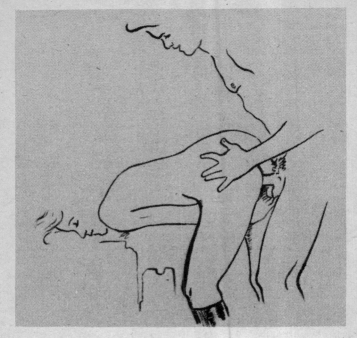

Fig. 21-6: The Standing Position.

Is There an Ideal Position?

The main problem with most positions in sexual intercourse is that the woman's clitoris is located high up in front of her vagina and therefore usually receives only indirect stimulation. This affects the amount of time it takes her to achieve orgasm. A more rapid, explosive orgasm can be achieved if the woman receives direct clitoral stimulation. Some sex researchers have suggested that the "ideal position" might be with the woman sitting on top of the man, but facing away from him. This allows her all the pleasureful freedom of the female superior position, combined with the ability to rub her clitoris on the back of the shaft of the man's penis, stimulating sensitive areas on both herself and the man. Furthermore, this position brings together the woman's vagina and the man's penis at the most natural and comfortable angle for both. The drawback in this

Fig. 21–7: The Ideal Position? The ideal position for any couple is the position in which two people find the most mutual enjoyment. It has been suggested by some that the ideal position might be the woman superior position with the woman facing away from the man. This gives her all the advantages of the superior position while giving her more direct stimulation of the clitoris by rubbing the back side of the penis. The drawback of this position is that the couple loses the visual contact and exchange of expression during the love-making.

and all positions in which the woman faces away from the man is the loss of visual contact and exchange of expressions.

There can be many variations on these basic positions, of course. It is not possible in this brief space to mention them all, nor to suggest that they are all necessary to a happy sexual relationship. A couple ought to feel open and adventurous enough with each other to try anything. But at the same time, they ought to feel equally free to be simple in their tastes and enjoy sex in as unsophisticated a way as they want. Variety is the spice of sex life, but simple, honest enjoyment is the meat and potatoes.

ORAL SEX

Cunnilingus, the oral stimulation of the vulva and vagina, and *fellatio,* the oral stimulation of the penis, are the main features of oral sex. It has been illustrated on pottery and described in poetry from the earliest known human societies, and appears in every culture on earth, from the most advanced to the most primitive. Only in Western, Judeo-Christian societies has oral sex been viewed with hostility and taboo. This has resulted in many people remaining ignorant of and superstitious about it. Oral sex occurs commonly in animals, birds, and reptiles, yet human beings often suffer guilty insecurity if they practice it and certainly lose a source of tremendous pleasure if they avoid it. Emotional conflicts about oral sex can create pain and stress in individuals of any age, seriously undermining a sexual relationship and bringing problems to a marriage.

The Kinsey Report sex researchers have confirmed that the higher a person's level of education, the more likely she or he is to perform and enjoy oral sex. This itself is a perfect example of the gain in pleasure from good sex education. Americans are becoming a highly educated people, and there is a new sexual frankness in today's society. No doubt oral sex occurs in well over 70 percent of the college-educated population—and this in spite of the prevalent legal penalties against it. More and more people are learning that oral sex is neither dirty nor unnatural, but rather a delightfully different and completely normal means of sexual enjoyment.

Technique of Oral Sex

The mouth is delicate, soft, flexible, and extremely sensitive—a perfect sexual organ. A very precise, subtle type of stimulation which is unavailable any other way can be achieved in oral sex. Most women enjoy having their vaginas licked and penetrated by their lovers' lips and tongues. Often, the lover separates or pulls the labia apart in order to gain greater access to the clitoris and, thereby, increases stimulation. Most women will be highly excited by having their clitorises caressed, al-

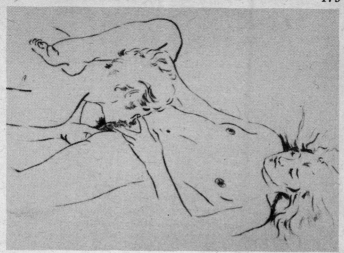

Fig. 21–8: Oral Sex. Cunnilingus is the oral stimulation of the vulva and the vagina. This is extremely pleasurable for a woman and many women cannot reach the pre-orgasmic phase without this stimulation. A woman should tell her partner where she enjoys being caressed; she can even help her partner by spreading the labia apart to achieve direct kissing of the clitoris. During cunnilingus, a man can caress and stimulate other parts of the woman's body with his hands.

though this degree of direct stimulation can prove too intense for some women. Sometimes during cunnilingus, a partner will feel like blowing into the woman's vagina to stimulate it: *This is extremely dangerous!* The pressure caused in the vagina can drive air bubbles into the blood stream, and there have been cases of women dying of embolism as a result.

Since the anus is an extremely sensitive area, many couples enjoy stimulating it by oral means *(analingus)*. As long as each partner is clean, this is not harmful. Lovers should be careful, though, to wash thoroughly before engaging in this practice.

Most men enjoy having their penises kissed, licked, and sucked, and many enjoy having their scrotums orally stimulated as well. During this form of sex play, a man enjoys the wetness of his lover's mouth. For this reason, many women take extra care to lubricate the penis with a large amount of saliva. If a woman's mouth gets too dry, she can fill her mouth with lukewarm water and release it around the penis while it is in her mouth. Although a complete *Deep Throat* technique is unnecessary, most men enjoy a fairly deep penetration in the mouth. At the same time, most men do not like to feel a woman's teeth, however lightly, during fellatio. In extreme cases, this can develop into a psychological condition of fear known as *vagina dentata*, or "teeth in the vagina," which is common in the folklore of many countries. Some men are unable to ejaculate in a woman's mouth. This may be due to a psychological factor; at other times, it is caused by insufficient friction. This problem can be aided by either partner manually stroking the base of the penis during fellatio.

Gourmet Sex

The pleasure of oral sex has recently been aided by the availability of such accessories as flavored douches, sex creams and oils, edible body powders, and the like. Many people enjoy covering their genitals with these products and having their partner "eat" them. Any imaginative couple can easily discover other suitable substances for themselves.

Variations of Oral Sex

Oral sex may be a part of foreplay, as a prelude to intercourse. A woman and man may engage in it mutually, each partner both giving and receiving simultaneously, or by turns. A woman may perform fellatio on a man and bring him to orgasm so that he can then enter into the prolonged act of intercourse which she requires. In a similar way, a man may perform cunnilingus on a woman and bring her to one or more orgasms before finally entering her so that they can enjoy an ultimate orgasm together.

When oral sex is continued to orgasm, it is usually performed by one member of the couple on the other, because the extreme excitement of the orgasm makes mutual stimulation difficult. Unlike intercourse, oral sex allows the two distinct sexual pleasures of giving and receiving to be individually savored to the fullest.

Is Oral Sex Unhealthy?

A great deal of the difficulty that people have in accepting and practicing oral sex comes from the vague notion that it is in some way dirty. This attitude is based on the common confusion of the reproductive and excretory functions of the genitals—functions which are totally independent of each other. Assuming that both partners maintain basic bodily hygiene, there is no reason why the genitals should be unpleasant either to the taste or the smell.

The internal situation of the vagina makes it more susceptible to odor, but if the vagina is in a clean and healthy condition, this odor will be minimal, and not distasteful or harmful. By now, most women are probably aware that the various vaginal deodorant sprays on the market, which capitalize on the hostility of Western societies to any natural smells, can be unsafe to use. Vaginal deodorant sprays commonly cause irritation, which develops into severe inflammation. If a woman is worried about vaginal odor, she would be well advised to use soap rather than the available sprays (which only mask odor, but do not remove it). The European bathroom fixture called a bidet is specifically designed for genital cleansing and is a much more medically sound answer to the problem. Men who are still uncertain about performing cunnilingus would do well to realize that the bacterial content of their own mouths is generally considerably higher than that of a normal woman's vagina. The danger of infection is probably greater for the woman. So instead of asking a woman to use a vaginal deodorant for his sake, a man would usually be better off using a mouthwash for her sake.

A woman, for her part, may worry about taking a man's semen in her mouth and swallowing it. She may think that this fluid is unclean and harmful to her. In fact, the chemical composition of semen is similar to that of saliva in the mouth. Rather than being harmful, semen is an extremely high-protein, low-calorie substance. The protein content in semen is 30 percent higher than the protein content in cow's milk, for example, while the fat and sugar content of semen are both one ninth as great as in milk.

Oral Sex and VD

Only under special circumstances can oral sex transmit venereal disease. There must be fresh syphilitic sores in or around the mouth for the germs to spread—a condition which is sure to be visible to the sex partner. Gonorrhea cannot survive in the mouth, so it cannot be transmitted or contracted during oral sex. In certain rare instances, gonorrhea can spread to the eyes, if the eye comes into close contact with an already infected area. In general, though, oral sex is very unlikely to lead to any kind of infection or disease. It is most likely to result in pleasure.

ANAL SEX

The area around the anus is an important erogenous zone, stimulating to both women and men. A woman often enjoys having a man put his finger in her anus during intercourse and especially just before her orgasm, so that she is twice penetrated. Many men, likewise, enjoy having a woman do this to them. Naturally, a woman with very long fingernails must proceed carefully. A vibrator is also excellent for this purpose.

A couple may start with frequent manual penetration of each other's anuses and decide to try anal intercourse. If a woman has never had anal intercourse before, it will probably be difficult for her to accommodate a man's penis at first. Oral and manual stimulation of the anus before intercourse will help to relax the anal sphincter. Using some lubricant such as K-Y, Vaseline, baby oil, or cold cream, the man should begin to dilate the woman's anus, first with one finger, then two, then three. This is a time for slow, gentle arousal. If the woman is not properly prepared, anal intercourse will be painful. When the woman feels excited and ready, the man can start to enter her gradually with his penis. He should not thrust or move quickly. Both his penis and her anus should be well lubricated. The woman should bear down slightly on her anus to relax it and facilitate initial penetration. Men who enjoy anal intercourse usually like the tight squeeze of the anus around their penises. This tightness also makes penetration more difficult, so the man must not go too quickly, nor penetrate too deeply. He must allow the woman to guide him.

There is, unfortunately, a certain amount of hypocrisy associated with almost all sexual practices and mores. So it is, too, with anal sex. In many religions and societies, anal intercourse is frequently performed just to safeguard the exalted virginity of the women. Since pregnancy is impossible during this practice, some couples use it as a form of birth control. In some societies, anal sex is illegal and referred to as *sodomy*.

Can a Woman Reach Orgasm through Anal Intercourse?

A few women can reach orgasm during anal intercourse, probably as a result of the pulling on the perineum, which is transmitted to the clitoris. Many women do not achieve orgasm, but do enjoy the sensation of anal intercourse. Some women, even after careful, slow arousal and dilation of their anuses, will still experience such pain from anal intercourse that it is not of interest to them. If a woman wishes to try this sexual practice, or has tried it and liked it, she ought to be frank about her

Masturbation and Orgasm

A high percentage of women are able to achieve multiple orgasm by masturbation. Many women bring themselves to three or four orgasms before they feel completely satisfied. The majority of women are multiorgasmic generally, and much more so during masturbation. Some women are happy with a single orgasm; others will continue up to seven or eight or more orgasms until they are exhausted.

Women who have difficulty concentrating on masturbation enough to reach an orgasm should try to fantasize some erotic situation to heighten their excitement. Women usually need to fantasize during masturbation, especially at first. A woman may need to masturbate for an extended period of time before relaxing enough to have an orgasm. Fantasy speeds up the process by creating a more complete sexual situation.

Every woman is capable of achieving orgasm through masturbation. In some difficult cases, a woman must first familiarize herself with a masturbation technique and liberate herself from guilt and other hang-ups. She must be relaxed; she must be *alone*. Initially, she may have to masturbate an hour a day for several weeks before reaching orgasm. Once the first orgasm has been reached, each subsequent orgasm is easier to

Fig. 21-9: Masturbation.

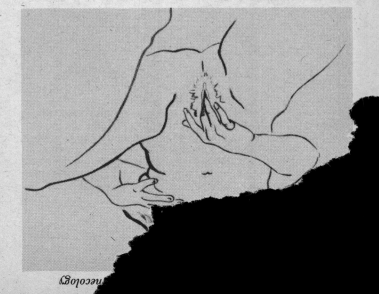

necology

desire with her ▒
and found it genera▒
about refusing it.

WARNING!

There is one common danger in anal intercour▒
wants to combine both anal and vaginal intercourse, ▒
tant for the man to take the time to wash his penis af▒
removes it from the woman's anus and before he enters h▒
vagina. The chance of vaginal infection is high if vaginal pene▒
tration immediately follows anal, because the *E. coli* bacteri▒
which predominate in the anus will be transferred to the vag▒
na. A man and woman may be reluctant to interrupt their sex
play for so mundane a task as hygiene, but the woman must
remember that she may pay for her impatience later.

MASTURBATION

For generations and generations, the act of masturbation has
been used to scare people. People were told that if they played
with their genitals, they would grow hair on the palms of their
hands, go blind, grow up crippled or malformed, or eventually
go insane. By now, it is hoped that everyone knows the truth,
which is that all these horror stories are only repressive scare
tactics. Scientific study has long since proven that masturbation
is not harmful to any individual in any way.

Sexual responsiveness develops at different rates in different
people. Girls are less likely to masturbate than boys, but very
young children of both sexes do touch their genitals and masturbate regularly. Many women do not begin to masturbate
until they are middle-aged.

Masturbation techniques have been studied in sex clinics, and
it has been found that no two women masturbate in the same
way. The majority of women do not like to masturbate on the
glans of their clitorises, because the concentration of nerve endings is so high that touch can be painful. Women usually masturbate by touching the surrounding area, a gentler stimulation
to the clitoris. If a woman masturbates for a long time, she will
want to keep her vagina moist with saliva or some other lubricant, such as vaginal secretions. Some women touch their nipples
as well during masturbation. This increases the amount and
variety of stimulation, and brings a more total sexual experience.

chapter 19

CORRECTIVE BREAST SURGERY

Many women are unhappy about the appearance of their breasts. Some who feel their breasts are too small undergo all forms of exercise and/or hormone treatments to enlarge the breasts and often finally decide that such efforts yield no results. Some of these women decide to have silicone injections or implantations, only to find that the silicone injections are frequently harmful. In some instances, the breasts become very hard and lumpy, resulting in fear of having them touched or caressed.

Other women, who consider their breasts to be great beauty assets, find that after childbearing, their breasts often become softer and start to sag. This often causes unhappiness. Some women feel they are not as attractive as before, and so decide to have corrective breast surgery.

Quite a few women have been happy with the results of corrective breast surgery. It should be emphasized, however, that if you decide to have breast augmentation surgery, you should be sure you choose a very competent surgeon, one familiar with the latest developments in this field.

In the last few years, surgical corrective procedures of the breast have developed into a fine art. Pendulous breasts can be made smaller; sagging breasts can be elevated; ugly scars can be excised, and small breasts can be enlarged. Most of these operations must be considered major procedures, but not in the risk-to-life category. Nevertheless, because these major procedures require general anesthesia, which in itself entails a certain risk to life, breast surgery should not be performed on every woman wishing a correction for minor abnormalities or a re-

desire with her sex partner. If she has tried anal intercourse
and found it generally unpleasant, she ought to be equally open
about refusing it.

WARNING!

There is one common danger in anal intercourse. If a couple
wants to combine both anal and vaginal intercourse, it is important for the man to take the time to wash his penis after he
removes it from the woman's anus and before he enters her
vagina. The chance of vaginal infection is high if vaginal penetration immediately follows anal, because the *E. coli* bacteria
which predominate in the anus will be transferred to the vagina. A man and woman may be reluctant to interrupt their sex
play for so mundane a task as hygiene, but the woman must
remember that she may pay for her impatience later.

MASTURBATION

For generations and generations, the act of masturbation has
been used to scare people. People were told that if they played
with their genitals, they would grow hair on the palms of their
hands, go blind, grow up crippled or malformed, or eventually
go insane. By now, it is hoped that everyone knows the truth,
which is that all these horror stories are only repressive scare
tactics. Scientific study has long since proven that masturbation
is not harmful to any individual in any way.

Sexual responsiveness develops at different rates in different
people. Girls are less likely to masturbate than boys, but very
young children of both sexes do touch their genitals and masturbate regularly. Many women do not begin to masturbate
until they are middle-aged.

Masturbation techniques have been studied in sex clinics, and
it has been found that no two women masturbate in the same
way. The majority of women do not like to masturbate on the
glans of their clitorises, because the concentration of nerve endings is so high that touch can be painful. Women usually masturbate by touching the surrounding area, a gentler stimulation
to the clitoris. If a woman masturbates for a long time, she will
want to keep her vagina moist with saliva or some other lubricant, such as vaginal secretions. Some women touch their nipples
as well during masturbation. This increases the amount and
variety of stimulation, and brings a more total sexual experience.

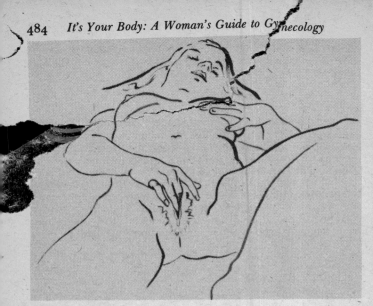

Fig. 21–9:   Masturbation.

Masturbation and Orgasm

A high percentage of women are able to achieve multiple orgasm by masturbation. Many women bring themselves to three or four orgasms before they feel completely satisfied. The majority of women are multiorgasmic generally, and much more so during masturbation. Some women are happy with a single orgasm; others will continue up to seven or eight or more orgasms until they are exhausted.

Women who have difficulty concentrating on masturbation enough to reach an orgasm should try to fantasize some erotic situation to heighten their excitement. Women usually need to fantasize during masturbation, especially at first. A woman may need to masturbate for an extended period of time before relaxing enough to have an orgasm. Fantasy speeds up the process by creating a more complete sexual situation.

Every woman is capable of achieving orgasm through masturbation. In some difficult cases, a woman must first familiarize herself with a masturbation technique and liberate herself from guilt and other hang-ups. She must be relaxed; she must be *alone*. Initially, she may have to masturbate an hour a day for several weeks before reaching orgasm. Once the first orgasm has been reached, each subsequent orgasm is easier to achieve. If manual masturbation becomes too strenuous, a vibrator can certainly help.

Placing a mirror between her legs allows a woman to watch her masturbation, and this added visual sensation often proves exciting.

Is Masturbation Addictive?

Many women are concerned about masturbation, wondering if it is addictive or if it robs them of the enjoyment of other sexual pleasures. Masturbation is addictive, but in the same way that breathing is habit forming. It is not harmful and it does not prevent you from enjoying any other sexual pleasures. On the contrary, masturbation conditions you in such a way that you more greatly appreciate all other sexual activities.

Masturbation is the ideal solution to the sexual tension of a woman who is alone for any reason—traveling, divorced, isolated. Furthermore, any woman who is familiar enough with her own body to understand exactly what pleases her will also be a more open, responsive sex partner. Masturbation does not have to be practiced alone. Many couples enjoy masturbating themselves and each other, either as a part of sexual foreplay or before continuing to mutual orgasm.

Masturbation presents no problem to the older woman. Women who have begun masturbating in their twenties and thirties usually continue to do so throughout their lives. Older women who are widowed may then begin to practice masturbation, or may return to it after abstaining during marriage.

FANTASIES AND FANCIES

If the sexiest part of a woman is her mind, then the role of imagination in sex is central. One of the biggest sexual stimulants of all is fantasy. People fantasize about making love to people they desire, either people who are known to them or utter strangers. The object of one's fantasy can be a person who is a part of one's everyday life or the misty vision of a favorite movie star. Some people fantasize about watching sexual intercourse, usually between their own sex partners and someone else. Others fantasize that they and their accustomed sex partners are meeting each other as strangers for the first time, or that they are both different people, or in a new location, and so on.

A woman may fantasize while she is alone, masturbating, or while she is having intercourse with a man. She may prefer to keep her fantasies private. Some people can live for years in a world of complete sexual fantasy, and have intercourse with their partners only as a mechanical act. To this degree, fantasizing is certainly destructive to a couple's relationship, because it is being used to substitute or conceal the fact that there is some sexual difficulty. The most successful and enjoyable fantasies are those that are shared.

A couple can use their imaginations in as simple or complex a fashion as they desire. Their fantasies may be unique or regularly continuing, habitual or experimental, consisting of nothing more than a mutually arousing verbal exchange in bed or ranging to epic, costumed dramas.

Telephone Sex

Mutual arousal over the telephone is practiced by couples who are temporarily separated from each other as a means to relieve their sexual tension and can be a perfectly pleasurable experience. Telephone sex is itself a variation of sex talk in general, which many couples enjoy. Sex talk, in bed or over the telephone, can range from tender to coarse, from elegant to vulgar. Two people who are both open about sex can usually improvise a telephone conversation in sex talk that will be exciting enough to bring each other to orgasm with or without simultaneous masturbation.

Sex in Airplanes

Many people feel sexually aroused when they take off in an airplane. The fact is that a person usually becomes more sexually stimulated as the oxygen supply to the brain decreases. This fact has been a part of sexual knowledge for centuries, practiced by heterosexuals and homosexuals alike. Thus, during intercourse, one partner will press forcibly against the arteries of the neck of the other, closing the amount of oxygen-carrying blood to the brain and bringing heightened arousal. People are sometimes strangled to death in the excitement of intercourse by improvised nooses intended for this purpose. The pressure change in the passenger cabin of an airplane produces the same effect.

Underwater Sex

The idea of underwater sex is delightful. The smooth, slippery feel of skin in water, the stimulating coolness of the liquid, and perhaps the setting—a sun-baked ocean beach or a floodlit swimming pool at night. A whirlpool bath offers still another level of sensation, the lovers' bodies being stroked by the swirling water. Whirlpool also offers a pleasant sensation when the genitals are placed in front of the constantly flowing hot-water stream. A soap massage is a pleasant addition to bathtub sex. A hand shower can provide a woman with enough stimulation for many orgasms all by itself.

In reality, though, sexual intercourse underwater is often unsuccessful. Water washes away the very vaginal secretions which serve as lubrication for the man's penis, leaving the vagina dry and tight. This makes penetration by the man more difficult, which in turn is painful to the woman. If, however, the couple is extremely aroused and the man's entry is quick, the water can be an exciting sexual playground.

Vibrators

Women who have difficulty achieving orgasm in intercourse often find that the purchase of a vibrator revolutionizes their lives. A vibrator may be used as an aid to masturbation or as a

Fig. 21–10:   Vibrators. Women who have difficulty reaching orgasm have found that vibrators can give the sufficient stimulation needed for satisfaction.

part of a couple's sex play. Indeed, a vibrator seems to excite both the man who is using it and the woman who is feeling it; to a couple it can be as much a novelty as a new sex position. Also, a woman can use a vibrator to keep herself aroused while the man rests between orgasms.

Vibrators come in many sizes, but one basic shape, which is like a penis. Some women tend to use a vibrator mainly for clitoral stimulation. Most avoid direct contact with the clitoris, choosing instead to place a towel or some other light fabric, like panties, over the clitoris to avoid burning. Other women use the vibrator for deep vaginal penetration, like a dildo. A lubricated vibrator may be used to penetrate a woman anally while she is having vaginal intercourse; the vibrating sensation is in this case felt throughout the pelvic area. A newly marketed vibrator has two extensions for simultaneous penetration of the vagina and anus.

While vibrators have become very popular with women today, artificial penises (dildos) seem to have little appeal. Even among lesbians, manual or oral stimulation is preferred to intercourse with one of these devices. A vibrator does the same, and better.

Medically speaking, vibrators are neither dangerous nor harmful. They are no more or less addicting than manual masturbation.

Gadgets

Artificial vaginas are as available to men in sex shops and by mail order as artificial penises are to women, and the response is about the same. Although a few men buy them, most do not. Younger men may be curious about the various artificial vaginas [from simple soft rubber sheaths to complex suction devices like milking machines]. Most older men prefer massage parlors or prostitutes as a sexual outlet.

A *penis ring* is a rubber or metal band which is placed around the erect penis. By preventing the blood from leaving the penis, it maintains a hard erection as long as it is worn. Certain of these devices have attached rubber knobs which rub against the woman's clitoris during intercourse, giving her extra stimulation which may be either exciting or painful, depending on the woman. The newest-developed penis ring has a miniature vibrator with a battery attachment. This supposedly stimulates both the penis and the clitoris.

Metal penis rings can be extremely dangerous for the man, since the penis can become so swollen that the band can only be removed surgically. The rubber and leather rings are therefore safest. In fact, a simple rubber band can do the job. It's important not to leave a penis ring on more than an hour, since prolonged use can cause damage to the penis. It does not make the penis permanently longer, although the size of the penis may be temporarily increased while a penis ring is worn.

Many sex gadgets are bought for fun as novelty items. People may buy one, take it home, and put it in a drawer, but they'll remember the fun they had buying it. Anything that adds extra enjoyment to one's sex life is welcome. Sex gadgets make provocative presents. But it isn't necessary to visit a sex shop to find sex gadgets, because everyday life is full of possibilities.

As mentioned, certain women find a hand shower attachment to be far more exciting than a vibrator. A woman may lie under a running bathtub faucet and let the water pounding her clitoris bring her to orgasm. Hair dryers and hot combs project a firm jet of hot air which, when trained on the clitoris, arouses some women. Care must be taken in this situation to avoid burning, irritating, or excessively drying the vaginal labia. Many women enjoy masturbating or being penetrated with a bottle, its size and coolness being stimulating. Because the vagina and uterus enlarge as a woman is aroused, there is a suction in the vagina which can draw up smaller items and even beer bottles. If this happens, a woman must have a doctor remove the object before it causes permanent damage. Thus a woman and her partner must be extremely cautious when engaging in such sex play.

With sex gadgets, as with sexual activity in general, the important thing to remember is that there is no perfect way to reach orgasm. There is a vast number of slightly imperfect, giddily exciting ways. Mix them up, and vary your pleasure. There's a lot to choose from.

Group Sex

At one time or another, most people think about group sex. Sex counselors and psychologists are split between those who advocate experimentation with group sex and those who are against it. Since a good sexual relationship is a difficult thing to achieve between even two people, it is still more precarious when a number of people are involved. Obviously, then, the success of a group-sex venture depends on the people.

The essential rule is that no one should be forced to participate. If a couple engages in this activity, it must be at the desire of both partners. The woman and man should consider and discuss how each feels about having sex with others, about watching each other having sex, and about being watched.

Reactions should be honest. Although group sex is considered very hip in certain circles, it simply may not appeal to some people.

Once a couple decides to try a sexual experience involving other people, they must consider carefully whom they will choose. Generally, group sex with old friends is difficult, since sexual and social sides develop at a different rate. It's advisable to find new people with whom you can begin a fresh relationship that is both sexual and social. Compatibility is important. Everyone must feel relaxed and comfortable with everyone else. It's better to wait and choose well than to rush into an unpleasant, tense experience.

In a culture still shaped by Puritan tradition, "swingers" (people who enjoy sex with two or more couples) are a threatening subculture with a shared secret. They seek out like-minded people, sometimes sight unseen through advertisements in sex newspapers and magazines. They frequent bars known as swingers' meeting places. Certain sex-therapy centers promote group sex sessions among their patients. All of these situations have the potential for success or failure.

Group sex is a rather epic way to live out a common sexual fantasy. If all the participants possess the two important characteristics of healthy sexuality—that is, openness and imagination—then the reality can be even better than the fantasy.

Threesomes

The simplest form of group sex is the threesome; either two men and one woman, or two women and one man. Given the different orgasmic abilities of women and men, the man with two women may find himself unable to satisfy them continuously, while the woman with two men is likely to satisfy her desire for several orgasms as she alternately fulfills the men. This can be an enormously stimulating experience for a woman. A man with two women will often employ a vibrator on one as he enters the other, in order to keep them both aroused. In many cases, two women will engage in mutual fondling and, perhaps, masturbation while the man rests.

Swinging

In its ordinary usage, the term *swinging* refers to sex between two or more couples. Each person has a partner, which reduces the potential for jealousy, which can be a major problem in threesomes. Each couple will probably engage in sex at their own pace. Sometimes they may combine in larger groups. Couples may be in separate rooms, or all together so that they can watch each other. When a large number of couples are together, spontaneity seems to increase. Some people will be having a lot of sex with a lot of people, some will be having a lot with one person, some will be having a little sex with everybody. You do as you please. It's perfectly all right to refuse, and no hard feelings. It's perfectly all right to *be* refused. In large gatherings, sex may be going on only in one area, with couples joining and leaving continuously; elsewhere people might be conversing, dancing, or whatever. In smaller groups of two or three couples, sex is more intimate and intense, each person being more aware of each of the others. The impersonality of large groups will be exciting to some people; the intimacy of small groups will please others.

Orgies

A session of swinging can be a pleasant, straightforward, shared sexual experience. An orgy, on the other hand, is a frantic, anything-goes situation. There will be lesbian, homosexual, and heterosexual activities, often involving everyone present with or without their consent. A woman having intercourse with a man may find him replaced by another woman with a dildo; a man may find himself fellated by a woman and man in turn. Participation is obligatory, on every level.

Orgies are a much more casual, haphazard sexual environment than swing parties. Swingers tend to gather in homogeneous groups. An orgy involves people of all backgrounds. People rarely know each other at all. The sexual pressure is greater, and it is difficult to refuse anything with anyone. Therefore, there is a very real chance of contracting venereal disease of some kind at an orgy. This is the main physical danger of all group sex experiences, but in the more selective situations of threesomes or swinging, the chance of venereal disease is far less.

Voyeurism and Exhibitionism

With voyeurism and exhibitionism, we have reached the fine line where normal sexual pleasure sometimes shades into perversion. Seeing and being seen are two of the most basic sexual stimulations, for animals and people alike. As a part of sex play with a free, imaginative partner, the display of one's body and the enjoyment of someone else's can become an exquisite erotic delight. But if these fancies are forced on an unwilling stranger or are practiced as a substitute for intercourse, they have clearly crossed the line into sexual aberration.

Can Voyeurism Be Normal?

A *voyeur* is one who gets pleasure from seeing other persons in the nude, undressing, masturbating, or having intercourse. Everyone is, to some extent, a voyeur. Traditionally, men have seemed more inclined to voyeurism than women, but with the freer sexual mores and successful women's movement in today's society, both sexes are now enjoying looking at each other. We have *Playgirl* and *Playboy.* Women are joining men in the audiences of X-rated feature films, and of hard-core porno flicks, too. Many couples having sex like to watch themselves in a mirror. Usually this visual stimulation is a means of arousal leading to orgasm.

In earlier societies, nudity was no cause for shame, either in a woman or a man. Sex was a natural function like eating, and to cover one's sex organ would have been as silly as to cover one's mouth. Indeed, many cultures featured nudity as a proper subject of public appreciation. The Greeks adorned their public squares and buildings with fully nude statues, for example, and fashions for the women of ancient Egypt bared their breasts completely. Then came the long period of sexual gloom brought by Western religions, when nudity was considered savage and immoral. It is against these centuries of inhibition that the sexual energy of modern times is rebelling.

Can Exhibitionism Be Normal?

Exhibitionism, the pleasure of displaying one's body, is the normal complement of voyeurism. Today more and more people, both women and men, realize this. This recognition has rejected generations of shame, and people are again becoming proud of their bodies. The most widespread and obvious example of this is on a beach in summer. Nowadays, both women and men are wearing extremely minimal bathing suits designed to cling to the body and reveal what they must legally cover up. Women are going braless and men are wearing tight pants. The popularity of slenderizing diets and exercise these days undoubtedly has as much to do with the desire to have an attractive body as to have a healthy one.

Thus, in most circumstances, voyeurism and exhibitionism are healthy, natural sexual activities for women and men.

When Does This Behavior Become Abnormal?

Although the women's movement is changing the behavioral patterns of both sexes, men have generally been socially conditioned to be more aggressive in all areas. It is precisely when the pursuit of pleasure from voyeurism and exhibitionism becomes an act of aggression that it becomes a sexual problem.

Thus, most cases of this sort involve men either spying on or exposing themselves to women who are usually strangers. These acts generally arise from sexual guilt and/or repression, not sexual freedom. The "peeping Tom" is excited by the forbidden view of nudity or sexual activity; the "flasher" is excited by the forbidden display of his genitals. As with group sex or any other practice, all participants in voyeurism and exhibitionism must be willing, but the women who are the objects of peeping Toms and flashers are in no sense partners in the act. They are victims of it.

Exhibitionism is one of the commonest sex crimes in many countries. In general, an exhibitionist is likely to be harmless and is often impotent. After exposing himself, he will run off and disappear until the next incident. Voyeurs, on the other hand, may become so sexually stimulated by watching a woman that they will try to gain access to the woman and rape her.

Voyeurism, Exhibitionism, and the Law

Although there are no certain cures for peeping Toms or flashers, the social and legal penalties are severe.

This behavior has been condemned since biblical times. Throughout history, the penalties have been stiff. Legend has it that Lady Godiva rode nude through the town of Coventry in protest to a tax levied by her husband against the townspeople. Her husband forbade anyone to watch the ride and all complied with his wishes—all but one. The city tailor, named Tom, secretly watched, or "peeped," through the shutters of his store window. This action made him famous, for the term "peeping Tom" originated with him, but it also provoked Lady Godiva's husband to strike him blind as a punishment.

Today, prison sentences are common penalties. Sadly, this is not the answer, since it does not cure the problem; it just punishes it. Perhaps the solution will come when the sexual revolution has succeeded in instilling in everyone a positive, open view about the nature of the human body.

KINKY SEX

"Kinky" sex is the twilight zone of erotic behavior. Most people would agree, for example, that intercourse is perfectly normal sex and necrophilia (sex with the dead) is downright perverted. But, as in the case of voyeurism and exhibitionism, there is a hazy line between the two obvious extremes. Kinky sex walks that line.

What is considered normal or perverted at any one time and place is largely a matter of fashion. Homosexuality is a good example of this. Other sex practices may be normal or perverted depending on the degree to which they are practiced—if they're indulged in slightly or only occasionally, they're harmless; but if they're regular or extreme acts, they then become dangerous. Voyeurism is one such practice.

A further distinction may be made. All the sex practices discussed so far have been motivated by distinctly sexual stimuli. As one enters the murky gray area of kinky sex, one finds more and more nonsexual causes behind the sexual activities. What is considered sexy has more to do with particular personal associations than with one's general cultural conditioning. Of course, this kind of very personal stimulus is a part of every normal sexual relationship—it's what makes sex different with different people.

The following pages will discuss certain of the more extreme kinds of sexual displacement. These particular pleasures are not for everyone. These are the exotic fruits of kinky sex. In some cases they seem very normal, while other examples seem decidedly less than normal.

Fetishism

Probably the most popularly practiced type of kinky sex is *fetishism*. It is so popular that most people would not consider it kinky—at least, not what *they* do.

A fetishist is a person who receives sexual stimulation from some sexual or nonsexual feature of other people or from some objects. It is most often hair, feet, shoes, or special kinds of clothing that turn such people on, although the list of possible fetish objects is practically endless; some women get pleasure from making love to a partially clothed man; some men get extra kicks from making love to a woman who wears boots or shoes during the sexual act.

Hair—The Most Common Fetish

The most common fetish is hair. From the earliest recorded times, hair has played an important role in sexual stimulation. The story of Samson makes hair the symbol—even the source—of virility. Throughout history, women have had to cover their heads in public. Until recently, the custom of women wearing hats in church was strictly observed, based on the belief that by covering their hair, the women would arouse no lustful thoughts in the men present. Other religions, such as the Jewish Orthodox, forced a woman to shave her head after marriage to deprive her of the means to seduce other men. The tremendous change in men's hairstyles in the last decade is intimately connected with the general social trend toward a more natural, free expression of sensuality and emotion.

Pubic hair has an even more specific sexual connotation. An Arab legend tells that when the Queen of Sheba visited King Solomon, he refused to go to bed with her until she had shaved off all her pubic hair. On the other hand, among certain Oriental peoples, it is considered unlucky for a man to have intercourse with a woman who has shaved her pubic hair. The two different attitudes continue into the present day. Some men like the appearance and scratchy feel when the pubic hair is shaved, others enjoy the sight and pleasant tickle of unshaved pubes. Still others may playfully urge a woman to shave her pubic hair in the form of a heart or other design. It should be pointed out that if a woman does shave her pubic hair for a time, she will find it rather itchy as the hair grows back in.

Women tend not to have such particular feelings about men's pubic hair, but they do have definite preferences about men's body hair. Studies have shown that men with extensive body hair are no sexier or more potent than men with very little hair. The difference is simply genetic. Still, for whatever reason, some women are attracted to men with hairy chests and backs, while others find this type of man unappealing. What's virile to one woman is brutish to another. On the level of pure physical sensation, too, some women like the rough texture of a man's body hair against their naked bodies during sex, while other women like the softer touch of skin against skin.

Smell

Smell can also be a fetish. Many persons get sexual stimulation from different types of smells. Of course, what smells good to one person might not smell good to another. Many European women, for example, do not shave under their arms or use deodorant, because European men are excited by the natural smell of the body. Other smells may be exciting because of personal associations. The smell of horses, for example, could be extremely stimulating to some people. One woman recently admitted that she became sexually aroused at the slightest smell of a horse. This was apparently because her first sexual experience, which still carried a very strong impression, took place in a stable. On the other hand, a particular perfume might remind a man of *his* first intercourse.

A certain amount of fetishism is present in everyone's sexual behavior. Some people, though, are unable to enjoy any sexual activity that does not include their fetishes. They may even withdraw entirely from intercourse and all other mutual sex activities and respond only to the fetishes. There are people who develop a fetish for crippled or deformed partners. In fact, the particular choice of a fetish is probably not as important to one's sexual health as the degree of exclusivity the fetish occupies in one's sex life.

S and M

Sadism and *masochism* are two kinds of kinky sex that are closely related. The essential element in both is a sexual arousal based on pain or suffering. The sadist delights in watching or making other people suffer. The masochist delights in experiencing this suffering. Sadism and masochism have existed since the beginning of human life, but only recently have they been identified and named.

Sadism

Sadism is named for the Marquis de Sade. Born in Paris in 1740, he was enrolled in the French army at the age of fourteen. The extreme daily cruelty he witnessed during his next twelve years as a soldier—beatings, rapes, and torture—undoubtedly colored the rest of his life. De Sade left the army and began hiring prostitutes, with whom he indulged his passion for cruelty. This activity led to his repeated arrest and imprisonment. During his life, de Sade spent a total of twenty-seven years in prisons. He died in a mental hospital at the age of seventy-four.

While he was in prison, he wrote the books for which he is now famous, principally *Juliette* and *Justine*. He described various types of torture that had existed since ancient times, but it was not until de Sade publicized sadistic behavior and its sexual satisfaction that people focused attention on this activity.

In its earliest manifestation, sadism was a feature of religious ceremonies. The infliction of pain was a necessary step in various rites of atonement. The citizens of imperial Rome were extremely enthusiastic about spectacles of human agony, the most obvious example being the gladiatorial shows. Men and women fought each other to the death or faced wild beasts, and the crowds were thrilled. The same sadism underlies the pleasure people have today viewing boxing matches, automobile races, bullfights, or any other sport where the chance of death or mutilation is high. There is a little of the sadist in everyone.

Love and hate are closely linked passions. The desire to cause pain to those we love is normal. In some cases, this duality is reinforced by forgotten childhood incidents. Freud writes of a child who saw his parents having intercourse and imagined that his father was assaulting his mother in a terrible fight. A child frequently beaten severely by his father or mother may associate this pain with the love he feels for them.

The confusion of pain and pleasure may also come from some experience in later life. Men in wartime combat view the killing of their enemy as a positive, rewarding action. For poor or oppressed people, beatings and cruelty are an important means of release from the feeling of powerlessness that fills their lives. There are as many other examples as there are varieties of individual human experience.

CAN SADISM FIT WITHIN NORMAL HUMAN BEHAVIOR? Underlying all forms of sadistic behavior is a completely natural instinct: the instinct to seek dominance over others. It is an instinct which motivates our greatest achievements and all our ambitions, but also our worst atrocities. This is the difficulty with attempting to pinpoint the causes of such particular kinds of behavior as sadism. The texture of human behavior, sexual or otherwise, is a continuous weaving of contrasts. Everything has its cause in everything else.

SNUFF. Sadistic sex can involve nothing worse than a playful spanking given by a man to a woman during foreplay, or it can be as horrifying as the brutalization and sexual murder of children. De Sade himself enjoyed inflicting the torments of whips, knives, and poison on the prostitutes he hired. This extremely sick form of sadism is very much with us today, in the proliferation of the so-called snuff movies. In these films, a woman is shown being dismembered or killed after performing various acts of sex. Many of these films are fakes, but not all. A few women every year are kidnaped and forced to participate unwittingly in these films, losing not only the essence of their human dignity but their lives as well. That there is a definite audience for these films is not only shocking; it illustrates the utter depravity and sickness that is possible in the human condition. It is not only sick sex, it is murder, and anyone who participates on either side of the camera desperately needs urgent psychiatric help. These are potentially the most dangerous people in any society—they have an undeniable attraction to murder and are highly likely one day to satiate this urge directly. If you know anyone involved in any way with the so-called snuff movement, you should report him or her to the police, who can and should monitor their actions. There is, unfortunately, a definite audience for these grotesque spectacles.

Masochism

Just as sadism is basically an act of aggression, masochism is basically an act of submission. Masochism is named for the Austrian writer Leopold von Sacher-Masoch, born in 1838. His father was a local chief of police. He was an exceptionally bright student, a distinguished physician, and a decorated officer in the French-Austrian War. In addition, he wrote several notorious books, in particular *Legacy of Cain* and *Venus in Furs,* in which he vividly portrayed the enjoyment of suffering and pain at the hands of a beautiful woman.

There are three incidents in the life of von Sacher-Masoch which seem to have influenced this behavior. First, it was said that as a child, von Sacher-Masoch was fascinated by stories of the Andean mountain martyrs and their terrible suffering. Then, during puberty, von Sacher-Masoch had a dream which continued to haunt him for the rest of his life. In the dream, he was the slave and victim of a cruel woman. This dream was probably the result of an experience he had as a boy. Lastly, while hiding in a closet in his aunt's bedroom, he witnessed her making love to a strange man and then being caught by her husband, who gave her a beating. Later, when she discovered young Leopold in the closet and realized that he had seen everything, she gave vent to her guilt by beating the boy. Certainly these three incidents in many ways may be responsible for the behavior for which von Sacher-Masoch became known.

Eight years before he died in 1895, France elected him a member of the Legion of Honor, in recognition of his literary achievement in the twenty-four books that were published there.

Masochism has had a significant place in the development of human culture, in the very heart of Western religion. For the glory of God, men and women inflicted upon themselves wounds which they would not allow to heal, but aggravated by rubbing salt into them. They donned hair shirts and slept on beds of thorns. They practiced long periods of thirst, then drank contaminated water to honor God. People tried to outdo each other in the search for ever more horrible methods of self-torture. Christine of St. Troud, for example, fastened herself to a wheel, had herself racked, and was hung on a gallows beside a corpse. Bands of penitents flagellated themselves in public processions for the sins of the world. Many of these men and women were praised for their holiness, and some were canonized as saints. Their example is undoubtedly inspiring—and undeniably masochistic. What are we to think?

The immense popularity of the book and the movie versions

of *The Story of O* indicates a current high level of public interest in, and curiosity about, the masochistic experience.

As in the case of sadism, there are a variety of theories which explain the cause of masochistic behavior, but people cannot agree which is right. It is seen as a manifestation of a sense of unworthiness in the individual, as a desire for humiliation. It is seen as an attempt by the individual to absolve her or his own guilt about sadistic tendencies. It is seen as a low-grade death wish. It is the opposite of sadism, and therefore—like love and hate, pain and pleasure—very much like it in many ways—including its elusiveness.

Discipline and Bondage

"D and B" is actually a special kind of "S-M," or sado-masochistic, behavior. The focus in discipline and bondage situations is not the act of sexual intercourse, but the sexual stimulation derived from seeing a woman or man bound in leather harnesses which emphasize and reveal the sexual organs, or tied with ropes or chains, or perhaps gagged with a mask. The idea of being helpless, or of rendering someone else helpless, and thus subject to any whim, is extremely stimulating to some women and men.

A certain level of discipline and bondage is within the scope of normal sexual activity and has recently become popular among both straights and gays, providing their lovemaking with an extra kick.

It is a completely normal fantasy of young girls and women to be bound and raped. Such a fantasy often fulfills their desires to have intercourse without feeling blame or guilt for the act. Many men who seek to be tied and beaten are highly educated and extremely powerful, yet deeply guilty about their success, feeling unworthy of it. They tend to have difficulty expressing this feeling to their wives, and instead seek prostitutes or massage parlors that offer "English therapy"—discipline and bondage.

Some couples are strong enough to be frank about such preferences. Other couples are just curious, or interested in experimenting sexually. Whatever the case, mild forms of discipline and bondage are a frequent spice in many people's sex lives. A woman or man will tie up the other with twine or leather belts or neckties. Another simple form of bondage is blindfolding, which can be accomplished with a mask, a scarf, or even a towel. Blindfolded, a woman or man cannot see and prepare for whatever the other partner is going to do, and sexual stimulation in this situation is heightened for some people. Also, being blindfolded allows the subject to fantasize freely about the identity of the other partner and/or the setting in which the sexual activity is taking place.

For some people, the enjoyment of discipline and bondage is intimately connected with the sexually stimulating properties of leather, which is often the substance of the variety of available "D and B" accessories. There is nothing more sexy than skin, and leather, of course, is just that. It is not known whether the orgasm is caused by the tightness of the apparel or by the textural quality of the leather; it is probably a little bit of both. Prostitutes have long recognized the attraction of leather boots and garments in plying their trade.

Saliromania

Saliromania, from the French verb *salir*, meaning "to soil," or "to make dirty," is a type of sexual stimulation derived from urine or feces. Some people get excited by urinating or defecating on others; some people get excited being urinated or defecated upon. Obviously, this is another variation of sadomasochistic behavior.

The different forms of saliromania are undoubtedly distasteful to the majority of people. Yet this extremely kinky activity has certainly maintained a steady appeal to people in all periods of history and in all parts of the world.

Necrophilia

This is a practice named from the Greek word *nekros*, which means "dead body," and describes the sexual stimulation some people get from intercourse with a dead person. Even psychiatrists have found it difficult to explain exactly what causes this behavior.

Zoophilia

This is a term describing sexual intercourse with animals. In many cases, this is less a perversion than a need. It is known to be a common practice of farm workers who are isolated from any other sexual outlet, and therefore enter into sexual activities with farm animals. This was confirmed by the Kinsey Report.

Pornographic literature and films often feature a woman having intercourse with a dog, a donkey, a pig, or some other animal. These seem to provide great stimulation to certain voyeurs.

Can an Animal Impregnate a Woman?

There have never been any confirmed reports of pregnancy in women as a result of having sex with dogs or other animals. Nor, in the reverse situation, can a man's semen successfully cause pregnancy in any animal.

Obscenities

Naturally, the potential variety of kinky sex is as unlimited as the human imagination. Many persons get some sexual stimulation from the use of "dirty" words, a practice known as *coprolalia*. The most familiar form of this activity is the obscene telephone call. This can be extremely upsetting and frightening for women who receive such calls. In fact, it is just this sort of response which usually excites and has motivated the caller—a person who is very sick, but is also usually impotent. If you get such a call, do not engage in any conversation. Hang up immediately and report the incident to both the police and the phone company.

Such calls, when unsolicited, are criminal acts; which is one reason, perhaps, that many of these people are now calling prostitutes instead. Other people enjoy screaming dirty words at people they pass on the street; some shout at the height of the sexual act.

Kleptomania

Kleptomania, the persistent impulse to steal, often has a sexual cause. Studies have indicated that a woman's desire to steal actually changes throughout her menstrual cycle, becoming strongest just prior to the onset of her period and also during the time of her menopause. The sexual stimulation which some women feel in kleptomania is thought to be influenced by hormone levels. Every teenage girl who shoplifts a pack of cigarettes for a kick or in rebellion is obviously not a true kleptomaniac, but if the behavior is recurrent, it may indeed have a sexual association. A similar behavioral pattern is pyromania, the enjoyment of setting fires, which is generally considered to have a sexual basis.

The examples proliferate. The fact remains that there's a lot more to sex than just intercourse, and a lot more to sexual arousal than just sex.

HOMOSEXUALITY

The word *homosexual* is not derived, as most people think, from the Latin meaning of *homo,* which is "man," but rather from the Greek *homo,* which means "identical." Thus the term applies to either sex.

Female Homosexuality

Although the written history of female homosexuality (lesbianism) is incomplete—another example of a male-dominated society—it has the same classical roots and historical occurrences as male homosexuality. The word *lesbian* comes from the Greek island of Lesbos. Sappho, who lived on Lesbos in ancient times, opened a school for young women, to whom she taught poetry, music, and dancing. She, who was not married, referred to her pupils as "companions" and fell in love with one after another of these girls, writing several poems about them. This led scholars of antiquity to debate whether these poems were, in fact, expressions of sexual love between women.

Male Homosexuality

The practice of homosexuality has been found in many primitive tribes. The Zunis greatly honored such "men-women." In some regions of the world—Babylonia, Mexico, Peru—it was this group of "men-women" who often made up the tribe's magicians, medicine men, and priests. Certain tribes supplied a man temporarily without a sex partner with a "substitute" female in the form of a boy or young man.

Greek mythology attributed homosexual behavior to some of its gods, including Zeus and Apollo. The Greek civilization valued the nude male figure even more highly than the female, as characterized by the nude male athletes of the Olympic games and the idealized beauty of the prevalent sculptures called *kouros.* The phenomenon of a love relationship between an older, well-educated man (*Erastis,* meaning "lover") who held a prominent place in society and a young boy (*Eromenos,* meaning "beloved person") whom he was to prepare for his future place in that society was very much a part of the ancient Greek culture. Homosexuality was considered a proper aspect of a man's total education. Later, when the boy was older, he himself would take on a younger pupil.

The Romans adopted homosexuality from the Greeks, but debased it into a simple act of pleasure, without the noble aims it had once served. Homosexuality was pervasive throughout

Roman society. The elder Curio, a Roman senator, taunted Julius Caesar as "every woman's man and every man's woman."

Religious Disapproval

The Christian religion reacted against the easy vices of the Romans that were everywhere evident. The Bible considered the begetting of children as the only justification for sex. Any other sexual activity was looked upon as an abuse of the worst sort; sex for pleasure was a sin. Homosexuality, according to the Christians, was against God and nature. Christianity has spread throughout the world in the centuries since then, but homosexuality has survived.

Are Homosexuals Different?

Studies indicate that, in general, homosexual individuals do not differ from other people in any physical way. Rather, homosexuality is a pattern of behavior which is very likely established in childhood. Although homosexuality is not inherited, there is probably, in the opinion of most psychologists, a complex interrelation of familial and social factors which develops it.

Kinsey reported in his first study that 37 percent of American men and 20 percent of American women have some kind of homosexual experience at least once in their lives, although the percentage of people who were exclusively homosexual was far smaller. Given the greater sexual freedom and awareness of our contemporary society, these percentages are higher today. Recently it has become a matter of one's "liberation" in certain circles to participate in a homosexual experience. Whether this is an actual trend or simply "bisexual chic" is impossible to determine yet.

Do Homosexuals Marry?

Many homosexuals are married, often for the sake of appearance. Lawyers, doctors, men and women in business, and others in positions of "respectability" in society may be homosexual, yet may marry and have children, maintaining happy family lives and engaging in homosexual activity on the side. It is, of course, impossible to determine the exact frequency of marriage involving homosexuals. Recent research indicates that 35 percent of white women homosexuals and 20 percent of their male counterparts have been married at least once.

Many homosexuals live together as married couples. Some have even secretly performed marriage rites that seem to be as sacred and meaningful to them as marriage is to heterosexuals. Society has not yet fully understood homosexual marriages, and they are not legally binding or governmentally recognized in the United States. Some European countries are more enlightened on the subject and do recognize such marriages.

What Do Homosexuals Do Sexually?

The manner in which homosexuals behave in their sexual relationships does not differ much from the way heterosexuals behave. Homosexuals often maintain that a member of one's own sex is far more capable of understanding one's sexual needs than a member of the opposite sex. Female homosexuals, or lesbians, know exactly how and where to stimulate each other's clitorises, and perform sex at their own proper pace. Touching, caressing, and massaging are important expressions of lesbian love. Lesbians also perform cunnilingus and often engage in mutual vaginal penetration with their fingers. Lesbians may use dildos or vibrators to simulate intercourse.

The most common sexual activity between male homosexuals is oral sex. Anal intercourse is practiced by some male homosexuals, but not all.

Attitudes and Behavior

Homosexuality is more predominant in large cities. Homosexuals find themselves too easily recognizable as "different" in smaller communities, and are usually deprived of easy contact with other homosexuals. Large cities offer an entire homosexual subculture and afford a degree of anonymity which permits the homosexual to live her or his own life free of interference.

With homosexuality becoming more generally accepted, or at least tolerated, in today's society, many lasting long-term homosexual relationships have become possible. Still, the old prejudices live on, and for many homosexuals the usual pattern involves a number of short affairs, perhaps with strangers, in which the threat of exposure is kept to a minimum. Homosexuals tend to be more promiscuous in their sexual activities than most heterosexuals. Therefore the incidence of venereal disease among homosexuals is considerably higher than in the general population.

Many homosexuals are completely happy and fulfilled, particularly when they are younger. However, those who do not have permanent partners will often find themselves lonely as they grow older. This is also true with heterosexuals; it just occurs more frequently with homosexuals and is probably due to the transitory nature of their life.

There is now a nationwide movement toward Gay Liberation—the recognition of the right to live a homosexual life without harassment and disapproval. Homosexual newspapers and magazines are appearing in every major city. The theater, movies, and even TV have begun to treat the topic with seriousness and respect. This new openness among homosexuals and the freedom with which they are voicing their needs is, in a sense, a return to the past—a journey to the days of the ancient Greeks, when homosexuality was not looked upon as scandalous or abnormal, but rather as a particular sexual identity which had its rightful place in the society of mankind.

TRANSVESTISM

Transvestism is derived from the Latin words for "cross clothing," and describes the practice of dressing in the clothes of the opposite sex.

Like most other forms of sexual behavior, transvestism is nothing new. The Greeks spoke of the androgynous nature of human beings and included among their gods Hermaphroditus, who was both man and woman. Transvestism played a part in the fertility rites of the cult of Astarte, where women carried spears and lances and wore false beards, while men wore earrings and other feminine accoutrements.

Although the primary cause of transvestism is no doubt a sexual stimulation, this is not the sole factor responsible for the practice. Wearing the clothes of the opposite sex was thought by early peoples to allow one to assume certain characteristics of that sex. Women facing a situation that demanded they be valorous and brave, for example, might don men's garb to gain a man's strength.

Some women and men feel a great deal of satisfaction in dressing as the opposite sex. Certain people desire to do so only in the privacy of their homes; others want to parade in the streets. This practice has never been confined only to homosexuals, as is often wrongly assumed. A transvestite may be quite happy with her or his sex and dress up as the opposite sex just for fun. Homosexuals, of course, are not unhappy with their present sex, only with the sexual behavior that is expected of them. Thus most homosexuals are as far from wanting to switch clothing as heterosexuals. Other homosexuals, however, enjoy transvestism as a variety of sex play, as an escape from the pressure of socially expected behavior, or as a means to lure "straight" men into a sexual experience with them. It is not uncommon for a man to discover that the woman who has just performed oral sex on him is in fact another man. Other people may feel a tremendous, uncontrollable desire actually to become the opposite sex, and will practice transvestism as a first step toward that end. These people are not true transvestites, but transsexuals, and will be discussed later.

Often a transvestite is simply turned on by the feel of wearing the clothing of the opposite sex. True transvestite women generally achieve a sexual satisfaction by wearing identifiably "male" clothing. This could be due either to the rougher tactile quality of the so-called male fabrics, or to the power transference inherent in such a switch, since society has, up to now, been male dominated. Transvestite men achieve satisfaction wearing women's clothing, which is generally softer in its fabrics than men's and more tightly fitted to the body, another feature of the stimulation.

One of the most visible aspects of the great revolution in manners and morals that has taken place in America over the last decades owes its inspiration to the same pleasure which motivates transvestism. The sight of a woman in pants is now virtually universal in Western society, no matter whether the setting is a business office, a weekend's relaxation, or a formal evening affair. It is increasingly common to see women wearing not only pants of whatever variety, but also man-tailored shirts and suit-coats to go with them. The change in men's fashions is equally great. Flowered shirts with billowing sleeves, tank tops skintight to the body, jackets with shaped waists which give a man an "hourglass" figure, high-heeled shoes, and more are being worn by men of all walks of life. The pleasure these women and men get from crossing the once-rigid sexual barriers to dress in the style of the other is hardly a perverted or abnormal desire. It is a celebration of the freedom to experience all things more fully. Many designers predict that unisex fashions will soon be universal. This will obviously lessen the visibility of transvestism.

THE THIRD SEX

Every human being carries in her or his body vestiges of the opposite sex. A woman has a vestigial penis in her clitoris; a man has rudimentary breasts and nipples. In a like manner, every person produces both female and male hormones.

Under the circumstances, it is not surprising that there exists a significant amount of sexual crossover among women and men of all eras and cultures. Certain individuals find themselves irresistibly attracted to members of their own sex. Still others feel they are, in fact, trapped in the wrong bodies, in the wrong sex, and transform their sexuality entirely through an arduous and complex series of medical procedures.

Whatever the nature or degree of the sexual crossover which occurs in some people, the process is a normal part of the vast sweep of sex and in no way a perversion. This type of sexual crossover is viewed today as a psychologically *special*, not abnormal, form of behavior.

What Does Transsexualism Mean?

The word comes from the Latin, meaning to "cross sexes." Transsexuals define themselves as women or men whose mental representations of themselves—their gender identities—are at odds with their anatomies. A man with an entirely male body believes he is a woman; a woman with a female body believes she is a man. In such cases, one solution is the series of surgical and psychiatric procedures popularly known as a "sex-change" operation. A person who undergoes such a change of gender is called a transsexual.

Are Transsexuals Really Homosexuals?

Emphatically, no. A transsexual lives with the burden of an intense psychological certainty that she or he was "meant" to be the opposite sex.

In homosexuality, the factor which differentiates the homosexual from the heterosexual is the chosen object of sexual desire. A heterosexual chooses someone of the opposite sex and a homosexual chooses someone of the same sex.

In the more complex situation of transsexualism, the differentiating factor is *the person's perception of herself or himself*—that he or she is trapped in a body of the wrong sex.

More explicitly, a homosexual wants to use her or his sex organs with like partners. A transsexual, on the other hand, is usually repulsed by her or his sex organs and does not want to use them. In fact, transsexuals view their natural sex organs as so repulsive that they rid themselves of them.

How Many Transsexuals Are There?

There might be as many as twenty thousand transsexuals living in the United States, but the exact number is unknown. There is great resistance, not only among the public but in the

medical community as well, to the procedure, which many consider tampers with God's handiwork. Until recently, most such
operations were performed abroad, particularly in Casablanca.

In the last ten years, the operation has become more accepted
in the United States, and approximately five thousand sex-
change operations have been performed. Still, the prejudice
continues both within and without the medical community.
That prejudice is, according to most doctors, the chief difficulty
every transsexual encounters.

Surgical Preparation

People who want to change their sex should be screened
carefully before any irreversible decision is made. In most
cases, a complete evaluation from a psychiatrist is required.
Counseling about future life and the problems the transsexual
will probably encounter should also be a mandatory part of the
preparation. Also, a year-long series of hormone treatments is
administered. During that time, the person must live, dress,
and act as a member of the opposite sex. If, at the end of this
year, the person is still certain that she or he wishes to continue,
the actual surgery is performed.

The Sex-Change Operation

The man-to-woman procedure is performed approximately
ten times more often than the woman-to-man procedure. It is
also easier. In this operation, the penis is excised at its base.
This exposes the nerves, which become the foundation of the
clitoris. Although the new structure is never as sensitive as a
woman's clitoris because of the resultant scar tissue, the transsexual can derive pleasure and sensation from the artificial organ. The man is castrated—the testes and some of the scrotal
tissue are removed. An artificial vagina is then surgically
created an inch or so above the anus, where the tissue is softer
and easier to manipulate and where there is no bone structure.
An opening is made that is wide enough to admit two fingers
and approximately seven to eight inches deep. In order to ensure that this opening does not close, it is lined with a skin graft.

A special machine removes only a superficial layer of skin,
usually obtained from the inner thigh. This skin graft is sutured around a plastic rod which has the same dimensions of
the new vagina. It is inserted into the surgical opening. The rod
remains in the opening until the skin graft has taken in this new
location, a process which usually takes three to five weeks. This,
of course, creates a great susceptibility to infections, which, in

turn, may delay the healing process. When the rod is removed, dilators are used to prevent collapse or closure until complete healing occurs and intercourse is allowed (about six to eight weeks after the operation). Some surgeons use the skin of the excised penis instead, folded inside out around the plastic rod, for the new vaginal lining. A few surgeons even use bowel tissue for this purpose. The remaining scrotal tissue is pulled down and sutured around the edge of the newly created vaginal opening, forming the labia. The breasts, which have already enlarged slightly due to the hormone therapy, can now undergo silastic implantation. Many people choose not to have this performed.

The woman-to-man procedure is considerably more difficult and surgically not as successful. During hormonal therapy, the breasts decrease in size, while the clitoris becomes larger. A total hysterectomy and an oophorectomy (removal of the uterus and ovaries) are performed, in conjunction with a double simple mastectomy. Due to the extent of this procedure, it is often done in several stages. The vaginal mucosa is excised and the vaginal opening is closed. Skin grafts from the clitoral area are implemented to create the penile tissue. The new penis does not contain erectile tissue and silicone rods are inserted inside to provide sufficient stiffness. It is not a true erection, but it is sufficient for intercourse when *manually* inserted into a vagina. The manual insertion is necessary since this constantly stiff penis always hangs down. The main difficulty lies in creating a functional urinary conduit, so the new man can urinate from a standing position. The scrotum is made from labial tissue, and artificial (nonfunctional) testes are implanted inside this newly created scrotum. Since silicone is a body-friendly substance, the artificial testes are made from this material. Sexual activity is usually not possible for at least eight weeks following surgery.

The hospital stay for both operations is usually between one and two weeks. The cost of this operation is minimally around $5,000, although in some instances, insurance may cover a portion of this.

Are Orgasms Possible after This Operation?

The normal male ejaculates during orgasm, but since the penis in a surgical male is nonerectile and no semen is produced in the artificial testes, ejaculation is impossible. Still, the surgical male can achieve *orgasmic sensation*. This sensation is similar to the orgasmic response of the normal woman and focuses in the area of the removed clitoris. Because of this, the surgical male cannot achieve orgasm during intercourse or masturbation which stimulates only the shaft of the penis. Orgasm is, instead, brought about by stimulation to the area of the former clitoris.

The surgical female can achieve orgasm, although many do not. Orgasm in the surgical female is more difficult to achieve than in the normal woman, since no real clitoris exists and some of the nerves are usually damaged during the operation. Orgasm during intercourse probably occurs as a result of pulling the new vulvar tissue surrounding the artificial clitoris. This pulling stimulates the area of the former penis and orgasmic sensation is achieved.

Are There Any Postoperative Problems?

Of those who have undergone the sex-change operation in controlled conditions, a great number have experienced serious post-op complications. The Stanford University Gender Dysphoria Program in 1974 reported that eighteen of thirty-eight patients—almost *half*—had post-op problems.

In female-to-male surgeries, these problems were broken down to include rejection of testicular implants, infection, and "a desire to take a shotgun and shoot off the genitals of the surgeon."

Are Transsexuals Happier after the Operation?

Happiness is always a difficult quality to measure. With transsexuals, there are many factors affecting happiness—community prejudice, postoperative problems, and the many psychological factors that inevitably arise from any personality change of this magnitude.

According to the Erickson Educational Foundation, a national clearinghouse which disseminates information on the phenomenon of transsexuality, only two out of every ten transsexuals make happy adjustments after the operation. That is a very discouraging number for some, and hopefully society and medical research can effect a change for the better.

Still, the two out of ten who do adjust are supposedly living lives of emotional contentment that were not available to them in their previous genders.

Are Unnecessary Sex-Change Operations Performed?

Without any doubt, too many sex-change operations are performed. In the United States, applicants are carefully screened, and in most cases, from 75 to 90 percent of all applicants are *rejected* for surgery.

Of course, we in the United States cannot control the operations that proliferate outside our country, especially in Casablanca. In many foreign clinics, all a person need do to qualify for the sex-change operation is to show up at the clinic. This is a deplorable situation and one in which even the low twenty-percent success rate is reduced.

Most experts feel that at least ten times as many people apply for the surgery as should have it.

Who Should Have It Done?

Without recommending this arduous procedure, those people who fit the profile for potential success fulfill the following criteria: (1) They are over thirty and under fifty. These people have reached an emotional maturity and still have time to make an adjustment for the rest of their lives. (2) They absolutely hate their natural sex organs, sometimes to the extent of wanting to mutilate them. (3) They see no other viable alternatives to living their lives. The sex-change operation is, in all successful cases, a last-chance procedure.

Societal Benefits of Transsexualism

Many people are extremely prejudiced against transsexuals. Certainly the people who can honestly be defined as transsexuals are extremely rare, and understanding of their dilemma is lacking. But the rarity of this psychological circumstance makes it no less worthy of serious study.

Since Christine Jorgensen became the first "surgical female" in 1952, society has come a long way in accepting these people. Recently, writer Jan Morris and the American tennis-playing doctor Renée Richards have revealed themselves as transsexuals. Their admissions have helped focus public attention on a little-known problem.

It is logical to assume that if modern doctors can change a person's sex by clinical, exterior means—that is, by switching genitalia—there must already be a great similarity between the sexes. If transsexualism forces an examination of this similarity and promotes a greater understanding between all sexes—male, female, and transsexual—then it has been worth the trouble.

RAPE

In the past few years there has been a sharp increase in the number of reported rapes, and rape is now considered one of the fastest growing crimes today. Recent statistics have shown that there is an increase of more than 240 percent in the number of rapists admitted to New York State prisons during the past five years over the previous five years. It cannot be ascertained whether these statistics reflect an increase in the number of rapes committed or an increase in the number of rapes reported. Statistics indicate that 17 percent of reported rapes involve victims below the age of fourteen. Approximately 55,000 rapes are reported annually in the United States.

Physical Trauma during Rape

Women who have borne children or who have had previous intercourse may have minimal physical trauma following rape. However, the physical trauma, such as vaginal lacerations, to a virgin or a child may be severe. As soon as a rape has occurred, a woman should seek medical help either in the emergency room of a local hospital, or from her physician. Vaginal lacerations are occasionally so severe that surgery is necessary to repair the damage and to control bleeding. This vaginal repair should be performed as soon as possible after the assault to prevent infection or extensive blood loss, and to ensure proper healing. If the assault victim is a child, the child must be admitted to a hospital. A child often needs general anesthesia for proper examination and treatment since she may be so frightened that proper examination cannot otherwise be carried out.

What Should a Woman Do While She Is Being Physically Assaulted?

Unfortunately there are no clear gynecological instructions for the woman being raped that will help her avoid either physical or emotional trauma, since each rape case is so completely individual. If escape is not possible and screaming is useless, it might be advisable to let the rapist proceed with the sexual act without physical resistance. Fighting may provoke further violence and physical harm. It has been suggested that as some means of protection, a woman perform some act that might "turn off" her assailant such as vomiting, taking off a wig and throwing it at him, pulling out false teeth, or even urinating. These acts should not anger a potential rapist, but rather shock him.

What Should a Woman Do if She Has Been Raped?

If a woman has been raped she should immediately contact her physician or go to the closest hospital emergency room. She

should also contact the police to give a clear description of the
assailant and the circumstances of the assault. If there has been
trauma to the genital organs, immediate medical aid must be
sought. However, even if there is no trauma a woman should
seek medical assistance for two important reasons. First, in this
emergency situation, if the rape has exposed her to the possibility of pregnancy she can receive DES, "the morning-after pill"
(see Chapter 9, Modern Methods of Contraception) to prevent
conception, and secondly she should be tested for VD. If there
is any suspicion of venereal disease, antibiotics should be administered. Another important reason for the examination by
a physician is to obtain physical evidence of the rape such
as vaginal smears of sperm or a description of any genital
laceration.

Since rape victims have often been mistreated and humiliated
by the very people who are supposed to help them—the physicians and the police—women are often ashamed to seek medical
and legal help. Because of this, many rapes go unreported.
Luckily, attitudes are changing and rape victims are given
priority treatment in many emergency rooms and psychological
assistance is readily available.

Psychological Trauma After Rape

Even when there is minimal physical trauma, there is often
severe psychological trauma following a rape. This psychological trauma can be so severe that it will permanently influence a
woman's view of sex, men, and herself. Women are often
shocked and fearful that this crime might happen again. Voluntary intercourse with a desired partner can be disturbed by
the fear of the past rape and even vaginismus may develop. A
number of counseling services are available throughout the
country to help women over the shock of rape. NOW, the National Organization for Women, has set up a number of such
centers and may be contacted by telephone in case of rape for
reference to the appropriate counseling organization.

How To Prevent Rape

It is as difficult to prevent rape as it is to prevent many other
crimes; and you take the same precautions to avoid being raped
as you would to avoid being mugged or having your home
burglarized. A woman alone should avoid deserted streets at
night. If she is followed by a car, she should reverse direction
and run. If attacked in a building it is far better to scream FIRE
than to scream RAPE to get doors open. Locks on windows and

doors should be adequate, and unidentified strangers should never be let in. The list of warnings could go on and on; the major warning is simply to be careful and prudent and to avoid, rather than confront, the dangerous situation. Parents should always know the whereabouts of their children and warn them against strangers.

PROSTITUTION

A prostitute is a person, usually a woman, who engages in sexual activity in exchange for money. A prostitute is also referred to as a hooker, a call girl, a working girl, a party girl, a whore, or a street walker.

The practice of prostitution has existed for centuries but today it is more openly talked about. One of the main problems related to prostitution is the spread of venereal disease, and this has been minimized in countries where prostitution is legalized. Governmental regulations there require prostitutes to have frequent physical examinations to check for VD. The legalization of prostitution has allegedly reduced sex-related crimes in these countries also. In most of these countries, women must work in so-called red light districts and must constantly carry a health certificate indicating the date of their last medical check-up.

In countries including the United States in which prostitution is not legal, it is too often carried out in back streets and in high crime areas. Prostitution in the United States is therefore often associated with muggings, assaults, and murders, in addition to a higher incidence of VD than in countries where prostitution is legal.

What Do Prostitutes Do?

The sexual services offered by a prostitute often depend on her status in the profession. Many "call girls" have relations only with a limited number of regular clients whom they see on an established basis. The range of sexual practices available in brothels and so-called massage parlors depends on the predisposition and the wallet of the client.

There is a growing demand for exotic sex, and some brothels specialize entirely in sadomasochistic practices. "English therapy" and other S-M activities seem to be in demand particularly among well-educated, successful executives.

Massage parlors offer a variety of services with international designations. The least expensive service is manual masturbation. The French massage is oral sex. Swedish massage usually refers to penile massage between the woman's breasts. Danish massage, also referred to as "straight," is vaginal intercourse without manual stimulation. Greek massage is the professional term for anal intercourse. The most common practice is the so-called "half & half." During this practice the prostitute initially stimulates the client manually, then orally, and finishes with vaginal intercourse.

Since call girls are usually sophisticated professionals sexual relations with them are usually safe and rarely associated with real criminality. They will inspect new clients carefully for any obvious signs of VD prior to indulging in sex.

Brothels and massage parlors are so concerned about the spread of VD that often two women will at the outset inspect a client for any syphilitic sores, then milk the penis to make sure that there is no discharge that indicates gonorrhea. The women will then carefully wash the man's genitalia as well as their own before indulging in any sexual practices. Intercourse is only carried out with the aid of a condom.

The most dangerous prostitutes are the so-called "street walkers" or the women picked up on street corners. Many of these women offer their services in high crime areas. They are often involved with drugs and may be addicts or former addicts. They are usually under the control of pimps and are not careful about their bodies to prevent the spread of VD.

The Profession

There is a lot of money to be made in this profession and it is hard to judge those women who cannot find other suitable or well-paying jobs. It is, however, not as easy to earn money as one might think, and many professionals are unhappy and depressed. The happiest women in the profession seem to be those who have steady relationships or marriages in which their partners accept their work completely.

The women who are usually most satisfied with their jobs are those who have a steady clientele and thus a steady income. The most unhappy are probably those women who are drug addicts and who had to resort to prostitution to maintain their habits. There is, furthermore, a great psychological pressure inherent in working as a prostitute, since they must indulge in sexual relationships with many unappealing men. Any worker who feels this stress should immediately find a new profession.

Before any woman works as a prostitute she should be sure that she is familiar with all the signs and symptoms of venereal disease. She should know how to examine a man properly for VD and should wash both the man and herself with soap and water prior to intercourse. She should, furthermore, never indulge with any stranger without the use of a condom. Above all she should have regular medical examinations.

chapter 22

SEXUAL DYSFUNCTIONS

Many sexual problems are a result of lack of information and understanding and can be solved with nothing more than a greater awareness and openness between the two partners in a sexual relationship. The colorful variety of sexuality already presented has been, it is hoped, a step in that direction.

Despite all the openness and understanding in the world, there are sexual problems, or *dysfunctions*—such as frigidity, vaginismus, impotence, premature ejaculation—for which professional help is usually needed. These problems have many complex causes rooted in more serious psychological factors or marital problems which may result in a complete failure to enjoy, or even experience, sex. If a couple finds themselves with a major sexual problem of this type which cannot be improved by discussion and understanding and freedom between the two individuals, and which does not in the opinion of a gynecologist or urologist stem from any physical malfunction, the couple should seek counseling at a reputable sex clinic.

It is important that good professional help be obtained. This is not always easy. In recent years, there has been a burgeoning number of sex therapists to meet the public demand for this kind of treatment. Unfortunately, a great number of these physicians are not qualified to act as sex therapists, and may do more harm than good. Unless a doctor has participated in postgraduate study and training in the specific area of sexual dysfunction, he does not have adequate knowledge to treat sexual problems. This is equally true of general practitioners, urologists, and gynecologists and also of marriage counselors and psychiatrists. A doctor may be highly skilled in one of these related fields, yet be incompetent as a sex counselor. Today we believe completely in medical specialization: If one has heart trouble, one goes to a cardiologist; if one has sexual problems, one should go only to a reputable, trained sex therapist.

People often suppose that a doctor's knowledge of sex must be greater than the layperson's, and that doctors generally have more open, balanced attitudes toward sex in their own lives. This isn't necessarily true. Quite often medical students are so busy studying and specializing that they themselves have little specific sex education and perhaps only minimal sex lives. Sexual problems abound as much among physicians as among people of other professions. Doctors are not immune to the social pressures which produce guilt in so many people. Indeed, a physician may acquire a feeling of hostility toward sex as easily as anyone. There are many cases of gynecologists who are reluctant to treat women with venereal infections because this is "proof" that the woman has a promiscuous sex life in the eyes of the doctor.

Doctors who are uninformed or guilt-ridden about sex present an obvious problem to a couple seeking sexual therapy. An even more serious problem is the proliferation of downright quacks who infest the field of sex counseling, especially since the success of Masters and Johnson's groundbreaking clinic in St. Louis. It has been widely advertised, for example, that hypnosis is being used to treat sexual dysfunctions in certain clinics, although most responsible sex counselors say there is no proof that this has ever been successful.

Therefore, a couple seeking help for a sexual dysfunction would do best to consult one of the organizations listed below for referral to a reputable, effective sex clinic in their area. These organizations are the recognized leaders in the field:

Masters and Johnson, in St. Louis, were, as mentioned, the first physicians to study expertly and report on human sexual behavior. They have personally trained numbers of other physicians in this field.

Dr. Helen Kaplan, associate professor of psychiatry at Cornell University and head of the sex therapy program at the Payne-Whitney Clinic of New York Hospital in New York City, is another acknowledged expert in human sexuality.

Dr. Harold Lief, director of the Marriage Council of Philadelphia.

In addition, most U.S. medical schools and university centers now have, or are in the process of establishing, human sexuality programs which treat patients and train professionals. Therefore, the best way to find a well-trained sex therapist in your area is to contact your local medical school's hospital facility. But good qualifications are not enough. The same rules apply in choosing your sex therapist as in choosing your gynecologist: he or she must have good training, but, most importantly, you should feel good and comfortable and "right" with him or her or them.

Competent sex clinics deal with several major kinds of sexual dysfunction. The remainder of this chapter involves the most common of these dysfunctions—what they are and what they aren't, how a couple can recognize and deal with a big sexual problem at the outset, and what to expect if you decide to seek help at a sex clinic.

FRIGIDITY

A woman's orgasm can fall anywhere along a wide spectrum of sensation. Some women can reach orgasm simply by fantasizing. Some reach orgasm just by squeezing their thighs together. Some can reach orgasm if only their breasts are stroked. Some reach orgasm being penetrated by a man's penis. Some need direct clitoral stimulation.

Other women can become aroused during sex play and intercourse, and yet are unable to reach orgasm. Some women do not respond to any form of sexual stimulation and have a total inhibition of orgasm.

Although sex therapists still have no single, widely accepted definition of frigidity, it is certainly safe to say that women who fall into the last two categories of sexual response may be considered frigid.

Frigidity is a term that is used loosely by many people. If a couple is having a fight, the man may accuse the woman of being frigid. A woman who has never been as excited about sex

Fig. 22–1:   Foreplay. The most important step in treating any sexual dysfunction is for the couple to openly discuss their problems and try to find ways to solve them.

as she thinks she should be may think she is frigid. These are usually cases of sexual disappointment, not sexual dysfunction. Sexual disappointment between two people can almost always be cured by better information and greater openness.

What Is Frigidity?

True frigidity, by contrast, is a serious sexual impairment for a woman. If a woman is capable of being aroused at all, there is a good chance she can be brought to orgasm. A woman whose sexuality is totally inhibited is in the more complex situation of having actually to relearn her sensual awareness before she can enjoy any sexual experience whatsoever.

In the first case—that of a woman who gets aroused but no more—the usual culprit is fear. The woman is nervous about letting go, either physically or emotionally. Her feelings about the act of sex are probably ambivalent, and therefore her feelings about her sex partner or partners are also ambivalent. She may be uncomfortable about showing affection toward a man. She may be afraid of crying out during her orgasm, or of losing control of herself in front of someone else. She may be afraid of what she might say. She may want to keep her sex life superficial, without realizing that this condemns it to being unsatisfactory. Perhaps she wants to enjoy sex, yet punishes herself at the same time for enjoying it. Or she may simply have an excessive fear of pregnancy.

The second kind of frigidity—total sexual inhibition—is an extreme form of the first. At least 10 percent of all women have this problem. The reasons are many—often a combination of factors such as family and religious upbringing, childhood trauma (rape, for example), severe depression, and so on.

Mutual Responsibility

Sexual problems are private failures that a person is reluctant to admit, even to a spouse. This can start a pattern of snowballing misery for a couple. A frigid woman may let her husband have intercourse with her just to avoid a fight. She may even fake orgasm. But her continuous lack of pleasure will drive her further and further into resentment. She begins to make excuses: She's sick, she's tired. She may start a fight to avoid having intercourse. The couple has less and less sex. They withdraw from each other, making discussion of their problem impossible.

According to Masters and Johnson, there can be no uninvolved person in a sexual relationship. Both members of the relationship bear equal responsibility for its success or failure. Nearly every reputable sex clinic, therefore, requires both partners to undergo treatment for any type of sexual dysfunction. Once a couple realizes this, they should be able to confront each other about their sexual behavior without any feelings of hostility on one side or embarrassment on the other.

If a woman finds herself unable to achieve orgasm, there are certain immediate measures she and her sex partner can take. She must be sure the man knows exactly what pleases her. The man should be careful to arouse her slowly and at length, with a variety of foreplay. During intercourse, she may wish to take the superior position. The man might stimulate her clitoris with his fingers or a vibrator. New kinds of sex can be tried. In some cases, the problem can be solved by honesty, openness, and understanding.

Professional Treatment

If the problem persists, the couple should seek help at a sex clinic. There are several schools of thought about the treatment

Fig. 22–2: Sexual Stimulation. If a woman cannot reach orgasm during sexual intercourse alone, she should be honest with her partner and discuss with him how to achieve better stimulation. If a woman masturbates with a vibrator during sexual intercourse and her partner at the same time caresses her with kissing and touching, mutual pleasure can often be enjoyed.

of frigidity, but all of them in one way or another emphasize the retraining of the woman's body to its natural sensuality.

The most frequently employed treatment is that which Masters and Johnson developed during their research on human sexuality. The couple is examined to be certain there are no physical causes for the sexual problem and interviewed together to discuss the situation. The couple is not allowed any sexual activity for a few days prior to beginning the treatment. The treatment begins with the couple clothed or unclothed, engaging in mild kissing and touching. The woman plays with the man, and the man with the woman, first by gentle body caresses and then, eventually, by direct genital stimulation. Intercourse is not permitted until the woman is ready for it, aroused by the sex play. Then the woman usually takes the superior position, accepting the man's penis only as little or as much, as slowly or as fast, as she wants. As the woman progresses from being tense and afraid to accepting and enjoying sexual activity, she is carefully guided closer and closer to orgasm, until it is finally achieved. This treatment may at first seem uncomfortable or upsetting to the woman, but if she has the encouragement and support of her partner, she has an excellent chance of reaching the satisfaction that has been so long absent from her life.

Treatment by Masturbation Training

A newer theory prevails in some sex clinics, where the treatment for frigidity involves counseling for the woman alone, followed by masturbation training. Proponents of this type of therapy maintain that a woman must first be capable of exciting herself and bringing herself to orgasm before she can expect to be excited by anyone else. The women being treated will meet as a group to discuss their individual versions of the common problem. Then they will be given thorough instruction on techniques of masturbation. They will be told about the different erogenous zones of their bodies and how to stimulate each one. Usually they will be told to fantasize while masturbating, to create a total sexual environment for themselves. The women then meet once or twice a week in a group to discuss their progress and share experiences. Many women find they are not alone in needing to masturbate for an hour or more before becoming excited. One by one, the women will find themselves at last reaching orgasms, and helping each other to find the way in their discussions. After a woman has been able to stimulate herself successfully, she will in turn teach her sex partner how to masturbate her.

IMPOTENCE

Impotence is the approximate male equivalent of frigidity. It is an inhibition of the man's erectile reflex.

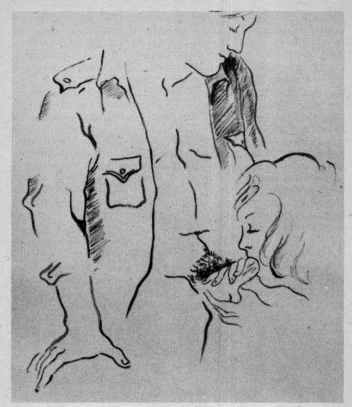

Fig. 22–3: Impotence. Many men easily achieve sensation and erection when they are fully clothed, but lose their erection as soon as they are naked. This is a typical example of impotence caused by the fear of performing. In clothing, the man knows he is safe and intercourse will not be demanded. Men with this problem should be caressed and stimulated by their partners while fully or partially clothed.

Impotence can occur in teenagers just beginning to experience sex, in men at their peak of sexual vigor, and in older men who feel their age is showing. In fact, it is estimated that about one half of all men have known an occasional incident of impotence. Impotence, furthermore, crosses all racial and socioeconomic lines. It occurs among whites, blacks, and Chinese and from the ghetto to Beverly Hills.

What Is Impotence?

Some men have such severe impotence that they have never been able to achieve an erection with a woman, although they may when they are alone. Other men experience more limited, particular kinds of impotence in certain situations.

An impotent man might feel aroused by and want to have intercourse with a woman, yet still be unable to get an erection. Some men get erections during foreplay but lose them as they are about to enter the woman's vagina. Some men are impotent in intercourse, but can maintain an erection during manual stimulation or oral sex. Some men can only achieve erections when they are clothed, and fall soft as soon as their penises are exposed to view. Some men have erections when they are in a situation where intercourse is impossible, but lose their potency when intercourse is feasible and expected. Some men can only get erections when the woman is dominating the sexual activity; others become impotent whenever their partners try to take control. Some men get erections when they are with a prostitute but not when they are with their wives. Other men couldn't be unfaithful to their wives if they tried—with anyone else, they are impotent. Some men are impotent with their wives but respond to homosexual experiences.

Causes of Impotence

There are as many kinds of impotence, and as many causes for them as there are different circumstances in different men's lives.

Impotence can have a variety of purely physical causes, too. Chronic hormone imbalance, or the natural decrease in testosterone that occurs in a man's later life, can cause impotence. It can occur after the man has suffered an accident or disease in which the nerves involved in the erectile reflex are damaged. In severe cases of diabetes, for example, the high blood-sugar level will damage these nerves and make a man impotent. Habitual, excessive use of alcohol or barbiturates can damage the body and lead to impotence. Men who have cancer of the prostate and are treated with estrogen compounds, or men who are given medications to combat high blood pressure, might experience an adverse effect from these substances on their erectile reflex.

Therefore, if a man begins to experience recurring impotence, he should have a complete physical examination to determine whether there is some neurological or physiological explanation. In each of the situations mentioned above, there is a specific course of treatment that can be prescribed by a doctor to eliminate the man's sexual dysfunction.

Most often, though, the causes are emotional or psychological and related, in some way, to anxiety. The anxiety may have roots in the childhood conflicts of the Oedipal (mother-son relationship) period of development. It might have to do with the indelible anxiety of a man's first sexual experience. It might reflect a man's worry about proving himself through his sexual performance. The anxiety may result from a man's rigid moral upbringing: he wants to have "dirty" sex with his "nice" wife, and can't reconcile the two. The anxiety can be of a completely nonsexual kind, as well. A man's nervousness or depression over his job, his marriage, or a problem can produce a sufficient psychological pressure on him to make him impotent. No relationship between impotence and any single psychodynamic pattern has been established; it is a serious sexual problem precisely because it is such a complex one.

Impotence does not mean sterility. A man can become aroused and ejaculate with a soft penis. Men suffering from impotence have been able to impregnate their wives, but this is only the most fundamental, reproductive level of sex. Impotence affects myriad other functions of sexual activity— pleasure, relaxation, and love, both given and received.

Professional Treatment

A man who experiences severe impotence and has been examined and found in good health should seek help from a sex clinic. As in the case of frigidity, both partners will usually be required to participate in the treatment.

Most treatment follows the basic principles developed by Masters and Johnson to diminish a man's sexual anxiety and restore his positive view of himself. The immediate goal is one successful act of intercourse, on the assumption that this success will give the man confidence and break the block to his sexual pleasure, although treatment may be continued beyond this point.

Again, as in the case of frigidity, the treatment must be preceded by several days of sexual abstinence. Then the couple is told to engage in mutual caressing, both bodily and genitally. The man is told not to *expect* to get an erection, not to *try* to get an erection, and not to worry about *losing* his erection if one does occur. Thus the man is under no pressure. He is permitted to remain clothed at first if he so desires. The situation is made as comfortable as possible for him. When, with continued mutual stimulation, the man does achieve an erection, he is told not to have intercourse until he is ready for it.

The "Squeeze" Technique

Some men are tremendously encouraged when they discover they can have erections, and promptly undermine the therapeutic gain by becoming obsessively concerned with whether they can keep it, and if, once lost, it will ever happen again. This is a fairly common, understandable reaction, and Masters and Johnson chose to meet it directly by forcing the man to lose his erection and regain it several times before allowing him to continue into intercourse. This is accomplished with what they term the "squeeze technique." At the height of the man's erection, his partner is instructed to squeeze his penis tightly just under the head, which causes his erection to weaken and disappear. He is then stimulated by the woman to achieve another erection, and squeezed again until he loses it. Once the

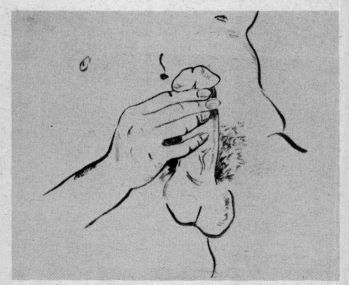

Fig. 22–4: The Squeeze. Introduced as a part of the treatment for both impotence and premature ejaculation by Masters and Johnson. By squeezing the penis when fully erect, as shown in the illustration, a man will lose his erection.

man becomes confident of his ability to continue to have erections, he is guided into the act of intercourse.

Final Treatment Stage

At this time, the man lies on his back and the woman mounts him. The couple then separates without building toward orgasm. The important step is that the man now knows he can maintain an erection and penetrate the woman, yet he does not have to perform or satisfy her. This is repeated until the man is confident that he can maintain his erection inside her. In subsequent acts of intercourse, the man proceeds at his own rate toward orgasm until he has finally achieved it. The initial coital experience is a critical landmark in the treatment of impotence. Further treatment focuses on making the sexual act ever more pleasant and mutually satisfying for both partners.

DYSPAREUNIA

Dyspareunia means "badly mated" in Greek, but what it means medically to a woman is *painful sexual intercourse*. This is one of the most common sexual dysfunctions affecting women. If a woman experiences regular pain during sex, she should see a physician—a gynecologist, however, since the majority of cases fall into the category of pelvic diseases.

Causes of Dyspareunia

Unlike frigidity and impotence, dyspareunia is often a result of one of several physical causes. Yet, as in any sexual problem, there may be psychological factors as well.

An inconsiderate or clumsy sex partner, for example, may fail to arouse a woman sufficiently before having intercourse with her. Since she is not excited, her vagina might not have gone through the changes necessary to accommodate a man's penis—that is, lubrication and enlargement. The friction of the man's penis against the dry, relaxed tissues of her vagina will be painful for the woman.

Psychological factors involved in situations of dyspareunia include a woman's own personal history of sexual trauma, misinformation, or simple embarrassment. Indeed, a woman's embarrassment is one of the chief obstacles to her successful treatment for dyspareunia, since many women are extremely reticent about discussing painful intercourse with their doctors and often invent other, less intimate, complaints instead.

There are a variety of physical conditions that may produce dyspareunia. One of the most common is infection. If a woman has contracted a venereal or other pelvic infection, and if the infection has traveled up through the uterus and into the fallopian tubes or the abdominal cavity, it can cause tremendous pain to her during intercourse. One trouble with such disease is that a woman can have a severe infection in her pelvic organs without having a significant temperature elevation, so self-diagnosis is not always easy.

Painful intercourse can also be due to adhesions—the phenomenon of unconnected tissues growing together—after an operation. During intercourse, there will be a pulling on those tissues which causes tension and pain. Similarly, if a woman has a fibroid tumor in her uterus, intercourse could cause a pressure on the tumor which might be painful.

Another reason for dyspareunia is the condition known as endometriosis, in which the tissue lining the uterus which is usually passed in the blood flow of menstruation, has instead spread up into the fallopian tubes and the abdominal cavity, where it grows like a foreign body. Some women can have such severe pain from endometriosis that sexual intercourse is impossible. A tilted uterus or other uterine abnormalities may also be at fault.

Treatments

There are effective, specific medical treatments for each of the physical problems mentioned above. The benefit is a double one: relief from the physical abnormality, and an end to painful sex.

A partially intact hymen, for instance, may require several acts of sexual intercourse to open a woman's vagina fully, and until this happens, intercourse may be painful. A woman with a *tipped uterus* often experiences pain when the man's penis strikes her uterus during sex. Vaginal or abdominal operations—the most common of these is the *episiotomy,* an incision made at childbirth to enlarge the vaginal opening—may leave scar tissue or may heal so that the vagina is smaller, thus causing a structural change in the woman which makes sex painful for her. In the case of organic defects such as these, doctors recommend that each woman experiment with different coital positions to find one that changes the angle or lessens the depth of the man's penetration. A woman with a tipped uterus, for example, may find that by lying on her back and pulling her knees to her chest, she can enjoy full vaginal penetration without pain.

If no physical causes are found for dyspareunia, it is probably caused by deeper psychological problems. In this case, a sex therapist or psychiatrist should be consulted.

VAGINISMUS

Vaginismus is the involuntary spasm of the muscles surrounding the vaginal opening which causes the vagina to close so tightly that it is impossible for a man to enter. This can occur in women who are organically normal and sexually active.

Vaginismus often serves as a woman's unconscious reaction against fear of vaginal pain. This may stem from an incident of infection or painful medical treatment that the woman experienced as a child. It may be a fear of the pain of pregnancy and childbirth. It may be a reaction against the pain of intercourse with a brutal, incompatible, or insensitive sex partner.

Causes of Vaginismus

This tight closing of the vaginal opening makes penile entry extremely painful, if not impossible. Thus vaginismus can lead to dyspareunia. And in the reverse situation, dyspareunia can lead to vaginismus. The painful intercourse that results from some internal physical problem can so frighten a woman that she develops vaginismus in reaction to it.

Masters and Johnson have discovered that one main cause of vaginismus is an impotent sex partner. The man's continual failure to enjoy sex will affect the woman so that she will want to avoid his problem and protect herself from further frustration. She can do this by, literally, closing herself off from sex.

Vaginismus can be the result of a deep-seated hostility the woman has toward men in general or her man in particular. The hostility may not be specifically toward men, but toward the sexual act itself, because of a woman's stern moral upbringing. If her distaste for sex or her sex partner causes her unresolvable conflicts, her subconscious may react and her vagina close.

A Myth Regarding Vaginismus

One of the most widespread and persistent of all sexual myths relates to vaginismus. This is the myth of *penis captivus*— the situation in which, during intercourse, the woman's vagina snaps so tightly around the man's penis that he is unable to

withdraw it. Supposedly, the couple is taken by surprise while
having sex, and must go, with the man still firmly clutched
inside the woman, to a hospital, where they are separated either
surgically or by being doused with a bucket of cold water. It is a
fascinating picture, no doubt, but not true. Although it has
occurred in animals, no medically recorded instance of such
penis captivus exists in humans.

Treatment of Vaginismus

Treatment for vaginismus focuses first on finding the underlying psychological problem and dealing with it through ap-

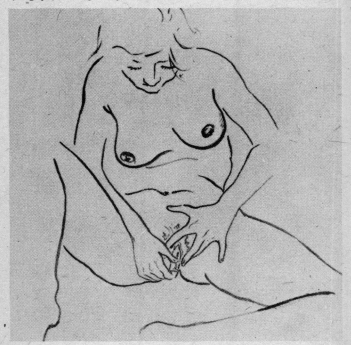

Fig. 22–5: One of the initial steps in treatment of vaginismus is for a
woman, in a relaxed atmosphere, to be taught to insert a vaginal
dilator into the vagina. When she has become familiar with one size
dilator, she is given dilators with increasing diameters. As this
progression becomes successful, she will perform the same procedure
with her sex partner before intercourse is allowed.

propriate counseling. Thereafter, the mechanics are dealt with. The woman is placed in a relaxing situation and her vagina is progressively dilated with dilators of increasing diameters. Then she attempts to penetrate herself with a lubricated finger. When this is successful, the same procedure is performed in a relaxed atmosphere with her sex partner. One lubricated finger is tried first—gently. Then two fingers (other therapists prefer the use of vaginal dilators). If this direct manual stimulation does not make the woman nervous or fearful, the couple will be guided into simple penile penetration, and finally into intercourse.

PREMATURE EJACULATION

This is probably the most common sexual problem in men. The exact definition of premature ejaculation differs from authority to authority. One textbook defines it as a male orgasm occurring within thirty seconds of vaginal entry. Kinsey defined it as ejaculation within two minutes of stimulation. Some clinicians accept the criterion of ejaculation in less than ten penile thrusts. Masters and Johnson diagnosed premature ejaculation if a man reached orgasm ahead of his wife more than fifty percent of the time.

Perhaps the best basic definition of premature ejaculation is orgasm happening before the man wants it.

A man's ability to control his ejaculation is vital to good sexual relations and his own self-confidence. The effective lover must be able to continue sex play even after he has become highly aroused, so that the woman, who will take longer to respond, can be satisfied. Also, if a man is secure about his ability to control his orgasm, lengthy foreplay gives the couple an opportunity to explore and extend their range of sexual activities and pleasures. This is why boys and young men, although more sexually energetic than older men, are poorer lovers—they do not know how to control their reflexes and usually, in their excitement, reach orgasm too quickly.

A man who knows he cannot control himself will feel depressed and incompetent, an attitude which may carry into other areas of his life. In bed, it is impossible for him to be sensitive and responsive to his partner while he is worried about becoming too aroused himself. A woman will usually be unaware of her partner's effort to restrain his excitement and interpret his behavior as cool and uninterested instead. While he tries to hold himself back to please her more, she feels rejected. Premature ejaculation is a serious sexual dysfunction which can ruin a couple's sex life and maybe their relationship as well.

Causes of Premature Ejaculation

There are a number of psychological factors that may contribute to, or cause, premature ejaculation. Many times premature ejaculation is almost like a habit for a man whose first sexual experiences were sneaky, speedy gropings for pleasure with the dire threat of discovery always imminent. Masters and Johnson stated that when a man's first sexual experience occurs with a prostitute who imposes time restrictions on him, premature ejaculation sometimes becomes a problem in later life because of the time associations he places on the act. Premature ejaculation may also be a response to some unresolved psychological problem that exists between a couple. A husband who no longer desires his wife will dutifully have intercourse with her, yet want to get it out of the way as fast as possible. A husband who is angry at his wife may try to punish her by ejaculating quickly and denying her her orgasm.

There are also physical abnormalities that can cause premature ejaculation. A man might have some infection of his urethra or prostate which causes this problem. It can be associated with some diseases of the nervous system.

Home Remedies

The great majority of men who seek treatment for premature ejaculation are involved in friendly or loving relationships and are in good health. Often these men have already tried to deal with their problem at home, perhaps by desensitizing their penises in some way—like rubbing powdered aspirin, Novocain jelly, or cocaine on the tip—or by treating the penis with a substance which reduces friction—oil, Vaseline, or a lubricated condom. Some try taking their minds off sex by thinking of other things while arousing their partners. This last home remedy is, admittedly, difficult. Home remedies can help in cases of minor dysfunction, but more profound problems require professional aid.

Professional Treatment

The prevailing opinion among sex clinicians is that most cases of premature ejaculation are caused by a state of excessive sensitivity in the man, which leads to an overly active ejaculatory reflex. Dr. James Semans, a urologist, developed the basic elements of the treatment procedure that is now widely used for this problem. The general therapeutic approach consists, initially, of several days of discussion and counseling. Episodes of mutual man-woman arousal and sensual-focus exercises, during which intercourse is prohibited, are then employed. The woman is directed to stimulate the man's penis manually or orally until the man feels close to ejaculation. At this time, the stimulation is stopped until his excitement decreases. Then she begins stimulating again. This "stop-start" technique is repeated over and over so that the man can become accustomed to the sensation of sexual pleasure over a long period.

Masters and Johnson advocate a slight variation of Dr. Semans's technique. When the woman has stimulated the man's penis just short of bringing him to orgasm, he will tell her to stop, at which point she squeezes his penis just below the head, which makes it impossible for him to ejaculate. Then he will lose his erection and be restimulated back to arousal, and squeezed again. This "squeeze technique" can be used by any man to retard his orgasm in any situation.

After the man has been manually stimulated a given number of times, he is directed to lie down and the woman directed to take his penis into her vagina. When he feels close to orgasm, she stops moving completely and sits with his penis in her until he begins to lose his erection. Then the woman begins to move again to excite him. It is important for the man to remain passive during this initial intercourse and allow the woman to do the moving. Also, the woman must be in the superior position, because the male-superior position provides too much stimulation for the man. In the case of a man with premature ejaculation, this extreme sensation can be too much.

It is possible for a man with clinical supervision to reach ejaculatory control using the female-superior position in intercourse within a month. Once a man learns this control, it is usually permanent, although complete control in missionary intercourse may take somewhat longer.

RETARDED EJACULATION

This is a much less common problem among men than premature ejaculation. Many men may experience occasional incidents when they have difficulty coming to orgasm, or may not be able to reach orgasm. This can be due to any of a variety of minor temporary upsets or illnesses, or simple fatigue.

The man who cannot ejaculate after extended periods of

Fig. 22–6: As one treatment for retarded ejaculation, the woman can reach down and touch the man's penis, stimulating the scrotum as well as stroking the penis during intercourse to achieve orgasm. Where a sufficient erection cannot be achieved, the woman's hand can also be held as shown to direct the penis into the vagina.

stimulation, intercourse, or fantasy, or the man who must withdraw from the woman and masturbate in order to reach an orgasm, suffers from a much more serious degree of retarded ejaculation. The cause of the problem may be a chronic illness, such as diabetes, or a long-term physical condition, such as alcoholism, or a persistent psychological block of some type. Whatever the cause, the man constantly finds that he does not experience sufficient sensation to ejaculate.

Treatment of Retarded Ejaculation

Except in situations in which the man suffers from the effect of damage to his nervous reflex system, the treatment for retarded ejaculation involves providing a heightened level of stimulation to the man during intercourse. The woman is directed to reach down and grasp the man's penis while he is penetrating her, stroking it with her fingers near the base of the shaft, an action which is very stimulating for her partner. She is also directed to cup and caress, gently and lightly, the man's testicles. These techniques provide the man with greatly increased sensation. A woman may excite a man this way during oral sex if she desires to bring him to ejaculation in her mouth. The extra excitement is a good bet to bring an end to a man's difficulties with retarded ejaculation.

CONCLUSION

Sex and sexual problems used to be "private" matters fraught with unspoken fears and angers. Modern women and men should realize that major advances have been made—and continue to be made—in our understanding of the complex physical and psychological mechanisms which control sexual response. Reputable sex clinics are often able to pinpoint a problem and proceed with a specific program of effective treatment, as thousands of happy couples can testify. There is no longer any reason for anyone to suffer in private misery about a bad sex life.

chapter 23

SEX THROUGHOUT YOUR LIFETIME

Everybody has a sex life. A kid has one and Granny does, too. Good or bad, sex is with you your whole life long. This is the most urgent reason for having the most rewarding sex life possible.

Because of our cultural conditioning, we tend to forget or ignore how really sexy we all are. Yet self-denial is a more twisted form of behavior than any act of sex. Sex is our connection with the processes of the universe and nature, with the history of our people and our planet, with the deepest sensibilities of others and of ourselves. Our sex lives begin near birth and end near death.

FREUD'S THREE STAGES OF PSYCHOLOGICAL DEVELOPMENT

According to Freud, children move through three stages of psychosexual development. The first is the *oral stage,* from birth to about eighteen months of age. During this stage, the infant's main pleasure is oral: the purely selfish delight in feeling and tasting with the mouth. This is followed by the *anal stage,* from eighteen months to four years old. This is the toilet-training period, when the infant must learn to control and direct a free, natural bodily function to conform to an external authority. The final stage is the *genital stage,* from age four to about six, when the child's pleasure becomes erotically located in the genitals. This is the period in which children pass through their Oedipal or Electral conflicts, which complicate their sexual feelings forever afterward. The child chooses the parent of the opposite sex as the object of her or his erotic focus; necessarily, this attraction brings frustration, anxiety, and guilt and, frequently, a conflict with the parent of the same sex. As the child grows older, these dilemmas usually disappear.

PARENTS' ROLE IN SEX EDUCATION

Children should be exposed to the truths of sex at every age. Children living in the country will routinely observe sexual activity between animals, and this is a good, natural time for parents to put in a few words of explanation. A pregnant mother has another perfect opportunity to mention sex in a comfortable, conversational way. A couple's own sexual behavior with each other will fix a strong image, for better or worse, in a child's mind. A wife and husband ought to be equally natural about nudity and privacy alike, because both are parts of healthy sexuality. What a child sees is what becomes "normal" for that child. A child should see Mommy and Daddy happy together, kissing and touching affectionately.

On the other hand, exposure to overly explicit sex is probably more confusing than helpful to a child. What may register on the child's mind is not the specific details of what it sees, but only the sheer intensity of the physical act. For children, intensity is usually a hostile feeling and a little frightening.

The most important thing to remember about a child's sexual education is *not to wait*. Parents may be tempted to put it off, assuming that school will take care of it. The act of *not* telling a child about sex in itself tells the child a lot about sex. In fact, sex education ought to be a simple, fundamental part of a child's family life.

The Language Barrier

One of the problems with discussing sex with a child is the language barrier. The child is exposed to words like *fuck, cunt,* and *cock,* yet parents and sex educators teach words like *intercourse, vagina,* and *penis* for the same function or genital parts. What the child is being taught is not the same as what the child hears on the street. Thus sex begins to have a dual existence in the child's mind: the split personality of sex and Official Sex. One of them comes to have an importance it doesn't deserve. Sex is too much fun ever to have to be Official. Some societies already realize this problem. In the Scandinavian countries, sex educators use both sets of words when teaching children.

Many cities have clinics which recognize the problems and dispense both information and methods of contraception to minors without parental consent.

TEENAGE SEX

Teenage pregnancy has been called the No. 1 population problem and it is estimated that more than 11 million teenagers are sexually active. Many teenagers have more sex than their parents. This is usually astonishing and threatening to the parents. Yet while teenagers may be having a lot of sex, they don't know a lot about it. The average teenager is likely to be only vaguely informed about orgasm, menstruation, contraception, childbirth, and venereal disease. Parents are (or ought to be) wiser than their children and ought to help them adapt to their new sexual expression, rather than hinder it. Punishment doesn't hinder, anyway; it only drives it out of sight.

In adolescence, as in adulthood, a person's motives for sexual activity reflect the full spectrum of human needs, from purely erotic sensation to completely nonsexual factors. Sexual activity, for example, might be a teenager's attempt to gain peer approval and popularity by doing the "in" thing. It might be a means of rebellion from and a blatant expression of hostility to the teenager's parents. Those parents who are uneasy, anxious, and threatened by their children's sexuality are the most vulnerable to its effect as a weapon. Sexual activity may be a teenager's means of forcing a marriage to escape from the home environment. Children from cold, hostile families may try to produce babies to have something to love.

Recent studies show that more than 30 percent of teenagers who engage in sexual intercourse do not use any form of contraception, because they don't dare try to get it. In some instances, it is easier for a girl to get an abortion than a contraceptive. This is a shocking fact. Among other people standing in the way are physicians, who are often unwilling to supply a minor with any means of birth control without her parent's consent. The dilemma here is that a girl may know that her parents don't, and won't, approve. It should be pointed out that parental disapproval is unlikely to keep a girl from having sex if she wants it; but disapproval might keep her from having it safely. Many parents worry that if they make birth control available to their children, they are encouraging their children's promiscuity. Studies have proven that a teenager's rate of sexual activity *does not change after beginning use of contraceptives.* It is also interesting to note that a majority of gynecologists give their own daughters some form of contraceptive as soon as the girls become sexually active.

There has been a statistically enormous increase in the number of childbirths among girls under the age of seventeen, even with birth control and abortion becoming more readily available.

It is estimated that there are one million teenage pregnancies per year and two-thirds of these are unwanted. A teenage girl should know that both she and her boyfriend are in the most fertile period of their lives, and she should get contraceptive advice. In order to avoid the physical and emotional trauma of teenage pregnancy, it is strongly advised that contraception be available when wanted and needed.

VD and Teenagers

Another large problem in the sex lives of teenagers is venereal disease. Most teenagers are virtually ignorant of the symptoms, transmission, and treatment of gonorrhea and syphilis. Because adolescence is, in every area, an age of experimentation, teenagers often engage in sex with an enthusiasm that blinds them to practical concerns. This is another area in which parents can help a great deal by informing—not lecturing—their children on the subject. Parents who care about their children, and not just about a social code, will do this. A girl ought to know that a boy who has a discharge from his penis may have gonorrhea. She should realize that if she finds a sore on her vagina, she may have syphilis. These diseases can be treated effectively if they are caught at the beginning. But if, for reasons of embarrassment or ignorance, a teenager waits too long to see a doctor, the consequences can be far-reaching, and can include sterility.

THE TWENTIES AND THIRTIES

After the primitive conflicts of childhood and the psychological holocaust of adolescence, the twenties and thirties are a time of comparative sexual fulfillment for most people. People in this age group are at their most physically fit and attractive. Whatever problems occur sexually have usually been at least identified, and perhaps dealt with, by most people. The chances of a successful sexual life are good.

During their thirties, women usually start to find themselves. They have finally begun to overcome their inhibitions, they know their own bodies enough to know how they want to be satisfied, they know enough about men to be able to be satisfying sex partners, and they are close to their peak of sexual response. A man's sexual peak occurs earlier, in his twenties. At this time, the man's testosterone level, as well as his sperm production, is at its highest and he is able to reach an orgasm with minimal stimulation and with only a short pause between orgasms. As the man moves into his thirties, his sexual capacity gradually begins to decline.

It is for these reasons that a woman may take a younger man as a lover at this time in her life. The match is ideal, sexually speaking. Both partners are in the primes of their sex lives and have the capacity for extended sessions of intercourse, with multiple orgasms for woman and man alike.

On the other hand, a younger man may not satisfy a woman in other areas; he may very well be far less sophisticated and sensitive than she. His great sexual energy means the younger man has less control over his orgasm than an older man, and may not be as skillful a sex partner for a mature woman.

THE FORTIES

A woman and a man are most similar sexually in their teens and most different at about forty. Many women feel that their sexuality is heightened and their need increased as they get older. This is because of the removal by that time of the majority of psychological blocks the woman has about sex. She wants sex more because she has fewer inhibitions about it. She is inclined to try oral and anal sex if she has been reluctant to have these experiences before. As a woman enters menopause, her hormone level usually decreases, making her vagina drier during intercourse, but this minor problem can be treated effectively with a medically-supervised regimen of anti-aging substances. A woman's sex life can continue to improve right through menopause.

A man in his forties is in the male menopause and usually experiences some decrease in his sexual desire. This is caused by a combination of factors. There is a decrease in his hormone level, although the decrease is small for most men. Testosterone treatments can quickly restore a proper balance. A man at this time in his life is often devoting the greater amount of his energy to his work or business and has little left over for sex. Family responsibilities are at their most burdensome, with children to put through school or college, house or car payments to be met, and so on, so the potential for worry and depression is very high for the middle-aged man. His physical condition may not be the best.

It is a fact that overweight people of any age experience a change of body metabolism which produces a decreased interest in sexual activity. In the middle-aged man, this weight problem is often combined with a general loss of strength and youthful vigor, which renders him less capable of sustaining what sexual activity he does desire. Other medical factors associated with middle age can affect sexual performance: overuse of alcohol or drugs, for example, or diabetes.

Thus, just as a woman is experiencing increased desire in her forties, a man is experiencing a decrease. The difference can make a man temporarily impotent. A woman's newfound sexual appetite and freedom are threatening to a man who finds his erections coming more slowly than they used to, and not as firmly, and who needs more direct stimulation to become aroused—especially when once a mere fantasy was enough. This is a time for understanding all around. The man in his forties usually has overcome his inhibitions and is more sensitive to women from experience. Thus he will be a skillful, thrilling lover, if a somewhat slower one.

THE FIFTIES AND SIXTIES

A woman's sexuality decreases to a slight degree in her fifties and sixties, which brings women and men back to a state of sexual compatibility at this age. One of the main problems now likely to affect a couple's sex life is the real possibility of the man suffering a heart attack. The new medical opinion on treatment of coronary disease recommends a speedy return to all kinds of physical activity as a way to strengthen the heart and prevent recurrence of the problem. A patient will be advised to begin walking as soon as possible, and a program of daily exercise will be prescribed for him. Once a doctor has indicated that a man can resume a relatively normal degree of exercise, it means he can usually resume sexual relations as well. Naturally the man must be careful not to overdo it. A heart attack is a warning signal. But it need not be a stoplight to a couple's future sexual pleasure.

SEX AND THE ELDERLY

Our youth-oriented society has shrouded most of the processes of aging with a veil of embarrassment, discomfort, and ignorance. The gradual deterioration of body and mind which occurs in the elderly is frightening to those still in the flush of good health. We don't want it to happen to us. It is, of course, inevitable. A lot of the fear and distaste we feel about aging might be dispelled if we could realize that old people do just about the same things everybody else does. Age makes things take longer (and more difficult to do), but age does not necessarily rob us of our joys. That most emphatically includes sex.

Sexual activity, particularly among happily married couples, continues through the sixties and seventies and even into the eighties. Studies have found that this activity is somewhat higher among elderly blacks than among elderly whites, somewhat higher among men than women, and somewhat higher among lower socioeconomic groups than among the more well-to-do. More than 60 percent of couples over the age of sixty enjoy regular sexual intercourse. By the age of eighty-five, the incidence of sexual activity drops to about 10 percent of couples studied. In short, older people may well enjoy the varieties of sexual delights until the day they die.

This lovely truth ought to be a source of hope and delight for us all. Yet many people are upset at the idea of elderly women and men engaging in sex. Some middle-aged couples have tried to commit their aged relatives to mental institutions when the old people struck up lively romances instead of behaving "properly" and fading away. There are actually people who think that sex among the elderly is a sign of insanity, but if you think about it at all, what could be more sane?

SEX AND THE UNIVERSE

Sex is the proof that the natural—which is to say the universal—will prevail. From the minute we gain consciousness until the minute we lose it, we are affected by conflicts, inhibitions, and repressions about our sex lives by the entire panoply of dark forces spawned by our Puritanical heritage. Thus it has been for ages. Yet we cannot keep the unwitting infant from gleefully masturbating at any time; we cannot keep the adolescent from plunging into the glorious fun of unmasking sexual secrets; we cannot any of us resist having sex for more reasons than simple reproduction; we cannot and will not give up the good feeling of sex, even in our last years on earth. For all the mighty foes it faces, sex just keeps winning.

We began with the question: What is "normal" sex? We end by saying that sex is what keeps us normal.

INDEX

Page numbers for illustrations are in italics.